SOMEONE'S
LISTENING

SOMEONE'S LISTENING

SERAPHINA
NOVA
GLASS

GRAYDON
HOUSE

GRAYDON HOUSE®

Recycling programs
for this product may
not exist in your area.

ISBN-13: 978-1-525-83674-9

Someone's Listening

This edition published by arrangement with Harlequin Books S.A.

Graydon House
22 Adelaide St. West, 40th Floor
Toronto, Ontario M5H 4E3, Canada
www.GraydonHouseBooks.com
www.BookClubbish.com

Printed in U.S.A.

For Mark Glass. Always.

SOMEONE'S LISTENING

PROLOGUE

WHEN I WAKE UP, IT'S BLACK AND STILL; I FEEL A light, icy snow that floats rather than falls, and I can't open my eyes. I don't know where I am, but it's so quiet, the silence rings in my ears. My fingertips try to grip the ground, but I feel only a sheet of ice beneath me, splintered with bits of imbedded gravel. The air is sharp, and I try to call for him, but I can't speak. How long have I been here? I drift back out of consciousness. The next time I wake, I hear the crunching of ice under the boots of EMTs who rush around my body. I know where I am. I'm lying in the middle of County Road 6. There has been a crash. There's a swirling red light, a strobe light in the vast blackness: they tell me not to move.

"Where's my husband?" I whimper. They tell me to try not to talk either. "Liam!" I try to yell for him, but it barely escapes my lips; they're numb, near frozen, and it comes out in a hoarse whisper. How has this happened?

I think of the party and how I hate driving at night, and how I was careful not to drink too much. I nursed a glass or two, stayed in control. Liam had a lot more. It wasn't like him to get loaded, and I knew it was his way of getting back at me. He was irritated with me, with the position I'd put him in, even though he had never said it in so many words. I wanted to please him because this whole horrible situation was my fault, and I was sorry.

When I wake up again I'm in a hospital room, connected to tubes and machines. The IV needle is stuck into a bruised, purple vein in the back of my hand that aches. In the dim light, I sip juice from a tiny plastic cup, and the soft beep of the EKG tries to lull me back to sleep, but I fight it. I want answers. I need to appear stabilized and alert. Another dose of painkiller is released into my IV; the momentary euphoria forces me to heave a sigh. I need to keep my eyes open. I can hear the cops arrive and talk to someone at a desk outside my door. They'll tell me what happened.

There's a nurse who calls me "sweetie" and changes the subject when I ask about the accident. She gives the cops a sideways look when they come in to talk to me, and tells them they only have a few minutes and that I need to rest.

Detective John Sterling greets me with a soft "Hello, ma'am." I almost forget about my shattered femur and groan after I move too quickly. Another officer lingers by the door, a tall, stern-looking woman with her light hair pulled into a tight bun at the base of her skull. She tells me I'm lucky to be alive, and if it had dropped below freezing, I wouldn't have lasted those couple hours before a passing car stopped and called 911. I ask where Liam is, but she just looks to Sterling. Something is terribly wrong.

"Why won't anyone tell me what happened to him?" I plead. I watch Detective Sterling as he picks his way through a response.

"The nurse tells me that you believe he was in the car with you at the time of the accident," he says. I can hear the condescension in his voice. He's speaking to me like I'm a child.

"They said 'I believe' he was? That's not a— That's a fact. We came from a party—a book signing party. Anyone, anyone can tell you that he was with me. Please. Is he hurt?" I look down at my

body for the first time and see the jagged stitches holding together the bruised flesh of my right arm. They look exaggerated, like the kind you might draw on with makeup and glue for a Halloween costume. I close my eyes, holding back nausea. I try to walk through the series of events—trying to piece together what happened and when.

Liam had been quiet in the car. I knew he'd believed me after the accusations started. I knew he trusted me, but maybe I'd underestimated the seeds of doubt that had been planted in his mind. I tried to lighten the mood when we got in the car by making some joke about the fourteen-dollar domestic beers; he'd given a weak chuckle and rested his head on the passenger window.

The detective looks at me with something resembling sympathy but closer to pity.

"Do you recall how much you had to drink last night?" he asks accusingly.

"What? You think…? No. I drove because he… No! Where is he?" I ask, not recognizing my own voice. It's haggard and raw.

"Do you recall taking anything to help you relax? Anything that might impair your driving?"

"No," I snap, nearly in tears again.

"So, you didn't take any benzodiazepine maybe? Yesterday…at some point?"

"No— I— Please." I choke back tears. "I don't…" He looks at me pointedly, then scribbles something on his stupid notepad. I didn't know what to say. Liam must be dead, and they think I'm too fragile to take the news. Why would they ask me this?

"Ma'am," he says, standing. He softens his tone. This is it. He's going to tell me something I'll never recover from.

"You were the only one in the car when medics got there," he says, studying me for my response, waiting to detect a lie that he can use against me later. His patronizing look infuriates me.

"What?" The blood thumps in my ears. They think I'm crazy; that soft tone isn't a sympathetic one reserved for delivery of the news *that a loved one has died—it's the careful language chosen when speaking to someone unstable. They think I'm some addict or a drunk. Maybe they think the impact had made me lose the details, but he was there. I swear to God. His cry came too late and there was a crash. It was deafening, and I saw him reach for me, his face distorted in terror. He tried to shield me. He was there. He was next to me, screaming my name when we saw the truck headlights appear only feet in front of us—too late.*

ONE

NOW

WHEN THE CLOCK ON THE STOVE HITS NOON, I POUR a tumbler of pinot grigio. I make myself wait until noon so that I know I still have a modicum of control. I pull my robe tight and slip onto the front porch to sit. The sky is dark—a pebble gray—and the air is crisp. Across the street a car pulls into the driveway. Ginny DaLuca has forgotten something, it appears. She opens the car door, and the speakers inside exhale light jazz music as she runs in and then back out of the house quickly, holding her forgotten item. I notice an autumn wreath on her door. It's barely September, but she can't help herself. The same bronze and orange wreath of twisted twigs and foliage with a tacky scarecrow face in the middle welcomes her guests, of which I no longer am one. I don't bother to wave the way I once did because she'd pretend not to see me, or maybe give an uncomfortable smile and nod. I used to be someone who secretly (very secretly) swelled with delight when I saw a row of Christmas decorations pop up next to the back-to-school supplies in late August, but now, this forcing ahead of time is intolerable. If anything, I want to slow it down. Reverse it even.

The Sunday newspaper, in its plastic sheath, lies at the end of the driveway, half of it immersed in a puddle from last night's rain. How many times have I said I'd go online and change my subscription to digital only? It's so wasteful. Liam liked the feel of the paper though. He liked the inky film it left on his hands, the smell of it. He didn't want to look at his laptop on Sundays. "It's exactly why we have a big front porch," he'd say, after promising to recycle the paper. I sip my drink, wishing I would have poured a red—more suited for the weather—and wonder how many newspapers would have to pile up at the end of the drive before one of the neighbors would check to see if I were dead.

A soft tapping of rain starts up again. The Pattersons give up on raking leaves from their sugar maple that's shedding early this year. They laugh at their attempt to spend the gloomy Sunday in the yard, and with a shrug of defeat, Al Patterson puts an arm around his wife as she shields her head with her hands and rushes inside. How I long for Liam's hand on the small of my back for any reason at all. If he were here, he'd comment on how illogical it is for them to rake before all the leaves have fallen for the season. There's a small window between the end of fall and the first snow, and he'd always plucked out those few days, like feeling the rain coming in one's bones, and timed it perfectly.

I rescue the paper from floating down the gutter. It's bloated with rainwater, but I take it inside and lay out the swollen pages on the kitchen table anyway. I'm relieved not to see my face looking back at me; maybe enough time has passed and they're finally on to the next life to ravage with speculation and statements of "alleged" involvement. At my desktop, a chat bubble blooms on my screen. It's Ellie, and although she means well, the sisterly concern she tries to communicate with daily check-ins is becoming exhausting. There are only so many times you can circle the same conversation and get nowhere. She's sorry for my loss. I know she is. She wants to make sure I'm eating. She encourages me to work.

Her intentions are golden, but it will take a shift into vodka gimlets before I breach that tired conversation today. I ignore the bubble asking me how the weather is holding up, and I try to do a little work.

Since taking a leave of absence from my practice, I still communicate with a few patients who didn't take the news of my time away very well. Paula Day is suffering from stage four breast cancer and no matter my own hardships, I would never abandon my weekly video chat with dear Paula. Eddie Tolson's panic disorder exploded when I explained I'd be away, so I chat with him now and then. In my private practice, I've pretty much kept on anyone who wildly protested my leave, but most of them took my referrals quietly and sympathetically with the promise of my speedy return. I respond to a few emails, but it's hard not to think of Liam. It's hard to concentrate on anything else.

I click on a folder on my desktop titled "Liam." I've kept every email and photo, even the everyday notes he used to leave around the house that I took photos of because I thought they were so sweet. I uploaded them all to the computer over the years: "Sorry I drank all the almond milk, I'll pick up more tonight," taped inside the fridge; "Meet me at Luigi's at 7?" on a stick-it note on my car. It's silly to keep such mundane remnants, but it was all part of our evolution together.

I never wanted to forget, even when he was here, the swoosh at the top of the L in his signature or the inside jokes we exhausted. "Hardy Har" scrolled at the bottom of dozens of these old notes, a secret, stupid one-liner, just between us, which we'd stolen from some long-forgotten TV comedy sketch and made our own language. I cherished each one. All of the photos and instant messages strung together; this was our life. Even our ranting text arguments—I never deleted those from my phone. Now, the pettiness of them fills me with shame.

I scroll through some of the last photos of him—of us. His work as a food and wine critic meant the lion's share of our photos were at restaurants. We're pictured together, with that stagey, for-the-camera pose, sharing a Scotch egg at a gastropub, or taking giant bites of lobster rolls off a pier in Cape Cod. There's a short video of him explaining why romesco sauce can go on darn near anything. I click to play it even though I've watched it countless times. I took the little clip with my phone at an Italian place in New York that I don't recall the name of, but I remember so clearly the drippy candles and the Dean Martin song playing in the background.

We'd taken a cab there right from the airport to make our reservation on time, so we were dressed too casually for the place, and we'd had a few Makers Mark and sodas on the plane to celebrate a television spot I'd gotten. It wasn't like him to drink often and certainly not before he reviewed a restaurant; I guess that's why I love this clip. Just thirty-two seconds of Liam preaching the utilitarian nature of romesco sauce with a dot of it on his cheek, slightly buzzed.

My face has become rinsed with tears before I notice, so I close the folder and graduate from wine to vodka and turn a house-flipping show on TV to fill the silence. After a couple of miraculous and seamless home renovations, I pull on a wool coat and start my daily work. I print a hundred more missing persons posters from my office printer and head out. I look at Liam's face on the poster. It's a photo we took at Sapori Trattoria last year. My face, along with the veal scaloppini we shared that night, are cropped out. I thought it was the clear-est photo of him I could find.

Today I'll just go to shops, hang them inside restaurant front windows so the rain doesn't dissolve him.

TWO

THEN

ON A BITTER FEBRUARY NIGHT, I CAME HOME TO FIND Liam in the kitchen in socks and sweats, the table covered with takeout boxes that looked like carefully wrapped gifts. They each held different desserts and dishes from the French restaurant that he'd written a rave review about the week before.

"Try this." Liam handed me a glass. I took a sip and handed it back. He looked surprised. "You can't tell me you don't like it."

"It's too sweet. Ugh," I say, rejecting it as he tried handing it back to me.

"This is a tawny port. Forty years old."

"It tastes like a rancid fruit pie."

He smiles and pours my glass into his own.

"More for me," he says. "So this is a 'no' for your book launch party then?"

"You're cute." I smile.

"I am?"

"Yes, you're treating this party like a wedding. Are we going to taste a sampling of cakes next?" I say, picking at boxes on the table.

"No. But there is a Pots de Creme I figured you'd at least want to try. The owner of Le Bouchon is practically falling over himself at the opportunity to host it, so I thought I'd take advantage of that."

"Free Pots de Creme. How could I say no to that?" I placed the port he was holding on the counter and wrapped my arms around him, kissing him. "Thank you. For being so support-ive." He kissed me back. I rubbed my hands together, eyes wide. "What flavor?"

"Mocha." He opened a box and grabbed two forks. I was so grateful that he was embracing my new book and getting used to my new role in the spotlight. Since my first book (*Starting Over: Life After Abuse*) had done so well, I was asked to ap-pear on many shows for guest spots until landing a weekly advice slot on a talk radio program: *Someone's Listening, with Dr. Faith Finley.*

It wasn't fame exactly, but locally I guess you could say it was. It was a bit overwhelming to be recognized here and there, to be invited to bourgeois cocktail parties and black-tie dinners where I would often be asked to speak. Liam was the one who was used to that role—the feared and respected critic whom every chef in town went to great lengths to impress when he sat down at their tables. He supported my success, but I can't help but feel that he missed the way it was before, when he was the gatekeeper to charity dinners and Bears sea-son tickets and all things social and exciting. I was the quiet academic and he was the charming foodie, revered for his swift and honest opinions on everything from the authenticity of the latest taco truck to James Beard Award–worthy restaurants.

My colleagues quietly disapproved of my new role when I started the radio spots a few years back. It was the McDonald's of therapy, after all—a few minutes on the air and I'm wield-ing life-altering advice? It was hard to tell if their judgment was based on their keen moral compasses or...envy. I shared office space with a few other clinical psychologists and an analyst whom I only saw in passing now and then. The curt nods and smiles I started receiving from Alan and Thomas in place of the once obligatory but genuine small talk we used to engage in told me all I needed to know about their feelings regarding my media presence. I did help people though, no matter what they thought.

Liam and I kept a condo in the city that we got away to now and then, and where I occasionally stayed when I was writing my book—a glorious brownstone built in the late 1800s with a sliver of balcony overlooking the busy street below. I remembered a woman staring at my mailbox then back up at me one afternoon when I stabbed a key into the box and flipped through a pile of junk mail in the shared lobby. As I tossed an oil change coupon into the recycling, she put together who I was.

"You're Dr. Faith Finley." She beamed ear to ear and began rambling about how she'd written into Dr. Phil four times but couldn't get through and could I help her.

"I don't usually offer advice in the lobby like this, and I'm heading..." I started to say.

"Of course. I'm so sorry. You're headed out. You must be so busy. I'm Lettie." She reached her hand out to shake mine. "It's so nice to meet you. I can't believe you live in my building!"

"Nice to meet you too, Lettie. How about you call into the show on Friday, and I'll let the producer know to put you through," I said.

"Oh my God. Really? Thank you! Yes!" She beamed.

She did call in to the show. Sadly, she had the same story I hear almost every week. It started with a flared temper and an apology, but her husband's verbal abuse has turned into rage and physical altercations, and she doesn't understand why she keeps going back.

I counseled her the way I would anyone in her position, and referred her to my book where there was a whole chapter on creating a safe plan to leave. The station even sent her a copy of the book after the call. A couple of weeks later she called back to report that she'd taken the advice and was singing my praises and thanking me on air, safely away from her abuser. So, I had proof I wasn't just some sellout. I was making a difference in more lives than I could in private practice. Maybe it wasn't the same, but it was still valuable.

It wasn't just Lettie. The same week a woman called about her out-of-control teen and then reported, months later, that the recovery center I suggested for her was a miracle, and her daughter was sober and that she was like a different person. I remember calling the New Hope Recovery Center myself and coordinating with the mother after the call. It wasn't fast-food advice, and I resented the implications otherwise. I tried to keep my defensiveness in check.

Mostly, I just received fan admiration, but it was the people in my practice—the people whose opinions I thought mattered more—that robbed me of my breath anytime I let myself think about the things they undoubtedly said about me out of earshot.

Liam would just say "Screw 'em. Jealous old dinosaurs. Clearly they didn't read your book or they'd know how damaging passive aggression can be. You lay it right out for them." I loved it when he'd try to defend my honor, no matter how nonsensical and unnecessary.

I would do anything. Anything in the whole world if we'd never hosted that party—if that night had never happened. Anything.

THREE

NOW

I'VE BEEN WALKING IN THE COLD RAIN LONGER THAN intended. It's already dark and I'm out of posters so I duck into a tavern for a drink. We bought our house out here a few years ago. It's only fifty miles outside of Chicago, but feels like a small town where you can't escape seeing someone you know. As I slip in through the massive wooden door to the tavern, I'm grateful to be out of the cold and hope I don't recognize anyone inside.

The light is soft and red, and the ancient carpet is dotted with black gum spots and outlines of stains from years of neglect. I'm comforted by the warmth and low light. I aim for the restroom first, but when I go in, I'm assaulted by stinging fluorescent light and the smell of bleach as a Shakira song plays too loudly through a distorted speaker. It changes my mood instantly from temporarily comforted to irritated, and out of nowhere I'm suddenly fighting an overwhelming feeling to break down sobbing—a feeling I fight back a lot these days—but I don't. I go out and scan the place quickly, and when I don't see any familiar faces, I belly up to the bar.

It's been nearly seven months since the accident. I know I'm supposed to feel thankful that I'm up and walking again. It's hard to do. The only thing I'm thankful for is that I'm more mobile, so I can better spearhead search initiatives for my husband.

Now that I can get around, I hope the darkest times are behind me—long stretches of nights unable to sleep, utterly confined by my fractured ribs and broken leg, dependent on a home health aide for nearly everything. I didn't get to choose who they sent. Insurance just sent whoever, and I got Barb, a heavyset twentysomething who smelled like cigarette smoke covered up by drugstore body spray that left a charred plastic scent in every room she lounged in. That's mostly all she did unless I needed help to the bathroom or getting something to eat.

She wore a Garfield T-shirt, stained, with a quip about hating Mondays while she played Candy Crush on her phone and wolfed down Arby's smokehouse brisket and curly fries. Meal prep was on her list of skills, but she looked at the vegetables I had her buy like foreign objects. After serving me a silo of blue cheese dressing with a few leaves of lettuce, I had to coach her to simply throw a salad together. The fatigue from my injuries left me aching, and the depression I tried to fight, on a minute-by-minute basis, did not allow me any patience with the situation. I heard her call me a bitch once, on the phone, talking to a friend. I didn't care. I would have if it were another time, but I was starting to wonder if I was capable of caring about anything ever again.

In the early mornings, I usually tried to sleep on the couch. Adult Swim, infomercials with knives that cut through bricks, and repeats of Jimmy Swaggart sweating into a handkerchief with a hand to heaven, distracted me just enough to keep me from ending up back in the hospital with a panic attack. I almost called for an ambulance one night a few months back, when an invasion of anxiety left me hyperventilating so severely my limbs went numb and I thought was having a heart attack. It's something I'd heard all the time from patients, and I knew exactly how I'd approach this if it were someone else—what advice and treatment I'd proffer—but the grief would simply not allow me to react rationally.

Now though, I can do more than cry and post desperate social media pleas offering a reward for any information about Liam. When it happened, they treated me like some unstable drunk in the hospital who was making up stories. When they learned who I was, the pacifying condescension shifted into something else. I was credible enough, I surmised, that they would at least not dismiss what I was saying, no matter how implausible it seemed. But they were the ones on the scene, and they assured me I was the only one in the car. They weren't looking for a second person at the time, though, so I'm sure they did only a half-assed look around. After a few days, when Liam Finley did not show up at his wife's side in the hospital, nor did he show up to work or his Saturday pickup basketball game at the Y, they finally started to ask real questions, not just bullshit ones, half-accusing me of being a pill popper and therefore an unreliable voice on what had happened in that car. Even with the new evidence, they still didn't believe me.

I hate this bar. A string of lights spelling out "live, laugh, love" blink above the front door, sluggishly, weary from the task of boosting spirits. Tacky plaques with obscene quotes decorate the wall behind the long, ancient, oak bar. Every surface of wood is scratched and weathered; mirrored rows of glass bottles are disordered and dressed with sugary overspill. The smell of stale cigarettes and urine are only circulated, not alleviated, by the dusty ceiling fans.

Liam loved the nostalgia of the place, the mammoth Pac-Man game in the back, the jukebox with real vinyl in it. I

SOMEONE'S LISTENING   25

loved it because he loved it, and we spent nights here, dancing to Neil Young on the makeshift dance floor on Saturday
nights and relishing our quiet escape from the city that we'd
discovered. But now it's just the closest place to numb myself.

I want to believe that the impossible things the detectives
are telling me are lies. *Liam withdrew money before the accident;
it looks like he planned to disappear.* It's outrageous, laughable.
Except that I discovered his passport missing, and I'm running
out of plausible reasons for him to have taken out a large sum
of money without telling me. I wish I never opened the goddamn drawer our passports live in. I was looking for a receipt
for some stupid thing. I never even thought to check to see if
his passport was in its place, and I wish I didn't know. I wish
I never looked. The bartender places another drink in front of
me before I need to order one; I gulp it down in a few swallows, and push the dark thoughts away.

The waitress, Pearl, smiles at me as she sits in a booth with
her scratch-offs. I order an Old Fashioned and nod in her direction to passively say hello. After her husband died, the bar
owner gave her a job even though she is clumsy and forget-
ful and the customers complain about her. The regulars look
out for her, though, because of the tragedy. The stories about
her misfortune vary. The most consistent version is that her
husband worked for a metal factory in town until one night,
on the graveyard shift, he fell asleep and his sleeve was pulled
into a three-roller press. He was squeezed all the way through
until all of his insides were pressed out, leaving only strips of
papery flesh behind to gum up the cogs and gears.

It's said that Pearl always packed him a lunch basket full of
things like sweet potato cakes, candied figs, heaps of pasta,
and warm buttered bread, and she'd always drop it off for him
before she went to bed at night. She didn't witness the accident, but she did arrive at the factory just after it happened—

in time to see bloody strips of him left behind—his skin and tissue flooding over the sides of the press. Some say she lost her mind that night.

I offered her my services once, no charge, if she ever wanted to talk. She never took me up on it. It's true she's not quite lucid all the time, so she mostly just chain smokes and drinks translucent coffee until it's time to clean up for closing. She looks smaller than usual tonight, slunk in her stool, swimming in her big sweater that was meant to match her earrings. Across the front is a cross-stitched jack-o'-lantern, whose triangle cut-out eyes and nose are meant to light up, but the sweater has no batteries and the pumpkin's dead face makes her look even more lifeless than usual.

I want her to mother me. I want to ask how she coped with such devastating loss, so she might comfort me and tell me to be strong, but she hasn't coped, and that's why she scares the hell out of me. She laughs abruptly, her square jaw bobbing like a ventriloquist's doll. Then she stops and looks around, offended as if some phantom person has asked her to be quiet.

I order another drink. My phone vibrates across the bar top. It's Ellie again. I can picture the conversation already. I know that she is, at this moment, standing in her kitchen over a pot of Hamburger Helper, browning the meat with a diapered baby on her hip and a toddler nearby in a bounce chair. I'd be at the counter with a glass of wine, picking at the fresh baked, from a tube, sheet of cookies, no doubt contaminated by greasy little kid fingers. This is Sunday night. I suppose there is a comfort in the routine of it. I answer. She finishes hollering to her husband before saying hello.

"Joey! Like, it's not hard. You want poop in your green beans, fine by me," she yells. Then a pause. "Then take him. Diapers are in the trunk. I forgot to bring them in." I can hear Joe sigh or scoff as he takes the baby.

"Ell?" I'm not sure if she forgot she called.

"Faith. Hey. Sorry 'bout that. How are you doin'?" she asked, changing her tone dramatically from the moment before with Joe.

"I'm okay." I down my drink in one swallow and gesture for another. There are a few minutes of talk about the cold front, her call to Sprint customer service earlier, how little Hannah is going to go as a cupcake for Halloween because she found the sweetest little costume at Pottery Barn. I remember when Ellie and I were little and she went as Bob Ross. She sported an epic afro and carried around a little painting of woodland creatures. A cupcake? I guess parenthood does weird things to a person. She finally squeezes in hints that I should come back to the city.

"We're gonna pawn the kids off on Joe's parents and do like an adult dinner in a couple weeks. Do you think you might be in town…wanna come?" she asks carefully. Joe is a Chicago cop, and she is an overwhelmed stay-at-home mom, so they rarely get any time away. She never asks me to watch the kids, thank God, but I feel a little bad she knows it would be hell for me.

"Um… I mean, maybe," is all I have to offer at the moment. Sometimes I wonder if she was right about going back to the city. It was Liam's idea to move out here. He wanted an idyllic little corner for us. We were still in the city several days a week usually, but he had grand plans for this small town life he'd never had. We both grew up in the city, grad school on both respective coasts. We traveled, we had months, maybe years, where our careers could have easily splintered our relationship if we weren't so committed…and yes, in love.

He'd thought Sugar Grove would be our place. A house you couldn't even dream of in Chicago for the price point— with a hot tub on the deck, an acre for future dogs to run in, and a big ole BBQ pit he dug himself. He adored it. All of it. It even had a small airport, and since he reviewed all over the country, he could use it for last-minute trips if he needed to without driving to Chicago.

I split my practice. Three days a week in Chicago, a couple in Sugar Grove. If I'm honest, it wasn't what I would have chosen, but with him, it's hard to explain; it was perfect. He made it that way. I did prefer the lull of sirens at night and self-righteous baristas with man buns, microbreweries, and a public radio station I could tune into without static, but now... I didn't know what to say to Ellie. I tell her I'll think about it.

The night it all happened, we left the restaurant in Logan Square. We were fourteen miles from home when we crashed. On a highway of vast nothingness. Maybe I associate finding him with being closer to the house in Sugar Grove than the condo we had barely been to in the last year in Chicago. It's nonsensical. If someone took him...or if he left, like they think he did, it would be unlikely he was hanging out in Sugar Grove, population 8,997. I know that. It's a logical argument as Ellie has made on more than one occasion, but I can't help but feel that if I leave, I'll—I don't know—abandon him. I *should* search in Chicago, but this is where I last saw him...in a way. Now that I'm mobile again, it has crossed my mind, but I don't want to think about it now. I just want the liquid euphoria to buzz between my temples and warm my chest. I close my eyes and trace the rim of my glass with my finger as I listen to her.

"Oh, Jiminy Crickets. Joe's got Ned out on the fire escape changing diapers so he doesn't stink up the kitchen. It's a miracle any of this family is still alive." I hear her stop hard in the middle of her last word. I can tell she wishes she didn't say it. She starts at an apology.

"Oh, Faith—I meant—"

"I know. Hey, I gotta go, but I'll talk to you this week," I say. There is a beat of silence. Knowing Ellie, she wants to say something to end on a better note, but knows I just want to go.

"Okay, love you," she says with a forced lightness. I hang up.

Nobody thinks Liam is dead. But it's the tiptoeing around the topic and the way the register of someone's voice changes when they speak to me, like I'm a child around whom you must use simple and carefully chosen words, that makes me crave solitude.

I pay my tab and walk the fifteen minutes home. Since being restricted from walking for months, now it's all I want to do. It's already dropping down to the midforties at night, and I never wear a warm enough coat. "Fashion before function," I'd tell Liam, but that was when I was used to dipping into cabs a few feet from a warm building in the winter. I pass a sad, man-made lake and feel sorry for the birds gliding on top of it, suddenly concerned for their body temperature. A sparrow swoops past the dried stocks of goldenrod along the road, which, even after an early frost the other night, still reveals hints of growth. Fragile veins cling to life inside the brittle, russet stems.

When I round the corner to my street, I see a car I don't recognize in the drive. It's idling, and the person inside sits with a square of blue light puncturing the dark that is beginning to fall so early now. I freeze a moment, trying to imagine who it could be. Then I walk up slowly and tap on the window, startling the man inside.

"Jesus!" He leaps. I see that it's Len Turlson from Liam's office. What the hell could he possibly be doing here?

"Faith, hi." He puts his phone down and opens the door. Len was always my favorite of Liam's colleagues. A stout man with a round, ruddy face but always uniquely fashionable in his Irish fisherman sweaters and wool newsboy caps. He wrote for Arts and Culture, but we've been on a few trips abroad with him when he and Liam had crossover stories, and my memories of him are mostly laughing, and once drinking too much whisky at a pub in Scotland, him getting into an embarrassing arm-wrestling match with Liam. I have no earthly idea what could bring him all the way to Sugar Grove. For a second I wonder if he has news that Liam's okay, but his face would have communicated that immediately, so now I feel a hollow wave of nausea, wondering what else would bring a man this far out of his way besides in-person sort of news.

"Len. Um…hi."

"Sorry to drop in like this, but I wondered if we could talk a minute," he says.

"Of course. Yeah." I lead the way to the front door. Inside, he takes off his newsboy hat and holds it, a gentlemanly gesture. I invite him to sit. He does, but holds himself at the edge of the sofa like someone ready to leave.

"Can I get you a drink?"

"A drink sounds great. Whatever you're having." He smiles. When I return with two scotch whiskies in lowball glasses, he's taken out some documents from somewhere. His jacket pocket? They just sort of materialized and are now smoothed out in his lap. I hand him a glass.

"So…there must be a good reason you're here. As much as I'd like to chitchat about the early cold, could you please just tell me."

"Bonnie didn't think I should come. I guess I'm not completely sure it's the right thing to do either." My instinct was to ask how his wife, Bonnie, was. She'd suffered an illness earlier in the year, and I hadn't seen much of her recently, but instead I sat, paralyzed, waiting for what he could possibly

have to say. He was waiting for a response, to give him permission, I suppose, to potentially devastate me.

"What is it?"

"We finally cleaned out Liam's office down at the *Tribune*."

"What? Like they—got rid of his office?" Is this what he
wanted to tell me?

"John thought it was time. They're sending his things. You
should get everything soon, I'm sure." He takes a sip of his
drink and looks at the papers on his lap nervously.

"Okay." I wait. There's more.

"Faith, we had his assistant go through his email, so we
could retrieve some things we needed and forward contacts.
And...anyway, the point is, there was an email that...I thought
you should know about." He hands it to me. A printout of
something that Liam emailed to himself, as a reminder to print
it perhaps, or send it to someone? Me? Was it a draft of a suicide letter? Was it a portion of a letter that was meant to explain his sudden move to some far-off place? South America or
something? I read it. It's not addressed to anyone, it just starts.

I wish there were a more eloquent way to put this. One that
wouldn't look so cowardly, but...I want out. I need to take
a break, maybe a permanent one. I don't know yet. There's
so much I wish I could explain to make this all make sense,
but it's complex, and frankly, I'm so tired of being misunderstood. I don't want to explain to everyone what's happened,
I just want out. Of all of it.

I realize that my hands are trembling so intensely, that I'm
barely able to finish reading it. I look up at Len, choking back
tears. I can't bring myself to say anything. It was like Liam to
use an ellipsis to show his pause in that second sentence, but

feeling misunderstood? I didn't understand. He "didn't want to explain what's happened"? What *had* happened?

"Faith." Len tries to take my trembling hand in his, but I stand up and turn away. I have no idea how to behave in this situation.

"I've heard that there was a series of…things. Evidence. That made the police decide not to investigate this as a missing persons case." His face is red and downcast. I know how difficult it is for Len to be here—to be saying these things, but I wasn't going to make it easier for him. I go into the kitchen and return with the bottle of whisky. I sit down again and pour two more glasses silently.

"Should I go?" he asks.

"No," is all I can muster, burying my face in my drink. I associate Len with Liam, and his presence is still a comfort in some intangible way.

"Listen," he continues reluctantly. "I was with you. Everyone was. He'd never just…walk off. I don't know what I'm trying to say here except that if it were me…I'd want someone to tell me the truth. I'd want this email. I hate that the cops were right. *If* they were right. But they had reasons to not pursue it, and it left you…fucked. I know." He sits down to contain himself and sips the topped-off drink I poured him.

"I thought maybe seeing this could help provide…some, I don't know…closure." He closes his eyes. I give him nothing.

"And even if it doesn't, well, goddamn it, Faith, how could I not tell you?" he says.

Provide some closure? Is he a writer or a fucking therapist? I nod to him, suck my teeth, blink back tears. He is so sincere. He is trying to do the right thing, but I hate him right now. My skin feels hot and electric. I don't want to break down in front of Len Turlson.

"Thank you, Len," I say coldly. I stand. I do want him to go.

"God, Faith. I'm so sorry."

I let my tears escape silently. "I know." I flick them away, quickly, and try to do the Midwest thing we do—the compulsion to divert attention away from ourselves. "Hug Bonnie for me, and thanks for letting me know." *Thanks for letting me know?* That's a response you give when someone tells you you've made a grammar error. My body language makes Len feel unwelcome enough that he decides to let himself out after an awkward, sympathetic hug. I pour his full glass of whisky into mine and sob the minute I hear him pull away from the driveway.

Liam chose to leave. I'm holding proof. How could he do this?

FOUR

THEN

IT HAD BEEN JUST OVER EIGHT YEARS SINCE I MET Liam—at a chocolate festival, of all places. Ellie had coaxed me into going. She adored her fall traditions and forced everyone to go along, and she expected a smile and fun to be had. Genuine or forged, it didn't matter. We were making memories, damn it. This was before kids. Apple picking, pumpkin farms—it was forced family fun that included just her and me back then. These days, though, wine tastings have morphed into hayrides full of sticky-fingered kids wielding pumpkin-shaped candy corns and seasonally wrapped Reese's cups.

Last year, instead of getting buzzed off mulled wine, I spent the better part of an hour talking Hannah down from a candy-induced meltdown. Turns out if you try to explain to a kid that although Rudy Gutman stole your three-cent chocolate Milk Dud, you are still holding six pounds of even more valuable candy, they can't be reasoned with. The economics of it was totally lost on a two-year-old who just released inconsolable, snotty howls until distracted by Ellie digging out an equally valueless, hairy Milk Dud from the bottom of her goody bag and saying, "Look." That's all it took, and I'd never once even considered that.

One of the first things that drew me to Liam was his position on kids. I had just turned thirty and was starting to get fatuous comments about "clocks ticking" just when Ellie was in a fit of baby fever. When two women at the festival stood dipping knots of bread under the chocolate fountain at one of the kiosks, I heard one of the women complain about her kids, and then say something like "but what is a home without children?" And uninvited, I answered, "quiet." It was probably the chocolate wine speaking. They just looked at each other and shuffled themselves over to the chocolate macaroon castle.

Liam was sitting at a nearby table with a sampler of fruit and truffles, holding a pad and paper. He'd just started with the *Tribune* and was writing a piece on one of the chocolatiers. He made a joke about how people with toddlers refer to them in months, and stated that if they're over a year old, you can just say "a year," not fifteen months. They're not aged cheese. I laughed. He offered me a strawberry wearing a chocolate tuxedo and gave me his card.

We fell in love hard and fast. We spent winter under comforters with takeout and whisky, sharing with each other our favorite music and movies, like college students—forcing one another to listen to a particular line in some angsty song that was reminiscent of the halcyon days of our youth, not so long ago.

It was barely a mile, we discovered, between my duplex in Wicker Park and his apartment in Ukrainian Village, so we'd walk to one another's place after work and make love fiercely before going out to one of the infinite number of restaurants Liam had to show me. My freshly straightened, sandy hair hung long and neat down my back until he came over and pushed into the door when I opened it, and kissed me.

We'd stumble into the bedroom, or sometimes not even make it that far and end up on an area rug in the living room, hot and groaning, my once sleek hair now in damp curls clinging to my sweaty neck.

Then, weary from our day and exhausted from the sex, we just wanted to stay naked, interwoven in each other's bodies and sleep, but there was a culinary world that had to be explored, so we'd always pile on layers and brave the cold night in search of a restaurant to impress us. Well, him. I was pretty impressed with every little haunt he took me to.

We'd stroll through evening snow flurries, through decidedly untrendy neighborhoods where he boasted we'd find the most authentic fare. He delighted in teaching me about food.

"This was an Irish Union working-class neighborhood," he said to me on a frigid night as we ducked into an old pub for bangers and mash. "It may be gentrifying, but there are untouched gems where you can really see what an old family-run place should be." We sat in old, wooden back booths sharing a bottle of wine or tiny cups of espresso, talking into the night, many nights. I had just started my postdoctoral placement in community mental health before getting my license and moving into private practice and I was working all the time, but the nights were all ours.

One night in November, we lay under the sheets with only the red flicker of the fireplace lighting our bodies. A Vito & Nick's pizza box sat open on the floor beside the bed next to an empty bottle of d'Arenberg shiraz. He asked about my family, my childhood memories—the sort of insightful questions that made me fall in love with him. The amount of therapy one undergoes to become a therapist leaves very few past traumas unexamined, but I still found, to my surprise, that he was the first person besides my therapists to ask; talking about it in an intimate context brought up a flood of emotion I swallowed back, but was shocked to experience.

His questions about my father prompted me to see flashes of incomplete, disjointed thoughts and memories that had no right showing up in that moment. I thought of a Barbie doll I had when I was very young and how I had swallowed both of her tiny pink shoes for no reason at all. I thought of my mother's instant coffee, of the sharp garlic smell of marinara sauce on the stove on days when the sun set long before it was ready to be nighttime, the sound of canned laughter from a sitcom played down the hall from my room where, without looking, I could see my mother on our yellow couch looking past the television at something so far away that I would never see.

I told him about my childhood home. I saw it clearly although I hadn't been home in years—the blistered paint and tawdry wicker furniture on the slanted balcony of the shitty apartment building. The rusty, archaic Radio Flyer that housed weary soil and dead plants, the years of unhappiness there. My mother was probably still spending her days sleeping in the back bedroom with a box of wine on the bedside table. My father was long gone.

I told Liam about my reasons for specializing in domestic abuse—the time my mother drove through the rain in our Pontiac Bonneville, searching all the bars in town for my father. She sat me on an overturned milk crate inside the front door of our apartment and handed me the Remington shotgun that she kept under the kitchen sink next to a bottle of Ajax and a pile of molded steel wool. She told me if he came back, warn him once to leave, and then shoot. I was eight.

She planned on finding him first and shooting him with the handgun she kept in her purse. It wasn't because the night before, he had forced her to lie on the bathroom floor and stomped the back of her head into the herringbone tiles, causing her to lose two teeth, and who knows what sort of head injury she'd sustained. He did this often. Maybe he was careful to use just the right amount of force to not cause life-altering wounds. More likely, though, it was so he wouldn't get stuck raising me and my sister. No, it wasn't retaliation for that. *That*, she didn't seem to react to anymore. In fact, she'd have two over-hard eggs and a bacon smiley face on his plate at breakfast the next morning after waking up on the bathroom floor. This particular night, she'd heard that he was seen with a hand up LeAnne Butler's skirt down at Shorty's bar.

When they came home in the small hours of the morning, together, I was asleep in the front hall with the Remington clasped in my arms. I don't know why I was surprised when they laughed at the sight of me and stumbled past me to the back bedroom. I didn't feel particularly protective of my mother, all told. She never protected me.

"Jesus," Liam said, stroking my hair mindlessly as I lay on his chest. "You don't still talk to the son of a bitch, do you?"

"No." I reached for a piece of pizza and sat cross-legged in a T-shirt and underwear, ready to be done with the conversation. It was making me more anxious than I had anticipated.

"Your mom?" he continued.

"Well, not really. She still lives in the same place. I guess I see her every few years by accident. She showed up at Ellie's wedding, uninvited and hammered," I laughed, humorlessly.

"God, Faith. I'm sorry."

"Yeah."

"When's the last time you saw your dad?" he asked, genuine care in his eyes.

"A long time. I wish I could say my mom finally grew a set and left, but he worked as a trucker, and met some 'bimbo in Missouri and moved into her trailer and just never came back.' That's the way my mom tells it, anyway." Even though

I'd mentioned once, in a similar late-night conversation over wine, that I'd worked through all of my shit, so not to worry. It was in a joking context. I was a little worried, though, that he'd see the piles of baggage I came with and I'd be regretful for opening up, but he just took the pizza out of my hand and dropped it in its box. He slipped off my T-shirt and kissed up my body, and although I was aware of the immeasurable gesture of unconditional love this was meant to be, although we'd only dropped the L-word a few weeks earlier in the infancy of our romance, I still hid the flood of tears streaming down my face as we made love. I turned over and pushed my face into the pillow to hide it as I felt him press his body into my back and kiss my neck. *What the hell was wrong with me? That was a million years ago.*

The concerned, loving Liam I saw in him that night was the Liam I got every day. It wasn't a best-foot-forward facade I got for a few months until the newness wore off and I'd begin to discover a gambling addiction, or that he was a closet smoker, or that he usually spent five hours playing Grand Theft Auto when he got home from work. There was no temper lying dormant, no looking over my shoulder at a prettier girl. He even found my 1930s jazz obsession "sort of adorable" and hummed along to Ella Fitzgerald when I had it singing from my laptop while we cooked together. When my dog, Potato, was still with us, he baked him a birthday cake. Could there really be such a thing as a perfect man?

FIVE

NOW

AFTER LEN LEAVES, I THROW UP, RUNNING TO THE toilet and retching myself sober. I cry for what seems like hours until fatigue and mundane thoughts drift in, easing me out of it. All the drinks I just had were gone now. A waste of money. And so I take a Klonopin and pour a glass of port to chase it with.

I sit at the kitchen table and open Liam's laptop. I have tried every password I can think of, from his beloved grandfather's name and his birthday with and without exclamation points after it, to "password" and "1234," which I know he'd never use, but I was desperate. I had welcomed the police to seize his computer so I could find out what was on it, what the hell I had missed, but as Len pointed out, "they had reasons not to pursue it." Meaning they had evidence that Liam had left of his own free will and didn't want to be found. And there was no law that could force him to return. Or so I was told by a detective whose downward glare insinuated that I wanted to "force" Liam to return.

Liam was an only child of a single mother who was deceased. So, no family was hovering around to insist it was out of character for him to walk away from his job and wife. His coworkers and friends echoed my statements that that was the case, but the police are nonetheless disinclined to spend precious money and manpower on a case that has "overwhelming" evidence the "subject" left of his own accord:

A. There was a large bank withdrawal made just before his disappearance. Approximately $6,000.

B. His bank card was used the day after the accident by the O'Hare Airport. Although no one with the name Liam Finley had flown from Chicago, he could have used an alias for a local flight and then flown internationally.

C. His passport is missing.

D. And now, I've discovered that he left a note on his work computer saying that he needed a break from everything. Maybe a permanent one. (Translation: *the scandal his wife was caught up in was reflecting badly on him.*)

So, friends may think it's out of character, but given the current stressful circumstances and all the evidence that he was alive and well, and perhaps just a coward, a side of him not seen before, there is no reason to treat this as a missing persons case.

Between fits and starts of sleep, I found myself mostly awake in the hospital for days after it happened, coming up with explanations for their findings. Someone might have stolen his phone and bank card to use them. Detective Sterling argued that the likelihood of someone obtaining his PIN number, and squaring that with the coincidence of a large withdrawal before the party and a missing passport was… He didn't even finish the sentence; he just looked at me, a fatherly look, telling me to be reasonable, put it together. Maybe if the phone and ATM were the only bits of evidence, it would have changed things, but all of that to-gether was implausible.

I'm the one who told them his passport was missing, after they'd asked me about it, and now I wish I hadn't. Maybe less information would have forced them to keep the investiga-tion open. I suggested they search our house in their initial half-assed investigation. I opened the locked file cabinet and whipped out folders and important papers. I showed Detec-tive Sterling the folder with our passports; I pointed mine out, sitting in a manila folder by itself. I thought it would be helpful, but it proved to be the last piece they needed to be certain Liam wanted out.

After I'd been home a few weeks, my leg still in a cast, I shot out of bed from a fevered sleep. I hobbled across the room to the light switch, knocking half a bottle of wine onto my white pillow, letting it glug out of the top as I felt around the sheets for my phone, making my bed look like the scene of a homicide. When I rescued my phone from a knot of bed-sheet, I called Sterling. He didn't answer. All my knowledge of police work was from bad crime shows that flung one-liners around shamelessly, but it seemed to me that when-ever you called a detective on a case like this, day or night, they answered. This was urgent. He did not answer. I leave a frantic voice mail.

"Detective Sterling, it's Faith Finley...um, I just... I'm sorry to call so late but...you said he made an ATM withdrawal after the accident. It was... I looked at the bank records, and it was the ATM at Wells Fargo near the airport. It has a camera. I've used it before. It has a camera. You could see if it was him...him who made the...who used it, right? Please call me back." I hung up shakily and fluttered my hands to my robe, clasping it closed, looking at the bloody cabernet puddle in my bed.

Completely unable to deal with it, I pull Liam's favorite fleece blanket from its folded spot at the end of the bed—the one Potato loved to curl up in, and drag it out to the couch to pour a vodka soda and wait.

The next morning when Sterling calls back, not only does he remind me that this is no longer an open case, therefore not *his* case any longer, he also tells me, not without a little condescension, that of course they'd checked the camera on the ATM, but that unfortunately, the camera had been out of commission for a few days. No evidence pointed to tampering or that it was linked to this case...*when it was a case*, he adds, trying to keep sympathy in his voice. He assures me if they'd found something of consequence like that when they were looking into it, they certainly would have mentioned it to me.

I can explain away any of that evidence to make a case that Liam was in danger—that he didn't leave. I even have a whiteboard of bullet lists that I drag from my office into the living room, outlining multiple scenarios that could explain away all the so-called evidence. But now, Len knocks on my door and hands me almost irrefutable confirmation that their theory is true.

But...the timing. I was driving. How could he have planned to disappear that night? Something *happened* to him. Maybe he was planning it. Maybe there's evidence of that, but that night? Is my life now a B movie about supernatural phenomena? *It's incomprehensible*, I think. I had held out a thread of hope with that thought—that it was just impossible—until Officer Bloom, a large woman with a pillow of girth beneath her uniformed pants, pulled high around her large waist, had told me that faking your own death was a pretty straightforward way to try to disappear. "If he had been planning to leave and not be found," she'd said, "maybe the opportunity just pre-

sented itself." That had never occurred to me. She'd said this
the day I got out of the hospital, after Liam had been almost
one month missing. I'd felt like crawling back into that sterile
bed and never getting out. I couldn't be left alone with that
idea, so I'd chosen not to believe it. *He loved me.*

But this fucking email printout? Fuck you, Len. I know
why Liam was angry that night. I know the months leading
up to the party were our toughest and that he'd tried not to
blame me—to be the kind and understanding man I knew.
But I saw the light in his eyes shine just a little dimmer, and
I heard his boisterous laugh less often, and the worst part is
that all the shit the press was saying about me—I saw it taking its toll on him more than me. Now it's possible he may
never know—never *really know*—that I did not do what they
were saying I did.

Liam's email log-in stares back at me. His smiling face in
a thumbnail photo beside the empty search bar, blinking,
waiting for me to type in his password. It's all I can do not
to smash the screen into pieces with a kitchen mallet, but the
Klonopin is settling into my bloodstream, and I simply give
up trying and close the laptop.

My job is to counsel. My specialty is mending abusive relationships and knowing the signs of narcissists, abusers, and
secret-keepers, yet here I am, shamefully unaware of Liam's
secret life. What other explanation could there be? I have
proof in hand. An elaborate plan had been set up to deceive
me while I handed out advice to other women about their
marriages—how to spot a scammer, a liar, a cheater.

I'm still going to find him. If grief could fuel months of
looking, anger can now carry me even further. He can't do
this without answering to me. I top off my vodka and sit on
the couch. I wait to start sobbing, a nightly ritual. By dusk
I can hear a few of the neighborhood kids playing kickball

in the cul-de-sac. I catch scraps of their conversation, petty protests about who's cheating and who's "it." Janie Stuart will sit on her porch with a cup of tea—something we'd done together before I turned into an inconsolable basket case with unkempt hair and dark circles under her eyes whom everyone avoided as politely as possible. It wasn't out of cruelty. People just don't know how to watch someone else in pain. It makes them uncomfortable, so they bring casseroles and "send prayers" for an acceptable amount of time, and then avoid contact and hope it goes away. I can't say I blame them.

I flip on a show about hoarders. I haven't started to sob yet. I watch a woman climb over a wall of garage sale toys and soiled clothes in order to make it to her kitchen, overrun with cat boxes and rat feces. This is completely normal to her. She pees in old soda cans because she can't find the bathroom any longer. It's covered by a barricade of newspapers dating back to 1942. I found myself watching this a moment with less judgment that I expected. It's not impossible for me to see how she could let it get that bad. I can see giving up, I really can.

Liam's keys still sit it in an organizer on the kitchen counter. We'd taken my car that night. I go to pour another drink and pick them up. I imagine his many pockets in which the keys had lived, doors they might open, and what faces or music, comfort or disappointment might lie behind those doors. Which one opened the door to his office? Were there secrets hidden there, meetings with a lover? I remembered the day they'd sat undisturbed on the bargain table at a used bookstore until we retraced our steps, and only then he remembered putting them down on that stack, where they left their toothed impression in a neglected dust pile. We laughed when we found them, and ran through a misty rain to get coffee across the street.

I imagined him in this kitchen, bare-chested with gym shorts and slippers, recipe cards askew and splashed with marinara sauce as he played Iron Chef, determined to impress me with his grandmother's beef bolognese.

I realize why I'm not succumbing to tears tonight. I don't know what I'm doing in this house. It feels haunted by his constant memory. In Chicago, I can hear neighbors on three sides—their arguments, their phones ringing, their TVs right through the walls. I'm forced to say hello to people when I go outside. How is there enough space in the world for me to walk all of these big empty, unused rooms alone? They should be filled with life, and I feel dead. I make a decision. I have to leave.

The next morning I wake up and try to remember the leftover wisps of a dream, but it's hazy and just out of reach. I grasp, mentally, for the memory. I dreamed that I set the house on fire. I should be horrified by the thought, but it seems gratifying for a moment. At least I'd be left with a crumb of satisfaction, knowing that nobody else would ever sleep in our bed or enjoy my coveted soaker tub with the must-have jets. They'd never cover up our memories with new ones.

Then I recall a flash of the dream. I watched our wedding album burn. The flames engulfing the bedroom first and the photos curling up on the sides, melting and boiling before meeting the rest of our earthly belongings as ash in a puff of rolling black smoke above our house.

I go into my office and start writing my description of the one-acre lot and updated, open-concept living space before promptly calling a real-estate agent to list it.

I call Ellie and tell her I'm moving back to the condo. She

screams in delight, almost deafening me, making girls' night and mani-pedi plans before I even finish my sentence, but I hurry her off the phone. I pack my bags right then and there, and hire a service for the rest. I get in my car and drive to Chicago.

SIX

THEN

I CAN PINPOINT THE EXACT MOMENT OUR LIFE started to crumble. It was a Saturday in January, a few weeks before my book signing party. My first book was a success, and my permanent radio spot *Someone's Listening* was turning into regular TV appearances, a few talk shows, guest spots, and even televised interviews. My agent, Paula, thought I should title my next book *Someone's Listening*, make it instantly recognizable from the radio show—an expansion on my first book that focuses on life after abuse.

This book would reveal some personal stories of my own abusive childhood, and offer safe plans for leaving an abusive relationship. "It should be really positive," Paula said. It would include all the tips to get help and a step-by-step guide for anyone trapped in an abusive situation, but the overarching message will be about overcoming destructive patterns and reclaiming yourself.

I liked it. Part of me may have liked it because it was a "screw you" message to Thomas and Alan, my colleagues, because it proved this wasn't some stroke of luck or a phase.

I was really establishing myself in this new role. I would not be "crawling back to private practice with my tail between my legs after being devoured by the media over one misstep or advice that backfired," as rumored by Alan, or so I'm told. Of course, he'd said it in jest, apparently, and in his defense, after he'd had a few scotches at a dinner party.

I'd been sent a few boxes of the new book, and they'd arrived that morning. Liam and I sat on the sofa in robes, sipping coffee. He was catching the end of the news while I was distracted with opening the boxes of books like Christmas presents, before I could get on a soapbox about the biased, sensationalized theater the news had become. I took one of the books from the neatly packed box. I smelled the glue, the paper, the ink. I examined my photo on the back. Liam complimented it, and started to change the channel when I saw it.

I saw my own face—the same photo I was holding in my hand appeared in a small, framed box next to the reporter's head. I felt a tapping of prickly heat climb my back. I froze and stared at the screen. Liam looked paralyzed a moment too, the remote held out in midair, his face a mix of confusion and shock.

"Dr. Faith Finley, a popular radio show doctor that you may better know from her appearances on *Get Up, America*, *The Chat*, and even an appearance here on *Weekend Edition*, is gaining fame for a different reason today. She's been accused of having a sexual relationship with an underage patient. Carter Daley, now twenty, talked to us about his experience with the doctor when he was just seventeen."

I dropped my coffee on top of the box of books. It seeped down through the creases, saturating and ruining them. I couldn't speak. Carter's face appeared on the screen. There were microphones everywhere. He looked frightened. A man stood next to him. Maybe a lawyer? It wasn't his father. I'd

met his father, Alex Daley. He was grateful for the progress I
was making with Carter. What the hell was happening? Reporters shouted questions at him. I couldn't discern one from
another, but he started saying something, quieting the chaos
a moment.

"I'm not pressing charges. I just think it's important that it's
out there so it doesn't happen to anyone else. That's all I want
to say about it," he said, looking at his feet. There were more
questions. Something about how he felt, being taken advantage of at his most vulnerable mental state. Another question
was shouted, asking whether he'd sue. But the story cut off
and transitioned back to Larry Green, who made an attempt
at sincerity when he remarked how sad the situation was for
all involved, and then moved to an update on the weather.

Liam turned off the TV and sat down. Neither of us moved.
We were in shock, I suppose. Then he just looked at me. I
hadn't seen the look before. Maybe it was a sort of pleading
in his eyes to tell him this wasn't true. Maybe it was disgust.
Maybe it was what a person's face looks like the exact moment trust is broken and they know they'll never be the same.
My hands were shaking and tears were clouding my eyes. My
heart was pounding in my ears.

"I…don't…" I had to catch my breath. I couldn't speak.
"That's Carter. That's—" I stood, then sat again.

"Faith. What's going on? What happened?" he said with
a forced calm.

"I don't know!" My voice was breaking. "I don't know! You
think I know? He's a patient! He— Oh my God."

"He's saying you had sex with him? What… Why would
he…?" Liam sat very still and stared at the floor. If I knew
him the way I thought I did, he was thinking about how to
handle this. "Did…?" Liam started again, but he didn't get
out another word before I exploded in defense.

"No! My God, are you kidding? Of course I didn't. Jesus Christ! Of course I— Why is he doing this?" Tears were falling now. I couldn't think; I just seethed with anger.

"Faith. Can you think of anything at all that he could have misinterpreted as…" Liam started to ask, and I cut his question off again.

"If I were able to discuss his diagnosis with you, you'd know that it is not surprising that he may misinterpret a lot of things, but I am telling you—nothing ever happened. I shouldn't have to tell you that. I have no idea why he'd do this!"

I stood and breathed, trying to stop my shaking. What I was ethically bound not to tell even Liam was that Carter struggled with paranoid delusions. One of which was erotomania, where one believes that a person, usually of higher social standing, is in love with him or her, contrary to evidence otherwise. He hadn't been in my care for almost a year. His parents were active in his therapy. He'd been doing really well last I'd heard. What would ever cause him to make an allegation like this, I could not imagine.

"You believe me, right?" I gave Liam a steely look.

"Why would he *say* it?" He was still looking at the floor. His head was in his hands, then he rubbed his temples and ran his hands through his hair nervously.

"Oh my God. Are you asking me that? I ask if you believe me, and that's your response?" I was fuming.

"No. Of course. Of course I believe you. I'm sorry." He sat back against the sofa arm and looked far away, already contemplating the mess this would be for both of our careers, I was sure, because that's all I could think of.

"I don't know why he'd say it!" I practically screamed. "I have no fucking clue why the fuck he would do this!"

"This is a mess," Liam said quietly. I started to cry, silently, and sat opposite him in an armchair.

Only an hour before, Liam had been so excited because we'd just booked tickets to visit Santiago, Chile, in May. The region was on his lengthy list of food destinations around the world where we needed to travel together, and while we'd crossed off many places, there were still a few must-sees, and Santiago was top of the list. He was scrolling through his iPad, verbally planning out our trip while I made eggs in the kitchen.

"We have to visit Barrio Lastarria first. We'll have coffee and breakfast at Colmado, order a cappuccino and a *pincho de tortilla* and eat in the courtyard. The weather will be perfect in May," he'd said. I'd covered the mist of sizzling bacon grease before it could pop out of the pan and burn my arm, and kissed him, pot holders on both hands, agreeing with his plan. Now, everything would change.

Liam went quietly into the kitchen and poured more coffee. He leaned against the counter and looked out the window.

"I'll call Paula," I said, looking for my phone. "See if she can start on damage control."

"Don't you think you should call Ralph first?" he said, without looking away from whatever he was mindlessly fixated on outside the window—a squirrel balancing on the fence, it looked like.

"You think I need a lawyer?" I stopped cold. "He said he's not pressing charges," I said, and Liam turned to me with a flushed face.

"Um…okay," he said, in a sarcastic way that was uncharacteristic.

"What?" I asked.

"The way you say that… I don't know." He stopped.

"What?" I snapped.

"Like you're relieved he's not pressing charges," he continued.

"Of course I am!" I was flustered, shocked. I didn't know what he was getting at.

"It's just a weird thing to say. It sounds like you have a reason to be relieved he's not pressing charges. I mean I'd expect you to say that you plan to press charges against him... for defamation of character or something. It just sounded... I don't know. Grateful."

"Oh my God." I sat down, a sob rising in my throat, but I swallowed it down and let anger lead. "You're doubting me."

"No," he said, trying to stay calm. I could tell by the controlled and forced way he was speaking.

"I'm sorry..." I said, now scrolling through my phone, looking for Paula's number. "If I haven't been falsely accused of a... I don't know, felony probably! In front of the entire country, and so I'm not sure of the etiquette."

"I just mean..." He still had that overly controlled tone that was beginning to piss me off. "That I can't imagine it matters whether the kid pursues action or not. The whole country knows now. I'm sure they'll investigate. Right? I mean..." He stopped. I put my phone down, not having thought of this in the five minutes I'd had to absorb the news. New panic began surfacing.

"Who's 'they'?" I asked him.

"I don't know. The state? I don't know."

My heart was racing. They couldn't convict me if I was innocent, right? I was trying to sort it out. *I could take a polygraph*, I thought. I realized this was something I'd learned from police dramas and was probably not regular practice.

But it was just the word of an unstable kid. I tried to think of anything that I may have said or done to cause this. No. He misinterpreted damn near everything. *That* was part of his diagnosis. I hated that I was doubting myself. Could I have brushed against his knee when leaning over to hand him a tissue? I'd hugged him once, but it was at his last session when I wouldn't be seeing him again, and his mother was standing right there. I'd hugged her too, in fact.

Then it hit me. Three years ago, when he'd started with me, he was seventeen. He'd lunged at me and tried to kiss me in one of our sessions, but I'd pushed him away in time. He had cried, apologized. We were working through his unhealthy sexual urges, so I made a careful record of the incident, and was firm with him about how inappropriate his behavior was, and if it happened again, I'd have to refer him elsewhere. He didn't have any more outbursts or make any advances after that. That must have been what he was talking about. He must have been jumbling his memories of it. Even under the circumstances, I couldn't explain this to Liam because of confidentiality purposes, but it must have been something to do with that. My phone rang. It was Paula.

"Hello," I answered.

"A heads-up about this would have been nice, Faith," she said, without even saying hello.

"Paula, I found out about this a few minutes ago when I saw it on the news. I don't even know what to say."

"So you do know the kid? It's not some crazy coming out of the woodwork?" she asked.

"He was a patient, and I might know how to handle this. He may have misconstrued something. I mean I can't talk to you about his case obviously, but I need to contact him, and..."

"I don't think you should do that just now. This is...really fucking bad. You have to make this go away," she said in a curt tone I'd never heard her use with me before.

"I will. I really think it's nothing, and that he's not altogether stable. It should be easily cleared up." I was gaining confidence as I said it.

"Well, the details are pretty…damning. I hope you're right, but get a lawyer."

"What details?" I asked. "All I heard was that he said something sexual happened a few years ago…which, of course, it didn't." My confidence was gone as quick as I'd acquired it, and I noticed my hands trembling again.

"You don't know?" she asked.

"No. What? What's he saying?" I practically yelled into the phone.

"Well, you'll find out in about five seconds if you look at any local papers or news today, so…" She stopped and took a pause that made me uneasy. "He says you tried to touch him, and he was scared…and…" She sighed.

"What? Is that all he said?" I demanded.

"This isn't easy for me, Faith. He said you were concerned about his drug use and were going to recommend him to chemical dependency treatment." She stopped.

"Yes. I was. And?"

"And he didn't want to be sent away again, or have his parents find out about his drug use."

"Okay, that's all true, so what then?" I was growing impatient. Then she blurted it out.

"He said you wouldn't make that recommendation on the condition he gave you…ah…certain sexual favors. Oral sex were actually the words he used." She cleared her throat, uncomfortable.

"Paula. Oh my God," I said in almost a whisper. "I…"

"Did you by any chance make the recommendation to chemical dependency treatment? Please say you did so we can sweep this under the rug," she said, hopeful.

"I didn't," I said.

"Goddamn it!" She cut me off. I heard something bang on the other end, like she'd thrown or punched something.

"I told him he needed to prove he could stay clean, and I gave him a few weeks before I made any moves. He did. He proved he could stay away from drugs, and he was really doing well. Jesus! How could he say that? Paula, this is—" I didn't even know what it was, how to describe it, process it.

"I'm sure the kid's a quack," she interrupted. "But you have a book coming out next month, and we need to make a public statement. Make it go away as soon as humanly possible. So, talk to a lawyer and work with the police," she said firmly.

"Police? Are you kidding me? Police?" I said defiantly. I looked up at Liam, who simply closed his eyes and took a deep breath. He dumped the rest of his coffee into the sink and started to walk out of the room when there was a knock at the front door. Through the slim glass panels on either side of it, I could clearly see who it was.

The police.

SEVEN

NOW

THE CONDO IS ON THE FIFTH FLOOR WITH A VIEW OF bustling shops below, a café with burnt coffee and an owner with body odor that's pretty much stunk out all his customers, and, lucky for me, a pub called Grady's. I stab the key into the lock of the condo door, and I don't want to look around. It feels better than the house, but I'm not going to stare at photos of us on the wall and then imagine him the way he was in that photo, the same wide smile and pale eyes, his chest and shoulders buttery with coconut sun block, standing on a beach in Cabo. For all I know, he's there right now with his arm around some other woman.

What wouldn't be the same are the orange swim trunks he was wearing. His favorite. He didn't take clothes. He didn't pack anything. Maybe a reminder of this life he apparently wanted to escape so badly. Maybe just because he had money, why have luggage weigh down his elaborate plan? He really would start over completely.

I don't even open the blinds. I place a key under the mat and call Merry Maids. Once they cleaned and took down the photos that I didn't want to touch at the moment, I would order groceries and booze for delivery, and stop by a Macy's down the block for new bedding. I might be able to work with the place then. For now, alcohol.

On my way out, I stop in the lobby. I remember Lettie and how I was able to help her. That seemed like another lifetime ago. I wonder if she stayed in Chicago after she left the shelter or left town to escape the ex. Just then, I see a woman trying to push open the door and balance a moving box on her hip. I hold open the door, and she rushes in. She is short and a bit disheveled, with wild hair and sweatpants. Not the usual sort of tenant the building attracts. It's on the higher end of amenities even though it's a historic building. It's in a sought-after neighborhood; lots of young professionals who get dressed up just to go to the grocery store live here, so she stands out a bit.

"Oh my God. Thank you, thank you," the woman says, out of breath. I notice that there is a cat in the box she's holding. Before I can say anything, she holds her hand out. "I'm such a fan."

"Oh." I shake her hand, taken aback.

"I see you in the news, and I just want you to know there are a lot of people in your corner. It's terrible what happened to you," she says.

"Thanks." I just want to be done with the conversation and have a drink in my hand.

"I'm just moving in. This is Mr. Pickle." She nods to the cat in the box. "And I'm Hilly."

"Well, welcome, Hilly. You'll like the neighborhood, I'm sure." She still stands there, staring at me. I notice a guy sliding some sort of flyer into the top cracks of each mailbox on the wall. He gives me an eye roll, seeming to understand how awkward this is as the woman stands there, too close I might add, smiling at me like I'm Beyoncé or something. He hands her one of the flyers, coming to my rescue.

"If you need any help with computer repair or set up in your new place, I'm at your service." He puts a flyer in the box, next to her cat.

"Oh. Thanks. Say, can you replace a cracked screen?" she asks, backing out of my personal bubble and into his.

"I can do everything from turning the power on to hacking the Russian government."

"I just need my screen fixed," she says seriously.

"That was a little joke. I mostly do simple repairs and software installation, so yes. Just give me a call." He smiles and continues tucking flyers into mailboxes.

"Thank you. Nice to meet you, Dr. Finley. I'm in 208 if you ever need anything, or want to come by for a cup of coffee, or anything," she says, now trying to calm a restless Mr. Pickle, which is likely the only reason she moves past me and to the elevators.

Before I head outside, I look to the flyer guy. I know he was making a joke about hacking, but I wonder what his skills really are. I can't ask him now, but I wonder how easy it would be for him to get into Liam's computer, and how I could approach it without seeming suspicious.

"Could I get one of those?" I ask, pointing to his stack of flyers.

"Oh. Yeah." He hands me one. "Need help with your computer?" he asks.

"Maybe." I look at it and see his name across the top: *Marty Nash*.

"Thanks, Marty." I slip it into my purse. "I'm Faith." I stretch my hand out to shake. "Nice to meet you."

"Nice to meet you." He shakes my hand.

"You live in the building?" I ask.

"Fourth floor," he says, pointing to his name on the mailbox that reads 429 and then turns back to finish stuffing the last few. I've never noticed our neighbors below us before. When we moved to Sugar Grove four years ago, we'd really just pop into the condo once in a while to grab mail or sleep after a late event, only to rush out again in the morning. I used to write here some weekends, but we didn't spend actual time here, so if Marty has only been in the building three years, it would make sense that I hadn't met him until the other day. Hell, I barely know any of the neighbors in the building. Another reason we thought smaller town life would be more fulfilling.

I want more information. I hadn't thought about hiring someone, but—as much as I wish it weren't the case—I need to know where Liam went…and with whom.

"How long have you lived here?" Why am I asking this? My attempt at conversation is sounding creepy.

"Three years, give or take," he answers, unoffended.

"You do this full time?" I ask. "The computer stuff?"

"Eh. I guess. I'm a software programmer, but I work from home mostly now, freelancing."

"Oh. Cool," I reply, not really knowing what else to say.

"I don't know about cool," he says, "but it pays the bills." He looks like he wants to finish his work, so I thank him again and walk down to Grady's.

At one in the afternoon, the pub does not have many inhabitants. The few men who line the bar—each claiming his respective bar stool with discarded coats and a hunched posture—are the embodiment of loneliness. It fills me with an intangible grief, like the permeating damp of a basement invading one's skin, one's mood, but it simultaneously feels like the comfort of finding home because of its safety or anonymity, I suppose.

I take a Klonopin from a zipped pocket inside my purse and chase it with a vodka tonic. I fit into this setting more than I would have a few months ago. If you look at the photo on my book jacket, I'm put together. My long, dark blond hair, always up-to-date on conditioning treatments and lowlights. My nails short but French-manicured, my thin frame mistaken for an athletic build, broad-shouldered and lanky—but really I'd simply won a genetic lottery; it allowed me to eat anything Liam needed to critique, from duck confit and butterscotch pound cake to lobster risotto and baklava at a new restaurant every week, and not worry about gaining weight.

I'm sure it will catch up with me one day, but in my late thirties, I'm still described as pretty. *Who gives a shit?* I think. Now, after pulling on dirty yoga pants and a down parka, and not washing my hair for a few days, I sort of fit into this shithole bar. I prefer it this way.

When all the stuff with Carter Daley began, two news anchors with tight neckties and graying temples questioned why someone so pretty and successful would need to trick a teenager into sex. I almost took a pair of rusty scissors from Liam's toolbox in the garage that day and cut all my hair off to make a point. But I didn't really know what point I'd be making, and rather than risk appearing crazy or unstable in light of everything I was facing, I decided against it.

The bartender slides another vodka tonic in front of me without me having to ask. It's old school at Grady's: you leave a small pile of singles and fives in cash on the bar, and he just subtracts the price of the drink from your pile each time, counting it out in front of you and leaving the rest of the cash, assuming, I suppose, that most of the clientele will be too drunk to count fairly shortly after taking their places on their stools. I'm one of them now. Each time I'm sure I've hit rock bottom, I find a new low.

I look around, almost hoping one of these drunks will talk to me because none of them knows who I am or cares, so they wouldn't have sympathy or judgment, just meaningless small talk, which I long for. I listen to a couple of them preach uneducated opinions about politics like they're an authority on the topic, then argue over a football play, gesturing wildly to the

TV above the bar, which I hadn't noticed until now. I heard one of the men complaining to another about how he's gonna spend Christmas down at the mission because his sister's a bitch.

I imagine him being invited just once a year to his family home. His bitch sister just hoping he can manage the forkful of green bean casserole from the plate to his mouth without trembling and making a mess, or worse yet, drinking too many mugs of mulled Christmas wine and making a scene in front of her in-laws.

No one wanted me either. In these recent months, all of the friends I held dear, one by one, stopped calling, stopped coming by. I wasn't sure if success simply attracted fairweather friends, or if they, at some point, had to give up on the task of consoling the inconsolable and move on with their lives. In all fairness I'd slept for weeks, never returned calls, didn't say much in the company of anyone who tried to see me. Should they be expected to keep trying to be there for me? I wasn't sure. I can't really say I fault them for quitting.

Now, three vodka tonics in, I find myself thinking of Hilly and Mr. Pickle. I think of knocking on Hilly's door. One year ago, if I knocked on the door of a new neighbor, I'd be carrying a gift basket of expensive wine, exotic teas, and assorted meats and cheeses. Now, I find myself wondering if I'd even remembered to order a box of cookies from the grocery delivery, so I could dump one of the plastic sleeves onto a plate, passing it off as my own, in order to go have a conversation that wasn't about "my loss." The problem is, Hilly knows me, or at least knows of me, and any attempt at chatter about coming snow flurries or the regal architecture of the brownstone building would turn to headlines and probing questions.

The headlines have mostly faded by now, the newest school shooting or celebrity scandal taking their place. My life, my career, also forgotten about, but left ruined in the wake of accusations and a runaway husband.

The friends I once had don't know what to say to me anymore. My personal life is splayed open, wet, raw, and exposed—I may as well be naked, spread wide on an exam table. Every detail, from the sexual intimacy I allegedly had with Carter Daley to my prescribed medications, were public knowledge.

Even when they tried to talk to me like a normal person at a dinner or the occasional obligatory event I still forced myself to attend until recently, there was something behind their eyes—a tinge of suspicion, maybe. Or worse yet, pity.

I guess that's the same reason I can only take Ellie in small doses these days. It's not just the perpetual shitty diaper and baby powder smell in her house and the squawks and shrieks of dancing puppets on the television that made me want to run (like literally run from her place directly to the gynecologist for a tubal ligation), it was that she'd been there through every turn, God love her, but to see her face is to see Liam. She was right next to me on our wedding day, and for almost every memory. His bare feet and white linen pants as we tried to ignore the hot wind and scorching sand beneath our feet on the beach for the ceremony. Late at night, when I'd talk to Ellie on the phone and tell her about our dates, in the early days, all the details of exotic foods and hours of lovemaking. All of the summer-soaked backyard barbecues, the Christmas Eves watching George Bailey curse the Building and Loan, the maternity ward when Ellie gave birth, the trips to Belize. It was the four of us. Ellie and Joe, me and Liam, and the reminder of a life robbed from me was too much sometimes.

I fish out a lime rind from my drink and suck on it. I remember someone telling me that lemon and lime peels have more bacteria than a toilet seat. I don't much care at the moment. I think about Marty the computer guy. Maybe he could be someone to drink with. He didn't even flinch when Hilly was gushing about being a fan. A fan of who? Who was I? He didn't give a shit. I liked that. That's the kind of uninvested stranger I need. How pathetic that I'm going to corner this poor guy because he gave me a flyer.

I know what I should do. I should call old friends. I'm back in the city, I'm standing upright, I've dressed myself. There is progress. And now, I have all the information I asked for. It's time to move on. I could work out a new book idea with Paula about self-reinvention, life after loss or something, get back into the world.

But I don't do any of that. I stumble out of Grady's, walk upstairs, get into bed, and don't leave the condo for days. I'm not sure how long I would have stayed like that if I hadn't seen something shocking.

I'm sitting with a bottle of wine on a dark October afternoon, icy rain tapping at the windows, and I'm trying to muster up the energy to pay a stack of bills. Then I see it. Something in a forgotten corner of Liam's desk that changes everything.

EIGHT

THEN

THERE WAS NO EVIDENCE, BUT IN THE TWITTER-sphere, that hardly matters when it comes to someone's reputation. The police asked me a series of questions about Carter Daley. His parents decided to push the matter with the district attorney and insisted they file a suit, so I was officially under investigation.

In the days that followed, I stayed home for the most part. I made the colossal mistake of looking in the comment threads of the posts about my case. It was now "a case." I knew enough after a couple years in the spotlight with my TV work to know that you *never* read the comments section. Even armed with a Klonopin and a bottle of moscato, doing so could easily cause one to slip into an unrecoverable depression, if not a homicidal rage. I couldn't help myself though.

A Facebook post blinked on my screen. It was a still shot of Carter in front of news mics when he gave his public statement—his random, out-of-the-blue, wild accusation, meant-to-ruin-me statement. I click it and read the comments:

Candy_grl7156: That ugly ass bitch should rot in jail. I hate her face and her stupid radio advice. "Leave your abuser." Oh, why didn't I think of that!? She needs a PhD for that shit advice?

RwrdyDawg001: Who you callin' ugly, fat stick? I'd let Faith Finley molest the shit outta me.

HyPnOTk1998: It's not something to make light of, I know, but you're right, like, why would that kid even complain. I'd eat that pussy all day. LOL.

Momoffour19_78: You all should be ashamed of yourselves. This kid is a victim. Educate yourselves. Sexual assault is sexual assault. No matter looks, or anything else.

There were hundreds of these. Some were on my side. Most weren't. People…really hated me. Paula tried to remind me that next week no one would even remember, and we could recover from this. I could tell she didn't believe that. And the more I scrolled through comments, the more I saw hate messages aimed at Carter too.

Jnk_n_Trnk96: What a faggot.

AllyCat0011: That kid's a liar, and like totally autistic or some shit.

Lrd!_!Voldemort: He goes to the media to make an accusation, and then cries like a bitch saying he doesn't want to get anyone in trouble. #goodjob #supersmart #douchecanoe

I hated these people. I didn't know why Carter was doing this, but I felt the urge to protect him—to stand up for him. I knew I couldn't say anything publicly, but if I could just talk to him, maybe this could all be resolved.

The lawyer Liam put me in contact with, Ralph Kinsey, was one that he used now and then when someone tried to sue him for a bad review of their restaurant or something of that nature. Kinsey came to the house and sat down with me for an expensive fifty-minute hour on the day after this all came out. He was a sweaty, red, impatient man with a neck too large for the tight white collar that pressed his flesh out over the sides. He looked very uncomfortable, as if it took effort just to be sitting upright. As off-putting as he was, I wondered how he garnered enough credibility to be the hard-hitting lawyer Liam assured me he was.

He sat in our front room; the sofa protested slightly. He wiped the beads of sweat from his forehead with a soiled handkerchief and told me, in no uncertain terms, that I was not to contact Carter Daley for any reason whatsoever.

"He said/she said cases are the hardest and most involved kind, especially if there is truly no evidence, as you claim. And for God's sake, don't talk to the press," he said, cramming the wet handkerchief back into his pocket. It was hard to believe my future could rest with this distracted, fidgety man, who looked at Liam when answering questions *I* asked. I didn't feel like I should do anything to hurt or otherwise disappoint Liam after causing him all of this upset, so I took Kinsey's card politely, nodded when he said he'd be in touch, and thanked Liam for his help recommending the guy. Liam hugged me into him, an "it will be okay" gesture, but he felt very far away from me already.

He was heading out to a new resort in Playa Del Carmen to review their restaurant. I stayed back even though he said some sun would be good for me. I had work to do. If I couldn't reason with Carter directly, I had every intention of talking to the press. Kinsey could fuck off. I would get to the bottom of this.

I got drunk faster than I intended after Liam left for the airport. I couldn't bring myself to eat, so the alcohol crept up on me. I found an unopened bottle of Diplomatico Ambassador rum in the pantry. Not what I would have chosen, but it would do. I lay on the couch and stared vacantly at the television as hours of an *Iron Chef* marathon played out in front of me. I missed Liam. He hated Alton Brown—always said he was smug—and if Liam were here, he'd be adding his insulting commentary—which, I realized, was the only reason I liked the show.

When I stood to go to the bathroom, I immediately fell back onto the couch. The bottle on the coffee table was half empty, and I couldn't remember the last time I had drunk so much. I knew it was pathetic, but I couldn't help but laugh at myself for literally falling over. I turned to the TV, where one of the competing chefs was using an inedible garnish on his presentation. "Have you ever seen the show?" I yelled. "Even I know you don't put a sprig of rosemary on top of your pork chop, idiot!"

I heard my words slur as I argued with the television. I needed to go to bed. I needed to stop drinking. I needed to bring a giant glass of water and some ibuprofen up to bed, but I didn't. I opened my laptop and...read the comments.

Brkn_tHe_Rlz: I heard Dr. "Fiddly Fingers" got canned from her radio show. That's karma, bitch!

That's not true, you little... I actually started typing this, then stopped. I understood the paper trail it would leave. I knew I shouldn't, but I was still sure that if I could see Carter, or maybe even just talk to him via phone or maybe even email,

I could clear up whatever delusion he was having. I'd always been able to work through these delusions with him in the past and get him to a good place. It was outrageous that the first course of action would not be to talk to him face-to-face and work this out. He was being protected like I was some sort of predator or child molester.

It was against policy to contact a former client, but I didn't care. The rum was making me unsteady, light-headed…and careless.

A text popped up from Liam, who was about to take off for Mexico—a photo of a wilty, eighteen-dollar ham sandwich and a sad face emoji. His last-second grab for dinner before he boarded, I assumed. He said he loved me and would see me Monday. Poor Liam, who'd done nothing, was going to pay for this situation too—it would be only a matter of time before the media pounced on him, as well. I was not going to let Carter destroy us both.

I decided I couldn't wait to see if Kinsey could rescue my career, reputation, and possibly even my marriage. I took a second Klonopin and sat outside on the front stoop. It was dark and very cold outside, but I wanted the air. Wet leaves clung to the base of the porch, and the air smelled like damp earth. I could see inside the Pattersons' front window, a square of warm light in the darkness. They sat having dinner together, just the two of them. It looked old-timey, the way they ate. Peas, meat, potatoes, with glasses of milk on the side and a plate of white bread between them. They'd probably been having a variation of this oddly formal sit-down dinner-for-two for years. I wished that were Liam and me right now. I wished I could escape this nightmare and be enjoying pot roast and milk instead of piecing together my life.

I don't have much of a history of antianxiety pill prescriptions. In fact, I hadn't taken more than an Advil in years, since college probably. I had a panic attack once, back then, when I was under tremendous stress. I was starting therapy during my postgraduate work, and I had started to unpack the experiences with my father, speaking about his abuse with my psychologist for the first time, and in doing so, I began having bouts of numbness and dizziness. Once my heart raced so hard, for seemingly no reason at all, that I went to the ER, positive I was having a heart attack.

They gave me a low dosage then, and it helped. I worked through the trauma in analysis over time, and stopped taking the pills after a couple years. That was over a decade ago. I was sure I had handled it, that it was behind me.

Since the story hit, and I saw Carter's face on my television saying unthinkable things about me, never mind the things the entire internet was saying about me, I'd started to feel panic creeping in again. There were three weeks to go before the book launch party, and no matter how devastated I was, I had to show my face. I was not going to roll over and let this derail everything I'd worked so hard for. I needed to keep it together, so I'd gone in a few times to see a therapist, someone new this time, as Dr. Whitman had retired. I'd been given another Klonopin prescription, and I felt like I just might be able to get through the coming weeks of hell until I could sort out this whole mess. And I *would* sort it out.

The thing is, how can I blame the world for believing him? We need to believe victims. If I'd seen this on the news, I wouldn't think twice about trusting his account, especially because his slight social awkwardness makes him appear even more traumatized to someone who doesn't know him. But they don't know about his diagnosis. If I explained it, if I could tell the world that his sexual delusions are part of his medical history, and the very reason he came to see me, *and* that it's not the first time he's made accusations about people in positions of authority, this might disappear as quickly as it materialized. But I can't. I legally and morally cannot betray that classified bit of information. So I am cornered. I need to deal with this in a different way.

I wrapped a blanket around myself as I sat in the sharp night air, thinking about what I'd say to Carter if I could. "Why the fuck are you doing this to me?" was all I wanted to ask. But no—first I'd check on his well-being. That was where I'd start. I'd express my concern and ask what was wrong, if he was okay. I'd tell him I wasn't angry, and that he could talk to me. I didn't know what I'd say exactly, truth be told. It would depend on his reaction to my call.

I took a swig of the rum I'd brought outside with me. My head was spinning. I fumbled with my phone. There was a tiny, sober part of me that knew it wasn't ethical to do what I was about to do, but I hushed that voice. I took a deep breath and called the cell number I had saved under his contact.

It hadn't occurred to me until I dialed that it might not be current any longer, and I felt that familiar wave of numbness…a gentle brush of tingling that spread up my legs and pricked at my spine. Then it rang. It rang several times, and then went to voice mail.

"You've reached Carter. Please leave a message." It was very polite, not a casual tone that tried to be funny or personable. Knowing Carter, I'm sure he practiced that simple line many times before settling on this particular recording. I choked a moment, but since it would already be in evidence that I'd called, there was no going back now. Maybe a message could get through to him somehow. Maybe, just maybe, he'd call back and we'd figure this out. I tried to concentrate very hard on sounding sober.

"Carter. Um…this is Dr. Finley. I, ah…hope you're doing okay. I really think we need to talk. I think there must be a lot of confusion, and I—I just, I hope we can talk. I know you don't believe these allegations. I… Okay, that's all, I guess. No, it's not. Listen. I care about you, so does your mom, your dad. We all—if you're struggling with something right now, we're here. You can tell the truth and no one will be upset with you. Please call me."

He didn't. I tried twice more between 10:00 p.m. and 1:00 a.m., and then sent an email asking him what on earth was happening, and why would he be saying these things. I started to wonder if he was working with some new, shitty therapist and was uncovering false memories or something, and maybe he actually believed the things he was saying. I wondered if he was back on drugs, or maybe he was desperate for money and thought this could end in a lucrative lawsuit. Then again, he was still maintaining that he didn't want to take legal action.

So *why*, then? Why would he want to go through all of this just to ruin me? Fame? Could it be that simple? Could he really just want this attention? Because most of the attention he was getting was attached to the terms *faggot* and *dickass*. So, if that was it, maybe it was backfiring and he'd come to his senses.

After a few days without a response to my calls and emails, I decided to call his mom, Penny Daley, and explain to her that this was a huge mistake and that we all really needed to sit down and figure out what was going on—that I would never, in a million years, do anything close to what was being reported. I knew this would essentially be me calling her son a liar, but she knew full well the propensity he had for delusional episodes. She'd listen to that. I'd assure her I wanted to help.

I had to look up her number online. I was getting desperate. I really did think at one point that maybe I could make this all go away in the three days Liam was gone, and he'd come home and everything would be just like it was.

I sat at my desk on Monday morning before Liam was due back and called her. No answer. Their lawyer had advised them not to speak to me, I was sure, but I couldn't accept that. Penny was a reasonable, kind person. If she weren't being brainwashed by the media and her lawyer, she'd be pushing pie and cookies on me the way she had anytime I'd seen her, with the portable Tupperware she seemed perpetually to be carrying. She'd pat my knee and smile, and listen without interruption the way she did when I had to tell her tough things for a mother to hear about her son's condition.

This was maddening. I spent the rest of the weekend finishing the rum, hunched over my computer, trying to watch and rewatch Carter's statement, trying to scour the thousands of comments to see if he'd responded, to see if anything was said that might clue me in to what was happening.

I was glad Ellie and Joe were away on vacation. If she'd heard, she would have called, so I was happy, at least, not to ruin their ski trip. A few friends, even Alan from the office, tried to call me in those days after the accusations, but I didn't answer. I stayed buzzed enough to keep a full-blown anxiety attack at bay, and tried to decide what sort of statement I would make. If they wouldn't talk to me—if Carter and his parents could not be reasoned with—I'd have to defend myself and make a statement. Double fuck Kinsey. I didn't trust his advice anyway.

By Monday morning, I'd made no progress. I checked my email. There was only one. It was from Steve Flynn, the radio station manager. I didn't open it. I knew that it was going to be a tough talk, and we'd have to figure out what I was going to say about it on my show that Friday, and how to handle it all, but I would go in later in the day and talk to him in person.

There were no calls back from the Daleys, and I started to worry about whether I'd lose patients in my private practice and what could really happen as a result of this situation. I wanted to try to pull myself together before Liam got home. I was terribly hungover; there were dark circles under my eyes, and everything hurt from lack of sleep and too much rum…and after the rum, gin and sodas. I made some coffee and turned on the TV so the house didn't feel so deadly quiet.

I felt a little more human after a few Advil and coffee, so I ran a searing hot bath—the first time I'd bathed since Liam had left on Friday. I settled into the water and stayed there until my fingers were soft and puckered. I thought about my book launch and if anyone would come now—I thought that if I hadn't put myself in the spotlight in the first place, this probably would never have happened. I'd be in Playa Del Carmen right now with Liam, reading a romance novel under an umbrella by the sea, with crumbs of white sand dusting my tanned legs.

Attention was the only plausible reason for Carter to be doing this. I had eliminated all other possibilities. When I stepped out of the bath, I heard something on the television down the hall—my name. I wrapped a towel around myself, rushed down into the living room, and stood in front of the TV with my mouth gaping open. A well-endowed blonde in a tight sweater was giving the news headlines, and I was one of them.

"Dr. Faith Finley will not be returning to her radio show, *Someone's Listening*, and it sounds like her spot on *Wake Up, Chicago* is also on hold. This news comes from the stations themselves, when questioned by our own Chris Christoph who reported on this after serious allegations from an underage patient surfaced last week. More about this as it unfolds. Back to you, Brian."

I instantly flipped open my computer to look at that email from Steve at the station. Attached was a termination letter. Not even a call, let alone an in-person conversation. I could not believe it. Just a shitty few sentences saying how sorry he was, but that he'd lose his nerve if we made a big to-do about it and his job was on the line too—that it just looked bad, like the station was supporting sexual assault or something. And that again, he was really sorry.

"Fuck!" I yelled. "Fuck, fuck, fuck!" The doorbell rang. I was still dripping wet and draped in a towel, but the man at the front door could see me because of the stupid glass side panels around the front door that are pointless, I might add, and should be stained glass at the very least. I mean, he was right there. He looked like a UPS guy, but I didn't remember ordering anything. He smiled weakly and waved. I opened the door.

"Yes?" I said curtly.

"Are you Faith Finley?"

"Yeah. What? What do you want?" I said impatiently.

"Here." He handed me an envelope. "I need you to sign for this." I sighed as I signed his form, assuming it was a work thing for Liam. I grabbed the envelope from him and shut the door. I sat on the staircase a few feet away to force myself to take some slow breaths and keep it together. Breathe in: *one, two, three, four.*

As I glanced down at the envelope, I saw that it was addressed to me, not Liam. I picked it back up off the stair next to me and opened it, carefully. I read it, then read it again.

I stared at the paper in my hand in utter disbelief. I looked at the name on the envelope again, sure there must be a mistake.

Penny Daley had filed a harassment complaint, and I'd been served a restraining order.

NINE

NOW

I'M PARALYZED, STARING. I CAN'T BELIEVE WHAT I'M looking at. Inside Liam's desk, almost falling out the back end of the drawer, is his passport. Attached to it, a yellow stick-it note that reads "Renew before Santiago." I lose my breath a moment, then open it and see the thumbnail photo of his face and the date. We were set to go to Santiago in May; it was now October. This passport expired months ago. My first thought is that he renewed it and had a new one, in whatever country he'd disappeared to with his new lover. But no. He didn't renew this. He couldn't have. Why would the note still be on it? Why wouldn't this old one be back in the file cabinet at the house if he'd renewed it? He's completely anal when it comes to organization and important documents being in alphabetical order in a locked cabinet.

It would make sense that he'd bring it to the condo because there were no passport offices in Sugar Grove. He was in Chicago all the time. He must have left it here so he could get it renewed next time he was in town, but he never had. Oh my God. If he didn't have this, it changed everything.

Besides the lame investigation they did in Sugar Grove—
for a few perfunctory days until they presented me with evidence that it wasn't a missing persons case—they also did
some basic searching in Chicago. They talked to friends, coworkers, looked through the condo, but they certainly didn't
get to any deep searching because of the speed at which Liam
had taken off.

I'd looked in every file, every drawer, every possible hiding place for clues, for love letters, a burner phone like those
used by people up to no good, maybe for a list of passwords
in order to log in and see his computer contents, but I hadn't
seen this—his expired passport, caught by its weathered corner in the roller of the desk drawer.

A familiar tingling grazes my shoulders and taps down
my arms and spine. Panic. Then, a flash, a warmth like alcohol hitting the bloodstream. My heart pounds in my ears.
What does this mean? My first instinct is to call Detective
Sterling—to tell him he was wrong and Liam is here, somewhere, and something terrible has happened to him. But,
so far, despite his attempts at compassion or professional-
ism (which one, I'm not quite sure), he'd treated me like a
hysterical drunk who had driven her husband away. Reading people this way is a blessing and a curse. Underneath his
thin smile and shifty eye contact, it was clear exactly what
he thought of me.

I need to be prepared when I present this so I won't be politely dismissed, Sterling unaffectedly reiterating the other
evidence and offering a simple explanation for the expired
passport. But what could explain it?

I pull out a fat pack of Liam's beloved stick-it notes and
look around the condo for a place to work this out. The
condo is small but neat. The brick around the fireplace wraps
around half the living room, creating a cozy vibe. The win-

dows that face the busy alley and overlook miles of rooftops and busy shops below reach from floor to ceiling; they lead out to the fire escape that we've always treated as a tiny balcony—enough room for a few flowering plants and a couple small chairs if you place them on rubber mats so the legs don't slip through the grated slats. You had to shimmy over the low windowsill to get out and pretend the fire escape was a balcony, but everyone did so, and it was a deliciously urban way to live.

The interior, with its hundred-year-old crown molding and ornate wooden detail along the banister and built-in cabinets, is also worlds away from our grand house in Sugar Grove. I take down a painting that hangs on the brick wall above the table in the tiny dining room, and fill the wall with stick-it notes.

Each note lists a reason Sterling has for deciding there was no foul play involved.

"Liam withdrew money after the accident, near airport." Underneath, I list possible reasons for this besides their theory that he was heading out of town. Like, what if he was forced at gunpoint to do so? What if they forced him to give them his PIN?

"His phone was pinging all the next day after he disappeared. (Until, what? He left the country?)" What if he were in someone's trunk? What if they were using his phone? When I write these things down rather than just think them, it starts to sound a little more implausible, maybe even like a bad *Law & Order* episode. All together on paper, it seems…well, crazy. I continue anyway.

"He took out a large sum of money shortly before the accident." I don't have an explanation for this one. No money was found in the house or condo. The first few weeks after the accident, I wanted to believe he'd planned to surprise

me with something—that Zales would call and ask for Liam
Finley to tell him the diamond pendant he'd ordered was in.
Ridiculous, I know, but my mind reaches, desperate for an
explanation. If he'd purchased something, I'd know by now.
Even if it were the motorcycle he'd always wanted, and I'd
found out he'd bought it and was keeping it in the neighbor's
shed, or something, until he had the courage to tell me, I'd
jump for joy, but there was no trail to follow. If he'd taken
this "large sum," this six thousand dollars somewhere, then
what does that mean?

I wrote "drug dealer?" on another stick-it note and placed
it under the one that said "large withdrawal." I immediately
peel it back off the wall and crumple it up, whipping it to
the floor.

That light whisper of panic pricking down my arms returns.
It always snuck in without warning: when I had to hit the
brakes too hard in traffic; when I was struck with the knowledge I was going to be late for something, or the horror of realizing I'd hit Reply All. Once, when Potato dug beneath the
fence and disappeared for an afternoon before showing back
up at the screen door at dinnertime, the same unexpected in-
trusion took over my body. A tremor, a sweep of numb.

I fight it. I open a fresh bottle of red and sit at the dining
table, staring at the crumpled note.

"Drug dealer." No. Not Liam. But if he did take the money
with him, why only six thousand? Why not wipe out sav-
ings, or do exactly what would be in his character to do, and
take half? He'd be fair, that's who he was; even in the throes
of this insanity, he'd still do that. I know he would. Besides,
six thousand was specific, and it had to mean something. I
write a question mark on another note and placed it beneath
the words "large withdrawal."

"Passport NOT missing" goes up on the wall next. I pour

another drink and sit again, studying this phrase. It's the first sliver of hope I've had in so very long—the thought of Liam stopping at the condo at lunch to collect the mail and grabbing the suit I told him he should wear to the book signing party, the one I liked, and scribbling a quick reminder for himself to "Renew before Santiago." He'd never leave something as important as a passport sitting out in the open. He'd put it in a drawer the way he did. I'd laugh at him for that and ask him what could possibly happen to it on top of the desk versus in the desk, and he would, without a doubt, tell me that it's the principle. You conceal your valuables.

I wouldn't have smiled and let it go. I would have said, "Maybe if a city window washer happened to be rapelling down the side of our building and spotted it inside our locked windows on the fifth floor, and concocted a master plan to come back later to break in and steal your expired passport so he could assume your identity and flee the country, then you have a point." He would appreciate the joke and smirk, but he'd still put it in the drawer. I smile at the memory of him for the first time since Len had given me the letter.

Then a thought stops me cold. My hopefulness dissolving into pure, distilled panic. What if he'd told the passport office that his passport was lost or stolen? When my car was broken into and mine was stolen, that's how I reported it. We'd just come back from a trip, and I shouldn't have left it on the seat, but I had my back turned for thirty seconds, max. This was the difference between us. I'd take that thirty-second risk, thinking the odds were stacked in my favor. He would hide his valuables, even in the security of his home. If anyone thought that one of the people in this relationship would do something impulsive, it would be me, a hundred times over. The way I did moving into radio and TV seemingly out of nowhere. It wasn't a negative thing, necessarily, but it would never be like Liam to lead with impulse.

I don't remember if I just had to pay a little more for the new passport because it was stolen, but I remember it wasn't a problem. They reported it as just that: stolen, and then they'd issued me a new one as normal. He could have gotten a new one and still have had his old one, if he'd never found this one stuck in the drawer. There must be a simple way to check this. But even as his spouse, I can't imagine they'd give me information like this. I'd have to tell Sterling. He'd have to look into it, but would he take it seriously?

I feel close to losing my mind. What earthly reason would he have to leave a note on an expired passport, just to report it lost and get a new one? He didn't try to cover up any of the other so-called "pieces of evidence." It just doesn't add up, so I decide to keep the twinge of hope I'd felt upon finding it. He didn't leave me. He's in trouble somewhere, and he needs my help.

Another thought strikes me, and I leap to my feet, feeling instantly sober and alert.

"Holy fucking shit," I murmur, rifling through a file folder I had on the counter that contained all of my missing persons posters, news articles, everything connected to his disappearance, including the letter Len brought me. A printed email, folded once, and slipped into a small envelope. I pull it out violently and read it again. It's not addressed to anyone. There isn't even a "to whom it may concern." It reads like an email draft he might add a name to and send later. I look at each word carefully.

I wish there were a more eloquent way to put this. One that wouldn't look so cowardly, but... I want out. I need to take a break, maybe a permanent one. I don't know yet. There's

so much I wish I could explain to make this all make sense,
but it's complex, and frankly, I'm so tired of being misunderstood. I don't want to explain to everyone what's happened,
I just want out. Of all of it.

Jesus. He could have been writing this to his boss, Samuel
Richter, for all I know. This could have easily been a resignation letter as a breakup letter. It reads like thoughts that
he'd polish up later—like the subtext of a play. It might have
been how he felt, but since it wasn't sent and wasn't even addressed to anyone, maybe it was just the ramblings of a guy
fed up with his job. I know he was tired of traveling so often.
I know he was growing weary from the backlash after a bad
review. The night we found our car covered in eggs in the
parking lot after we left a food and wine festival was the first
time he'd verbalized it—that maybe he'd like to take a year
off and write a cookbook—that he'd loved his run as a critic,
but he still wanted to do other things, maybe a sommelier
certification, something new and exciting.

I feel a flood of comfort. I almost cry with relief, like a
person escaping captivity—there is a split second where the
realization that he may not have abandoned me on purpose
jolts my heart and forces spontaneous tears, but if I'm honest,
Liam lying on a beach with someone else would be best-case
scenario at this point. At least he'd be safe.

I cry until my face is pink from exhaustion and my eyes are
swollen into thin slits; then, when I'm aching from the exer-
tion, I take the half joint out of a tea tin it's been in for over a
year, easily, and I climb out onto the fire escape and sit looking into the unremarkable evening, swelling with envy for
the folks below, going about their normal lives.

The building behind us creates a partial view of a brick
wall, but below, you can see the busy shops and an Italian

restaurant we used to frequent. I see a couple walk into it. They look small from my fifth-floor vantage point, but I notice the man place his hand on the small of her back to guide her inside. Such a small gesture, but it makes me throb with longing for Liam.

I am distracted by a sound I can't place, a crackling. If I weren't so drunk, I may have thought to snuff out my joint instinctually upon hearing someone else, but instead I inhale slowly and look around for the noise. One fire escape over and down a floor, I see a man carefully placing plastic bags over the remaining hanging plants on his fire escape to shield them from the coming frost.

I admire the care he takes, tucking in each delicate leaf. I hear something playing in the background, coming from his cracked window and spilling out into the night air. Billie Holiday? After a while he sits and opens a beer. I can see his profile. It's Marty Nash, the computer guy.

I'm surprised at the delicate way he cares for the plants because his apathetic demeanor the other day doesn't seem to match the careful botanist listening to Billie Holiday (of all things) that I'm seeing now.

I think of his business card and almost say hello, to start a conversation, so if I do try to hire him at some point, he may not think I'm some scorned wife, stalking her ex or something. I don't know why it matters. I just want to be discreet. And I'm pretty sure asking someone to legitimately hack someone else's account is at least a misdemeanor. Illegal for sure, at any rate. I need him to be on my side.

Suddenly, he sniffs the air and looks around. *Oh, God. He can smell the marijuana. Smart. Great!* I smash it out on the arm of my chair, but he's already looked up and sees me there, frantically stamping out the cherry that had fallen on the rubber mat beneath my chair like a lunatic.

"Sorry," I holler, "for all the noise—my—I dropped my… clove cigarette." Did I just say that? Do they even make clove cigarettes anymore? I'm glad he can't see my cheeks flush with embarrassment.

"That's okay," he says.

"Sorry," is all I could manage, again.

"I have an extra…clove," he says, concealing a smirk.

"Huh?" Is he making fun of me? I'm not sure what he means.

"Looks like you really smashed the hell out of that one. Just saying, I have another if you need it." He holds out a joint. I can see it in his hand, the right side of his body illuminated by the stream of warm light from the lamp inside his apartment. I let out a shrill laugh—a sound that I didn't intend to make. Liam liked to smoke a joint now and then, but I tried it exactly twice. Once in Amsterdam and once on a camping trip. Maybe it was just the paranoia, but I felt like I was being trapped in some undercover cop show every time I did it.

"Oh," was all I could answer, with a tone of surprise and uncertainty. I didn't dare climb the few stairs over to his unit. The alcohol and pot mixed together made me slur my words slightly, and I imagine, in my dizzying fog, slipping to my death. Would I die from a fall off the fifth floor? Probably. I read that once, that five stories was the cutoff. You'd *maybe* survive. Any higher, guaranteed death. I think I'd rather fall from higher. The stairs that connect one escape to the other are safe enough, just not in my condition.

"I'm okay, thanks," I finally say, but already he has, with the ease of a sober person, scaled the few stairs and handed me a joint. I take it, surprised, and he just steps back down to his escape and drinks his beer. No attempt at small talk— more like the flyer guy I remember him being in the lobby.

"Thanks," I say down in his direction.

"You look like you could use it," he says matter-of-factly. It doesn't sound like an insult, just an observation followed by a generous gesture, but I'm still mortified. Had he heard me sobbing? He could certainly see my bloated, red face as he reached over the railing to hand me the joint. It would be nice to finally have anonymous neighbors who don't know me or see me as a walking train wreck for a change.

I thank him again and climb back inside my window, embarrassed and drunk. I puff down the joint in long, sharp inhales and fall asleep on the couch—not the choppy, painful bursts of sleep that deposit me into the fresh shock of recognition of my situation every time I wake up, but a dreamless and heavy sleep I've craved for weeks.

It's still dark when a series of bangs pound my front door. I shoot up, trying to control my heart beating in my throat and my limbs trembling from the startle. The clock on the cable box across the room blinks 5:22 a.m. It gets dark early this time of year. Is it evening? Have I slept through another day? It wouldn't be the first time. The television is still on, flickering in the dark room. A tight-faced woman is wishing everyone a good morning, so I'd only been asleep a few hours. Who the hell could this be? Who would be at my door at this hour, or at all, for that matter?

I look through the peephole to see who it is, and then I fumble to open the lock as quickly as I can, trembling even more than I was at being startled awake, tears beginning to well up and already escaping my eyes before I open the door. I unlatch the security chain and stare at him.

Detective Sterling stands there, asking if he can come in. I can't even answer. I wonder if I'd called him in a drunken haze to tell him about the passport. God, I must have. He steps inside, and I shut the door. I must have nodded for him to enter; I don't even recall.

He doesn't have to ask me to sit down. He doesn't need to say anything. He simply takes off his hat and holds it to his chest before saying those words, and I already know what they are. They come out as "Mrs. Finley, I'm so sorry," but they translate to "Liam was found dead."

TEN

THEN

WHEN LIAM RETURNED FROM PLAYA DEL CARMEN, I didn't even need to tell him about the restraining order because he'd seen it on a television behind the airport bar. I was curled up in the media room in a blanket with a cup of tea, my eyes swollen, looking like hell when he came in, a bag full of tacos from some new "authentic mom and pop" place he'd stopped at to bring me dinner. He pretended not to notice my state.

"I was still craving Mexican when I got back," was all he said. He kissed my forehead and added, "Hungry?" I married a saint. That's all there was to it. I nodded, and he got under the blanket with me and handed me a taco. He inclined his head to the cooking competition on TV.

"What's the secret ingredient?"

"Horseradish," I answered through my chewing. Liam paused the show and looked at me.

"I'm not going to ask why you contacted him. I understand why you felt like—"

"It was stupid," I interrupted.

"Yes," he agreed. "It was a mistake. It doesn't make you look innocent, it makes you look… I don't know, Faith, but we have to have a plan to handle this. You can't go rogue on me."

"I know." I shoved the tacos away on the coffee table and pulled my knees up to my chest, hugging them. "We should cancel the book event, and I'll just lay low until the news shifts to the next scandal. At least that's what Paula said to do."

"First off, Paula is an agent, not a publicist, and she doesn't know what she's talking about. If you hide, you look guilty," he said firmly. I smiled at him for the first time in days. He believed me. He was on my side.

"But Kinsey said not to make a statement, and the show, they…" I tried to explain that I'd been terminated, but he'd heard it all already.

"The show would probably love to keep you on. Scandal is great for ratings, but I mean you know how it goes. It looks like they support what you did."

"But I—" I started to protest, but he interrupted.

"I don't mean that you did it. You know what I mean. Forget about the show. We'll focus on your party, and we'll discuss with Kinsey what you'll say if…well, not if, when the media show up. We'll have a plan."

"Okay," I agreed. "What if no one comes to the signing now, though?" I pushed my feet under his warm hip and rested my head on my knees.

"RSVPs have almost tripled," he said matter-of-factly.

"What?" I sprung up, in total disbelief.

"This is a totally fucked up thing, like nightmarish, but like I said, people like a scandal. You may have lost your show, but the timing of your book coming out right now… I hate to say it, but people are sort of awful. You'll sell." He picked up a taco and ate it. I had never even considered this. It was the last thing I cared about right now, but if there could be a shining light from all of this, maybe I could say my bit at the event, a polished, lawyer-approved, brief statement of defense, and maybe I would sell like crazy. Maybe my book would even help more people. Maybe this would blow over.

One would expect Liam to act a little strangely with everything going on. When people start to recognize you from sleezy news coverage and you constantly have to defend to people that your wife is not a deranged child molester, it can get under one's skin. At that time I wouldn't have been looking for signs of him pulling away, or making excuses for staying late at the office because he had every right to be on edge and guarded. Our world was upside down, so how could I have noticed it odd that he was removed, anxious, falling apart even? Why wouldn't he be? We both were.

He maintained that everything would be fine. He was keeping busy with his work, and with coordinating the menu items with the chef at Le Bouchon for the book signing event. But maybe there was more to his distance than the stress of it all. The smiles he gave me before leaving for work at times felt vacant. The distracted, polite kind where the eyes don't match the expression. He told me to show my face and keep my head up, but he didn't invite me to any of the new restaurants he was reviewing in those couple weeks before the event. I was sure he believed me, but now, I don't know. Now, the thought of him being…ashamed of me was unbearable.

I saw my regular clients. Only one stopped seeing me—a younger guy, late teens, probably at the insistence of a parent. The others seemed to genuinely accept my explanation and the nature of being in a high-profile position, and at least for the time being stayed. Although I felt reservation from many of them—a self-editing that I knew wouldn't allow us to make progress if it kept on. If they felt uncomfortable or self-conscious around me, it defeated the purpose of therapy. I would wait, though. Things would get back to normal.

Liam started to call from his office a few times too many, saying he was going to stay and finish an article or do some research before an event the next day. He rarely worked in his office. His job was flexible. He often worked from his laptop out of a Starbucks, and in the evenings he was always by my side. If there was a deadline to meet, he'd tap away at the keyboard while I cooked mediocre pasta or flipped channels on the couch, but he always wanted to be with me at night. The joys of a child-free life: good wine whenever we felt like it, sex, travel, and some expendable cash.

We were never one of those couples who passed each other on our way out to separate lives. We shared everything. It sounds trite to say it out loud, but we truly were best friends. Now, he wanted space, and it crushed me.

"I made zucchini bread, and *Survivor*'s on. Can't you just finish it up at home?" I asked, and when he didn't respond right away, I imagined him taking the phone away from his ear, closing his eyes and sighing, trying to find a delicate way to tell me he needed time away from me—from my pajamas, and my unwashed hair, and my obsessive retelling of the internet's latest gossip about me.

From my grief.

"Never mind." I recovered quickly because I didn't want to hear a made-up excuse. "I'll see you later then." I hung up before he could say anything.

I tried to think about how I would handle this if the tables were reversed. If a woman from Liam's paper said he'd abused his power to make her have sex with him and then he'd covered it up, would I doubt him? All the headlines that we thought would be buried in more interesting scandals in the press hadn't gone anywhere, not since the voice mails

were played on an *Inside Edition* episode. Liam had just been
flipping past the station, looking for something to watch. His
hand stopped halfway to his mouth when he saw it. A slice of
pizza, limp in his hand, his mouth agape. A terrible photo of
me filled the screen, and my voice mail was broadcast to the
world, but it was edited. I know what I'd said, but they took
out a few sentences and strung the rest together to make it
sound like I was luring him in.

"Carter. Um…this is Dr. Finley. I, ah…hope you're doing
okay. I really think we need to talk." Liam looked up at me
as if in slow motion. I came in from the kitchen, wiping my
hands on a tea towel, and stood frozen behind the couch,
watching. He looked, just as slowly, back to the TV. The sound
bites continued, out of order. "I care about you." No mention
of his mom and dad caring about him too. That was omitted.
They cut the rest of what I'd said about telling the truth and
no one being upset with him if he did. But they made sure to
play "Please call me." I switched the TV off in a rage. Liam
still stared at it, unsure of what to say. He just pointed at it
mutely, as if to ask, "What the hell?"

"I did not say 'Carter. Um…this is Dr. Finley. I care about
you. Please call me.' I don't know if Carter sent this to them
edited this way, or if his mother got a fat paycheck for handing the voice mail over and they had a field day themselves."

"What *did* you say? Wait, forget that. Why in the HELL
would you call him at all? Jesus Christ. I just—" He got up
to charge out of the room, but turned back around momentarily as I shouted back.

"That's not how it was! I needed to understand why—
Liam, my words were twisted. That's not what I said."

"Okay," he said dismissively. He wanted to get away from
me in that moment. I whimpered, pleading.

"Do you believe me?"

"Sure." Then he turned on his heel and went into the bedroom, closing the door behind him. The clip played over and over on different news outlets, and Liam stopped coming home when he usually did.

I didn't press him. I didn't relentlessly ask, "Are you okay?" I tried that a few times, but his hollow responses made us both feel worse. Up until now, he had tried to be there for me, standing up for me when strangers at the grocery store pointed and whispered. Last week he'd literally just stared back and pointed at them, and then whispered something to me. I couldn't help but burst out laughing at how ridiculous it was as they scurried away.

Once, he saw a woman in a restaurant parking lot who was stuffed into a pantsuit and teetering on heels; when she tried to covertly snap a shot of us with her phone, Liam just lifted his arms in a "gotcha" pose and said "Boo!", and she tripped on her heels and scurried off, humiliated. Maybe he simply had nothing left to give after days of constant self-defense. We were both exhausted.

The day of the book launch event, Ellie came over to the condo, and I drove in from Sugar Grove and met her so she could help me organize the stacks of books and rehearse what I was going to say to any press. Since I'd had to talk her down when she called, bawling after seeing the news story when she got home from vacation, she had tried to respect that I didn't want to discuss it. I wanted to talk about the record cold weekend ahead, her Valentine's day plans with Joe at the Signature Room, Ned's cold, anything else. So, while Hannah sat, delighted, watching *Doc McStuffins* on my iPad, Ellie told me all about her recent failings with Weight Watchers, and how she and Joe had a cheat night when they brought the kids to Chucky Cheese and had never got back on the wagon. Liam and Joe were close. I forget how much Joe is hurting too sometimes. Ellie opened a Dove chocolate I keep in a bowl on the table and ate it.

I had always felt for Ellie and her struggles with weight. She was very open about it and would promptly tell anyone who said "she has such a pretty face if she'd just lose a few pounds..." to fuck off. She called me once, crying after Ned was born, feeling impossibly fat and tired. She laughed at herself crying over the phone through bites of a Baby Ruth. She said something that surprised me though. She admitted that she never got to unpack all of the shit from our childhood the way I did, so she probably just eats instead. It seemed self-aware of her to know that there was an underlying reason for her binging, but it also felt a little blamey, like I was lucky I got to work through it somehow.

I just listened though, the way I did, as she neatly packed my book into boxes and bounced Ned on her knee at the same time, telling me all about her new, foolproof keto diet plan, and I was grateful for the mundane topic and the distraction.

The night of the book launch party, Liam was dressed in his tweed herringbone suit that I love, with its slim, hipster-looking fit. I erred on the conservative side, wearing a lace dress, high-necked and long-sleeved, hoping I could keep my coat on most of the night, considering the freezing temperatures. I didn't want anyone even looking at me. It was silly maybe, but it felt like a violation at the moment, the judgmental gazes masked behind smiles, kiss-kisses on the cheek, and clinked glasses. I didn't even want to do this at all. What was once going to be a fun night with French food, good wine, and friends, was now something to be tolerated for a few hours.

The restaurant was beautifully decorated, with elegantly strung lights illuminating the dimly lit lounge area, where a table was set up for me to sign. Canapés, bacon-wrapped brussels sprouts, onion tartlets, and foie gras crostinis all lined the white linen appetizer table in tidy rows like little hors d'oeuvres soldiers. Wineglasses sparkled in the light from hanging paper lamps; it was exquisite.

But the night was honestly sort of a blur. Like your own wedding—never enough time to talk to or even greet everyone. There were a few folks from the press. Liam had instructed Marcel, the owner of the restaurant, to let them get a few shots of the event, but after I offered them a statement, they'd have to go. I gave a rehearsed paragraph saying that the allegations were false, that Mr. Daley was not pressing charges because he knew this to be true, and there was no evidence to the contrary, which was why the DA didn't have a case—that I had no plans to stop practicing, and we'd be happy when this whole thing was behind us.

A scattering of guests, who were near the cameras at the time, clapped. Liam gave me a wink to praise me for sticking to the script with poise. All of that was true, so we did feel like (despite the voice mail messages I left, which the DA did hear the whole of eventually) this was bound to fizzle out fairly soon. My show would be a casualty in all of it, but my marriage, and maybe even my book, would not be. I could live with that.

I smiled and greeted people as I scrawled my signature inside the front cover of my book, one after another. I told myself that I'd have only one glass of wine, which I was feeling in desperate need of halfway through the signing. So I was grateful when a waiter handed me one, saying that the guy at the bar had sent it over. Liam was next to me, so it wasn't him. I looked around, straining to see who'd sent it. Always show gratitude and kindness to all of your fans, Paula would say. I didn't see anyone, and the line was too long for me to leave, so I told the waiter to thank him and kept on.

For a split second, I imagined Carter at the bar, having snuck in, sending me an anonymous drink, a few minutes away from creating a huge scene. The ripple of numbness swept my cheeks, and I shook off the ridiculous thought. Was I becoming paranoid, anxiety setting in so easily as the result of one irrational thought?

Then I saw someone walk through the front doors who made me stop cold. I excused myself from the table and went to the restroom before he could see me. It was Will Holloway. What the hell was he doing here?

Will was a childhood friend who I reunited with again in college, after losing touch for a few years. We'd dated for a couple years before I met Liam. I'd broken it off because it was just too much on my shoulders at the time. He was fresh out of law school, and I needed to put all my focus in starting my practice. I couldn't handle a relationship—didn't want to, I suppose. He was always really sensitive, and the more late nights and rescheduled dinners I had, the more suspicious and moody he became. We stayed close friends though, and when I met Liam, they hit it off too. I was honest with Liam about the fact that we'd dated, although I never mentioned the seriousness or length of the relationship to him. I wasn't hiding it, but once Liam and I were engaged, Will, seemingly out of nowhere, couldn't handle it. He told me that he wasn't over me and couldn't watch me get married and that he was sorry.

He took a job in Boston not long after, and so it was easy to explain to Liam why we didn't hang out with Will anymore. I don't feel like I lied to Liam, exactly, but we were planning a wedding, and I didn't want to hash through it all and taint the special time. No one had done anything wrong; I just chose not to explain it. I was utterly surprised at Will, after two years of post-breakup friendship, to find out he wasn't over me romantically. If anyone should have felt lied to, it was me. At least that's what I told myself. Any other time, I would have been thrilled to see him. But now, the thought that I'd kept a secret from Liam—and that it could surface—made me feel physically sick.

I ran the fancy waterfall faucet in the bathroom and looked in the mirror a moment. I smoothed my hair with my hands, keeping the long, blond strands inside the bun on top of my head, and then I took a deep breath and went back to the signing table.

Liam and Will were near the table doing their vigorous handshake, man-back-pat thing, and clinking their pints of beer together by the time I came back. Liam had put a Fifteen Minute Break sign on the book signing table in my unannounced absence, telling the folks in line to come back in a little while. His mood seemed lighter now.

"Look. It's Will!" Liam said, and I could tell he was more buzzed than I'd noticed before.

"It sure is. Will Holloway, I'll be damned," I said, hugging him.

"Faith, you look great." He pointed to my photo on the many books stacked up behind me. "That's you all over the place, that's crazy. Good for you. Congrats."

"Thanks. What brings you here?" I ask.

"He's back," Liam interjects.

"Oh? Cool," was all I could come up with.

"I partnered at a new law office in town, so I moved back from Boston a few months ago, actually."

"Really?" I said. I guess he thought I was offended he didn't contact us earlier because he started to make excuses.

"I've been too busy with the move and new job to really

reconnect with all the old Chicago gang, but I saw that you had this event, and I, wow, I knew you were doing well, but look at you. I wanted to stop in and get my copy before you sell out."

"Well, that's very nice of you to say, considering all the…" I didn't even know how I was going to finish that sentence; I just make a twisty gesture with my finger to signify "craziness."

"I heard. I'm sorry. I'm sure nobody besides bored, daytime TV watchers really believe any of that. It will blow over," he said, smiling.

"That's what I keep telling her!" Liam said, as if he were astonished to hear an ally agree with his profound point of view. "Hey, what part of town are you in?" Liam asked. It was weird to see Liam like this. He never got *drunk*-drunk. A little loose off dinner wine, but not like this. Not that I blame him.

"Just over in Wrigleyville," Will said, chugging his beer.

"No way. We got a Tuesday night ice hockey thing over there. You gotta come out."

"Hell yeah, I'll come out." Will matched Liam's tipsy enthusiasm.

"Another beer?" Liam asked, and they headed to the cash bar, Liam's arm draped around Will's neck. I blinked in disbelief a few times, then shook it off and sat back down at the signing table, pushing off processing what just happened until later.

After another hour of smiles and scribbling my name on book copies, the event was pretty much over. People were still drinking and mingling, but my bit was done and I wanted to go home. I was about to look for Liam and Will when Liam came toward me, both our coats in hand, an angry expression on his face.

"Can we go please?" he asked, his face flushed and lips pursed.

"What's wrong? You okay?" I stood, concerned.

"I'm fine. I just want to go…if you're done, I mean, I'm not trying to…" He stopped himself, probably remembering that it was my event and he shouldn't push me out the door, or maybe he just didn't want other people to know we were arguing.

"Yeah. Of course." I put on my coat, and we headed to the door. Will was standing near the bar and I caught a glimpse of him, looking apologetic. I didn't say goodbye, I just helped Liam to the car.

"I'm driving, I take it?" I joked bitterly, annoyed at his recklessness and chumminess with Will, although I had no right to really be angry about either.

"Looks like," he said, his response annoying me even more.

"Why don't we just go to the condo tonight, take the train."

"The train?" he complained, slurring his words.

"An Uber then," I said.

"I really want to go home. You didn't drink, right?" He opened the car door and slunk in.

"A little wine. Not much," I said. He shut the door and buckled up as if it were settled, and I drove into the icy night. We didn't say anything for a while. Once we were out of the city on the long stretch of black, unlit road that led to Sugar Grove, I broke the silence.

"Did you and Will get in an argument or something?" I asked tentatively.

"What? No. Why would you think that?" he asked.

"Well, then, what's wrong?"

"Nothing. I'm…drunk." He sort of laughed at this admission. I let it go. I tried to lighten the mood by making a joke about the fourteen-dollar domestic beers, and he gave a weak chuckle and rested his head on the passenger window.

A second later he screamed my name, pointing to the road ahead. Truck headlights appeared only feet in front of us— too late. The crash was deafening.

ELEVEN

NOW

STERLING CALLS AN AMBULANCE WHEN HE SEES ME hunched over, gasping for breath, in full panic, sobbing. By the time the EMTs get there, I'm sitting at the table with a double vodka keeping me calm enough to avoid going with them, not giving a shit what Sterling thinks of me or if it might make me look even less stable than he thinks I am. I had barely noticed his partner, Ramirez, lingering behind him, mumbling something into her police radio. Now they both sit across from me at the dining table under the mess of stick-it notes on the wall above us.

"You don't know for sure," I repeat.

"There are many identifying factors, including the photo from the event that you provided. The clothes match. It's what he had on that night, down to his wedding ring and a money clip with his initials and a little cash inside his jacket pocket. I'm so sorry." I wished he would stop saying he was sorry. "We'd like to ask you to release dental records to confirm. The medical examiner could court-order them, but it's

easier…it's been several months so the only way to identify
is—" He stopped when I cut him off.

"I don't know…" I start to say that I'm not sure which
dentist he switched to, but I trail off; they don't care. They'll
find it I guess. He hands me something to sign. "It's not him,
though," I whimper.

"Faith…" Ramirez starts to console me.

"Was it at the accident scene? Is that where you found him?
How did they miss finding him?" I demand. The tears won't
stop. I imagine he must have been thrown from the car, and
they didn't find him under the brush or water of the ravine.
I angrily brush away tears and wait for them to admit they'd
screwed up, and I'd been right all along.

"No," Sterling says. "They scoured that area thoroughly
and there was still no trace of him." He looks me in the eye.
"But we're treating this as a homicide."

"What?" I ask, shocked.

"There was—there was ah…a gunshot wound to the head."
He studies me for my reaction.

"That's not possible. He was talking about ice hockey,
and—and he had too many drinks, and he got his coat, all
mad, and wanted to go home and we, and so we—I mean,
and then we were driving home, and…that's not—that's not,
no that's not possible." The trembling and sobs don't stop, and
Sterling goes to the kitchen and peels a paper towel from its
roll on the counter and hands it to me.

"A couple of guys fishing on Lake Michigan found him.
Just south of Lakeview…offshore. I'm so sorry." His head is
lowered. He and Ramirez exchange a helpless look.

"In the city? But we were almost to Sugar Grove. I don't—
I… What?" I shake my head, trying to force myself to breathe.

"I know this is a lot to take in. I need to—we'd like it if you
could give us your account of that evening one more time in

light of the new circumstances. You don't have to do it right now. You could come down tomorrow. We'll have to just get some official statements on record." He tries to offer a tender look—a thin white, bloodless line across his face, masquerading as a smile.

I am a suspect.

He doesn't have to say it. They want a recorded statement. I was the last one to see him. The whole state knows about our problems. I'm not stupid. High most of the time? Okay. Fooled by this? No.

"Is there anyone we can call for you, to be with you?" he asks. I have no friends left, it appears. No real ones I could call. I don't want to put Ellie through this again, after what she went through during my weeks in the hospital.

"That's okay," I say coldly and stand up. I open the front door, signaling them to leave. They stand up and nod to me, politely. I stop Sterling before he exits the door.

"How do you know that… How can you tell that the gunshot wasn't…that he didn't…" I can't say it, but Sterling seems to understand.

"It wasn't self-inflicted. Forensics can tell how far away the firearm was. It would be impossible," he says, and then he puts his hat back on and disappears down the stairs to the lobby. I'm still nodding through my tears after they're gone, standing in shock.

Liam isn't on a beach somewhere. He is gone, and I am a suspect.

TWELVE

THEN

I REMEMBER BEING SO COLD. I THOUGHT THERE WAS fire—there was a red flickering behind my eyelids, but it was the lights from the cop cars and the ambulance. They were right: Liam wasn't next to me when I flitted into brief consciousness on an icy embankment next to the road, but I thought he was either still in the car, not thrown through the windshield the way I was, or close by somewhere. I'm not sure how long I was lucid, lying there in the snow, and then next thing I knew I was looking at the white squares of a hospital room ceiling, waking up in terrible pain.

"Where's my husband?" I demanded. "No one will tell me anything." That's the first thing I really remember saying, although I must have been pleading for information beforehand, groggy with pain meds they'd given me. When they told me that Liam wasn't in the car—that he wasn't found, the shock made the following moments, maybe even days, a blur.

Ellie was there. She came every day, trying hard to straddle the line between solemnly supportive and encouragingly cheerful. She brought a noodly casserole in Tupperware and some sort of M&M-filled brownies or confetti cake on the side that she and Hannah ended up eating while they squished together into the impossibly small, institutional love seat in my room to watch *Peppa Pig* and keep me company. Ellie had a newborn, and I told her repeatedly she didn't need to come, but she just rocked Ned in a little bassinet they provided in the room, and continued to bring me sudokus, magazines, and sweets while I healed.

All of it went untouched, but she buzzed around, fluffing pillows and ignoring my insistence on being alone, and I could never repay her for all of it, no matter how much I protested.

They told me early on that there was Klonopin and alcohol found in my system. I called them liars. I told a nurse to fuck herself at one point and declared that I was being set up—that Liam wasn't gone, and they were hiding facts from me, that I know I didn't take any pills that night, so someone was trying to make me feel crazy. They were lying to me. I pulled out my IV the third night there, and went crying down the halls, calling for Liam.

I was almost admitted to a twenty-four-hour watch in the psych ward, but they first brought in a counselor from the unit who tried explaining that between the trauma of the accident and the disorienting medication, I was confused. He went through the security clearances and blood testing accuracies with me, appealing to my logic, and basically spelling out for me that I was in a paranoid and perhaps delusional state, but that it would pass.

Ellie sat scarlet-cheeked and silent at my outbursts at the staff. She didn't disagree with my claims that I'd had one, maybe two glasses of wine over the four-hour event, and that I did not take any pills. I know she'd heard me slurring my words on the phone with her over the last weeks before the accident. She even saw me on the couch once, through the side windows around the front door, with a full glass of wine spilled down my chest, as the delicate stem was still lightly draped in my sleeping hand. My head was cocked to the side, and a thread of drool spilled onto my shoulder, or so Ellie tells me. Not the sight she was expecting when she stopped by after a trip out my way to an outlet mall. She'd wanted to surprise me. It looked briefly like a murder scene—the red wine down my front, bloody evidence of an intruder. She'd screamed and covered Hannah's eyes. Only her banging the door repeatedly woke me up to discover the unseemly situation I found myself in.

Even so, she didn't let on that she doubted my reliability when recounting how much I'd self-medicated that night. Surely I'd lost track of the times and amounts of booze and pills I kept myself numb with over the difficult weeks. She just smiled supportively and held my hand between her time spent knitting a tiny cap for Ned and reheating loaded mac and cheese.

After a few days, they finally did come to believe that Liam was missing, but only because friends and coworkers made statements as well, that he'd not returned calls, shown up to work, or to Tuesday hockey. They sent out a Want to Locate report, which was assigned to a missing persons detective. The detective conducted an investigation that included contacting relatives and friends, checking with other local hospitals to see if he was admitted, checking with the medical examiner's office to see if they had any unidentified bodies arrive since the last date he was seen, and running his name through databases and arrest records to see if he'd encountered the police or had been arrested. If police anywhere in the nation encountered him and checked for him on National Crime Information Center, Liam would receive a notice that Chicago PD wanted to know where he was.

Sterling made sure it was clear that this investigation was usually basic since adults have the right to wander off or leave someone. It didn't matter though, because there was no trace of him. That's when all of the so-called evidence mounted and they stopped looking. It was clear, they said, that there was no foul play here. He'd likely left the country.

I told Sterling again and again that Liam was with me—that people saw us leave together. I said there were witnesses. We'd walked out of a busy restaurant in the middle of Chicago and got in our car.

"Will!" I'd hollered at Sterling, one of the last times I saw him before they stopped looking. "Will Holloway. He was there. He's a friend—he…he watched us walk out together. He can tell you that Liam didn't—that he was with me."

"We've talked to the guests that were there, and the staff," Sterling said. "The owner supplied us with the guest list."

"Did you talk to Will?" I demanded, pushing hard for answers, desperate to make sense out of it all, but feeling invaded. They'd already spoken with our private guests.

"We did talk to him," he said. "He saw you leave together, yes."

"Okay!" I exclaimed.

"But he didn't watch you go to your car. He was at the bar. All he saw was the two of you walk out the door. That doesn't explain all the time afterward that's unaccounted for," he explained. It was such a stupid insistence on my part. Of course he didn't watch us go to our car.

"But that guest list was just family, friends, VIP people," I insisted. "It was a public event otherwise. There were a lot of people you may not have the names of, someone must have seen him get in the car—the valet!"

"The valet sees hundreds of people a night. He doesn't remember you." He said it like he was trying to take me down a notch, like I thought I was so famous or important.

"It's not relevant though, Faith. Between driving away and the accident…" He stopped. I knew he didn't want to imply what he was going to say. He probably thought I was too fragile or too nuts to bother spelling it out for me, but I knew what he was thinking, and what he would later investigate—that anything could have happened between driving away from Le Bouchon and ending up in a ditch near Sugar Grove.

We could have fought. We could have stopped somewhere, and with all the stress of the scandal and the book—with the alcohol and drugs in my system—perhaps the fight escalated and I did something unthinkable. Or maybe Liam had just forced me to pull over and had gotten out, walking away from our life together as it appeared he'd planned to do.

No matter what they didn't say at the time, with each passing day, with each snippet of new evidence that surfaced, the withdrawal of money the day before, the phone pinging, all of it, it added up to the police quietly dismissing me as an unreliable witness. The police even brought up things that weren't official evidence, things that made me look culpable for whatever had happened. For example, Liam had stayed at his friend Nate's one night because there was a press van in front of our house when he'd returned from work, and he just couldn't face it. It had been a long day, and he wanted a hot shower and peace, and so I'd suggested he meet up with Nate. They'd gone to the Spirit Room, and Liam had spent the night in Nate's spare room. He didn't tell Nate what was wrong, so now it looks like Liam and I were on the rocks. Whether Nate intended that or not, it's another sandbag stacked against the river of my perceived guilt.

Somewhere in those initial weeks, I began to doubt my own story. Was it more feasible that in the haze of tears and

rum and life-shattering rumors, that under the insurmount-
able weight of speculation from strangers and the splintering
shards of doubt that I started to see in Liam's eyes that I *did*
take a pill at Le Bouchon and forgot? Was that more reasonable than assuming some big conspiracy? Fine, I could yield
to that hypothesis. But what I would never waiver on was that
Liam was in the car with me.

Even under a bit of artificial relaxation, I was not inebri-
ated. I was not hallucinating. I remember him screaming my
name and pointing to the headlights that crossed the middle
line. I remember so clearly that fragment in time that would
change my whole life forever. We were inches away from a
head-on collision, and so I swerved; it was too late to avoid
impact, hard impact, so I swerved and we hit a tree with a
force so violent that it threw me from the car and shattered
bones, that it took Liam. Somehow, some way, it took him
from me.

When they told me that there was no other car at the scene
of the accident, my first thought was that I knew the headlights had come from a truck, and it had seemed like a huge
truck. All I could think was that it was a hit-and-run, though
they didn't technically hit us. Or, because I've heard of this
before, maybe the driver slipped over the line a little, barely
noticing, to reach for his phone or something, and jerked back
over, like people do all the time when trying to text or something stupid, just a moment too long, and he didn't even notice us swerve off. It was a big truck, not a semi or anything,
just a huge Ford model. Could it be possible they didn't see
us? Or did they flee?

Whatever the answer, according to detectives, the truck
didn't exist, Liam up and left, and I was popping pills. I would
have to do the work myself. It was now my job to find out the
truth. I was the only one who didn't doubt the elemental facts

that would help me find him, and find out what happened: that Liam was there. That there was another car involved.

I made a whispered promise to Liam, late one night, alone in my hospital bed. My hands were clasping my pillow and I sobbed into it, making choking sounds I couldn't control. I promised Liam that I would find him—that I'd make everything right again. Then I begged his forgiveness.

THIRTEEN

NOW

LIAM'S FUNERAL IS NONTRADITIONAL, THE WAY HE always talked about. We both wrote up wills the spring after his father, Henry, died. Henry hadn't bothered to do so himself, but Liam, being the only immediately family alive, would inherit anything Henry left behind anyway. At least we'd always assumed the little his dad held dear would go to him, but Liam's stepmother swooped in during the months Henry was dying and coerced him into signing a number of documents in his vulnerable state, leaving her everything.

Liam never fought it. We didn't need anything, after all, but it was the principle. He would walk away from any fights in court if she'd just give him his dad's prized golf clubs (which she was happy to get rid of) so he could have something special to remember him by. Liam always wanted to protect us from something like that happening. As a married couple it was pretty straightforward as far as the big stuff was concerned (house, accounts, cars), but I was grateful he'd specified some of his less orthodox requests in the will, like having the wake at his favorite bar—a quaint little speakeasy we frequented.

As far as burial was concerned, all he asked was to have his ashes spread near the sea.

I don't need to explain to people that we'd laid on a blanket in the dewy grass behind our house on summer evenings, looking out into backyard trees with a bottle of pinot noir, on more than one occasion, and talked about what we'd want—a party celebrating life instead of a depressing funeral. The sea. Someday we'd live seaside in some exotic little country, and so that's where we wanted to rest. It's all typed up for someone else to justify now. One less thing for me to be questioned about.

The wake is well attended, crowded even. It had been a few weeks since Liam's remains were identified. Dental records confirmed. I had gone down and positively identified his jacket and money clip, his shoes we bought in Italy together, and his ring that they finally let me keep. For months and months I've had to deal with the reality that something tragic happened to him because, with the exception of a brief upset after Len gave me that email, I never doubted that Liam was in danger, and wasn't just a coward who'd left his life with no explanation. So, in a sense, I have been mourning for almost eight months now. Some sense of relief might be expected—to at least have a sort of finality or some answers—but there is none. More questions have been raised than before, and the weeks and months of weeping and fear are now turning into anger and greater motivation to find justice for him.

I walk around the speakeasy, stoic, suffering through the niceties and sorry-for-your-losses. I have the bartender pour double shots of whisky into my coffee cup, so the fairweather friends and acquaintances, who are eyeing me sideways when they think I'm not looking, won't also judge me for drinking too much. I shouldn't care, but I tell myself being discreet is for Liam's honor. I won't make a scene. I won't tell all of these people what I think of their subtle disappearance from my life over the last year.

Ellie takes over playing hostess, and despite the waitress hired for the evening, she is asking people if they had enough to eat and taking empties off bar tables. I try to shrink into a back corner as often as possible, avoiding any conversation that wasn't absolutely necessary. Two couples we often went out with—Karen and Seth, Tracy and Paul—are feigning concern for me, offering hugs and "hand to heart" gestures, emphasizing just how gutted they are about the whole thing. I know they are, for Liam. But they'd stopped calling even before the accident, back at the beginning of the Carter Daley story. That's when they quietly stopped being friends with me.

When I am finally able to steal away from the four of them, standing in a huddle near the bar, I turn and see Ellie and roll my eyes. Instinctively, we both look to the front door for the tenth time of the evening, and then give each other a mutual "hang in there" look, a weak one, but one of solidarity. I'd invited our mother, and Ellie and I were both on edge. I don't know what made me make the call. Grief, perhaps. Maybe that primal need for your mother when you're in pain, because no matter how abandoned she's left you, no matter how many years have passed, you still carry an illogical hope that maybe…maybe she'll be there this time. We both know she won't show, but that flutter of hope, the very same that kept me looking for Liam—it doesn't die away easily.

In the eight years I spent with Liam, she met him once. Not at the wedding she didn't show up to, but when she was hospitalized for an overdose five years ago, and asked me to bring her her handbag and a change of clothes because nobody in her Section 8 building had a car. Her best friend Sissy's cell had been shut off by the phone carrier, and her boyfriend, Kenny, had run off again. Like a fool, I was so happy to be needed by her that I drove the hour and a half to bring her what she needed, completely unaware that I'd just smuggled in her meth, tucked away in a secret pocket inside her purse. That was the only contact in going on ten years, and I'm looking at the door like she'll walk through and make it all better?

I gulp my whisky coffee and sit in a corner booth, watching the guests. Some forgetting they are at a wake, knocking back drinks and laughing, then catching themselves and lowering their tone. I look out the window across the street at the fancy hotel lounge. It's nearing the holidays now, and the place is filled with men in suits loosening their ties, talking and negotiating over papers and happy hour drinks; a mother smacking the hand of her son, who is trying to put his hands into the hot plate of dinner rolls on the buffet; a woman with a slick bun in her hair, wrapped up in a shawl, asking the concierge for a taxi it looks like, probably to the theater, I imagine.

She looks to the bar for her date to finish paying the check so they can hurry. There is a flurry of activity and people, the Christmas season fanning the blazing fire of their day-to-day lives. I was just like these people such a short time ago, and now I can't imagine even a day so carefree and happy.

I am jolted back into reality by someone saying my name. I look up to see Len and Bonnie Turlson. Bonnie takes both my hands and says how sorry she is, then excuses herself to fetch drinks at the bar after a kiss on the cheek from Len, which looks like a sign for her to give him a minute alone with me.

Len surprises me by sitting next to me in the booth instead of across the table. He looks at me, then pulls me into a hard hug, forcing an overly dramatic moment I wasn't expecting.

"Oh, Faith. I'm so sorry." He holds the hug for an uncomfortably long time and rubs my back. My eyes scan the bar behind him for Bonnie. What is he doing? I pull out of the hug and he looks at me, shaking his head in disbelief.

"What can we do to help you through this?" he asks, still sitting too close. Had he been drinking before he came?

"I… Thanks, Len. I appreciate that. I don't really know." I do know though. I want information from him, but I need to ease into that. It may not be the ideal time to have this discussion, but I don't feel like I have a second to wait. Months have already gone by without anybody looking for a killer, and now it's so late in the game I have no idea how I'll do it, but I will find out what happened.

"I just don't believe it," Len says. "Are there any suspects?" As soon as he says it, he apologizes.

"It's okay," I say. "I don't know much yet." I notice Bonnie holding two drinks. She stops by Gerald and Anne from the *Tribune* and chats a moment, across the room. I don't waste time.

"Len, that email you brought me…" I say. His face crumples.

"God, now that this has all happened, I wish I wouldn't have. It could have been nothing. At the time, I thought it might help. I hope you know that," he says, still sitting too close. I scoot back to create some space between us.

"I just want to know why you assumed that it was meant for me. It could have been for Sam Richter, a resignation letter that he planned to revise before sending, I don't know, but it just seemed like you knew it was for me." He looks stunned.

"What?" I demand.

"It's just that Bonnie pointed out something to me about the letter, but she said I should butt out, so I didn't want to tell you and make things worse."

"Jesus, Len. What?" An electric buzzing of panic is tingling in my cheeks.

"The…woman who kept coming to the office… I mean, I was under the impression you knew about her. The woman he was seeing?" He says, looking genuinely confused that I don't know. I push out of the booth, forcing him to stand up as I push past. Bonnie approaches with the drinks, handing him one. I don't acknowledge her.

"What the hell does that mean? What the fuck are you talking about?" I am trying not to raise my voice. Bonnie's smile quickly vanishes, and she stands there glancing between the two of us.

"I don't know her name. I just—" he stutters.

"Oh, Len," Bonnie says, glaring at him and shaking her head.

"Shit. I might be misinterpreting." He looks to Bonnie for help.

"For God's sake. Tell me what you know. Why would you think I knew?" I'm furious. Tears want to come, but are suppressed by anger and full-body numbness and tingling.

"Oh, honey." Bonnie is clearly trying very hard to be kind. "I don't think this is the place to..." She touches my shoulder and I pull away.

"You brought me the email. You owe me an explanation!" This could be the clue I need to at least have a starting place. I won't wait for the cops. I tried that once. Bonnie gives Len a look as she sits, patting her large hair into place and sipping her pink cocktail. It was a look that said, "You'd better fix this."

"You're right. I—" But he can't finish. I look to Bonnie.

"We were at Bowen's. The steakhouse," she starts to say, then Len pipes up.

"They're a sponsor of the paper. Liam's there a lot for events, and—"

"You've helped enough," Bonnie says, cutting him off. She continues. "Len was writing about the new live music thing they were trying out..."

"When? When was this?" I say before she can finish.

"Not long…uh… I guess just days before the accident," Len says.

"He didn't see us. Reservations were supposed to be made for me by the office, but there was an oversight, which is why we had to sit in the bar. He came out of the back room with a woman. She was…" Bonnie stops.

"What?" I say impatiently.

"I feel so bad talking about it here, at Liam's…"

"Tell me," I demand again.

"The woman was zipping up her dress from the back as they came in the side entrance behind the bar. Len happened to be looking, and she saw him. I guess she recognized Len from the times she'd been to their office because after Liam was out of sight, she walked over and said 'Don't give me that look. His wife knows.'" Bonnie stops, swallows hard. Len chimes in.

"If she hadn't approached me, I wouldn't have thought it was odd. I would have thought that he was there for a story, and she happened to be adjusting her dress, but… I guess, I don't know." He is sweating and Bonnie takes over again.

"Sweetheart," she says, resting a hand on mine, her long, corn-chip-shaped fingernails painted black for the occasion. "Len got to thinking that maybe the email was him cutting it off with her, and that he had it wrong." She looks to Len. "And he should have kept his nose out in the first place," she adds. Len looks down shamefully at his drink and sips.

I can't speak. The room looks blurry and feels suddenly very hot and small. I walk away from them, mutely, and start for the door. I need air. Will Holloway is there, standing in my way, trying to greet me. I push past him and go out into the wintry air. I spot a wooden bench and walk down the side-walk, which is crackling with frost, to sit a moment, coatless in the icy air. I try to control my breathing. *One, two, three, four* breaths in through the nose, *one, two, three, four* breaths out through the mouth.

If he truly was having an affair, and I was the last one to see him, I was about to be the prime suspect. I have no choice but to tell the police, because even though they'll suspect me, I know that they need to be looking at whoever this woman is—or maybe her jealous husband. It will come out eventually; everything always does. I need to be armed with as much information as I can find.

I am shaking violently from the cold. I will not allow myself to cry. If I start to question if this was Liam's revenge for Carter, if he really hadn't believed me—if I start sobbing, asking why, I'll never stop. I'll genuinely hyperventilate myself into the ER. Breathe in, *one, two, three, four*. I feel someone's presence and look up to see Will, his coat outstretched. He puts it around my shoulders before I can protest.

"Hey," he says tenderly as he sits next to me. "You're gonna freeze to death out here. You okay?" I look at him determinedly.

"I need a lawyer. Can you help me?"

FOURTEEN

THE NEXT NIGHT, I ADD STICK-IT NOTES TO THE WALL, notating what I'd learned from Len and Bonnie. I have columns now. One for hard evidence, one for leads to follow, and one for suspects. Under the "suspects" column, I write "Woman X" and stick it to the wall and stare at it. How could I ever find out who this woman is?

I need Marty Nash. He seems to be a permanent fixture on the fire escape, always a drink in hand. I can relate, and I learned a few days ago that he has a little terrier named Figgy. Seems like a cutesy thing for a guy to name his dog, so maybe that could be a conversation starter. I could ask about the dog and try to rope him into conversation that way. Ease into asking him to spy on my deceased husband.

I go to mix a drink and bundle myself in a blanket so I can sit on the fire escape and wait for Marty's nightly smoke break when there is a knock at the door. I freeze a moment. Every unexpected call or visit puts me on edge. I keep fearing it will be the cops with some arrest warrant before I can clear myself—before I can do their job for them and actually focus on the true murderer who's still out there.

I look through the peephole and see that it's Hilly, the new neighbor in 208. Shit. This is not what I want to deal with right now.

"Hellooooo," she sings. "It's Hilly Lancaster! I brought a meat loaf!" She smiles up into the glass dot that my eye is peering through. I close my eyes and let out a long sigh before opening the door and forcing a smile.

"Hilly. Hi there. What brings you by?" I ask.

"I watched *Wake Up, America* and heard all about the terrible time you've been going through. I wanted to bring you a little, I don't know, cheer-up gift." She pushes the meat loaf at me. I can see she's holding something else that I don't recognize right away, and then I do.

"You brought your...cat," I say, trying not to show my confusion. She's holding a cat carrier in one arm and poking at the opening with her free hand.

"Well, animals are the best stress reducer. Proven science. I thought Mr. Pickle could help cheer you up. You could even borrow him if you want, isn't that right, Mr. Pickle?" She starts to talk to the cat, but it hisses and recoils into the back of its carrier, so she puts it down.

"Well, he needs to get used to a new place. I'll just leave him right here for now if that's all right." She opens the carrier door for him to wander out when he feels like it, before waiting for my response.

"Uh, yeah. Sure. Can I...get you anything?" I ask, hoping that all she wanted was to drop by a dry brick of meat loaf and be on her way.

"Oh, well, do you have Black Cherry Fresca by any chance?" she asks.

"I have wine. And...tea, I think...somewhere," I say, wondering if my lack of beverage options might expedite the visit.

"Tea is good. Herbal, I hope," she adds. I walk into the kitchen and dig through the back reaches of the spice cupboard, looking for tea bags, until I finally pull out a box that must have been back there for years. Liam and I are coffee and wine people. Tea is flavored water. He must have used the tea for some holiday baking recipe a decade ago.

"Earl Grey," I say apologetically.

"That'll do." She smiles, but looks somehow disappointed. How did I go from gratifying isolation to having an uninvited stranger in my living room who is dissatisfied with my hospitality? She makes herself comfortable in an armchair by the fireplace, and I stick a mug in the microwave. I guess I should own a teapot like most adults, but I don't. I pour a large glass of cabernet for myself and bring the drinks to the living room. I sit across from her on the couch and see her eye the size of my glass. I ignore it.

"So..." I say, not volunteering any more effort than that for this awkward conversation.

"I just loved your book," she says, beaming. "I read it three times already. Planning another read too."

"Thanks," I say, taking a soothing gulp of the wine, comforted by the familiar peppery, smoky undertones that instantly relax me just a little.

"I'm such a fan. And now we're neighbors!" She pulls something out of her bag. My book.

"You've got a lot of stuff in there," I say, noticing the giant, misshapen bag she has on the floor next to her.

"Would you mind terribly?" she asks, holding out my book. I take it, scrawl my name inside the front cover, and hand it back.

"Could you write a little note?" she asks. "If it's not too much trouble." She gives one of those irritating, childlike smiles as if a grown woman in a Charlie Brown sweatshirt and a grannyish, tight-curl hairdo is going to appeal to me by being cutesy.

"I can't," I say, lying simply because she's annoying me. "My agent won't allow personal messages. Just a covering-our-butts sort of legal thing." I take another long sip and eye the bottle at the counter, knowing I'll want a top-off before this woman leaves.

"Oh, because of all the terrible press. Right. Of course. I'll cherish your signature, anyway." She pulls out yet another item from her bottomless bag. She takes out a box of gluten-free animal crackers and nibbles on the edge of one.

"So, what it is that you do again?" I ask.

"Oh my, your husband never mentioned me?" she says, sorting out all of the lion crackers and sequestering them on her knee for whatever insane reason.

"What?" I snap.

"I'm sorry, I thought maybe you'd know who I was, not that I'm famous like you. Gosh, you must meet a million people a day. Of course you don't remember."

"What are you talking about? You knew Liam?" My words come out quick and caustic.

"I used to own Hilly's Honey. It was a bakery over on 12th. A gluten-free bakery. Gluten is poison, but I'm sure you knew that. Anyway, Liam reviewed it. You came in once with him," she says matter-of-factly. I don't know what's making my skin crawl more, the thoughts that the name Hilly's Honey evoked or Liam's name in this weird stranger's mouth.

"I was so starstruck by the both of you, my goodness." She is still smiling, nibbling. Liam must have written a glowing review.

"Did he…write a positive review?" I ask, still worried that this is going down a bizarre path, but hoping for the best.

"Oh, goodness, no," she says, but still oddly jovial. "He said my mint candies tasted like toothpaste and that gluten-free means taste-free. He said my cupcakes were dry, but I assure you, my cupcakes are very moist." She is still smiling. I want to throw up in my mouth. I'm sure she's talking about literal cupcakes, but she says it in a disturbingly sensual way.

"I'm very sorry about that. I…" What could I say?

"It's okay," she says, offering me an animal cracker. I put my hand up in a "no thank you" gesture and drain the rest of my wine.

"I'm sure there were other good reviews and the negative stuff passed, as, I'm learning, these things tend to do," I say, even though I know the opposite to be true.

"Oh, no. I had to close a couple months later. Liam Finley's word is God in the food business." She crunches her cookies and sips her tea.

"God, Hilly, I'm so sorry." I'm so confused by her upbeat demeanor and how it does not match her words.

"No, no, no. It's fine. It was meant to be. I wasn't enjoying the baking business. I loved it for a while, but I think it's what needed to happen, really. I'm grateful even. My passion was always arts and crafts, and it pushed me to do that. Full time. I sell on Etsy now," she says joyfully. I don't know whether she's being serious.

"Wow. That's…great then." I'm wondering how the hell she affords a place in this building selling crafts in an Etsy store. I wouldn't have asked something like that, but she offers it up.

"My mother died. She'd been in this building for thirty-four years, if you can believe that. She didn't own her unit, but it's still rent-controlled, so, you know, when I lost everything with the bakery, it was hard, but now that I have this place, I can follow my passion. It worked out the way God wanted, I guess."

"Well that's… I'm still so sorry to hear that. I know Liam hated that part of his job. He'd be sick to know someone closed because of him."

"C'est la vie," she says, with a dismissive hand gesture. A scratching noise comes from the cat carrier as Mr. Pickle starts to peek his head out, curious.

"Oh, Mr. Pickle!" she says in a baby voice. "Someone is fussy." It seems like she's going to leave, so I try to punctuate the situation.

"Well, I'm really glad you found your…passion."

"Oh, and I made something for you." She pulls out a hairy-looking something and holds it out to me. "It's a pin. For your sweater," she says. I look closer and it's a crocheted Thanksgiving turkey wearing a hat, fastened to a pin setting.

"Oh, wow. It sure is." I smile and take it.

"I don't know. I thought you'd like it. It's festive. It's my best seller on Etsy." She smiles proudly.

"Well, it's beautiful. And…thoughtful. Thanks so much."

"I knew you could use a pick-me-up." Her work here finished, I suppose, she goes and picks up Mr. Pickle. Shit, she's not leaving. "Maybe Mr. Pickle wants to explore. Dr. Finley might give you a tour of her beautiful place," she says, kissing the cat on the head.

"Actually," I say, "I was just headed out. Meeting friends. I'm running a little late, so maybe a rain check on that." She looks angry. I wonder if she thinks I owe her for the meat loaf and perhaps for the demise of her restaurant. She crams Mr. Pickle back into his carrier and sighs.

"Well, next time then," she says in a curt tone, but gathers her giant bag obediently. I open the front door. "I know where you live." I think she's making an attempt to be funny with the tired cliché, but it comes off a bit threatening. It may be her social awkwardness that just doesn't allow me to read her, but it's still unsettling. She holds up the carrier and says goodbye in a baby voice as if the cat is speaking and then starts to go.

"Enjoy your meat loaf. I'll come back for the dish," she says as she exits. I nod and shut the door. Shit. She's trapped me with the fucking dish.

I go over to my stick-it note wall and make another column. I write "weird shit to keep an eye on" and I stick the turkey pin right into the wall beneath the new heading. Not that I think chunky, awkward Hilly Lancaster is a killer, but I do think she's off her rocker, and I don't like that she came in to my home, knowing who I am—who Liam is. Losing everything after her bakery closed is nothing to take lightly. She wants something. I just don't know what yet.

I take her teacup to the sink and pour another glass of wine. I wrap up in a fleece blanket and slip out onto the fire escape. The night is electric with activity, and the streets below buzz with shoppers and diners. The cold is refreshing, and it feels safe—my tiny little corner of the world, suspended above the chaos and life below.

I hear Figgy whimper. I strain my eyes to see if Marty Nash is sitting on his fire escape. He's there. He reaches down to give the dog a scrap of something he's eating. Figgy takes it and goes to the safety of the living room inside to eat. I don't want to waste time in case he's about to go in too.

"Hey, Marty," I call. He looks up and gives a sort of stilted wave back, but he doesn't say anything. He always looks sort of sad. Damn. He's not even gonna throw me a bone here and allow for conversation. I try again.

"I opened a single-malt Macallan the other day," I lie. "You look like a scotch whisky guy. Wanna have a taste?" I didn't open it, but I know where it's stashed in the pantry. Marty gives a shrug like "Sure, why not?"

"Cool. I'll come down." I'm not drunk yet, so I can manage the ladder. I go inside and find the bottle in the pantry. I open it and pour a little out, so it doesn't look like I was lying about dipping into it earlier, and then I go back out and climb down to Marty's.

He's brought out a couple of glasses, and I hand him the bottle.

"Thanks," he says, and pulls out the other chair, carefully, so the legs don't catch between the grated floor below us. He pours two glasses and takes a sip.

"It's great. Very generous of you to share it. Thanks," he says. The dog looks out from the window, perched on his hind legs. Marty leans over and opens the window for him to come out.

"Oh, hi there," I say to the little guy. He sniffs and tries to get on my lap. "What's her name?" I ask, not letting on that I've heard him call the dog by name before. I don't want to look like a stalker.

"Figgy," he says. "He's a boy though."

"Oh. Sorry. Figgy. Well, that's a cute name." I'm talking more to the dog than to him.

"My wife named him."

"Oh," I say. I hadn't seen a ring, so that surprised me, but explained the cutesy, feminine name.

"Before she passed," he adds, and takes a drink.

"I'm sorry." I take a drink too. Maybe that's why he's so quiet and solemn all the time. Of course I don't ask about it further. We sit in silence a few moments.

"You've been here in the building a few years, you said?" I ask, trying to generate some natural conversation, but it's not easy.

"Yup," he says. I top off his drink. We are the same. It's clear to me that we are both in mourning.

"Hey, I was gonna shoot you an email actually."

"Email?" he asks, confused.

"Your flyer. For computer help. I was gonna see if I could hire you to help with some stuff," I say, realizing, all of a sudden, that my inviting myself over and bringing booze could easily be interpreted as hitting on this guy. Now I'm asking if he wants to come and help me with my computer, which at this point, probably sounds like a pathetic plot for something more than that. If the tables were turned, that's how I'd see it, anyway.

That's the last thing I want him to think. He's an attractive guy in a sort of unconventional way—tall, broad-shouldered. Kind eyes, and obviously very fit. A gym guy, for sure. I like the clean-cut look, so the shaggy haircut and goatee he's got going on aren't my thing, but I could see it appealing to women. It's not remotely what I'm after though, and I pray I'm not coming off that way.

"Sure," he answers. "What do you need help with exactly? And first, did you try rebooting?" he adds dryly. I release a short laugh because I'm not expecting an attempt at humor from him.

"You wouldn't believe how many jobs I get called to, and the solution is plugging and unplugging the computer. But hey, I still get my service fee, so I guess it's not the worst thing."

"Not a bad gig," I say. "No, nothing like that. I actually need to…" I try to choose my phrasing carefully and avoid the word *hack*.

"I need to access computer files, and an email account… and a social media account. I don't actually have the passwords. Per se." I stop. I swig my drink and look nervously to him for a reply.

"You want me to hack into someone else's account?" he asks.

"Um…yeah. Yes. Sort of." I guess I have to be honest. He'll need to know before he starts, obviously. Might as well just say it.

"Sure," he says. That simply.

"Oh. Really? Wow. Great, 'cause, I…it's a sensitive sort of… I just…it…" But he stops me.

"I don't ask questions. Just let me know when." He leans back and Figgy jumps on his lap. He looks over the puffs of smoke coming from rooftop chimneys and swirls his drink.

"Thank you, yeah. That's—great. Would tomorrow work?" I'm so relieved that it's just that easy. Maybe he does this all the time. He's like a journalist. He stays removed and objective and just does the job he's hired to do. I remember my appointment at Will's office in the morning. "Evening? I can text a time tomorrow?"

"Sounds good." He is a man a few words. I knock back the last swallow of my drink and pat Figgy on the head.

"Thanks. Night." I start to go. He gestures to the very expensive bottle of scotch whisky on the tiny iron table in front of him.

"Don't forget your Macallan," he says. Honesty. I genuinely forgot about grabbing it, but he didn't wait until I left to at least get another pour in on the sly before I came back for it. Good sign.

"Keep it," I say. "Consider it a down payment."

"Um, it's a twenty-five-year-old single malt," he says, almost smiling for the first time. "That's really not…"

"Night," I repeat, and climb the small ladder up to my fire escape and go into the warmth of my condo. I realize I'm shivering with cold, so I sit by the fireplace and look up at my stick-it note wall. *Woman X* is a heading with no information below it. If Liam was having an affair, I'll discover something in his emails or Facebook.

And if I do discover something, I'll go and I'll find her.

FIFTEEN

WILL'S OFFICE SITS ON THE EIGHTEENTH FLOOR OF A
downtown building. The interior is rich and dark. The wallpaper between the large wooden beams and crown molding is muted with greens and browns, mixing into a faded, old-European-style pattern. His executive desk is in front of a window with an impressive view of the river and the rest of downtown. I sit in a wingback chair of burgundy leather, looking at the stretch of law books that takes over the entire north wall. It's the opposite of modern, but it has a stately, sophisticated feel. Warm lamplight replaces the usual fluorescent lighting you expect in an office space, and it's comforting. There's even a fire roaring in the gas fireplace. The propane log might be the only updated thing on the entire floor.

I hold my coffee with both hands and look around the room, wondering how I got here. Will enters in a suit. He's patting the back of another lawyer, I guess, at the doorway before the other man disappears down the hall and Will turns his focus to me. It's strange to see him like this. A real grown-up who's done well for himself. His suit is tailored to his fit frame, and his once-unruly hair is now cut very short with the sides shaved close to his skin. He is no longer the tearful man, crying in the passenger seat of my car, telling me he couldn't watch me get married. He's a confident, revered lawyer, comfortable in his skin.

"Hi," he says exuberantly, and hugs me before sitting in the impossibly large leather chair behind his desk.

"Quite the office," I say, picking at the cardboard coffee sleeve.

"Thanks. Faith, I'm— I can't believe this is all happening. I mean, how are you handling it?" he asks with genuine concern.

"I've had months to get used to the idea. Doesn't make it easier, but right now I just want to find out why. Who would want to hurt him. I have to track down some leads, so I—"

"But," he interrupts, "you know that's the cops' job and you need to let them do their work. I hope when you say you 'have to track down leads,' you mean *they* need to." He opens his briefcase and pulls out some files.

"Why wouldn't I do everything I can to help?" I ask.

"Because that's the last thing you should do. You don't want to interfere with the investigation, and you don't want to put yourself in danger," he says emphatically.

"Well, I don't think they're competent, Will. They're looking at *me* while some maniac is on the loose."

"Faith, you know that they have to look at the spouse and the last person to see him, and you're both. You don't need to worry about that. You just need to make sure you tell them absolutely everything you know. They can't catch you in a lie if you don't tell any," he says, eyeing me to see if I react.

"All they need to do if they want to know every last detail of my life is turn on a news station," I say sharply.

"I can't imagine how tough this must be, I really can't.

You have no reason to trust the process or system after what you've been through with the Carter Daley stuff. I say that solely based on knowing you, and knowing that his claims are completely outrageous," he says.

"Is Carter a suspect?"

"I don't know yet. You gave me a ton of info at the wake on Friday, but it's only Monday morning, and I haven't really spoken to anyone yet. I'll call what's-his-face, Sterling, later on. The point is, you need to lie low and let them investigate. Keep your face out of the press as much as humanly possible."

"Okay," I agree.

"You're not technically a suspect at this point. Right now we are just in the phase of gathering information, and you'll have to try to—I know it's not a Faith Bennett thing to do, but—" He stops himself. "Sorry." He blushes.

"It's okay," I say. A name slip is the least of my worries. He continues.

"I know it's not a Faith *Finley* thing to do, but you have to butt the hell out and be patient." He sighs and looks at me. Maybe he's wondering what he got himself into, agreeing to help me.

"I said okay," I repeat, but we both know I'm lying.

"Is there anything you didn't mention at the wake? Anything else I need to know?" He looks right in my eyes.

"A weird neighbor came by. She lives in the building, sort of invited herself in. Then she says Liam reviewed her bakery and it closed because of his bad review," I say, and blow on my coffee. He stops writing notes and looks at me pointedly.

"Really? Well, that's definitely worth looking at. Weird how?" he asks, writing something down.

"Like you get the idea she could be an animal hoarder or have an unhealthy collection of stuffed animals sort of weird.

It's probably not the kind of thing that's relevant, but she gave me a creepy vibe."

"No," Will says. "Relevant or not, I need you to do just what you're doing. Any little thing you think is noteworthy, tell me. Be consistent too. Sterling will have more questions. Just say everything you know and don't change any details."

"Got it," I say.

"Anything else I need to know right now?" He looks at me in a familiar way, but I'm still not sure how to read it. To me, Will Holloway is everything good about my childhood: kick-ball, and candy at the 7/11, and smashing June bugs, basement parties. There was so little good back then, and looking at him feels...safe. In the midst of my crisis, I'm happy he's here.

He knows me so well. He was my first kiss. We were sit-ting in the sun-scorched grass behind the football scoreboard after a game. All the people and the light had gone, and we were drinking some cloyingly sweet alcohol from a flask he'd smuggled into the game under his shirt. We told stories that stopped and started with no beginning or end—the kids we knew, the places we wanted to see, the world that was wait-ing for us—threads of thoughts, or observations, or dreams were pushed out of our mouths and curled like smoke under the soft purple light.

Then, the sound of the field sprinklers hissed at us like rat-tlesnakes, and my startled yelp and giggle launched me into him for protection, and that was the beginning of a couple decades of Will Holloway threading in and out of my life like needlepoint. I need him right now, and I know we're both long over a love affair a decade dead, but I pray that the past stays buried and that we can trust one another.

"I think Liam was having an affair," I blurt out. As much as it breaks me to say this out loud, it will come out, and truth be told, it's better if the stupid police are looking for someone else, or at least have someone else on their list. It will look worse for me if I don't say it now.

"What?" Will asks, his face still and genuinely astonished.

"That gives me motive, right?" I ask. I'm not an idiot. I know it looks worse for me than it does for mystery woman.

"Wh-why do you think that he was having an affair?" He stumbles over his words.

"A colleague of Liam, Len Turlson, told me. First I heard was on Friday."

"Jesus," is all he says at first. I explain where Len had seen them, what the woman had said to him, that Len had seen the two of them in Liam's office a few times. I try to stay factual and removed in my description so I don't start sobbing in Will Holloway's office.

"Faith. God, I'm…" I stop him before he says he's sorry.

"Please don't," I say. "Just tell me what to do."

"They'll want computer records. They'll scour his accounts and his phone if they haven't already."

"They have phone records. I looked at our statements too. There's no odd numbers—at least none with a pattern that are called or texted more than once or twice. Nothing to indicate that kind of contact with someone. They have his work computer, so I'm sure they accessed his accounts that way. I have his personal laptop. Don't they need a warrant or something for it if I'm not under arrest?"

"They didn't ask for it when they brought you in for questioning?"

"Yes. I said he just had a work computer." I don't care if Will freaks out. It's not theirs, it's mine, and at the time I had felt desperate to keep it.

"You seriously—you fucking lied to the investigator?"

"I'll say I didn't know and that I found it when I was packing up the house or something. I don't know what's on it,

Will," I say, feeling ashamed, feeling angry that I'm even in this position—that they can take whatever they want of Liam's.

"Jesus. What if there's something that could really help? You need to tell them it exists, Faith," he says, irritation in his voice. But I already know that, which is why I have Marty the computer guy beating them to the punch this very evening. They can do whatever they want with his files, but so can I.

Will has left his door ajar, and a woman pokes her head in, apologizing for the interruption.

"I didn't realize, sorry," she says, but then points to her watch. "We have a meeting with Russo in five."

"Thanks," Will says, and she nods to me, flattens her lips in an apologetic look and ducks out. Will looks at me.

"Sorry," he says, "but I'll know more in a few days anyway, once I can look through everything and talk to the investigators." I stand and gather my coat. He puts his hands on my shoulders and looks at me intently.

"Please take care of yourself in the meantime, and let me know if you need anything. We're still friends, you know." He hugs me again, and I hug back.

"Thanks." I force a watery smile, turn on my heel, and leave.

I decide to walk awhile. I cross the State Street Bridge and stroll along the Riverwalk. I'm afraid of the quiet—of the empty hours and days stretched in front of me—that the stillness might allow regrets and grief to collect like dust. But if I stay in motion, perhaps the dust won't have an unwelcome opportunity to settle.

I'm told Carter Daley flips burgers at the Egg's Nest Diner off 18th Street. I know this because, as part of the restraining order, I'm not supposed to go there. I jump on the train and take it south a few stops to 18th. I won't talk to him. I just want to see if he's still there.

In the moments before sleep, when most people can easily descend into dark places in their mind, I sometimes catch a fragment of a dream starting, or maybe the end of a last lucid thought before I slip into sleep. I often see Carter and his parents. I wonder about his father. I know little about the man, but it seems like if he believes I hurt his son, he would be the more likely person to exact revenge. Then again, part of Carter's condition is the fantasy that I'm in love with him. He is likely genuinely confused about why I would reject him or deny my love. In his mind—with his disorder—he's completely convinced it's true. He's not faking those feelings. He believes, to his core, that the person he's zeroed in on, the person in authority he's chosen as the object of his affection, is in a mutual romantic relationship with him. Evidence to the contrary is very upsetting for him.

Violence doesn't usually accompany this sort of disorder, but it's not impossible that the lack of emotional control could cause unpredictable behavior. Isn't that true for any unrequited love story?

When I near the diner, I see a street vendor selling churros near an empty bench across the street, so I buy some and sit, as if the possession of street food will somehow make me less conspicuous. I'm still staring down the restaurant window across the street like a stalker. I see him inside.

It's a tiny place, a few stools snugly up against a counter, which is covered in holiday pies and a scattering of a few plastic menus. He wears a greasy apron and leans against the counter, talking with another guy around his age. The guy hands him a cigarette. The morning rush is over and only a few patrons are inside, finishing up mammoth plates of omelets and pancakes. Breakfast 24 Hours a Day is written on a large, cheap sign above the place. He looks small and unhappy as he disappears out of sight, out a back alley door, I assume, to smoke.

I think about the dreams he used to share with me in our sessions. College, a marketing job, a car, a road trip to Vegas with his friends one day. I don't know what all of this has done to him. Surely he's capitalized on my misery somehow. That was the point, after all. It had to be.

I don't know what his payouts were, but I can imagine he was instructed to keep his job, deny any ploy to exploit me in exchange for fame and money, and wait it out a bit. Act normal, continue to look like a victim from a struggling family, just a blue-collar kid trying to work hard and dream big until he was taken advantage of by a predator. He didn't need to press charges and try to sue me. He was bankrolled by TV stations and magazines. I'm sure of it.

I hand my untouched bag of churros to a man sitting on a door stoop holding a Will Work for Food sign, and I start for the train station when I feel my phone humming. I don't recognize the number, but I answer in case it's one of the detectives or Will's office.

"Hello?" I say cautiously. On the other end comes a voice I haven't heard in over six years. A voice the evokes instant rage and simultaneous comfort. I look at my phone to make sure I'm not imagining things, but it's her. I put the phone back to my ear in sheer bewilderment.

"Mom?"

SIXTEEN

I SET MYSELF UP WITH A BOTTLE OF SAUVIGNON blanc before I call Ellie. I have Liam's laptop open at the kitchen table in preparation for my appointment with Marty Nash, and click on the gas fireplace. The windows are ancient, and the draft through the condo forces me into fuzzy robe and slipper socks most of the time. I'd rather not answer the door for Marty in a housecoat or wrapped in a down blanket like some sad shut-in.

When it warms up a bit inside and I can relax a bit, I make the call. As soon as Ellie picks up, I hear a screaming Ned in the background. She sounds tired.

"Hey, what are you doing?" I ask casually.

"Hannah has chicken pox, so Joe taped mittens to her hands so she'll stop scratching, and Ned wants to play with the mittens, but I'm trying to keep him away from her. God, I don't know. They say you're supposed to expose them young. Did you know, people have chicken pox parties, so all the kids can get infected young, like it's safer or something? That's an actual thing. I just can't imagine him with the pox, he's so fussy already, I might literally die if I see him crying and miserable with itchy bumps. Ugh. I'm sorry. How are you? What are you up to?" She says all that in one breath. I start to tell her that our mother called. The words are climbing out of my mouth, but then I think how hurt she was when Lisa (as Ellie refers to our mother) didn't show up to Ned or Hannah's births, how she'd told Ellie she'd raised her kids already and her parenting was done—she didn't want to deal with any fucking kids— how Ellie has never gotten over the abandonment.

Ellie and I raised each other. We're only one year apart, and it was always just the two of us. I think of the winter when we tried to make a skating rink by flooding the backyard with the hose just before the temperature turned to freezing, but it only turned out to be a mess of lumps and grass tufts. I think of the Barbie graveyard we had in the garden where we'd buried fourteen Barbie dolls, in all, after Biff Larson's dog next door chewed up their heads. Each doll had its own name and gravestone, and each had a proper funeral with personalized eulogies. I think of our bedroom walls that had been painted every color of the rainbow over the years until finally, we changed from brilliant lavender and settled on bleu de France. I remember eating strawberries over the sink and throwing the green tops into a soggy pile in the drain—for every milestone, every heartache and celebration, there were no parents, just us.

"I'm okay," I say. I can't tell her. I'm the oldest, and I always have a nagging guilt about not being able to protect her from our father then, but I could shield her from the memories now, at least, in this moment.

I'm not the daughter of a great romance. We were born to parents who never really wanted kids—a war veteran father who treated us like little cadets, and a mother who never wanted children.

I have one memory of my mother happy, or maybe it was the one memory of me happy. I remembered it in therapy, and I have never asked Ellie if it was her last good memory too because we don't talk about it. It's such a simple string of images in my mind. It was the week we drove up to Minnesota to a cabin of some relative I can't remember. Ellie and I were small. My father put a little yellow shirt on me with hand-stitched, horizontal rows of openmouthed fish. He said I was gonna be his fishin' buddy. My mother laughed and touched him tenderly from the passenger's seat, and they sang along with the radio to music I don't remember hearing since. I gobbled big handfuls of cheese puffs in the backseat of the car. We slept on wooden beds in a cabin, and I got to feed an ostrich some corn right out of my hand.

My mother bought me a thimble with a little tiny lake engraved on it, and we lay around all day on the lake in inner tubes. It smelled like grass and fire, and my mother smiled the whole time. We took a few photos that weekend, and somewhere in a dusty basement box, my mother is still smiling. I never remember her really smiling much after that, not genuinely anyway, even with the pills that were supposed to make her smile. Those pills also made her sleep, so she spent afternoons sneaking pours of vodka into her iced teas and slipping into long naps, stretched out like a cat on the sofa.

That's where she stayed when our father made us lie on our bellies on the kitchen floor and took a bar of soap in a sock and whaled on our backs and said that's how it was done when a soldier got out of line. We were six and seven, maybe. Ellie had gotten into his record collection. And that's where she stayed all the times we spent the night locked in separate closets for running in the house or making a mess with Lego. Each time he squeezed our necks just a moment too long, until the stars came and we lost our breath, I saw the light in Ellie's eyes change.

I wanted her as an ally now. I wanted to ask her what in the world Lisa could possibly want, especially after not showing up to Liam's funeral. I can't come up with one thing she could have to say to me, but I decide not to tell Ellie. I would go and find out myself and let Ellie live her life. There is a knock on the door.

"Sorry. Ah, grocery delivery at the door. I'll call you later," I say. She's yelling Joe's name, telling him that Ned has his filthy keys in his mouth and to come and help out.

"Oh, okay, sorry. Ned is— Joe!" I hear her sigh impatiently. "For God's sake!" There is a rustling, handing off of a baby, I presume. "Sorry, yeah, let's talk later." She hangs up and I take a quick swallow of wine before opening the door to Marty.

"Evening," he says. I'd always assumed he was probably early forties, but looks younger now in his hoodie and jeans. He carries a bag of gadgets. I find that my heart is racing, and I'm far more afraid than excited to see what's in Liam's digital history.

"Come in. Can I pour you a glass? Not sure if you're a wine drinker. I have a full bar in the pantry, and...tea, as it turns out."

"Wine's great. Thanks." He nods to the laptop on the table. "This our patient?"

"Yes. Please, sit. Make yourself at home." I hand him the glass. He clicks the laptop's track pad, types a series of codes like a secret language. He logs into the computer itself as an administrator in minutes, making it seem like nothing. And then I see that Liam has a file, right on his desktop that holds his passwords. He opens Liam's email and turns the laptop to me to have a look.

I sit, prickles of heat tapping at my spine. I take a deep

breath and look. Nothing out of place so far. Lots of un-
answered work stuff, friends checking in on him, offers for
no-interest car loans, his gym membership expiring. There
were months of emails. I click into his deleted mail and scroll,
looking for anything out of place. Then I see a name. Rebecca
Lang. The subject line says *You looked really good last night*. My
stomach flips over as I click it open. *Maybe you can come and
see me again tonight.*

That's it. That's all it said. I don't know if he replied. My
heart races. I swallow. I feel tears trying to escape, but I turn
the screen to Marty instead and stay focused.

"How do I know if he replied to these emails?" I ask. He
clicks into Liam's sent box and nothing shows up, then he
clicks on Find Related Messages. More emails from her popu-
late the screen. All in his trash file. Marty gives a little grunt.

"Doesn't look like he tried too hard to hide them."

That's because he wouldn't need to, I think. That's because
I trusted him, and I would never look through his stuff, so
he wouldn't have to jump through hoops to hide it. I click
another one.

Your smell is still lingering, what is that cologne?

That was it. Each one, just a line or two. I click another one.

*The cucumber martini I bought you is my new favorite drink. You
should stop by so I can make you one.*

I miss you. I wish you'd come see me.

That's it. Just four short emails that changed everything.
I thought I knew about my husband and our love story, but
now it seems I was so, so wrong.

I pace behind Marty and gulp down drinks over the next
couple of hours, waiting for him to find anything that might
explain this. Liam's social media accounts don't offer any more
information. He wasn't friends with a Rebecca Lang on any
of the accounts. There's nothing else.

So now Sterling knows exactly what I know. They surely accessed his accounts from his work laptop and saw the emails from this woman already. I thought there might be something on his actual hard drive, or files that would give me any clue about who she was, or any indication at all about any trouble he may have been in that I didn't know about. I half expected him to have sent a threatening email to Carter, or maybe have a disgruntled restaurant owner sending threats, but nothing, not even porn in his browsing history.

Marty points out the desktop computer in the office, just inside the French doors.

"Did he use that one?" he asks.

"Um, not often, but what the hell do I know anymore?" I say. He could have snuck down and spent all his nights chatting up women and sending dick pics. It's worth looking at, I guess. I mean, I use it every day, but I don't know how to look at erased content or shit hidden somewhere on the hard drive or whatever the hell. I can basically push the power button and navigate Google and email. That's about it.

"I can do a quick scan," he says. He sits at the desk and clicks away. I top off my wine and sit by the fireplace. *You looked really good last night. Your smell is still lingering, what is that cologne?* That's the Dolce & Gabbana I got him for his birthday, bitch! I copy her email address down. It takes all of my self-control not to send that one-sentence reply back to her right now, but I breathe. *One, two, three, four.* I sip my wine and I think about how I'll find her.

"Wanna take a look?" Marty calls. I go in and he goes through readouts that I don't understand. He shows me a ton of deleted content. Everyday stuff that doesn't turn out to be anything of significance. I don't really know what else I was expecting. Finding out about Rebecca Lang was quite enough.

"What do I owe you?" I ask him.

"I worked for about nine minutes and you left a thousand-dollar bottle of whisky on my fire escape. I think we're square." He smiles. I didn't know he was capable of smiling until just then.

"Let me fill your drink at least." I go back to the bottle on the fireplace hearth and sit. Marty follows, and I pour more wine. He sits across from me on an armchair, but he looks uncomfortable to be socializing rather than working.

"I'm—uh...sorry to hear about your husband. I'm sorry you found what you found," he says softly. *He knows who I am now*, is all I can think. He probably looked me up and saw an endless supply of stories and gossip about me, about Carter, and now about Liam's murder. It's fizzled out of the headlines over the months. It popped back up a few weeks back when Liam was found, but I guess not everyone follows that sort of thing. Thousands of awful people who post in the comments section certainly do, but there have to be just as many who don't care.

"Thanks. I guess you saw a story about it?" I ask. I don't really care though. Everyone knows every personal thing about me now.

"Oh, uh, no. That lady from the lobby told me," he says.

"Hilly?" I ask.

"That sounds right. Carries her cat around?" he confirms. "She sort of cornered me."

"She tends to do that," I say. What is it with this lady? He stares down at his drink shyly. His eyes flicker in the firelight.

"When my wife..." He stops a moment, then continues. "Passed, a couple years back, I really just wanted everyone to leave me alone." Now I get his reserved demeanor. He probably still wants people to leave him alone. It's been months since I last saw Liam, and I can't imagine a day where I won't be crushed under the weight of the loss. I cannot conceive of a time where I'll have one solitary experience or even a simple conversation without him there, without Liam's face in my mind.

"I'm so sorry," I say, and then I cringe. I hate it when people say it to me because I hear it every day. They mean well, but I still hate it.

"How do you..." I start to ask, but I don't know how to finish.

"Get up in the morning?" he offers. I look up at him and meet his eyes. Yes, that's exactly what I want to know. Will I ever want to wake up in the morning again?

"Yeah," I say.

"I don't really know some days. It sounds stupid, but there's a support group I go to on Wednesdays. Sometimes again on Sunday if I'm having a rough week."

"Support group?"

"It's not like it helps, exactly...it's just nice sometimes to be around people who get why you're a mess—people who can relate a little since pretty much no one else in the world can know what you're going through."

"Like AA for mourners sort of thing?" I ask. He gives a shy laugh, and continues to look at his drink.

"I guess, kind of. I warned you that it sounds stupid." I can tell he feels self-conscious now. I wasn't mocking it, just trying to get a mental picture.

"It doesn't sound stupid. I'm glad you found something that gets you through." I smile.

"Yeah," he says dismissively. I want to ask how she died, but I don't. I wouldn't want to tell my story to a stranger. It has been refreshing to be in the company of someone who knows the same indescribable loss. I feel like he wants to invite me to the group, but he doesn't. He drains the last of his wine and stands. I feel a stab of anxiety. I find that I don't want him to leave. I don't want to fill the next empty hours researching my husband's lover. I don't want to face it yet. I just want to sit here by the fire and drink wine with a stranger who is as miserable as I am, but he picks up his gadget bag and goes to the door.

"If you have any more computer needs, just let me know."

"Thanks. Thanks for your help," I say, and then close the door behind him. He seemed embarrassed for opening up. He probably felt like I'm one of the few he could say all of that to. I could have asked more about the group and tried a little harder to hide my heartbreak, to make him stay longer, to stay distracted a bit longer, but he's gone.

I log on to my desktop and search Facebook. There are hundreds of results for Rebecca Lang. I narrow it down to Chicago and there is still an overwhelming number, but I don't know how to narrow it down from there, so I search. I scroll. I look at each of the Rebecca Lang profiles, seeing if I recognize one, or if there is a way to connect one of them back to Liam.

After clicking on thirty-seven Rebecca Langs, I've made note of only a few that are the right age and location. Then I click on "Becky" Lang. Occupation: bartender at Bowen's Steakhouse. I feel paralyzed for a moment. I click on her photo. She's young. Midtwenties, probably. I do what any woman in my position would do, and surrender to the compulsion to compare myself to her and wonder what she has that I don't. She has dark, shoulder-length hair. She's pretty, but not traffic-stopping, I think. A girl-next-door look. She wears a tight T-shirt with booty shorts in her photo, and gives bunny ears to a guy who's kissing her cheek. A boyfriend? Husband?

I forward the photo to Len and ask, Is this her? After about twenty minutes, I see the little dots pop up as if Len is texting back. They stop and start multiple times. I imagine he doesn't know what to say. He probably asks Bonnie how to handle it and she says, undoubtedly, to tell the poor girl the truth.

But all he texts back is Yes. Then, after a few more minutes, he asks, Are you all right? I just reply, Thanks, and grab my coat. I'll park outside Bowen's and wait, I decide. I won't talk to her yet. I'll follow her and see where she lives. There's no way to confront her at the steakhouse and guarantee that I'll get her alone a minute, or that she won't make a scene, say I'm harassing her—anything like that. Hell, she might act the part of the victim being stalked by a murder suspect just for the temporary fame it might bring her. I guess that's what people do now, just to see themselves on TV, no matter how foolish it makes them look.

I circle the block for a long time before a metered spot opens up in sight line of the front door. I can't see in the windows, so I need to first make sure she's there. I pay the meter and hug the side of the building as I approach so I'm not in plain sight of the large front windows. A light flurry of snow has started, and I'm underdressed for the cold. I hug my coat into my body and lower my head against the stinging air. Little Dr. Seuss–looking pine trees are trimmed in wooden planters in front of the main entrance. They're decorated with white twinkling lights, and Frank Sinatra music is piping out from the lounge to the sidewalk. I duck behind a planter and peer in the window sideways to get a view of the bar. I don't see her, just a young, thin guy with a hipster beard and a man bun. He greets a couple and places coasters in front of them at the bar.

I duck out of sight again. There are no other bars in the restaurant. I'd been here with Liam a few times, so I know the layout. A wave of nausea comes over me when I think that she might have been here then, sneaking covert winks and smiles, literally behind my back.

It's not a weekend, so maybe she's off. Although every night has weekend numbers at Bowen's. It's a popular place. I feel like I should be wearing a Groucho Marx mask the way I'm actually, in real life, ducking behind a planter, spying.

A cab tries to stop when he sees me looking. I wave him away and decide to bury my face in my phone, to blend in. I'm freezing, and after a couple minutes I need to shove my hands back in my pockets. This is a stupid plan. I peer in one more time, and... *Shit.* There she is. She carries a tray of empty glasses she's retrieved from the bar tables and sets them down behind the bar before taking an order from a patron.

Okay, I can wait. It's almost 9:00 p.m. now, and she should be off work anywhere between 10:00 p.m. and 2:00 a.m. I'll wait forever if I have to. I can do a few hours. I buy a cup of lukewarm coffee from the deli next door, hunker down in my car and listen to public radio. The plaid throw I keep in the trunk smells like oil, but I wrap it around my shoulders anyway, and I watch the front door of Bowen's.

I bolt up when I see something that my mind can't recon-cile. It's Joe. It's Ellie's Joe! He's in uniform. He walks out of Bowen's with a cup of coffee. He looks around and then gets into the passenger seat of his squad car. His partner, Marcus, is driving. I met him once. Why are they here? I watch them drive off and try to think what would bring him here. Is he watching me? Stop. I need to stop. I guess this would be con-sidered his jurisdiction, right? He met Liam for lunch here on duty before, so I guess it's not outrageous that he'd grab a bite or something. It's just a strange coincidence though.

Hours go by. It's almost 1:00 a.m. before she walks out the front doors. The steakhouse has a parking lot, and I am pray-ing she drove and parked there. If she takes the train home, that's it. She knows what I look like, so I can't just follow her to the same El car, but she doesn't. She stops in front of the entrance with another waitress. They talk for a brief moment and hug goodbye. She lights a cigarette, shielding it against the breeze with her hand, then blows the smoke out sideways and flips up the fuzzy hood of her jacket and walks to the parking lot. Yes. Thank God.

She gets into a rusted, late '90s Volkswagen and pulls out of the lot. *One, two, three, four.* I try to calm my nerves as I pull out and follow her. She drives north. I think she probably has some downtown loft or something. It's hard to tell her exact age, and there's no way of knowing if she's married, as I'm not close enough to tell if she's wearing a ring. I see her as a twenty-something, maybe post-college, living it up, single in the city with girls' nights and online dating…and affairs with married men, just because she can. But she keeps driving. When we pass Evanston, I start to have an irrational freak-out. What if she knows she's being followed and she's luring me to some remote location? Just when I'm considering turning around and pulling into an overly lit gas station for safety, she turns into a trailer park.

We're forty minutes out of the city now, almost in Des Plaines. I keep following as she turns into a dirt clearing on the side of a trailer. Does she live here? There's a small bonfire where a few people sit, drinking cans of beer. Is this just a party she's gone to? I turn into another trailer's dirt drive. I can hide here a few minutes. One of the guys hands her a beer when she gets out of the car, but she makes a gesture like it's too cold and goes in instead. I see the silhouette of a toddler in the glass door of the trailer. She picks the kid up and pokes her head out the door to yell at the guy who handed her the beer.

"Why the hell is she still up, Cal?" She doesn't wait for a response. She picks up the little girl, kisses her, and carries her off. Cal is the guy in the Facebook photo. I can see now. He scoffs and shouts back a response. "She's fine, she was watching TV." He rolls his eyes to the other guys and cracks the beer she didn't take.

I can't do this tonight, but I know who she is now. She's not a downtown loft, uptown bar girl. She's a mother, living in a trailer park way outside town. This doesn't make any sense. I need to get her alone. In daylight, not around a group of drunk men who are capable of God knows what.

When the front door is safely slammed behind her, I pull out and drive back to the city. The questions and confusion in my mind race and can't be quieted. I keep thinking the same thing over and over until tears start to flood my eyes and I finally say it out loud.

"Why, Liam? Why her?" My thoughts darken, and I can't ignore the image that keeps surfacing in the seconds between waking and sleeping, and under the deep haze of too much wine. The image of Liam, alive somewhere, the idea that his death could be staged, that this is some elaborate hoax. It's such a ridiculous thought that I push it down deep. I take deep breaths and shake off the unwanted images of him with a lover, him never really loving me. But why? What would he gain? No. He would never do that to me.

SEVENTEEN

THE NEXT MORNING I HAVE AN APPOINTMENT DOWN-
town with Will. I don't feel like dragging out more dark
details and explanations the way I have already done with Detective Sterling multiple times. All I can think of is Rebecca,
and when I see Ellie calling, my thoughts turn to my mother.

She's already playing games. She made it sound like seeing
me was urgent, and now she's telling me not to come until
Sunday. Four days to wonder, four days to suppress that naive
glint of hope that maybe she's getting clean and she knows
how much I need her right now, and just maybe she'll say she
wants to come and stay with me the way I've asked so many
times, and she'll sit at the fire with me and tell me what to do
with a parent's inimitable wisdom. Even in my thirties, I feel
like I need an adult—like I'm still a child, navigating a scary
world of police and lawyers that I have no business being a
part of yet.

Probably, though, she will put me off again and will eventually cancel the visit, or most likely, she got ahold of some
money and is on a binge for a few days. I'll never be able to

explain to Ellie, because I'll never understand myself why a mother who spilled blood for us, nursed us from her own body, sacrificed comfort and hours and days of her time and attention, could change her mind. And I can't explain why I still want to see her so desperately, and why I can't find the apathy that Ellie has discovered, out of necessity, and then skillfully mastered.

I decide to walk the three miles to Will's office. Winter is trying its best to announce itself, but yesterday's flurries have turned into a misty rain, and autumn leaves whisper around my ankles as I cross the street from the condo and stop at Brew House to buy a cup of coffee for my walk. I shake off my umbrella under the awning and see Marty standing in the rain in front of our building with Figgy at the end of his leash, sniffing around the iron fence, refusing to pee. He doesn't have an umbrella, and he looks like the saddest person in the world, alone, drenched. I wave, but he's not looking.

When I get my coffee and go outside, he's down the block, hopelessly trying to get his dog to do its business, but I do see Hilly in an enormous red parka, heading right over to the coffee shop as I exit. I quickly, almost involuntarily, make a left and then duck back into the lobby of the condo to wait until she's out of sight. I feel ridiculous hiding from a lonely cat lady. I truly need to get a grip, but I cannot have her corner me and invite herself up to get her meat loaf dish right now.

I stand next to the row of mailboxes in the lobby as I peer out the little window waiting for the coast to be clear. I decide to check my mail. I stab the tiny key in the lock and expect a handful of coupons and credit card offers, but then I see something that makes me gasp.

There is a white envelope with my name on it sticking out of the crease on top of the box. No address. It was hand delivered. My hands flutter as I open it and pull out its contents.

My mind is trying to make sense of what I see as I stand there, still, staring down at what's inside. It's a scrap of paper ripped out of a book. It reads:

Secure your new home:
Consider new window and door locks, outdoor lights, an alarm
system, steel doors and smoke detectors.

This snippet is part of a bullet list from my book *Someone's Listening*. The person has ripped out this phrase. I can still see the page number and the watermark of my name on the top corner. I actually wrote this list in both my books because it's a resource page for victims, a list of tips to help them escape harm and secure the safety they once had. This was just one of many tips in a bigger list. My heart is in my throat. Why would someone send this to me? My arms and legs are charged and tingling. This is a threat.

I look around a moment, as if the person would be standing right there, then I push the envelope down in my coat pocket and rush outside. When I look up, I see that Hilly is standing across the street in front of the coffee shop, looking at me. She gives me a wave, her body language odd, like she was staring at me hard and then pretended she just noticed me when she saw me notice her. Did I see that right? I don't wave back. I decide I need to drive instead, and I round the building to the back lot and get in my car. I try to catch my breath and slow my heart. *One, two, three, four.* When I catch my breath, I drive. I need to show this to Will.

In the car I call Sterling. All Will is going to tell me is to make sure the detective knows what's going on, so before I even get to him, I call, hoping this information goes a long way in starting to clear my name.

"Dr. Finley, hello." Sterling answers the phone in a friendly voice.

"Hi—um… I wanted to give you some information that might be helpful," I say, trying to mask my trembling voice.

"Oh? Are you all right?" he asks.

"Yes, fine. I think… I think that there may have been…an affair." I can't believe I have to say this out loud, and I resent Liam for putting me in this position, but if I offer this information now, it is less likely to look like I knew and covered it up.

"I think maybe Liam…it looks like…he may have been talking to someone. I guess I'm telling you because I don't know of anyone else who would—I'm sure you'd want to know—to talk to her, is what I'm trying to say." I take a deep breath and make a right on Lakeshore Drive.

"I appreciate that. We have been looking into that possibility," he says.

"What does that mean? Like in general you've been looking for evidence of an affair?" I'm angry because it makes it seem like they hope there is one, so they can nail me for a revenge or jealousy motive.

"When we took his work laptop into evidence, they examined the hard drive and his email and social accounts. There were some messages that could be interpreted as…romantic in nature, so we have been in contact with the sender of the messages."

On one hand, it's good they're actually trying to find answers, and I'm sort of impressed that they got that far already on a case that seems cold from the get-go, considering how long it was before he was found. On the other hand, the fact that they saw every exchange between us, every intimate, sweet instant message or email over the years, along with every curt "whatever" or " I don't care" at the tail end of a petty fight, is sickening. I'm sure they dissected my every word in hopes of finding some misstep that pointed to my culpability.

"Rebecca Lang? You've already talked to her? What the hell did she say? Why didn't you tell me this before?"

"I'm not at liberty to discuss any details." He pauses, and I wonder if he's going to say "with a suspect."

"Well, I got a threat in the mail today. A page torn out of the book I wrote, stuck in my mailbox with no address, just left there." I explain what it said, and that it was part of a resource list for victims. His silence gives away his surprise at this. I thought he was so sure it was me, he'd be dismissive, but he isn't.

"If that's the case, you may not be safe there. Anyone who really wanted to could easily find out where you live. Do you have family or friends you can stay with awhile?" he asks.

"No. I'm not gonna leave." I don't explain that the house in Sugar Grove has an offer on it and is basically sold, that my sister is in a two-bedroom with two young kids, and that my mother is a junky currently on a bender. I don't tell him that I used to have friends, but I don't think I do anymore.

"I can stop by and take a look at your security setup. We'll want to get that letter into evidence also." He sounds genuinely concerned.

"Okay," I say softly, angry that he has information he can't tell me.

"Are you somewhere safe now?"

"Yeah, I'm fine."

"Faith, this is nothing to take lightly. I can't force you, but I highly recommend you try to find a place to stay for a while," he says. I can hear his radio in the background with muffled dispatch voices calling for available units here and there.

"I'll think about it. Thanks."

Will's office is cold and quiet. I'm annoyed that he's too

busy to give me his focus for more than a few minutes at a time. After I tell him about the letter, he's called away a moment by a serious-looking senior partner carrying a towering stack of files in his arms. He says he'll be right back and steps out. I wait and listen to the sound of the rain tapping on his wall of windows. The city looks hazy and sleepy in the overcast day. I want to be home, in front of the fire, with a drink and a *Great British Baking Show* marathon. Alone. I want to be out of the damp, away from the burden of saying the same thing again and again to people who try to hide that fragment of doubt in their eyes that they can't fully conceal because they still wonder about me even if they don't want to. He comes back with an apologetic look. He pulls his chair up next to mine.

"I looked through all of the police reports and everything you've stated, and now, well, with this, I wonder... I'm not saying this to scare you, but have you considered that Liam wasn't the target?" he asks.

"What do you mean?" I ask. I have not considered this. I've spent months of my life focusing on finding him, and now I'm focusing on who would hurt him, and of course it crossed my mind that it could have to do with me, like if it were Carter, or a jealous lover, but not that they got the wrong person.

"Faith, I mean, it looks like from the police files, it was assumed that you were under the influence and hit a tree, and that Liam left on his own."

"Yes, they thought he was never in the car. That we fought, he left. I got loaded and hit a tree, and filing him missing was a desperate attempt to get back a man who was literally running from me. It's written a bit more kindly, but that's the general idea. Now, I guess the part where we fought means I killed him and then drove loaded and hit a tree." I'm not hiding my anger.

"Well, I believe what you're telling me. I'm on your side here. So, when you say there was another driver, coming head-on and you had to swerve, let's assume for a second that it wasn't an accident." He speaks softly, carefully. My eyes dart as I try to digest what he's proposing.

"You think someone was trying to kill me." This seems crazy, but just for a moment, and then I can't believe I haven't really thought about that before.

"You were driving. If they came at you head-on, sure, it could have been an accident, but you'd been all over the media. You had death threats on Twitter, among other places. Some believed you'd done something unthinkable. Now, you're getting more tangible threats. I think we should at least consider it as a possibility. The more I look at statements, evidence, all of it, the more I think we need to make sure you have a safe plan for yourself."

"Oh my God." If that's true, Liam's death was because of me. I can't even think about that.

"Do you have a security system?" he asks.

"Uh, I mean, no, but the building is gated. It's safe." I look out the window. My mind is reeling. Am I in danger? Could some crazed person who posts in the comments section really be on a mission to kill me? It seems so far-fetched, but there are senseless shootings damn near every day. There are a lot of crazies. I don't know what else to say.

"My grandma could get over that gate," he jokes, but neither of us laugh.

"Can you stay…" He starts to make suggestions like Sterling did, but I don't let him finish.

"I'm not moving again. There's no one to stay with," I say curtly. I'm not going to defend staying at the condo. But if this is all true, I'm not going to put Ellie in danger, or anyone else for that matter. The fifth floor of a busy, centrally located building is as safe as I'm going to get.

"Okay, then will you get an alarm at least? You need a security system," he says matter-of-factly.

"I'll get a security system."

"And you should check in with me or Sterling daily," he says, waiting for me to look at him. I pick up my coat and stand.

"Okay," I agree. "But I'm still a suspect?"

"Look, you were in the hospital when the pings on his phone happened and when his credit card was used. There's no gun, no evidence of you ever owning one, I mean. There is nothing to show you helped plan something like this. You have clean phone and computer records, so…" But he doesn't say that I'm not a suspect.

"But I still am?"

"It looks good for you, Faith, but you were the last one to see him under very strange circumstances, so until they know more, you won't be completely off their radar. The incident at the book signing points away from you also, so that's…"

"What incident? What do you mean?" I ask, confused. His face goes pale, and he suddenly looks ill. He didn't mean to say that.

"I didn't think it would be helpful for you to know right now, but in light of the letter you got…maybe…"

"What, for God's sake?"

"In the bathroom, at the party, Liam saw a copy of your book in the urinal. Someone had, uh, defaced your photo. You know, the photo on the back of the book jacket," he says uneasily.

"Defaced?" I realize that must be why Liam had the sudden mood change and wanted to leave that night.

"Yeah, they made a…mark, I guess. A slit on your neck. And…urinated on the book."

"Jesus Christ," I say, louder than intended.

"I don't know if Liam thought it was a threat, or some kids, or maybe just a nutjob who was on Team Carter and came by to make a passive intimidating gesture. I don't know. He pushed past me and left."

"And you thought, let's keep this from Faith? Seems like a great idea right now!" I am pissed, almost seething.

"I get that you're angry."

"Yeah, I'm fucking angry, Will. Why would you leave that out?"

"Listen, Sterling doesn't tell me any privileged information he wouldn't tell you. There must be a strategic reason he's not saying anything, but I didn't want to—you have so incredibly much to deal with, and at the time it happened, it seemed like an asshole prank. I told the detectives about it back when they questioned me. It didn't seem significant at the time."

"But, since I'm still a suspect, they don't tell me much."

"How much they disclose to you depends on a lot of things." I stare at him. He stops. "Okay, I should have told you. As a friend."

"I don't need you protecting me. I just need the whole truth." I try to take in a breath on a four count to keep calm without him noticing. *One, two, three, four.* I look at the ceiling a moment, then exhale.

"The good news is, it helps us. It shows a pattern of threats. So, as far as helping your name get cleared, it's a good thing. As far as your safety goes, I'm concerned."

"Well, I appreciate that, but I'm fine." I know he sees me close off. He knows my propensity for isolating myself and shutting down. He takes my hand.

"You're not alone. Really. I don't want you to worry. Just lie low for a little while, and we will get this figured out. I promise." He moves his hand to my shoulder and meets my eyes.

"Okay," I say, really at a loss for anything else. I'm overwhelmed by everything he's just told me.

"Thanks, Will." I open the door to leave his office. He
looks at me as if he wants to say more.

"Why don't we get dinner this weekend?" he says.

"Dinner?" I'm not in the mood for socializing, and I don't
get why he's asking.

"Strictly professional, of course. We can discuss all this in
more detail, no interruption for once." He gives me that familiar Will smile. At first I open my mouth to say that I can't,
the way I've done with every invitation over the last several
months, but I don't. I feel like he believes me, and I want so
badly to be believed the way only Ellie truly believes me. It's
nice to be around someone who knows me as well as Liam
did, and from whom I don't get pity looks.

"Yeah, that sounds good. Just let me know where," I say,
and he helps me on with my coat. As I start my way down
the hall to the elevator, he hollers, "A security system. Promise me." He gives a head tilt that looks parental, an "I mean
it" sort of gesture. I nod.

"I will," I say and disappear into the elevator. And I do
mean it.

I drive to Liberty Firearms on the west side of town, poorly
placed between a liquor store and a seedy gentleman's club.

They're right. There is "no evidence that I've owned a gun
before." I haven't. But now I walk in and purchase a security
system, as promised.

A .38 Special.

EIGHTEEN

AT HOME, ON MY STICK-IT NOTE WALL, THE EVIDENCE column is populating. The book signing "incident" goes up on a yellow sticky. Then I scribble other things of note and organize them:

"Car accident or target?"

"Note in mailbox."

"Hilly's behavior."

"Rebecca Lang."

"Carter."

"Len's email."

Things like the ping on his phone and money withdrawals seem less significant now. They were all I had when I was searching for him, but now it feels like some punk found his discarded phone and wallet somewhere stole them and used his card. Those things weren't found on him when he was discovered. Still, they're also on squares of paper on the wall. Why he took out a sum of money shortly before he disappeared still keeps me up at night. If it were some sort of blackmail, surely they would ask for more than a few grand.

The number of people who would want to hurt me seem endless after scrolling through social media sites and seeing all the hateful comments for months. However, the book being defaced at my event, the letter in my mailbox, it feels more personal. I need to go to talk to Rebecca Lang, but there is something I need to do first.

At Bullseye shooting range, I stand holding my gun like it's a dead fish. I don't plan to use the thing, but it's a better security system than a beeping noise with a one-minute delay before it notifies police, not to mention how long it would take for anyone to actually reach me. I need to know how to use it, even though it disgusts me to be touching it. It's come to this. Liam would be ashamed of me, I think. We pride ourselves on our antigun position; we even went to a march against guns once after one of the latest mass shootings. There are so many, I don't even remember which it was. But I have to. *I don't know what else to do.*

The guy giving lessons is the sort of guy who doesn't hide his narcissism. I hear him talking with a few other patrons at the range while I fill out the lengthy release paperwork before my instruction starts. I know the type of guy well. When someone is telling a story, all he can do is wait for them to finish so that he can tell his own story that's not only better, but also more directly involves him. He picks tobacco from his teeth and calls me "sweetie" and "lady" while he goes through the basics. I suffer through so I can meet my goal: leaving with this terrible weapon, confident I won't accidentally shoot myself before I arrive home.

I learn that a magazine is something other than *People* and *Time.* He shows me how to check the chamber. He goes on and on about the difference between a magazine and a clip. Even though that apparently doesn't apply to my gun and he's just showing off his vast knowledge on the wrong, unimpressed audience, he wastes another ten minutes of my life on how people use the terminology wrong. He goes through a long demonstration on safety, which is redundant as hell, but I guess I'm grateful for. Finally he lets me try it out.

I shoot a paper circle a couple dozen times. The giant earmuffs might be why, but it's not as horrifying as I thought it would be. After a few shots, I start to hit close to the middle of the circle. A long way from a bull's-eye, but good enough to feel like I can cower in a corner with this thing and aim it at someone if they broke into my home. Good enough to feel like I won't shoot myself by mistake, although I'm still sickened by the idea of having it in the house.

They upsell me on a lockbox for the gun, but I spend another ten minutes refusing the guy's attempts to try and get me to buy a cleaning kit and holster. He seems personally offended when I don't drop another several hundred dollars on gun accessories, and I can't wait to be out of there and not go back ever again. I had planned to take it with me when I showed up at Rebecca's, but find out there is a waiting period before I can take it home. I don't want to wait seventy-two hours before getting answers. Maybe I'll just go anyway.

I sit in my car, a little defeated, but decide to try and see if I can get some information about Rebecca's schedule before driving up there so I can be likely to catch her at home. If she has days off, maybe midday will be best. If, in fact, the boyfriend has a job. It's my best bet anyway. I pull away from the shooting range, just happy to be free of it, and make the call.

I pretend to be a friend trying to get in touch with Rebecca. I'm happy to get a hostess on the line, a woman who makes every sentence sound like a question.

"Thanks for calling Bowen's? This is Brittany?" I knew

immediately that it wouldn't be hard to get information from this girl.

"Yes," I say. "Um, is Rebecca Lang working tonight, by any chance?"

"Becky? Yeah, but she's busy now?" she says, and then I hear her welcome a guest. "I'll be right with you?"

"You know, actually, I wanted to come in and surprise her. I'm an old friend, and I thought I'd just pop in. I'm not in town yet, though. Do you know when else she works this week?"

"Oh, how fun! Okay, hold on, let me look?" She puts down the phone and clicks at the keyboard as she checks. In the background I hear the din of dinner conversations telling piecemeal stories. At one table, a woman laughing too loud, a snorting honk that pierces through the other voices. A guy, probably waiting for a table near the hostess stand, complaining about waiting for his whole party to arrive before being seated. I hear another voice going off about his phone carrier. "I had to restart the goddamn thing three times. They tell me it's water damage, and insurance won't cover that. What did I get the goddamn coverage for?" His voice is drowned out by a couple approaching the hostess, commenting on the cold and asking her to look up their reservation.

Sonder, I think. It's a word I never knew existed, and was delighted to learn about. It means: *the realization that each random passerby is living a life as vivid and complex as your own*. I envision all of the people having their very personal and different experiences there at dinner, while I listen in, scheming.

I remember the very table we sat in when we were there. I remember what I wore. I look at the gun in its box on the seat next to me, and it feels so incredibly surreal.

The hostess picks up again. "She has Thursday and Sunday

off, so any other day you come in, she should be here," she says, more distracted than before.

"Thank you," I say. I hang up and feel a surge of anxiety rush through me. I'll wait the few days and pick up the gun, then show up at her front door.

Ellie's name pops up on the phone, and I answer on Bluetooth as I drive home.

"Hey," she says, something recognizable in her voice. Disappointment? "I take it you're not coming?" she asks. I don't recall what I've forgotten.

"Um…" I say, but she doesn't let me dig myself a deeper hole.

"Dinner. Joe is at a work thing. You said you'd come over if I promised to have the kids in bed by eight." She's annoyed.

"I was kidding about that part," I say lightly.

"Were you?" she snaps, but then immediately changes the weight in her voice and tries to be light. I know she feels like she can't burden me with anything because of what I'm going through, so even when she needs something, feels something, she shuts it off and selflessly turns and makes it about me. She has every right to be upset. I screwed up, but she doesn't know what I'm dealing with, and I'm not keeping her informed about all of the developments. She's done enough, been through enough.

"It's okay. I know you're…" I'm not sure what she's going to say. She's not going to end that sentence with "busy." As far as she knows, I haven't left the couch in days, and it sure is where I wish I were right now. "Not feeling well," she lands on.

"I'm sorry, Ell," I say.

"It's okay."

"No, I forgot. That's not an excuse. There's no excuse." I say, genuinely sorry. As much as I try to mask my uncomfortableness around kids, she knows that's why we aren't as close. I mean it though; it's not an excuse. I need to make an effort. She's all I have, and I'm an asshole lately.

"It was just reheated chicken nuggets, it's fine." I cringe at the thought of microwaved nuggets. We live very different lives. "I just wanted an excuse to drink wine and put the kids to bed early," she says, with a little laugh to blow it off. Just the fact that she needs "an excuse" to drink wine is evidence of how opposite we really are. I could use a few excuses not to, however.

"I'm a jerk. I'm sorry. How about next week, and my treat? I'll bring takeout," I say. I should say that I can still come even though it's later than we planned, but all I want is my bed and a glass of wine and silence.

"Yes. That sounds perfect. I DVR'd *Housewives*. We can make a night of it," she says, and I don't let my voice give away the slightest bit of dread at the thought of watching *Housewives*.

"It's a plan. Love you," I say.

"You too," she says, hanging up. I feel like an asshole, so I drive over to her place anyway. It might be nice to listen to stories about spit-up and diapers for a few minutes to distract me. I'll just bring her a bottle of wine and some real food—a curry from Mai Thai.

When I arrive at her door with curry and wine as penance, she drops her shoulders in a "you didn't have to" gesture, but hugs me and takes it. We sit at a sticky dining table and slide away a pile of crayons to open the wine. She eats and tells some story about how Joe might be up for detective and about the long hours he's working—that she could use a nanny. She laughs and pours herself more wine, clearly only half-joking.

Before I leave she wants to show me the latest reason they can't "have nice things." In their bedroom, the once white wall is covered in Magic Marker drawings. I gasp and chuckle.

"It comes out though, right?" I say lightly, and then I see something. In the mess of their open closet sits a pair of jeans, thrown over the back of a folding chair. There are piles of both clean and dirty clothes in their walk-in, so it might go unnoticed by them, who are used to their mess, but they leap out at me. Those are Liam's. One of his favorite pairs. What the fuck? I silently walk to them, my mouth agape.

"Why do you have these?" I can't mask the horror on my face.

"What do you mean? Jeans?"

"These are Liam's." I study her for a look. Her face changes. Sympathy or guilt?

"Are you sure?" she asks. I don't want to point out how short and overweight Joe is compared to tall, fit Liam. If you take one second to look at them, you'd laugh at the idea that they could be Joe's. She looks them over.

"I don't know. Maybe he left them here?" She seems unconcerned and tells me to take them with if I want, as she is beckoned by Ned, wailing, and rushes into the other room. I take a few moments to compose myself before I leave so it's not in haste and she can't sense the terrible thoughts I'm having.

When I'm back in my car, I hate myself. I actually let it cross my mind that my sister was having an affair with him. I'm losing my mind. I just can't think of any time he would have changed clothes there or stayed there. They have a messy, tiny place crammed with kids' stuff. They always came to our place for any parties or overnight visits. God, I'm totally paranoid. I'm sure there is a perfectly benign reason for this. I take a few breaths and tell myself to pull it together.

When I near home, I see my usual lot is full, so I find a spot on the street a block away. I admire a storefront window displaying a family of happy snow-people gathered around a Christmas tree that stretches ten feet tall. Tinsel and glass icicles wink in the glow of Christmas lights, strung up the trees, in prisms of flickering colors. I see a horse and carriage standing in front of a busy restaurant. I watch the puffs of white breath stream from the wet nose of the horse's nostrils, and I feel sorry for it, the metal bits in his mouth and leather harness, standing in the sleet. I close my eyes and turn away.

Inside the lobby of my building, the homeowners' association has strung white lights around the banister of the stairs and through the branches of the potted trees. I take the elevator, and when I reach my door, I see a note taped to the outside of it.

I look around at other doors to see if it's a takeout menu that a delivery guy stuck there, but in that case, it would be fastened with a rubber band on the knob. But then I remember that every three months they send notice for pest control. The HOA was here today working in the lobby, so I breathe a sigh of relief. That's probably what it is. I'm becoming so paranoid. I need to remind myself to breathe, to be logical. When I pull the taped note from the door, I read it. I don't believe what I'm seeing, again. It's another torn quote from my book. It's from the same resource list as the last one.

Stay off social networking websites:
You don't want information about who you're friends with and what you're doing to be public.

There's nothing I can do to stop it: I'm dizzy, panting. I can't catch my breath. The panic attack is sweeping in, and I hate myself for not being able to control it. My hands are trembling so hard I can't hold my bag. I drop the letter and sit on the floor, holding back sobs.

Fuck, pull it together, I tell myself. But, I can't. *One, two, three, four.* It doesn't work. I'm having a panic attack. I don't know how bad it will be. My chest tightens. I put my head on my knees and lean against the wall, trying to breathe. *Fuck, fuck, fuck. Get a grip. Control it. Please.* But it rises up like bile in my throat.

NINETEEN

AFTER A FEW MINUTES OF TRYING TO SLOW MY breathing on the hallway floor, a dog comes bounding down the corridor and starts to force his nose under my chin to lift my head. I look up and see Marty running after him, leash in hand.

"Sorry," he hollers before he gets to me. Then he sees the state I'm in. "Oh my God, are you okay? What's the matter?" I can't answer. It takes me a second before I can catch my breath.

"Sss…sorry," I manage to say. "I'm okay." I try hard to speak. I'm so embarrassed.

"Christ. You're not okay. Can I help you inside?" He crouches next to me, offering to help me up. I go through my four breaths in my head one more time. I force myself to gain control. I dig in my purse, scrambling for a Klonopin. I find one and put it under my tongue.

"I can't. I don't want to go in," I say, pulling away as he offers a hand. He doesn't know what to do, I can tell. He probably wishes to God he didn't stumble upon me and now he feels stuck, but I really just want him to go.

"I'll be fine. Sorry. Thanks," I say, but he sits next to me and waits for me to calm down. Once I can speak normally, I apologize ten more times.

"I need to call the cops before I go in."

"Cops? Did something happen? What—did someone hurt you?" he asks, confused.

"No. I just—I've been getting some threats, and I found another one just now. I need to call… I don't know if it's safe to go in."

"Okay, I'll call. Don't worry." He stands and calls. After a minute of listening to him try to explain what he doesn't really understand, he hands the phone to me.

"They want to talk to you." As I walk them through the history, they put me through to Detective Sterling, and I'm sure Marty heard me explain the whole story, although he'd walked away down the hall to politely give me my space. When I hang up, he and Figgy come back over.

"They on their way?" he asks.

"Yeah." I am still shaking. "Thanks." We stand there awkwardly. He tries to fill the silence, which, from the little I know, doesn't seem like his quiet nature. He's obviously uncomfortable.

"You don't have to wait. It could take forever." I say this, but to my surprise, I don't want him to go.

"I don't mind. You don't really look like you should be alone."

"I look a mess. God, I'm so embarrassed."

"Don't be," he says, then silence again. "Sorry about Figgy. He won't take his walk in this sleet, so we were making our rounds down the halls. I should have had him on the leash."

"Oh, he's fine." I pat Figgy's head. "Helpful actually. Is he trained to help people…like a therapy dog or something?"

"Kind of, I guess. My wife brought him to some kind of

training like that. Not sure exactly what it was called, but yeah, he's good like that." He leashes Figgy and looks around. I peer at my watch, wondering how long I'll have to wait.

"I need a drink," I say.

"Why don't you let me go in and check it out? If anyone were inside, the door would probably show signs of someone prying it, right?"

"Oh my God, you don't have to do that," I say, but I really want to be inside. I'm cold and so tired.

"Figgy can go in first. He'll freak if anyone's in there," he says. I look at him a moment, contemplating this, then hand him my key.

"Thank you." I stuff the note from the door in my purse and peek in behind him as he and Figgy go in. I don't hear barking. After a few minutes, he resurfaces.

"All clear. Nothing gets by this little guy." He pats Figgy and makes a gesture for me to come inside. "Do you want me to wait with you?" he asks, and I really do, but I try not to let on.

"Oh. I'm sure you have things to do."

"It's okay." He smiles so kindly.

"Well, can I pour you a drink then?" I ask.

"Absolutely," he says. I invite him to sit at the kitchen counter and I open a red blend that's sitting out and pour us both a glass. He sees me shivering.

"Do you want me to light a fire? The heat in this building sucks."

"Old and drafty," I say in agreement. "Sure. Thanks." The Klonopin is kicking in, but I still need to warm up and calm down. I go and sit on the couch while he arranges wood in the fireplace. Figgy curls up next to me.

"Oh my God," I say, startling him. "It's Wednesday."

"It is," he confirms, puzzled.

"You said you have your support group Wednesdays. Were you headed to that? Did I make you miss it? I feel terrible." I'm not sure it's possible for me to feel worse, but I do.

"It'll be there next week. Please. Really. It's okay," he says. He's turned back to his task, striking a match and lighting the fire. He sits opposite me and picks up his glass.

"I'm glad it's something that you...found comfort in. I hate the idea of taking you away from that." I'm hoping he tells me more about the group. Maybe I just want to know there's hope to feel better at some point, but he doesn't offer much.

"I was looking for a reason to skip it tonight so I didn't have to go out in this crappy weather. A fire and a drink is better therapy at the moment."

"Well. Good," is all I can think to say. I hold my glass up in a toast, and smile at him. He smiles back warmly, and we drink. Figgy nestles into my hip, and I ache to stay right here and fall asleep, safe with someone else watching out for me, but there is a hard knock at the door.

"Faith! Hello!" It's Sterling, calling through the door. I leap up, and go to open it. He comes in and looks at Marty suspiciously.

"Is everything okay here?" he asks.

"Besides this? Yes." I hand him the letter. "This is Marty Nash, my neighbor. He helped me out," I say as Sterling eyes the note I gave him.

"You didn't see anything, anyone lurking around who may have left this?" he asks Marty pointedly.

"No, I didn't even see the note, just what Faith told me."

"He was coming by with his dog after I found it," I say.

"Sorry. I wish I could be of more help," Marty says, holding Figgy by the collar so he doesn't pounce on Sterling. "The security in the building is pretty abysmal," he adds. "Anyone could catch the front door if someone else held it for them.

The cameras at the gate are always out of service, same in the halls. There's always a sign pinned up, 'sorry for the inconvenience.'"

"Yeah," I agree. "They call it 'gated' and we sure pay for that perk, but there's just an iron gate in front. It's like never monitored or anything."

"Ultimately—" Sterling looks to me "—you should really think about staying elsewhere for a while. A friend?" He looks at Marty when he says this. I didn't know Marty could look more uncomfortable, but he does. His eyes flit around, looking for an out.

"I'll work on it," I say. "How are you going to find who's sending these?"

"Since the probability is high that it could be linked to the homicide investigation, it will be sent out for DNA, fingerprints. We'll keep working the leads we have for any more information. We'll try to get some more patrols on your block. Have you talked to the building's management company about security cameras?"

"A few times, actually, over the years. A whole HOA board has to approve it. It's not a quick thing if it ever happens. And they don't think it's necessary," I say.

"You can't put one up yourself?" Sterling asks. Marty snickers, because if you live here, you know how strict the rules are.

"You have to get permission to put a poinsettia on your fire escape," Marty says.

"It's a historic building," I agree. "So, no is the short answer."

"Do you have your own security system?" Sterling asks.

"I do," I say, still feeling shaky and disoriented.

"I'll need to keep this." Sterling indicates the note. "You sure you're okay tonight?"

"Yeah, I'll be fine."

"I'll check in with you tomorrow. If anything happens, you find anything else like this, even if it seems insignificant, call me." He opens the door. I nod in agreement and show him out.

"Thanks," I say, and Sterling disappears down the hall as he pulls out his phone and answers a call. Marty has Figgy ready to go and holds the open door.

"You're positive you'll be okay?" he asks.

"Yes. Thank you so much for staying. I still feel like an idiot, but I appreciate it. Maybe you can still make your group."

"Well, listen, you know where I live. Just call if you need anything."

"That's really nice of you. Thanks." I pat Figgy's head and close the door behind them.

The silence they leave behind makes my ears ring and gives me a hollow chill. I bring my drink to the bedroom, undress in the dim light, and slip on a robe, then wrap myself in the comforter to try to get warm. I lie on the bed, looking at the ceiling, thinking about what could make a person go this far. All the *Dateline*s and *20/20*s seem to have two scenarios: heat of passion murder by a jealous lover, or murder for insurance money. The spouse always kills for the life insurance. Of course they're looking at me, but whoever this is, whoever wants me hurt this badly, it's calculated and personal, and the cops have no clue where to start looking beyond me. I can tell by the way Sterling avoids my eyes and gives me sterile answers.

I pull out my phone, and still squashed in the blanket, I poke one hand out and hold my phone over my head, typing with my thumb. I look up Rebecca Lang again. I try "Becky Lang" now. There's just not much no matter how far I dig. I even tried one of those internet background companies for $19.99 that are supposed to pull up arrest records and any dirt in general. She was arrested twice for shoplifting, once at a Walmart and once at a Kohl's. Not much help. What had Liam wanted with her?

Did he just need to get back at me because I'd inadvertently ruined our lives? Did he have feelings for her—this young girl with a kid and a boyfriend, or maybe husband? Did he have a one-night stand, drunk after he closed down her bar, and she wanted more? I have to force myself to stop thinking about it. The stress is making my hair thin. When I looked in the mirror after my shower this morning, my ribs were visible through the pale skin stretched over my bones, tight as a drum. The makeup that I'm applying heavier these days only emphasized my watery skin tone and gaunt eyes. I officially am starting to look like hell. I need to sleep, but the Klonopin isn't as effective anymore. It takes two just to relax. I sit up and reach for my glass on the nightstand; I take a few gulps of wine and decide to look up Marty Nash.

Google provides many Marty Nashes. There are pages of them, but none that look like a match, no Twitter, no Facebook. That doesn't surprise me. I find a Marty Nash in Chicago with a Linkedin profile. He's a computer programmer, which matches, but no photo. I add +computer +Chicago to my search and scroll. I come across a church website, of all things, dated a few years ago. It's a public monthly newsletter.

Our thoughts and prayers are with a cherished member of our community today, Marty Nash, as we all mourn the terrible loss of his wife, Violet Marie Nash. Please sign up for the prayer chain, and give Marty and his family your love and support.

That must be him. I Google *Violet Marie Nash*. There's not as many results, but I come across an obituary for June 2016.

Violet Marie Nash will always be remembered for her courage during difficult times, and even though she took her life,
we know she is at rest without pain now.

I immediately feel like going over to Marty's door and just
embracing him, as trivial as it sounds. I know what it's like
to think your spouse would rather escape than be with you.
I know what it's like to have them gone. I feel sick for him.
I'm relieved I didn't make the mistake of asking him how she
died that night on the fire escape.

After a few more swills of wine, I decide to look up Hilly
Lancaster while I'm at it. I don't know that I've ever Googled
anyone before. Maybe a restaurant owner for Liam now and
again. It feels so invasive, but now, it's imperative.

It's not a super common name, so she pops up quickly.
When I go to images, she's there in a knitting circle. Shocker.
There are a few photos of her posed next to a tray of baked
goods and one of her bakery's grand opening. When I scroll
through articles, I see Liam's review and read it. It's everything she described. He did have a hard time tearing down
someone's dream, but he felt like he had a duty to be truthful
above all. The review was not kind. One of the harshest ones
I remember reading, actually.

A few clicks more and I see a local news article. It outlines
all the problems with pop-up bakeries and the god-awful re-
dundancy of cupcake shops. The writer is pretty brutal when
he bids Hilly's Honey a good riddance, and says that although
he's sad to see it go bankrupt a few months after opening, he's
glad the city is rejecting these wannabe home bakers ruining
pastry for the rest of us. He ends by thanking Liam Finley for
the review that swatted this bakery fly and flicked it off the
Chicago culinary landscape.

I sit up at the realization that she moved in the same day I moved back. Not only does she have motive, but she was there when I got the first note.

TWENTY

MORNING DRINKING ISN'T USUALLY MY STYLE, BUT I decide to go downstairs to Grady's before I pick up the gun and drive up to see Rebecca. "Becky," I guess it is. What I do know about her is that she took a perfectly nice name and white-trashed it. "Becky." I hated her. A rush of dread washes over me, tempered with something else: fear. I know I should let the detectives handle this, but I also know I can't.

Inside Grady's, I'm surprised to see other people. Not many—a few old goats gumming the rims of pint glasses. Bloody Marys and Hamms beer on tap are two-for-one before 5:00 p.m. What a steal. I planned on just one, but I double fist it since the second is free. Just two. I can still drive and keep my wits about me, I tell myself.

It's those first few sips that I love the most. The anticipation of momentary euphoria, the alcohol buzzing between my temples, warming my chest. After a couple drinks, though, I'm just chasing that initial feeling, and each subsequent drink isn't as satisfying as it is necessary. After pounding the drinks with hot sauce and sucking down both Bloodys, I walk out into the overcast morning and get a cup of coffee even though the dehydration is making me headachy and I should drink water instead.

As I drive, I think about all the ways this could play out. I've gone over what I'll say a thousand times, but I'm still not confident I know what will come out of my mouth. The fact that there is a gun under the seat is almost impossible for me to believe. I actually reach my hand under and feel for the box just to make sure I wasn't imagining the whole thing. It's there.

I picture Liam in my mind, and as angry as I am with him for betraying me, I can't help but talk to him, and still love and desperately miss him.

The thought about mass shootings only reiterates that it could be any nutjob in the world—a fortysomething guy still playing video games and living in his mother's basement who developed some sort of obsession with me, and I could be wasting precious time with futile pursuits, but where else can I look? I have to follow the threads I can see. It's all I have.

My heart races as I pull up, slowly, wheels popping the crunchy ice that has formed overnight. The trailer looks dark and uninhabited. The fire pit from the other night is full of empty beer cans and covered in frost. Her car isn't here. It doesn't look like the boyfriend is home either, but I have to find out. I keep my car running and walk to the front door, looking over my shoulder. It's quiet in the trailer park. The only sounds are the distant bark of a dog and a couple young kids wrapped in wool coats playing on a rusted swing set two yards over.

I swallow hard and then knock on the door and wait. There's no answer. I knock again.

"Hello? Becky?" I call. Nothing. I look around one more time to make sure none of the neighbors are taking notice, and then I step up on a cinder block on the side of the trailer and peer through a window to get a look inside.

I only see a baby bouncer in the living room (it looks like), a coffee table cluttered with sippy cups and beer bottles, baby books and pizza boxes. It's dark and there's no movement, so I go back to my car. I shiver a moment, blowing into my hands for warmth and shaking off the cold. I hadn't thought about whether I'd wait or not, but now I know I have to.

I wish I would have thought to bring a bottle of something. Maybe she's just taking him to work and will be back, so I turn on public radio and pull the hood of my coat over my head and wait. By 10:00 a.m. I doze off, and when the howling scream of a little neighbor kid jerks me awake, I'm horrified I slept like that. The blasting heater in the car and lack of sleep for days has gotten the better of me. I wrench my head to see where the noise is coming from, but it's just a boy, crying and red-faced with fury at his sister for taking his trike and riding off. A mother appears on a concrete step and stoops to pick him up and bring him inside.

I look at Becky's house. Still dark. No car. I'm starving after forgetting dinner last night and having Bloodys for breakfast, and I have to pee. I start to talk myself out of waiting, but decide I can pee behind my car. It's too cold for people to be around and the area feels deserted anyway, eerily quiet in the absence of the two screaming kids. I can't wait. I wouldn't even make it to a gas station.

I squat and try to keep an eye out at the same time without falling over. I remember a party Ellie and I went to years ago. A hot tub party in January. It was lightly snowing and maybe ten degrees, but Andy Sharp and his friends had gotten their hands on a bottle of peppermint schnapps. His parents were away for a few days, so we drank and flirted in his backyard hot tub, the steam meeting the cold air and enveloping us in a fog, lightly pierced by sprinkles of snow. It was magical and otherworldly. When Ellie and I had to pee, he didn't want us to drip water into the house, so we squatted in the snow in dripping swimsuits, the steam billowing from our bodies. We held hands to keep our balance and couldn't stop laughing. We used to be so close, and now I seem to widen the distance between us on purpose.

Three more hours go by with no sign of Becky. I find a stale snack pack of Fig Newtons in my glove compartment and eat a couple. Assuming the guy she's with has a job, I don't want to be here when he gets home. I need to talk about this with her alone. He probably doesn't know about the affair, just like I didn't, and the point is not to punish her, but to extract information I need, not that I care if it ruins her life. But it could blow up and certainly backfire if I handle it wrong. Even if he does know, speaking about it in front of him is a bad idea. I'll have to come back.

I stop at a roadside diner with World Famous Waffle Fries and order the special. A waitress named Trudy with spiky platinum hair and pineapple earrings delivers a plate of runny eggs and oily potatoes that I eat without protest, I'm so hungry. I drain a couple oversize cups of water, trying to ignore the bleach smell, and I feel a little better. I don't want to go home.

My mother has been unreachable since she called me, asking to see me. One of the games she plays. I'm already this far north, so I decide to drive to Elgin and drop in on her, whether she's high or not. I want to try to see what she wants. It's no doubt the police have talked to her in their investigation of me, and the days keep ticking past with no progress. Today has been a wash. I need to know something.

I get back in the car and head back to the dump I grew up in: the Crestwood apartments, a dejected, two-story building with a stony exterior and few windows. It rests on a bleak square plot with an overabundance of brown, overgrown grass and no trees. I find it astounding that my mother had managed to keep it this long without eviction. Section 8 and welfare probably cover just enough to provide the stability that enables her habit.

It hasn't changed. When I was a kid, I thought the girls in the front stoop with their glossy lips and hoop earrings were the coolest girls I'd ever see, and the prettiest. I asked to take them to my school for show-and-tell once. Now, it seems comical that anyone would not recognize them as "escorts," even a kid, but of course, we didn't see the world that way then.

I still have the same key she gave me when we changed the locks the day my father left. Geoffrey and Lisa Bennett are still written on a tiny insert of paper on the front of the mailbox. It's weird to see my father's name, even weirder that she never changed it. She's never gotten past him walking out. After a few knocks, I crack the door open and call out.

"Hello? Mom?" There's no answer. The smell of urine and stale air make me cough and take a step back outside for air. I cover my nose with my arm as I go in, but the stench of soiled linen and decaying food in the unwashed dishes that are littered around the place makes me feel ill, despite my attempts to take shallow breaths.

"Mom? Are you here? It's Faith." I hear a rustling from the back bedroom. A couple of guys from the next apartment fall into the hall, laughing, high. Then one falls into the other and it turns into a fight, so I close the apartment door. My mother appears in a bra and sweatpants. I was right. She's clearly been on a binge.

"The fuck? What are you doing here?"

"You called me," I say.

"The hell I did." She spits her response. I wonder if she really doesn't remember. It's very possible, so I don't explain that I came earlier than we agreed; I just go with the idea that she forgot.

"You did."

"Well, I ain't got nothin' to say to you, so you can go." She sits. Mascara is smeared around her eyes, and her hair is a nest on top of her head that once must have been a ponytail. She's sickly thin, but I'm not one to talk.

"Well, I came all this way, so maybe you can spare a few minutes." I push. After a few minutes taking me in, she shakes her head.

"Shit," is all she says, and then steps over the mounds of dirty clothes and booze bottles and boxes of God knows what. She manages to get herself to the kitchen, piled with dirty Tupperware and takeout boxes, blanketed with a fine, blue mold. She grabs a bottle of vodka and two plastic cups with Pizza Hut logos on them, and pours us a drink. She pushes some things off the small kitchen table to clear a spot. I stand there, watching her. It's been so long, and she looks like a shrunken, morose version of the mother I remember as a child.

"Well then sit, for Christ's sake," she orders. Her phone blasts a country song and I jump. It's an old pay-as-you-go flip phone, and she snatches it and answers.

"Yeah?" She disappears to the back room without a word to me. I can hear her explaining my presence to someone, the guy she's currently seeing, no doubt.

"Well, I don't the fuck know, do I, Jerry? Just get it yourself." She closes a door, I think, because her argument becomes muffled.

I close my eyes to absorb the stillness of the room and remember sitting here as a child, the sweet heavy odor of vanilla cakes baking in the oven. That was before my father changed. Before Lenny Dickson moved into the building and offered him a way to take the edge off after his long days laying shingles, and coming home to two screaming kids and a nagging wife.

I was so young, but I remember feeling the changes. They were slow. It didn't happen in days; it stretched over months. After he started to become different, I knew my mother felt like she was eternally walking on eggshells to assure his contentment. He was once a loving man, but he'd become so volatile. I know I remember that. She was not permitted to descend into unpleasant moods because there would be no one to keep us quiet in the evenings, assuaged with construction paper and crayons and our favorite television shows on the floor of the back bedroom. There would be no one to cook canned soup on the stovetop when he got home at night, or make excuses to the neighbors about the sounds they heard, or keep a part-time job to make sure the electricity bill was paid. These were her unspoken responsibilities.

I pick up my cup of vodka and look toward the living room. Before the change, the house was always warm and full of chaos, the TV always on in another room; it was filled with tacky afghans, doilies, Precious Moments figures, and kitsch. It's all still here and hasn't been updated since the midseventies; it's now just covered in a film of filth and neglect. The kitchen is still a dull rust and green color with rooster wallpaper. The living room has burnt orange carpet to match. Cookies sit stale inside old, yellow Tupperware on the counter, a corded phone rests on the wall, and there are too many saved magazines and ashtrays filling side tables and countertops. A place suspended in time.

There's a little snow globe up on top of the crown molding in the kitchen. I put that up there once when we were decorating for Christmas. That was probably twenty-five years ago. It seems impossible that I can go out in the world and find and lose jobs, fall in love, make unforgivable mistakes, hurt people, get my heart broken, develop wrinkles and cynicism, and change so completely from who I was in this house, and come home and that little Christmas globe hasn't moved, probably not even to be dusted, through all of this—through a person's whole life.

When my mother returns, she's pulled on a tattered robe that doesn't do much to conceal her bra. She picks up her vodka and lights a cigarette. When she sits, she wraps one leg around the other, and she's so thin that her legs almost twist around each other twice.

"Well?" she demands, saying nothing else.

"Well, what? You called me, so…? You don't remember why, I guess." I'm not gonna put up with any shit; I can see how it's going to be. Her fingers shake as she taps the ash off her cigarette.

"The cops are comin' around," she says, blowing out a nauseating wheeze of smoke.

"What did you say to them?" I ask urgently.

"Nothing. I told them to fuck off. But they'll be back, so?" She stops and stares at me, eyes bulging.

"So…what?"

"What did you do?" she asks coldly.

"I didn't do anything, Mother. What do you plan to say?" She could say any outrageous thing she was high enough to conjure up the next time they come.

"What do you want me to say?" she asks, and then I realize what this is about. She wants money.

"Well, what do you know about the situation?" I ask, knowing she barely knows her own name and might not even remember me telling her about Liam, inviting her to the funeral, any of it.

"Nothin'." She hacks, a deep smoker's cough rattling up

her chest into a phlegmy ball she swallows away. "That's why I'm askin' you."

"If you don't know anything, then I guess that's what you tell them." I give her a combative stare. "Right?" I should leave the vodka alone and keep myself sharp, but I want it too much. I pick it up and take a swallow, feeling so let down that this is all she wanted.

"Then I'll just tell them what I told the *National Examiner* when they was out here pokin' around."

"You spoke to a tabloid?" I feel the blood rush out of my face.

"They asked about your childhood. Said they'd give me five hundred dollars to talk with them. They was nice. I didn't think you'd care since you already said all those nasty things about us in your books."

"What do you know about my books? You didn't read them," I snap.

"Candace Lechers did, though. She told me all of the nasty stories you have in there, making us look like sickos to make a buck." She coughs and spits again.

"First of all, sharing my personal stories helps people. Other victims are comforted to know that I'm not just giving out advice I studied, but that I truly understand..." But she cuts me off.

"Victim, my ass!"

"What did you say to them?" I demand.

"They took photos of the apartment, said it was good to have a visual of where you grew up."

"Jesus," I whisper in disbelief.

"What? Too good for this place, are ya? You were fed, clothed..."

"Just what else did you say?" I'm not going to get stuck in

the same cyclical argument where she defends her parenting job because we didn't end up in foster care.

"They asked about the stuff you said about your father in the book, if it was true. I said no fuckin' way it was true." Her hands tremor, and she reaches for a small glass pipe; she makes no attempt to hide it from me. She lights the base and inhales the rest of the white substance. It doesn't take long before she's calm.

I look at her, her black-spotted teeth and pockmarked face that used to be quite beautiful in her day. I'm so angry that I have an urge to hurt her. How could she do this to me? On the other hand, why am I surprised? I feel a flush of shame rise up in my checks at the thought of pushing her up against the wall by her neck.

"That's what you told them? You told me to shoot him once, but I guess he wasn't abusive. That was just a whim you had…"

"Abusive. Oh, for Christ's sake, that therapy word. You overreact, Faith. You always have. It was his parenting style, that's all. You kids turned out just fine." She lights another cigarette off the first one. I catch a glimpse of the punishment closet in the hall leading back to the bedrooms. I wanted to ask her if she remembered when he found me filling his car with snow because I wanted to help him wash it. He raged like I'd never seen. I was only five or six. I tried to tell him I kept hearing "washed clean as snow" in Sunday school and I was trying to help. But there was water damage to the leather, and he pulled me by the arm and locked me in the closet. I know I was for at least two days, maybe more. That's where the panic attacks likely started, my first therapist told me. There's no point telling her this. She was there.

One, two, three, four. I take a long, silent breath and turn away from the closet.

"You can disagree, Mother, all you want, and say that his parenting style was the same as the way he was raised and it was fine, but if you actually read the stories, each one of them is a true account of what happened, no matter your opinion on it, and you can't deny the actual play-by-play, so you can't tell a national tabloid that they're lies." I'm trying to stay as controlled as possible.

I look at the burn marks down her arms, raised up in scar tissue, and I have been working with victims in denial long enough to know that nothing I say right now is going to change her mind. I know that she believes what she told the neighbors. Not that he held cigarettes to her flesh until they made weeping holes and finally extinguished, but that she's a clumsy cook. That's all.

She still believes the story she rehearsed hundreds of times. There's no point to any of this. I allow myself to be black-mailed because there's no other way to control her, and I can't have my own mother fanning the fire of lies and suspicion already burning out of control.

"How much do you want?" I stand; I'm done with this. I reach for my purse.

"Same as the paper gave me." She curls her scrawny knees into her body like a child, and crushes out her cigarette.

"I don't carry five hundred dollars in cash on me. I have forty. I'll have to come back." She takes the forty greedily.

"Okay," she says, satisfied.

"You tell them you don't know anything," I say, "because guess what? You fucking don't. Do you even know why they're trying to talk to you?" I cram my wallet back in my purse and cross my arms.

"You musta did something."

"Jesus," I mutter. "They're asking for current information that may help us figure out what happened to my husband.

And you have no current information about anything, and you didn't know him, and so you have nothing to say. That's all you're going to say. Leave anything having to do with my father out of it. That's ancient history."

"You think you just know everything. I bet your father is pretty goddamn pissed off at you for all the terrible things you wrote about him."

"What?" I freeze at the thought of this.

"They should go bother him and see what he has to say about you instead of botherin' me. Stupid fucking cops you got comin' around here, making everyone nervous."

"Do you know where he is?" I ask urgently.

"The cops should look for him and talk to him."

"I'm sure they probably tried. Nobody knows where he is…" I pause and study her face a moment to see if I'll get anything out of her. "Except maybe you."

"I don't know shit, I told you that a hundred times." She stands and walks to the door so I'll leave.

When my first book came out, I had the crazy idea that I might look for him after all the years that had passed, and maybe reconcile. Now that I was an adult and had money, maybe even get him help. It would be a sensational, touching redemption story. I found that he moved to Florida and only had a PO box. I wrote and emailed with no response. So much for that. I never cared to try again. Screw him. But now, what she said rings in my ears.

"I'll be back with cash when I can," I say. She doesn't push me about when. She knows that I can turn her in in a second or get the place raided if I really wanted to. She only has so much leverage. Holding out on my father's whereabouts is her best weapon.

She looks like a skeleton, standing in the dark backlight of the apartment door as I look back. I get in my car and exhale a long, slow sigh. I feel dirty and so tired. All I can think of is what she said.

I bet your father is pretty goddamn pissed off at you for all the terrible things you wrote about him. Not only might he be pissed off, he's also a violent psychopath with a severe addiction. And no one knows his exact whereabouts. I've exposed all of his sins and made him look like a deplorable, utterly sick man, which I believe he is. My God. I don't want to believe that he could be involved in this, but now it's all I can think about.

TWENTY-ONE

I BREAK MY RULE THE NEXT MORNING, AGAIN, AND I don't wait until noon. I bundle myself in a robe, drop a few pours of vodka into my coffee and stand in front of the living room window, looking down at people rushing in and out of cars and shops, through the flurries. It's a raw, unusual cold for November that forces people to cover themselves and hug their bodies tightly in the streets—to walk more quickly and with their heads bowed, the heaviness of winter settling in.

I wonder if Marty Nash can find Geoffrey Bennett. If he's too nice to take my money, I still have a bottle of Hennessy Richard that I can force on him. It will certainly cover his fee so I can feel less guilty about it. If I'm honest, I'm just tired of being the victim who relies on other people for help—I'm used to it being the other way around. I'll ask him, but today I've decided not to wait for Becky's day off.

She likely works nights. Most seasoned bartenders get the dinner shift. It's just as likely she'll be home during the day, I think, on a Friday with a kid, and that the guy will be away, than it is on a Sunday, a day off where they might go out. I just can't wait anymore. I need to start eliminating possibilities without waiting for invitations to my mother's or for Becky's damn day off. I want answers. If I have to sit outside her place in my car every day for weeks until she surfaces, I will.

I sit in the window seat and wipe a circle of fog away with my palm. Low voices from an old TV show and the smell of freshly brewed coffee make me long to take a few tramadol and sleep the day away to the tapping of sleet on the windows, but I can't let myself be still. I can't let the dark thoughts creep in through the silence and empty hours, turning me numb and apathetic.

I pick up my phone and click the *Chicago Tribune* app, scrolling through the headlines, then browsing the smaller stories. My name hasn't been in the press much lately. Headlines about Liam's death have fizzled out as midterm election news floods every channel. As I'm about to abandon the news and go and shower, I see something that stops me.

There is a mug shot of Carter Daley, just a tiny thumbnail photo with a brief story next to it:

Carter Daley, the young man at the center of the Dr. Faith Finley scandal, was arrested Thursday for assault and battery at a pub in Wrigleyville. He was released on bond early this morning. Some say his reckless behavior casts a shadow over his credibility regarding his accusations made against Dr. Finley. The case was dropped due to lack of cooperation on his part and lack of evidence for the DA to make charges, but that isn't keeping Mr. Daley out of the spotlight.

I look up at Carter's name on a stick-it note on my wall. He has a delusion disorder and is now proving to have a propensity for violence, and he doesn't even seem to be on Sterling's radar. When I meet with Will tomorrow, I need to make sure he knows that I don't trust this kid and they need to press him more than whatever desultory questioning might have done.

This is an ethical gray area. I want to tell Sterling and Will about his history, his diagnosis. I'd love to share his records so they know there is motive. He was obsessed with me. Plain and simple. The public doesn't know this because I can't divulge it, so I have to take all the vitriol spewed at me in the form of retreating friends, or assholes contributing to the comments section on various online rants on the matter.

There are a handful of situations where a psychologist might break confidentiality. The only one that may apply to Carter is if he'd threatened to assault or kill another person. He hasn't threatened though. Could he have been off meds and taken his obsession to the extreme? Could he have been the one in that truck that crossed the yellow line—that truck that was never proven to exist? Could he be trying to get my attention now, watching me, stalking me even? I think about my desperate emails to him months ago. Wouldn't he have responded and jumped at the chance to connect if this were all true? Maybe there are reasons he couldn't. Maybe his parents were monitoring his accounts. I know they'd done that in the past for his safety.

If someone in this situation asked me if the hunch about Carter coupled with his public defamation of my character was enough to break this sacred confidentiality, I'd advise that doing so could backfire; it could become a whole other potentially career-ending battle. I'd tell them to wait—to keep looking at these other leads and make Will be the one to look deeper at Carter and get some concrete evidence.

One more little pour of vodka to top off my coffee and pour into a to-go cup, and I dress and get ready to go back to Rebecca Lang's trailer. I'm prepared this time: water, a blanket, a bottle of wine in case, and leftover Chinese that I stuff in a linen bag like I'm packing for a lonely picnic.

I decide to take the long way, up Lakeshore Drive before cutting over west to the trailer park. I love seeing the lake. It's one of the things Liam loved most about the city. It was like our little ocean. I pull into a parking lot for a moment at a beach clearing we used to go to in the summer.

I sip the rest of my coffee and stare. I know I shouldn't put myself through it; I shouldn't work myself into a state before going to do something this important, but it hasn't even been a year without him, and I'm losing some of our memories and it scares me.

Before she passed, my aunt June used to make a drink called a Dark and Stormy; she would come over and sit on the tiny balcony at our apartment with my mother and list to her, between fits of deep smokers' wheezes, all the failings of my father, and I always imagined her drinking a thunderstorm and the sea beneath it—swallowing down black waves and lightning clouds. The lake felt like that to me now. The storm upset sediment from the lake floor, and debris from the trees blanketed the water's surface. The sand stirred and softened the water.

One very hot August night, Liam talked me into skinny-dipping. It was early in our love story, and I'm sure that I was trying to impress him even though I was scared of what crept beneath. I remember the water was warm and elastic as the dark wedges of waves bobbed around our heads softly. That was happiness. That was it. That moment, and I wish I had remembered to pay closer attention.

When I pull into the trailer park again, I'm more familiar with the layout. I pull over on the side road so I can still have a view of their lot. I ready myself to cozy into my blanket for a while, but there it is. Her car, the one I followed here that first night. It's parked next to the trailer. A prickly heat flitters across my chest under my coat. I touch under the seat to feel that the gun is still there.

It feels so ridiculous to be doing this. She's 120 pounds soaking wet with a baby in tow. But it's her guy friend and his buddies I'm more concerned about, and who knows what she's capable of? Everyone seems to have a gun these days. If you go down the dirt clearing they use as a road to enter the park grounds, you'd be surprised if everyone didn't have a gun or two. The properties have more than their share of gutted cars on cinder blocks, laundry hanging to dry, or in this case, freeze, in rows across ropes strung from rooftop to mobile rooftop. A couple of rusted-out bikes lie on a decaying mattress a few yards away from me, and kids' plastic toys scatter the landscape.

I realize I don't know what I'm going to do, all of a sudden. What if the boyfriend greets me with a shotgun in my face? I can hardly peek in the windows to see if she's alone. I'll try to speak to her no matter what I find. I take a deep breath, take the last long, astringent swig of coffee, and go up to the door. There is a light on, dimly visible on this gloomy day. I shield my head with my hood so I don't get soaked with the sleet that's now coming down again. I knock, a few hard raps, and stand back a step.

The door opens a crack and there she is. She looks through and takes me in; she opens it a hair more.

"Hello. Becky, right?" I don't know what the cheery tone is in my voice. Maybe an attempt at not getting the door slammed in my face.

"You're the wife," she says, unimpressed. My heart sinks.

A small part of me was hoping all of this is just a big misunderstanding.

"Do you think we could talk for a few minutes?" I ask.

"The police said I don't gotta talk to anyone 'cause it's my right. Plus I already said what I had to say to them."

"I'm not with the cops. I just really need to ask you some questions. It won't take long." She doesn't respond. "I'm not here to try to…punish you or anything. Please. It would mean a lot." After a moment of contemplating, she opens the door in one jerk and turns around, into the trailer, a passive invitation for me to come in. A baby is sitting on the floor in the living area; she picks her up and sits on a green floral couch.

"I got ten minutes before my husband comes home for lunch. I gotta get it going, and I sure as hell can't have him see you here."

"Oh. He…knows who I am?"

"He knows." She picks up a toy and tries to comfort the baby, whose chubby legs flex and kick against her mom's side.

"When Cal found those messages I sent Liam, he flipped out. I mean, he broke the TV. Look at the goddamn thing." She gestures across the room to a box television with a shattered screen. "Threw a full beer. Then he left for a couple days. So you better hurry with what you gotta ask."

"Cal is your husband?" I ask. She nods and crams some socks on the fussing baby's feet. I feel rage welling up at the way she casually says Liam's name. "I guess I just want to know…why? Why Liam? You're both married. He…" I start to realize I'm getting emotional, and pause. She fills the silence, and her response is not what I expect. Her tone is a mix of rehearsed lines and clear annoyance at having to talk about it.

"Look, I know it was wrong, okay? You think I don't get shit for it every single day from Cal? If you came here for an apology, I'm sorry I did it. I should have left him alone. Is that it?" She sighs and puts the baby in a bouncer. My neck tenses. With each bit of confirmation I get that this actually happened, I wish, fiercely, that I didn't know.

"Do you have anything to drink?" I ask, trying to stay controlled, but my palms are literally sweating. Until this moment I thought that was a vapid expression.

"I got beer. If you can drink it in less than ten minutes." She stands and gets a couple beers from the mini fridge.

"I can," I say, and take it from her, sucking down half in one breath. "Can you tell me what you said to the cops?" I ask shakily.

"Those pigs. I didn't tell them nothin', but Cal was home, and there was hell to pay when they brought it all back up and upset him, I'll tell you that. I thought we was over it. But he says to them it's illegal for them to come in, so that poor detective stood, freezing his ass off out there. I just said I didn't know nothin' and didn't want to talk. He said he'd be back, which sucks, 'cause I gotta deal with Cal punchin' walls and staying out at the bar all night for a week after. I hate those fuckers." She picks at the label of her beer as she talks and pushes the baby bouncer back and forth with her socked foot.

"I was sad to hear what happened to him," she adds. "But I really ain't got nothin' to tell them." She looks at me, and something she said stands out.

"You said Cal left for a couple days. When he came back, was he acting...different?" I try to ask this subtly and not advertise that I wonder if he went and found Liam to get his revenge.

"What are you trying to get at?" she asks, but not defensively, like I anticipated, but genuinely trying to understand the question.

"I mean, did you patch things up? Did he seem different, nervous, distant?" She looks at me, and I try to cover the pointed questioning. "Because I'm just thinking about clues Liam might have given me that something was going on."

"He acted plenty weird and distant, but what do you expect? Lots of people would have got divorced, but he stayed, so I gotta be extra careful now." She looks at the time and fidgets, wanting me to go. What else do I really need to know? She's sorry, not that I care. She didn't say anything helpful to the cops, and she's never going to tell me if Cal did something unthinkable. She's just happy to have him back.

I stand, drain my beer and head toward the door. Before I leave, I do ask one more question.

"Why did you pursue it with him? I mean, just…" I don't even want to bring myself to say it, but I need to know if he was in love with this girl. It's so hard to imagine he was. "Was it lust or more… I mean, why did you do it?"

"Why does anyone look outside a marriage? Same ole shitty reasons. Cal's gone too much. He didn't want me as much after the baby cause my stomach looks like cottage cheese. I wanted to feel sexy. The chase. It was stupid…and embarrassing, okay?" She shivers as a wind rushes and jerks the door open, slamming against the makeshift railing outside. I don't say "thanks" or "bye." I am going to start sobbing at any second and I have to just go. I turn and walk away.

"I know why you really came here," she says to my back. I turn and look at her.

"Huh?"

"I ain't givin' back that six thousand dollars. Already spent, so nothin' you can do about it now." I hear her pull the door shut. I walk as fast as I can to my car without running like a lunatic, and when I get in and crank the heat, I cry. I cry all the way back to the city. I wail. I pull over awhile when my vision is blurred with tears, and when I am done, I get angry.

She's ruined our love story—our history. Soon, memory will become the place where sorrow lives and suffering is shallowly buried, and I need to do something with myself besides think and cry and mourn, or the cancer of my sorrow will spread and anxiety may turn into a depression I'd never recover from.

TWENTY-TWO

WHEN I PULL MYSELF TOGETHER, I CALL WILL. WE'RE
supposed to meet tomorrow, but I need him. I don't want to
be alone, and although he'll be pissed I went, I want to tell
him about Cal and press him on Carter. He agrees to meet
for happy hour. I go home and get into bed until I have to get
ready to meet him. I just can't handle anything else today. I
ignore Ellie's call, hoping I didn't stand her up for anything,
and just take a couple Klonopin so I can meet precious sleep
and stay there all day.

It's already dark at 6:00 p.m. when I walk into the Hopleaf
and see Will in a booth. He stands before I even reach the
table, and he offers to take my coat, hanging it on the little
purse hooks on the side of the booth. He already has a drink,
and I can see him rushing to finish up what is probably a
work email on his phone. He quickly puts it away and looks
up at me.

"You look great." He smiles. And I'm glad he said so because
I actually tried tonight. I wanted to feel like a real person, like
everyone else here having a Friday night drink after work. I

used a flat iron on my hair, which I'd not touched in months. I went beyond a little mascara and applied lipstick and even some foundation and contouring. I look less gaunt. At certain angles, I look like my old self again. I'm wearing a dress for the first time since the funeral, a silky blue dress, and boots with my favorite fur-lined peacoat. I do look good under the circumstances. And I'm happy he noticed me like that. A little guilty about feeling happy about it, but I was aching to feel human again. I change the subject, though.

"Thanks for meeting tonight. Something came up tomorrow," I say, lying.

"Happy to. What'll you have?" A waitress passes and notices me.

"Double vodka tonic, please," I say, smiling up at her. She nods, writes it down, and disappears into the crowded bar. He doesn't make a snarky comment about the double. "Any new information?" I ask, getting down to business.

"Sterling talked to Rebecca Lang, the woman whose messages were discovered—"

"I know who she is," I interrupt sharply. He nods, understanding that the topic is painful. "And?"

"She wouldn't talk to him. I think it's the anticop vibe the whole area is known for. She's not obligated to talk, but we'll keep digging and hopefully find a reason to make her."

"I talked to her," I say. The waitress comes back quickly with my drink, and I suck half of it down through the tiny straw right away. I know this conversation isn't going to be fun, but I need his help.

"You what? Why would you do that? I told you you needed to…"

"Well, I thought you'd be thanking me since she willingly talked to me—even apologized for 'pursuing' things with Liam." I stand my ground.

"You just went to her house, or…?" He looks confused and a little miffed.

"I need answers, Will. Yes, I went to her house. I sat in her living room, and she said the affair nearly ruined her marriage. She said her husband, Cal, left for a few days and acted weird when he returned."

"Weird how?" he asks.

"Distant, volatile, it sounds like. He has a temper, broke the TV. So, he finds out about the affair, and disappears a few days, and comes back acting odd. I don't know when, like, the time line is, if it matches, but I'm pretty sure we should at least be looking into Calvin Lang," I say, firmly. He pulls out a notepad and jots down Cal's name, puts it away, and shakes his head at me.

"How do you know where she lives?" he says in a mix of disappointment and confusion. I shrug, silently rejecting his scrutiny.

"You put yourself in a lot of danger. It's not your job to—" I stop him though.

"It's not illegal. You can't talk me out of doing everything I can to clear my name and find out what happened to him." We are both quiet a moment. "I mean, I appreciate it. I know you're giving me standard advice or whatever, but I can't just sit at home and…hope." I suck the rest of my drink down. I see him notice, but he doesn't react.

"I get it," he says softly. "Can't say that I wouldn't do the same."

"Thank you." I stare into my empty glass. The waitress comes around with her tray, points at it and asks if I want another. Will answers.

"Another round for both of us. Thanks." He looks in my eyes after the waitress leaves. "It's helpful, even though I don't advise doing something like that again, and I promise to talk to Sterling and look into it as far as we can. He's already poking around over there to see if anything proves relevant, but there's no probable cause yet to search or arrest or any of that."

"Well, he was killed months ago, so it's pretty much a cold case, right? It feels pretty hopeless most days."

"It's not hopeless." He consoles me quickly. "We're doing all we can."

"I know." I try to smile.

"And I know Sterling comes off as a dick sometimes, but he's a good guy."

"He suspects me," I argue.

"Well, he suspects everyone. Wouldn't you want him to be thorough? I mean, if you could take yourself out of the equation, wouldn't you hope the person investigating this would keep being suspicious until there was certainty you weren't involved?"

"You think I might be?" I ask, hurt, even though I know what he's trying to say.

"No. I don't. I'm just trying to make a point that it's the sign of a good detecti—"

"I get your point. Fine. But he also needs to look at Carter Daley. I've already told him, and I feel like he's barely looked into it." Even just saying Carter's name out loud makes me angry.

"That's because the kid's got a solid alibi for the night of the accident," he says matter-of-factly.

"I know. He was at work, but we don't know if Liam was killed the same night. That's when he went missing. It could have been days later." I know Will already knows all this. There's no way to pin it down to that night.

If we'd fought and he walked off and something had happened to him, that's at least a digestible explanation. Vanishing

on a cold, rural road in the middle of nowhere from an accident scene? No one can wrap their head around how or why.
So I stay a suspect. And Carter Daley, with plenty of motive
that I can't discuss, continues to poach eggs at the diner and
keep his freedom.

"They've looked at him, Faith. There's nothing concrete
at the moment besides all the debacle in the press around that
time, which seems huge, I know, but the kid willingly came
in for questioning, almost like he wanted to help."

"Which you probably found odd in and of itself, yeah?"
I ask. "Like he's too eager to toss his useless alibi at you for
protection. Come on."

"Yes," he says. "At first, him coming forward before being
asked, as far as what Sterling told me, was…unusual, but he
has…very involved parents who made him talk before anything could hit the fan, I guess. He volunteered his house and
car to be searched. There's nothing but circumstantial motive.
You think he's involved?" he asks.

"Nobody volunteers their car and house to be searched
if there's gonna be fucking evidence found there. He could
have set it up that way—made sure those places were squeaky
clean. Who the hell knows who helped him or how he did it?
That shouldn't clear him!" The table next to us looks over and
then quickly back to each other. I was louder than I intended.

"No one is cleared entirely, but there's nothing else to go
on unless they can dig up some evidence that points to his
involvement. You know that. You know how this all goes by
now." Before I can say anything, he sees the wheels turning
as I twist my straw around my finger, and he reads my mind.
"Your restraining order was issued for a year, which means
there are a few months left, so don't even think about it."

"I wasn't," I say, but that's not true. Trying to talk to Carter is my next priority.

"You haven't changed at all, you know." He abruptly shifts the subject.

"I have," I say seriously, although he was clearly trying to be light and conversational.

"You never took any shit. Total determination with everything you do." He smiles warmly at me.

"I don't know about that." I smile back, trying to just let go and enjoy the luxury of meaningless small talk.

"Halloween, ninth grade. I heard that when Ginny Brewer started that rumor that you peed your pants in cheerleading practice, you invited her to your party at Grizzly's haunted house so you could punch her in the face in the pitch-black and no one would know it was you." He grins, and I convulse in a surprised burst of laughter, almost spitting out my drink.

"Untrue."

"I have solid sources," he jokes, leaning back in the booth. "She only started that rumor because she knew that Caleb Schroeder was in love with you and she couldn't have him."

"I think 'in love' might be a stretch."

"You're easy to fall in love with," he says, and then shifts nervously, looking as though he instantly regretted saying that. I know I broke his heart once, and it was never talked about. He just moved before my wedding and that was that. I don't know how to respond to him now. "I never believed you peed your pants, just so you know."

"Thanks. I didn't. For the record."

"Duly noted." We both sip our drinks in silence for a moment.

"How was life in Boston? Do you miss it?" I ask, curious

about the man he's become and how so many years can pass without someone, and still somehow their presence, after all that time, can instantly bring you back to the seventh grade Sadie Hawkins dance—to eating sleeves of Life Savers and chocolate Santas from his Christmas stocking until we got sick. And to first kisses.

"It's pretty much the same as here. I stay too busy to take much stock of my surroundings most of the time. My happiness is only gauged by which restaurants deliver to my office."

"That's...depressing."

"Yeah, well, it's not forever. I have a good chance at making partner in the next couple years. Gotta just keep your eyes on the prize, ya know?"

"You've slipped into speaking in clichés."

"Oh God. I have. I think we need another round. I apparently still haven't shed the day's stress." He makes a twirly gesture over our glasses when the waitress looks over.

"So what happens when you make partner? Don't you just get more busy?" I ask. He gives a sort of involuntary chuckle.

"I guess, probably." It's hard to think of him being lonely, but he must be if he doesn't make time for friends or relationships. Maybe he's exaggerating, but it seems like he's buried himself so deep in this career that he's left unbalanced and... sad. And he's done it on purpose.

"Oh, come on." I brighten my tone, but I can tell it sounds artificial. "You must be on a dozen dating sites. Those are for busy people, right? I'm sure you're quite the ladies' man." I wish to God I could shut up. Why would I say that?

"Oh, I'm sorry, I couldn't hear you over that loud cliché." He holds his hand up to his ear and looks around. I laugh. His sense of humor has always matched mine, and it's nice to be around. "I don't know," he continues. "Just not a priority right now." He doesn't elaborate. The waitress arrives at our table. I take my fresh drink from her hand. Kimmy, her name tag reads, and I wonder why a grown woman would call herself Kimmy if she wanted to be taken seriously. Then I silently chide myself. It's a silly observation, but I'm secretly afraid every day that I'm becoming an insurmountably judgmental person. I have to be aware of catching it before I lose myself altogether.

I don't know if I should bring up our past, but maybe it would clear the air and the palpable tension between us. Though I don't need to apologize: I ended things amicably and for the right reasons. He may have been hurt, destroyed even, but I was honest and kind about it. I *was* sorry for causing him pain, but how self-righteous does that sound?

"Sorry that you had to leave so abruptly and we didn't get a chance to, I don't know...not 'say goodbye,' but—" I begin, but he stops me.

"It's okay. I'm the one who should apologize for leaving like that. The job and everything just happened quickly."

"Yeah. Well." I don't really know what to say.

"I got over it," he says sharply, his words like a slap in the face.

"What? Over what?"

"You don't really need anything else on your plate, so I'm just saying I know I left things kinda shitty and I was not coping then, but obviously, it's been years. I got over it, eventually." His eyes are wet and shy when he says this.

"Oh, God. Of course you did... I...didn't mean to imply..." I stammer, taken off guard.

"Don't get me wrong. It took a very long time, and it was, well, embarrassing, frankly, the way I took off when I heard you were getting married, but sometimes you just gotta go and figure your shit out. It's good to be back, and we're… good?" I guess it's sort of a question.

"Of course," I say, thankful the elephant in the room has at least been addressed. The thought that he'd been pining over me had never crossed my mind. I hope to God I didn't make it sound in any way like I thought that's why he doesn't date.

"I'm glad you're back." I hold my drink up to toast, and I'm relieved that I had my say and am able to avoid thinking about the case for a brief time, because it's hard not to hate Liam right now, after everything I've learned.

We talk through another couple drinks. I talk about my practice and Ellie's kids, anything preaccident. He tells me about hiring a decorator for his new condo because he doesn't have the time or talent, but that he feels pretty guilty and bourgeois about it—not to mention his newfound obsession with froofy coffee drinks.

We're both buzzed, or maybe drunk, and I feel such a sense of elation. Just a couple of hours without gut-wrenching worry and strategizing through grief and exhaustion has made me feel like a new person.

"Did you drive?" he asks me, after we get the check and I lose the battle to pay for it.

"No. Uber," I say. He obviously can't offer to drive me, so I don't know what he's asking, but then I do.

"I live just up the block if you want to grab a nightcap, see Sylvia's genius interior decorating." I knew he lived on this street because it was part of the deal to push the meeting to tonight, since he'd be rushing. I can't lie; I want the company, but it seems wrong to go to a man's place after drinks. It feels like I'm doing something wrong.

"Okay, sure," I agree. He looks taken aback by my response,

but he gives a sideways smile and holds up my coat to help me into it. We walk, and he makes conversation about the great public transportation in Chicago and how much colder the wind makes everything seem, but I'm not really listening. I'm wondering what I'm doing going to his place.

A bus lumbers by on the street; laughter and music from a bar leaches out when a man flings open the door to come outside for a smoke. The paper birch trees hiss as they surrender dozens of dead leaves with each heavy gust of wind. I should go home.

Inside his condo, it's evident that whoever Sylvia is, she designs with a feminine touch because it's warm, inviting, and full of color and chic finishes. I lay my coat on a stool that looks like a piece of modern art and sit at the vast, marble kitchen island while he opens a bottle of red. With a tap of a remote, he clicks on a gas fireplace that is see-through, extending from the dining room into the living room.

"Fancy," I say, admiring the beautiful stone around it. I can't help but think about Liam, how he could have overcome the guilt—how he could reconcile betraying me the way he did. I'm doing nothing wrong here. I'm not.

Will hands me a delicate, stemmed glass of pinot as I wrap my coat back around my shoulders and shiver a little.

"Sorry it's still cold in here. I don't spend a lot of time at home. Let me turn up the heat a little." He darts into a back room where I guess the thermostat is. I see that he still has a remarkable view of the city, just like in his office. I think about Liam again, although I'm trying not to tonight. I decide I need to go. I can't shake the thoughts of Liam with *her*. Where did they meet? Her trailer? Not our bed. A hotel? She'd just had a baby. It was so absurd. Why? But the mind doesn't relent in these kinds of situations. It plays in my mind over and over—the ways he might have touched her, the lies he must have told me to pull it off, the two of them lying naked together, postsex, with drinks or room service, laughing, but about what? What could they have had in common? It feels like he just chose the first convenient person who showed him attention, which makes it so much worse. I fucking hate him.

Will comes back, and upon hearing the heat kick on in the vent he stops, points up, and gives an triumphant smile.

"There we go." He sits next to me on a stool and picks up his wine. I take it out of his hand and put it down. I stand in front of him, taking his face between my hands and kiss him, hard. He pulls back and looks at me, stunned. I know I shouldn't do this, but it's been so long, and I want something. I don't think it's really about revenge; I have been starting to fear that no amount of pushing and moaning and sighing can resurrect this frozen woman I've become.

It doesn't need to be mind-blowing. It could be clumsy and familiar, because even the achievement of mediocrity would feel like a fire, and I need to feel something besides pain.

"Sorry," is all I can say.

"No, no. Don't be, it's just…are you sure?" he asks, but he's halfway there already. I answer by pulling the edges of his neatly starched shirt from the waist of his tailored dress pants. I grab for his buckle and he kisses my neck. I feel the scratch of his five o'clock shadow and smell the expensive cologne as I grip his shoulders and pull him into me.

We pull off our clothes as we kiss and stumble our way to his bedroom. He says something I can scarcely hear under the panting and rustling of clothes. A joke, sort of, a mumble about how he'd lied about being "over it." It's at that moment that I know I should stop—that it's unfair of me to take advantage of the feelings he still clearly has just to benefit my own needs, but somewhere between my triumphant shame and inexorable desperation, we move into one another, drunkenly, passionately, completely, and then finally meet sleep under his designer sheets.

TWENTY-THREE

I WAKE WITH A VIOLENT POUNDING IN MY HEAD, naked, and tangled in the soiled bedding. Then, in a blend of confusion and remorse that becomes fierce and dizzying under the sharp daylight, I walk barefoot over the cold, wood floor to collect my scattered clothes, trying not to wake him up.

It's insensitive, but I have to get out of here and figure out what I've done. I'll send a text, saying I have a coffee date with my sister and I was going to be late. It's weak, but the truth is dangerous. The truth is that I may have just destroyed the only true friendship I have right now besides my sister, and I certainly can't tell him that, in actuality, I plan to find Carter Daley today. There's nothing he can say to talk me out of it.

When I'm dressed, I stand in the doorway of the bedroom and watch the slow rise and fall of his breath; he's still asleep. I hold my boots in my hand until I click the front door shut behind me and I put them on in the hall. I stop at the coffee shop near his building and then decide to catch the train home. It's a short ride and I can gather my thoughts. Part of me wants to call Ellie like we used to do in our twenties when one of us had done something crazy after a night out or taken someone home. It was instinctual to call and gush to each other, maybe because the admission alleviated some guilt from the reckless behavior. It was all fun and explorative back then. This is different, and I know she feels that I've gone beyond withdrawn and aloof, but it's to protect her from all of this.

I don't call. I tentatively enter my lobby and stare at my mailbox before quickly opening it like it might attack me. There's no note. I can breathe. All I want to do right now is take a hot shower and pop a Klonopin for the hangover. When I reach my door, I see Hilly standing there, holding something. She's knocking on my door. I only glimpse her from behind, but I can see her shoulders droop in disappointment as she turns and starts to leave. Damn it. She's coming toward me. If I had been thirty seconds later, I could have avoided this. Not now.

"There she is!" she almost squeals. I realize I'm still standing frozen in the middle of the hall, obviously ready to make a run for it.

"Hilly. Hello." I see she's carrying a plate of something. Christ.

"I brought you some of my famous sugar cookies. Vegan, just for you." She beams, but I'm confused.

"Vegan? Oh."

"Well, except for the eggs. You have a dairy intolerance, right?" She shoves the plate at me. "I thought I remembered that. Did you tell me that?"

"Doubt it." I dig in my purse for my keys.

"You know, I bet Liam mentioned it when I sent him home with a baker's dozen that time he was at the bakery." I hate his name in her mouth and don't know why she's going out of her way to bring him up right now.

"Well, that's very thoughtful of you," I say, taking the plate.

"I put them on a paper plate this time since you're not very good at returning people's dishes." She laughs too loud at her passive-aggressive joke.

"Right. Sorry about that."

"I came by a couple times for it, but you're not around much, are you?" She looks at me eagerly, wanting an invitation to come inside. I know that goddamn meat loaf is still in the fridge, probably covered in a layer of white mold. I think she would have a literal meltdown if she saw that I didn't eat it.

"It was delicious. I have been pretty busy lately. Could I bring that by on my way out in about an hour? I'm in a bit of a rush. Busy, busy," I say, sounding exactly like her.

"Oh, I'll take it now if it's not too much trouble," she says, on my heels as I open my door.

"Well, give me just a minute then." But she's already inside, looking around nosily. I walk over to the fridge and pull it out without her seeing, and dump the moldy loaf in the sink. I see her looking at photos on the mantel, so I crush the loaf down the garbage disposal with my fist.

"Where are you off to?" she asks.

"Just…some errands," I lie. What kind of person asks that in the first place? I'm wrestling with the meat loaf. There's no way I can wash the pan without her noticing, so I present the dirty dish.

"Gosh, I never ran the dishwasher. Sorry. Let me just wash this out quick."

"Oh, that's okay." She snatches it from me. "I know how it is living alone. Takes a long time to fill up the dishwasher when you're doing meals for one, doesn't it?" she says with sadness behind her voice.

"I guess so. Sorry about that."

"Any errands you need help with?" she asks, and I'm taken off guard.

"Uh…thank you. No, I'm just. I'm good. Thanks."

"Well, okay then. I guess you're in a hurry, so I'll leave you to it." She starts to go, then stops. "Hey, I know how hard it is to be on your own, so maybe you wanna come by and have dinner with me. I can show you my Etsy store." She looks at me, eagerly, holding her dirty meat loaf pan.

"Oh. Yeah. I mean, I don't know when right off the top of my head, but sure, sounds…good." I hope the look on my face is matching what I'm saying. She looks elated, so I guess so.

"Wonderful! I'll get on Pinterest and plan a menu."

"Great." I start to shut the door.

"And don't worry about returning the plate this time." She gives a shrill laugh. I smile and close the door.

I have no earthly idea what to think of her. She either put antifreeze in these cookies, or she's genuinely just the loneliest person in the world.

The room is too quiet after she leaves; I switch on PBS so the soothing British accents on Masterpiece Theatre can fill the space and keep me company. I want to curl up on the couch and sleep the rest of the day, but I don't let myself. I fear I'll never get up, so I make myself shower instead—I make myself behave like a normal, functioning person.

I stand under the scalding water and think about last night. I don't know what's worse, that I feel like I cheated on Liam or that I took advantage of Will. I hear my phone buzzing across the bathroom counter. I peek out and see Will's name on it. I shut off the water and step into a towel to answer. Not to would be petty.

"Hi there," I say brightly.

"Hi. I just wanted to see if you're okay. You didn't say anything when you left." I realize I never texted him.

"Oh my God. I'm so sorry. I was late for a…thing, and I planned to text you on my way home to let you know. I didn't want to wake you. I know you never get any sleep," I say apologetically.

"I wish you had," he says flirtatiously. "You're feeling okay though?" he asks. I guess he is either trying to gauge how drunk I was and how that translates into how much I remember about last night, or he's fishing in hopes I'll say something in regards to how I feel about him after last night. Or maybe I'm flattering myself and a one-night thing was all he wanted.

"Yes. Fine, just in a bit of a rush. Can I give you a call later?"

"Absolutely. Talk to you then," he says and we hang up. That was okay, I think. He wasn't upset. He's a busy guy. He gets it. It's a relief for now.

I decide I need to buy a burner phone. It sounds shady, but I tell the victims I work with to have a second phone in case of an emergency. At first I want to buy it so I can call Carter's restaurant without any possible way for them to trace it back to me. But then I think it's just a good idea to have it. With every new note left, threatening me, I have to think like the women I counsel.

I pay for it with cash at a downtrodden little cell store up the block. No record of purchase. I call the Egg's Nest diner immediately. I make my voice sound a little higher to mask it. I feel ridiculous and instantly don't know why I'm bothering. No kid picking up the phone knows what I sound like, or at this point, even who I am. I ask when Carter will be in. He doesn't ask any questions. He just tells me that he works nights usually, so probably around five or six.

I spend my day avoiding thoughts of Will and researching how to research so I can find some trace of my father. There must be ways to track down Geoffrey Bennett besides Google.

Just because Sterling hadn't mentioned it to me doesn't mean they didn't find him. I know this much: they provide the families of victims with information and a general idea of where they are on an investigation. How much, and what, they disclose to a family depends on the family members' level of involvement in the case: whether they will have to testify, what information they can offer police regarding the investigation, whether they are a target of the investigation. I am a target, so for all I know, Sterling could be chatting up my father as we speak and wouldn't feel the need to share that tidbit of information with me just yet.

Had he really moved to Florida—"God's waiting room," as my mother called it? A handful of "Geoffrey Bennetts" always came up when I'd searched before. None of them matched. I could see him in Bermuda shorts, living off welfare and food stamps in Key West—a permanent fixture at some beachside bar, having little awareness of social media or any technology past a flip phone. It's not a stretch.

My hours and days of searching over the years were certainly in vain, but now I need to talk to Marty. If he can't find anything, there's no way the detectives have. I'd planned to talk to Will about it, but I know he'd tell me to butt out of the investigation, so I'll do it on my own.

As I scroll through the latest news on my *Tribune* app, I see a story buried in Food and Culture. Liam's name has finally been replaced as head writer. I click to see who his replacement is. Len Turlson. A flash of fury makes my heart jump.

He took Liam's job? I know he's always wanted it because he'd joked about it in a way that you could tell it was not really a joke—a self-deprecating comment juxtaposed next to a boasting comment about Liam's success and "cushy" position. But Liam had worked a lifetime to achieve what Len thinks is "cushy." It certainly wasn't handed to him.

Why would he have never mentioned to me that he was in the running, or that he was seriously considering it? He can come over and ruin my life with an email, but he doesn't say anything about gunning for Liam's position? It's a ludicrous thought, I know. But now and again, I question this email that Len was so quick to show me. Could Len have deleted it? Shit, could he have written it himself?

Right now, everyone is a suspect. Some days I think it's Ellie's husband, Joe. I imagine him living a double life—going off to work in the morning, but really driving across town to his second family like in some Lifetime movie. Then I think Marty Nash, a guy who never met Liam and has lived quietly in the building is really some sociopath, who, despite many opportunities to kill me, is just biding his time. Then I think of a handful of others like Hilly who Liam gave bad reviews to, who may have wanted revenge, but what does that have to do with threatening me now? Everyone I meet is a suspect. There's no reason at all for the insane thoughts, but new ones come every day, my mind trying to sort truth from fiction, motive, opportunity.

Just yesterday I was rude to Bethany, the poor barista at the coffee shop across the street from us that Liam and I frequented, because a random thought grazed my mind—she's always so flirty, maybe he was having an affair with her too and she's watching me with her perfect view of my building. I think I'm going crazy some days. No one commits murder to take a person's job. That's not real life. But still, screw you, Len.

Around 4:00 p.m., I'm getting antsy, so I find a bar near the diner and wait with a couple of gin and tonics. Last time I stalked Carter at the diner, he was out smoking. I need to wait for a smoke break to get him alone, so if he starts at six, it will probably be a while, but I can't concentrate on anything else, so I'll camp outside in my car and watch so I don't miss an opportunity.

I down a third drink and make my way to the diner. It's only six o'clock, and already pitch-black. I park in the same spot as last time to get a view of the restaurant. I am completely aware of how wrong this is. But is it better than justifying disclosing his case to the detectives so they can press him? Probably not. At least I could find a way to defend that. I could have my license revoked, and I don't really care anymore. This is bigger than any of that, and I'm doing it.

I see him inside. Past the front counter with a couple customers picking at eggs and sipping watery coffee, I can see Carter in the back, sitting on a short utility ladder, shoulders drooped, just staring miserably at nothing.

He finally moves when the waitress slaps a paper ticket above the grill. I watch him rotely squirt a well of oil on the grill from a plastic bottle and drop a brick of frozen potatoes into it, stirring it around mindlessly. When he finally brings the greasy order up front, he glances out the front window. I duck instinctively, even though there is no way he'd see anything but his own reflection in the dark window. *Breathe. One, two, three, four.*

He takes a cigarette from behind his ear and pulls a coat on and heads to the back door. God. This is it. I get out of the car, beep the lock and round the building into the side alley. Carter is sitting on an overturned milk crate near the dumpster, puffing smoke into stringy clouds in the cold air.

"Carter," I say gently. He jumps up, startled. When he registers that it's me, he stands still a moment and looks around like an animal sensing danger. Then he flicks his cigarette away and starts for the door.

"Please, wait. Carter, please."

"You shouldn't be here. Wha— How do you know where I work?" He's anxious, frightened even, I think.

"I'm not upset with you. I didn't come here to yell at you or anything like that," I say calmly. He lights another cigarette.

"Then what do you want? I could get in trouble for talking to you."

"You won't get in trouble." I smile. "I would be the only one to get in trouble. I promise." But he just stands there, tucking his free hand under his armpit for warmth and looking at the frozen concrete on the ground. "I only want to know one thing."

"What?" he mumbles, still looking down.

"Why are you saying that I hurt you? Is someone telling you to do this, are you—"

"I have to go in."

"Carter. Look at me." He does. "We used to be friends, I thought. You can tell me if something's going on. Why are you saying these things?"

"'Cause it happened! That's why!" he snaps. My eyes widen and I step back. "You don't even remember that night?" His tone seems uncertain, although his words are confident, as if rehearsed. "I'm trying to move on with my life, okay?" He's softer now, taking a deep inhale of his cigarette.

"What night? Tell me about it, then," I say urgently, hoping to get any clue into what he's really thinking—his version of reality.

"I'm sorry," he says, looking me in the eye, "they won't let me talk about the rest of it. I'm... I'm sorry." He crushes out the rest of his cigarette with the toe of his boot and goes inside.

I want to scream. I practically run back to my car and sit while it heats up. What the hell is "the rest of it"? And who is "they"?

The feeling of self-doubt is like a zap of electricity. It's otherworldly and unexplainable because I know. I unequivocally *know* deep down that nothing sexual happened with Carter, but there's this little whisper that makes me question everything. *That night*, he said, so specifically as if I had been somewhere with him, as if we had shared a memorable night and it had gone too far and I was blocking it out.

Of course, the logical explanation is that with his diagnosis, he's imagined it. But what I think I know does not align with reality lately. I know that I didn't take any Klonopin the night of the accident. I know Liam was in the car with me. But the evidence seems to prove otherwise. Did I ever get blackout drunk back then? Could he have shown up at one of my events and I don't recall being alone with him? Was it possible I did something I don't remember?

TWENTY-FOUR

I CAN'T SLEEP. I KEEP SEEING CARTER'S FRIGHTENED face and wondering why he would be afraid. Of what? I realize I never called Will back. I feel like an asshole. I can't imagine what I'd say. It's not exactly regret I'm feeling. It was actually really nice to be close to him like that again. Surprising, and…exceptional, if I'm honest. But the weight of the guilt is too heavy. Besides, I still have to work with him, and I'm acting like a middle-schooler right now.

Ellie calls at 8:00 a.m., so I finally get up, without sleep, and trudge to the kitchen to put a pot of coffee on—a Kona Liam had shipped from Hawaii, convinced it's the best in the world and worth the sixty bucks a pound plus shipping. I don't tell her about Will, or going to Becky's, and of course I don't say anything about going to see Carter. She tells me about the Santa head Hannah made out of cotton balls and a paper plate, about Ned's snotty cold, and her turkey recipe for Christmas dinner, which I'm required to attend. We make plans for drinks next week, but I already think I'll probably cancel.

When we hang up, I sit in the window seat and watch the

happy people buzz around. Saturday brunch and preholiday shopping. There's no progress. After encounters with Becky and Carter, I feel like I'm back where I started. I need to know when Calvin Lang left for those few days—when he found out about Becky and Liam. It could change everything, and no one else is asking.

If I go back to her house, maybe there is a way I could get her to say more. Appeal to people's greed. It's the most effective way to get the result you want. I didn't see many toys in the trailer for the kid. Also, they both clearly like to drink. I can't say that I blame them. A case of beer and an expensive toy may get me in the door. It seems kind of cheap, but I need to know, and I was in shock I guess last time or I would have thought to ask. What do I have to lose at this point?

With a case of Bud Light and a Paddington Bear in the backseat, I drive back to the trailer park. As soon as I pull up, I see her car and I'm relieved, but I also feel instantly stupid having such shameless bribes. I can't carry a case of beer to the door and be taken seriously. I'll knock first and see if she's willing to talk. If she slams the door in my face or something, I'll embarrass myself with plan B.

When I knock, I hear footsteps. The trailer visibly shifts with the movement. A guy quickly whips the flimsy door open and stares at me. He stands in sweatpants and a stained white tank with a cigarette hanging from his lips.

"Yeah?" he barks. I freeze for a moment, then stutter.

"Oh. Um…shit. Is… Becky here?" I ask, ready to run.

"No." He leans against the doorway, not seeming to mind the frigid air. He looks me up and down.

"Okay. Thanks." I turn to go.

"You're the wife," he says. I stop cold and turn back around.

"Yeah."

"I know who you is. Cops were here asking about you," he

says, surprisingly calmly. "You wanna come in? Maybe I can help you." He's not exactly the raging lunatic I was expecting, but of course I shouldn't go in. He may be thrilled right now to be luring his prey in so effortlessly. But again, what do I have to lose. This may be my shot.

"I brought beer," I say, for lack of anything else coming to mind.

"For real?" He smiles. I nod and he watches me go over to the car and retrieve the case.

Inside, we sit across from one another in the same dingy living area and drink cans of Bud Light at 11:00 a.m.

"I heard what happened to your…" He gestures as if to indicate husband, I guess. "That sucks. I'm sorry." This is far more civility from him than I ever imagined, which is actually putting me on edge, because it doesn't make sense. Becky made it sound like he'd lose his mind if anyone mentioned Liam around him.

"Thanks," I say. "I…um, I thought you might be a little upset to see me." I probe a bit, wondering if it will unnerve him.

"Eh. I'm over it. I was pissed as fuck, but since nothin' happened, I guess I gotta get over it." He stops and then laughs suddenly. "Or kick the bitch out, but we's got a kid now, so."

"I'm sorry, what do you mean?" I ask, totally confused.

"Well, I mean she could go live with her stupid cow friend, Lacy, who started the whole damn thing up, if I didn't get her pregnant. Kinda stuck now."

"I mean—no, what? You said 'since nothing happened.' What does that mean?"

"You know, they never bumped uglies or nothin'." He cracks another beer and hands me one. I take it. I don't plan to hide my visit with Becky, since he's acting like he doesn't care.

"I talked to Becky. She…apologized for it. I asked why she

pursued him, and she never said 'nothing happened.' What are you talking about? That's what she told you, so you believe it?" I'm raising my voice and talking too fast. I need to stay in control.

"Whoa. You gotta slow your roll for a second. She was trying to get back at me, but it kinda backfired, that's all it was."

"I need to know what happened. I don't know what you're saying!" I yell, then stop. "Sorry. This—this is very important. I don't know if you know, but they're still trying to figure out what happened to him, and—" He interrupts me.

"I lost my ma last year. All of a sudden," he says, but I don't respond. I'm desperate for him to keep talking. "There's a lot unsaid, and so I get it. I mean, I feel like I can relate a little. I'm not a total dick. I don't mind giving you what you want to know. I just don't have all that much info. All's I know is she was all over him, and he told her to fuck off."

"What?"

"Stupid cow, Lacy, was telling her to get back at me just cause her husband cheated and she had a revenge fuck. I walked in on her tellin' Becky to go after this guy who was at her bar all the time—that he must like her if he's there alone so much."

"He's a critic. He was working," I say.

"Well, Lacy the cow says to fuck this guy out of revenge, but the difference is, I didn't cheat on Becky. I beat off to some chick over Skype. That's not the same thing. Right?" he asks.

"What makes you think nothing happened?" I ask urgently.

"'Cause she said. And there was a text from him." I have never seen his texts, of course, because his phone was gone, and the police had some forensic expert decoding it. I know from my research that that can also take a long time. Also, they may not tell me what they find. "It basically told her to fuck off, the text."

"What did it say, exactly?" I practically beg. He stops chugging his beer and looks at me sympathetically.

"You didn't know any of this." He says this not as a question, but as a statement, realizing. "Something like he doesn't want to have to report her and have her lose her job, but he's not interested and basically to leave him alone," he says, and I lose my breath. I put my beer down and stand up. *One, two, three, four.*

"I mean, she didn't want nothin' to do with me since the kid. Says she's all stretched out. What's a guy gonna do? I don't think internet beat offs is the same, though. Come on, right?"

"Right," I agree softly. *Keep him talking.*

"She just wanted the attention 'cause she was all depressed. But you can't go try to screw a real person, though. I mean, Jesus. She told me the rejection made her crazy, and she got obsessed and wouldn't leave him alone. I said I wanted a divorce, but anyhow. She eventually stopped being a fucking nutcase." He rubs his beard. I look at the floor, noticing a dirty toenail sticking out of a hole in his sock. I feel like I might throw up. I doubted Liam. I betrayed him by not trusting him.

"Did she go to his office?" I ask, trying to make sense of it all.

"I'm sure she fucking did. She done lost her mind with baby depression and revenge." His phone makes a sound. He pulls it out from his hip where he's been half sitting on it and taps on the shattered screen, then rolls his eyes and puts it back down.

"So you and Becky fought. About Liam."

"Fuck yeah, we did. I flipped the fuck out on her. Wouldn't you? Tellin' me I ain't as good as him, all that shit. But it's all the postmortem depression, that's what the doctors say. Well, not a doctor, but her cousin Angie who wants to be a nurse. It's real shit though. I looked it up. After chicks have babies and stuff." He lights another cigarette, and the smell is not helping my sudden nausea. I read somewhere that smoke curbs nausea, but I guess that's not true. It's so strange to think of these two strangers having knock-down, drag-out fights over my husband. Just a guy who was the subject of a bartender's crush at the wrong time.

"So you never actually met Liam? You never went down there to see him, talk to him?" I try to confirm that he never threatened him, to gauge his reaction to the question.

"I started hanging out at her bar every night, that's for damn sure, but I never saw him. He only came in now and again for an event or somethin'. But what the hell was I gonna do with him anyway? He told her to fuck off every chance he got. It's Becky and Cow I got the problem with."

"I'm sorry, when was this exactly? When did you find all this out?" I ask.

"February, I remember 'cause it was Valentine's day when I started checking her phone." It was just before the accident.

The small trailer is cloudy with smoke that stings my eyes, and I really can't think what else to say. I'm simultaneously comforted and heartsick by what he's said. Then I remember something that I can't get past.

"But Liam gave her money. Like six thousand dollars. That doesn't make sense," I say, starting to doubt his whole story.

"Oh, yeah. You ain't gettin' that back. Sorry. Been spent."

"I don't want it back. I just want to know why he'd do it."

"Oh. 'Cause she said I beat her and she was trying to get away from me. He tried to help her out. She said she needed money to move and shit. I think he was too nice, and she got even more crazy over him."

"Oh my God." It's such an enormous relief. "Really?"

"For the record, she's a lying bitch. I throw things some-times, but I don't beat my wife. She loves being the victim. I'm sure she told a great fucking story." He throws an empty

beer can across the room, and it hits the wood-paneled wall
and falls into a small pile of laundry. I'm sure the shock and
confusion on my face is visible.

"Thanks for talking to me," I say, standing to go.

"Well, I believe in the first amendment, so…" he says. I
have no idea what he means, but I just nod and set my beer
on a dusty end table.

"I appreciate it."

"You don't gotta go. We got all these beers to drink." He
follows me the four feet to the front door. Part of me considers
staying in case there's more to get out of him, but what else
could there be? That's the story. All the pieces have come together and, unless he's crafting a complex alibi, which I doubt
he's smart enough to do, it's clear, and it sounds exactly like
Liam to kindly dismiss her until he had to get firm. It made
sense he wouldn't tell me, brushing it off as trivial especially
compared to what I was going through with Carter.

I wonder why Len would tell me all of this and waste my
time leading me down a road that goes nowhere. I wonder
again about his behavior and if there's more to him than I
know.

"It's all yours," I say. He seems beside himself with joy.

"Whoa. Really? You—all of it?" His thin frame looks almost skeletal standing in the doorway as I walk to my car.
"Thanks!"

"Least I could do."

When I get on the main road back to the city, my mind is
reeling. Those messages I saw from her make sense in context.

You looked really good last night.

Your smell is still lingering, what is that cologne?

*The cucumber martini I bought you is my new favorite drink. You
should stop by so I can make you one.*

I miss you. I wish you'd come see me.

It wasn't a romance. It was her frantic attempt to seduce him. She "bought" him a drink, meaning she gave him one on the house to try to get his attention. It was good to see him because he was there sporadically when an assignment sent him there, and she was flirting or harassing relentlessly. From the other side of the bar. How could I have ever doubted him?

TWENTY-FIVE

IT'S SUNDAY MORNING, AND I'M WEEPING OVER THE
pancakes Ellie has lovingly made in my kitchen. It's only after
she's been at my place a half hour that I notice her fat lip. Am
I really that self-absorbed?

"What happened to your face?" I ask, and she looks annoyed at the question.

"Nothing."

"Your lip is blue and cut up. What the hell?"

"The kids were hurling toys. I got caught in the cross fire,"
she says, but seems really uneasy. I keep looking at it, and she
snaps.

"What?"

"Nothing. Okay," I say. She never snaps, so I leave it alone.
Besides, I am eager to confide in someone about what happened. I won't tell her everything, but I need her to tell me I'm
not a terrible person for what I did with Will and for doubting Liam's integrity. She does all of that, of course. She eats
the pancakes I push away as I go splash some booze into my
coffee and grab a wad of tissue to blow my nose.

"I can't believe you didn't tell me about this Becky chick. You're not alone, you know. You can talk to me." She talks with her mouth full. I sit back down at the kitchen island and bury my head in my arms on the countertop.

"I suck," I whine.

"If I saw the messages from her like you did, I woulda beat the shit out of Joe. I would file for divorce the next day. You did what any normal person would do," she reasons.

"But I knew in my gut he'd never do that. It wasn't his character."

"Well, you are under just a tiny bit of stress. I think you did what anyone would do. You should be happy that you know now. Why are you so upset about this?" she asks, still chewing.

"'Cause I did something horrible," I say.

"What?" She puts her fork down, ready for the gossip.

"Unspeakable."

"Oh my God. What, what?" she says eagerly.

"I…went home with Will Holloway the other night," I say shamefully. Ellie makes a high-pitched squeal and jumps up. She squeals again.

"Ahhhhh! You did not!" She slaps me playfully.

"I know." I frown.

"Man, he looked good when I saw him…" She stops before she says "at the funeral," realizing the weight of it. She changes gears. "Faith. It's been a long time now, since… Will's someone you've always been really close to. What's wrong?"

"Oh, God!" I bury my head again, overdramatically but I can get away with it, with Ellie. I want her to tell me more about how I'm not a monster.

"You think you were disloyal to Liam," she says. I whimper. "You did nothing wrong. You tracked down the truth with this Becky bitch because you believed in Liam—'cause you knew there was more to it. And Will…well, I say go for it."

She goes back to dousing pancakes in more syrup and shoveling them into her mouth.

"Ellie!"

"What!? Did you move in with him, did you promise to marry him? You just got laid. You probably, like, really need that right now." I just stare at her a moment. "What?" she repeats. Before I can say anything, there's a knock at the door.

"Oh, crap." I sort of duck like the person can see me. Ellie looks at me sideways.

"What?" Ellie asks, amused.

"There's a scary woman who keeps bringing me food. And once she brought her cat over, so we can't answer that."

"She did not," Ellie says flatly. I nod. "You got a lot going on over here." Ellie gets up and goes over to the door.

"No," I command, but she's giggling and tiptoeing over anyway.

"I gotta see what she looks like."

"Shhhh." I stay where I am. Ellie looks through the peephole. "It's a guy with a dog."

"Oh." I go over to open the door.

"God, you really do have a lot going on over here. Who's this guy? He's got a nerdy-sexy thing going on."

"For God's sake, are you sure you're not the one who needs to get laid?" I open the door and see Marty standing there.

"Hi. Sorry. I didn't mean to interrupt," he says politely.

"No, it's okay. This is my sister, Ellie. Ellie, Marty from the fourth floor," I say, patting Figgy on the head.

"Hi, Marty from the fourth floor," she says, and Marty just nods, not really embracing the humor. Ellie goes back over to her food.

"I was—I just wanted to check on you. See if you were feeling better, you know, from the other night. I should have done that sooner, but...yeah. You seem okay."

"I am. Feeling much better. Thanks," I say, eyeing Ellie because I don't want to have to explain that I had a panic attack—another thing I didn't tell her about.

"Great."

"You taking Figgy walking?" I ask.

"Just got back, actually."

"Would you like to come in for some coffee? Ellie made some breakfast if you like pancakes," I offer.

"Oh, thanks, but I'm actually headed to group today. I was just dropping him off." He smiles weakly. I remember him saying that he only goes on Sunday if he's having a particularly hard week.

"Oh, okay then," I say, and he lingers a moment.

"I should have offered before, but if you ever feel like you need it you're always welcome to come. I mean, you don't have to come with me if you don't want, but, I mean, it's there if you need it. Is all." Figgy gets restless on the leash and makes a couple circles, then sits.

"Oh, that's so nice. I have…" I look to Ellie, indicating that I can't right now, not that he was explicitly asking me to this minute. Ellie goes and grabs her coat off the ottoman.

"Faith was actually just telling me how she wants to get out of the house today 'cause she's going stir-crazy." She puts on her coat. "And I can only leave the kids with Joe for a two hour max before he melts down, so…" She looks at me with a ridiculously forced smile. "You should go." She's delighted with herself, and I give her a tight smile.

"Sounds good. Maybe I'll tag along," I say to him. "If that's okay."

"Oh. Sure. I'll just drop him off then."

"Great. I can meet you in the lobby in a few?"

"Yeah." He tugs on Figgy's leash and goes. I close the door and look sideways at Ellie.

"What's the group?" she says, smiling, still chewing.

"Maybe you should find out before you do that. It's a support group. He lost his wife."

"Oh. Man. Sorry." She packs up her stuff to go.

"Yeah."

"Well, that sounds good for you. And now you have two yummy men to hang out with to get you out of the house and out into the world. My work here is done." She kisses me on the cheek. "Have fun. You're welcome."

"Really?" I say, watching her whirlwind exit.

"I really do need to get home anyway. I'm still breastfeeding. Joe thinks he can do anything, but I'd like to see him try that one."

"Well, let me walk you down."

In the lobby, I hug her goodbye, rifle through my mail and wait for Marty. I suddenly feel like a nervous teenager waiting for a date. Probably because Ellie made it awkward. I wonder, for a moment, if he'll stand me up. Maybe he didn't actually want me to go, but felt obligated. But then, a few moments later, he comes bounding down the stairs and seems genuinely happy to see me, so I decide I will give the group a fair shot.

The meeting is in the basement of a community center within walking distance from our building. There's a circle of metal folding chairs in the center of a room that is probably used for kids craft activities, considering the glitter and elbow macaroni art on the otherwise dull walls. There is a coffeepot with some paper cups on a card table in the corner, and although I have never been to one, I feel like this is exactly what an AA meeting is like.

Everyone looks dejected. About a dozen people sit in the chair circle with their little cups; a cone of gray light streams through the only window, and it looks institutional. I don't want to be here anymore.

A portly woman with a big skirt sits, and uses her arm to help herself cross one big knee over the other and settle into her folding chair. She starts the meeting by introducing herself as Jodie and welcoming newcomers. Which is just me, I guess.

"Marty, do you want to introduce us to your guest?" she says, and I feel like she's talking to a kindergarten class.

"I'm Faith," I say, dismissing him of the duty Jodie has given him. I expect everyone to say "Hi, Faith," in unison, but they don't.

"Welcome. You can feel free to share at any time, or you can just listen, dear. That's totally up to you." She pauses a moment to see if I start sharing, but I just suck my teeth and give a little nod, suddenly feeling shy and out of place.

Another guy, Larry, starts off the meeting. His voice is booming, and he gets animated when he talks about how tough the holidays are. He ends most of his sentences with, "am I right?" and everyone murmurs in agreement. He says he's been drinking too much. Join the club, Larry. He gets tearful and stops talking after recounting the good Christmases he had with his late wife.

I feel my phone buzzing in my coat pocket. I sneak a look and see that it's Will. Shit. I never called him. Again. I want to walk right out of here and answer it. Maybe that could be my excuse, but no. Marty listens intently to everyone's sob story and this is his refuge. He's helped me out a lot, and I'd be a jerk to duck out. I can handle an hour.

I'm sure that talking it out does help some people. Maybe I'm just not ready because I still don't know what happened. I should be using this time to try to work through things, but it seems like hashing out details and reliving the pain every week would do more harm than good. A younger woman wearing a sweatshirt with the hood up over her head silently cries the whole time, making soft hiccup noises now and again.

Another woman with a nest of golden bangs straight out of the '80s tells the group that she thinks her daughter is appearing to her as a winter bird that keeps showing up on her fence every morning. She passes around a photo of the bird to get help identifying its breed.

The kicker for me was the old man, Earl, who lost his wife of fifty-four years in a house fire. He blames himself because she had dementia and he left her home alone for a half hour while he ran to the store. No wonder Marty is still this badly off. I would be worse too if I surrounded myself with this every week. I will never come back.

Will doesn't leave a voice mail. I think about him while people are talking, trying to drown out their stories with my thoughts. I need to face it eventually. I'm not sure how I feel anymore after talking to Ellie. She definitely made me feel less guilty. I decide to call him when I get out of here, and set up a meeting. All business.

Marty didn't share at the meeting, and he barely says a word after while people hover over the card table eating Hydrox sandwich cookies and sprinkling powdered creamer into their pale coffee. I stand in front of the window, looking across at some kids playing, their frozen hands on the long, chain-link swings in the courtyard. After Marty says his goodbyes, it's just us left. Tiny dust particles swirl in the window light making the air look fuzzy.

"I hope it wasn't torture for you," he says.

"Of course not," I reply quickly. "It was really nice of you to invite me." I smile. He looks at the sad plate with two half-eaten Hydrox cookies and a few leftover cups of gas station coffee and laughs.

"I want to spring for some Oreos and Starbucks, but I don't want to be insulting," he says, and I laugh out loud. *Marty made a joke*, I think. I sit in the oversize window arch.

"Can I ask you something?" I say, feeling like it's now or never.

"Sure." He pulls up a folding chair and sits in front of me. I don't know what makes me feel so free to really talk to him now. Maybe his vulnerability and bringing me here to connect in shared pain. Maybe it's everything that culminates in the overarching feeling that I really don't have anything to lose anymore.

"I was hoping you might help me look someone up again. I'll pay you actual money this time. It's... I need to find a guy named Geoffrey Bennett. I need to know where he is. If he's still living," I say, flicking crumbs of stale cookie on the table.

"I'm happy to see what I can do. Any birth date, last known city, all that will help."

"Yes. I can get that for you."

"Okay. Yeah."

"He's...um...my father. It's possible that he could be very angry with me because of things I've written about him." I look at Marty and take a deep breath.

"You're...worried for your safety?" he asks, concerned.

"Maybe. He's the reason I specialized in helping abuse victims, actually...if that tells you anything about his propensity for violence. You were there when I got that note—that threat on my door. I just need to rule him out. He's always been a...dangerous guy." I give a little involuntary laugh. "Understatement of the century. Anyway, knowing he's not living in Chicago at least will help. Maybe."

"I mean, yeah. Jesus. That's terrible. I can't say it will be quick or easy depending on what I have to go on, but of course I can give it a try. I'm better with an IP address than as an investigator, but there are a few things I can try."

"I'm paying you for your work," I quickly interject.

"Okay," he laughs, putting his hands up in an "I surrender"

motion. I pull on my coat and we leave the musty community center and walk the six cold blocks back to the condo building.

The sky is filled with dark, milky clouds. It wants to sleet or drop flurries. The sun has barely poked through in weeks. We don't say much on the walk. I don't know if I should ask more about his wife, because I'm someone who gets it, if I should initiate an attempt at comfort, but ultimately I decide to let him bring it up if he wants to.

When I think about him finding my father, I have to take a few deliberate breaths to suppress the waves of anxiety it brings. I think of the days I spent in that closet, my head to the floor so I could see the ribbon of light coming in underneath the door. Hours of crying until I went hoarse and just stared into the blackness, numb and tired. When my mother finally opened the door to let me out, I didn't even move. I was so dehydrated she had to carry me to the car and take me to the hospital.

I sigh to shake off the thoughts. Marty said something I didn't hear.

"Sorry. What?" I ask.

"I was just asking if you ever got that security system. Do you feel safe at your place?"

"Yeah. I mean... I'll be fine." We walk into the condo lobby and call for the elevator. I check the mail quickly while we wait.

"Well, you know where I am if you need anything. Just send me those details when you can so I can work up a search for you," he says, and gets out on the fourth floor.

"Thank you." I continue up to my floor. I leaf through my mail. No notes. I pause, looking toward my door. No note. I release the breath I didn't realize I was holding and open the door. At my feet is an envelope. My hands shake so violently,

I can barely open it, but I manage to pull out its contents. It's worse than I thought. I have to look away.

There is a photo of a naked woman, blindfolded, bound and gagged. It's an old Polaroid photo that looks like it was taken in a hotel. It's not printed from a nasty website. It's a real image. I turn it over. On the back it says, "Someone's Listening." I gasp, trying to find my breath, then run to the kitchen and throw up in the sink.

After a few minutes, I become enraged that no one can do anything about this. With everything at their disposal, all the cops can tell me to do is leave my home. I do the only thing I can right now. I go down to my car. I get my .38 Special. I'm ready.

TWENTY-SIX

"YOU CAN STAY WITH ME," WILL SAYS AS MY HANDS shake around my gin and tonic. "I mean, there's a guest room, I'm not…"

"I know." I stop him. It's Monday, and he's left work early to meet me at an Irish pub we went to a hundred times during college. We sit at the bar and I see that Carl, the owner, is still bartending. A lifetime later, he still perches behind the bar on a metal stool and tells the same stories about Vietnam. He's trying to make some extra money this year, it appears, by pushing stupid holiday drinks on people with preposterous names like "Nose Warmer" and "Melted Snowman," with lots of syrupy liqueur and whipped substances. I hate drinks with cinnamon and nutmeg and swirls of sickly sweet pinks and reds. I guess it's a way to try to be the alcoholic Starbucks, but the giant mudslide-looking drink in Will's hand is making me want to gag.

"And, Jesus. I wish you would have called yesterday when it happened." He puts his hand on mine and softens his tone. "You're not alone in all this, you know that, right?"

"Well, thank you, but I refuse to be chased out of my home—it's the last comfort I have. I mean, that's exactly what they're trying to do," I say. I *am* alone in all of this. He doesn't understand my loss. It's not only the loss of Liam—Will can't know how it feels to lose your credibility and reputation after working a lifetime to build it. It's not at home where I should have to look over my shoulder. "I appreciate it, but…it's all I have. Ya know?" He gives a conceding nod.

I tell him about Cal and Becky Lang. I don't think they're involved at this point, but any lead is worth following. Then I open my mouth to tell him about Len and my suspicions about the email and taking over Liam's job, but I decide against it. I remember a trip we took with Len and Bonnie one summer. Liam and Len were both assigned to write about a resort in Punta Cana. I thought it was so odd that Bonnie stayed up in their room most of the time. I never left the pool's swim-up bar the whole week. I stayed dripping in Hawaiian Tropic oils, smelling of sun and piña colada every day, and Len seemed to hover. He stayed drunk and always seemed to be peering at me over the novel he had resting on his pale, hairy belly on the poolside deck chairs.

I remember sipping a cranberry vodka in my white bikini at the swim-up bar, watching some poor resort staff member try to recruit guests for Marco Polo or some silly thing they were required to act enthusiastic about, when Len belly flopped onto an inflated flamingo and floated over to me, slurring his words and making crass jokes.

I told Liam after dinner that night that I thought Len was weird and if Liam had to work the next day, I'd like to go with him and avoid being ogled at the pool all day. When he explained that Bonnie had recently been diagnosed with ovarian cancer and that's why she was resting in the room, and that Len probably stayed shitcanned because he wasn't handling the thought of losing the love of his life, I'd felt like an utter piece of shit. She wanted so badly to go on the trip, Liam explained, but then had a bad few days, although she was thrilled to relax on their balcony and rest. She'd insisted Len mingle and get the story he'd come for. He added that he and I weren't supposed to know because she was very private about it.

I'd felt terrible for judging him so quickly and wondered how often I probably did that to other people without being corrected. I regretted jumping to conclusions about him then, and he's proven to be a man of character over the last few years, so I feel following other leads first is the best approach.

Will looks like he wants to address the elephant in the room, so I do instead. It's the least I can do, as I'd been ignoring him since. I think he's probably fed up with me and thinks I'm playing games.

"Hey, about the other night," I start to say.

"It's okay." He leaps in, grateful for the opportunity to have some control over the topic, it appears. "You don't have to. I get it, I mean. It was a one-night thing." Hearing him say this makes me feel annoyed. Or rejected. I'm the one who gets to say that. I swallow hard and look behind the bar at Carl, who has barely taken his eyes off the television since we got here. He laughs intermittently and washes and rewashes clean glassware, clearly aching to be somewhere else.

I remember his story. It was the same one over and over each night, and I wonder if he still told it. He almost saw Bob Hope once, and the *Hope Marathon* makes him strangely nostalgic for his days at Camp Bearcat. Even though when Hope came to Camp Bearcat with Raquel Welch that Christmas in 1967, he was stuck sitting in some goddamn hole, shitting his brains out from dysentery, missing the whole thing while everyone else at Long Binh got to see Bob and Raquel trade

sexual innuendos. After traveling twenty-three miles to give
Bob a shell with his name inscribed on it, Carl didn't even get
a glimpse of him or Miss World, who was right in his very
own camp flirting with Bob and some lucky bastard GIs who
got the front row.

I wonder if the memories of his once-vital life are what
makes him lurch into motion to find a distraction from his
thoughts, because he begins dumping all the untouched festive drinks down the bar sink. Ginger and nutmeg swirl up
from the sink like aroma threads in a cartoon pie, cooling in a
witch's window. The smell makes my heart tap in my throat.

"I should go," I say, gulping a few last swallows of my drink.
If I meet his eyes, he'll see a lonely longing for him in mine,
and it's confusing and a little troubling. Ellie tried to make
me feel okay about needing human contact, but the guilt is
acute and consuming. And now I may have gotten it wrong,
and it was just a one-off to him.

"I'd like to talk about some things Sterling brought up
this morning if you have time," he says professionally, and I
feel foolish for the confusing feelings I'm having as I watch
his hands, the hands that touched every part of my body the
other day, sweep away beads of water from his sweating glass.

"Of course," I say, pushing my empty glass toward Carl
for another.

"I know it's not something you probably want to get into,
but he spoke with your mother."

"Yeah," I say, knowing she didn't offer any information.

"Oh, you talked to her?" he asks, surprised.

"Briefly. She mentioned they came to see her."

"Well, she said that she has reason to believe your father is
living locally. Naperville, she said…" I look at him, stunned.
She told me she didn't say anything and not only did she talk

to them, she's making things up. I don't know why I'd be surprised she lied.

"Naperville?" I repeat.

"Sterling has actually been trying to track him down for a while with no luck quite yet." I didn't know this. Sterling asked me during one of the many times I went in for questioning where my father was, and I said last I heard was Florida, but that was years and years ago. He just took down the information. He never said anything about looking for him.

"They think he could be involved?" I ask.

"He's not a suspect at this point, but it would be good to get a location on him and talk to him. Your mother though… they brought her down to the station for questioning."

"What? They arrested her? Wait—wait—for what? I—"

"They didn't have to. Apparently, you can see the place is covered in meth paraphernalia from the doorway. They threatened arrest to get her to work with them, but thought it would be better if she came down semi-willingly."

"But what for?" I ask, totally confused.

"She tried to open a credit card in Liam's name," he says carefully.

"That doesn't actually surprise me," I say, hoping he had more of a lead that that. She'd steal from anyone she could, dead or alive.

"She was in possession of his driver's license. It's in evidence now."

"What! How?" I say so loudly, Carl looks over from his show and glares at me.

"She says he gave it to her." Will says this with a sort of scoff and shake of his head. "She was caught by the credit card company before using the card she was trying to open, but racked up a few small charges like fraud and identity theft. It really only amounts to some fines at this stage. But she's now a suspect. We don't have enough for an arrest, but we're looking into her."

"Jesus."

"I'm so sorry to have to tell you something like this. I mean it's your mom. I just… I'm sorry."

"How the hell did she get his driver's license? He didn't give it to her. He didn't even know her."

"Well, we know that. My question is, when did she get it? Did he have it the night of the accident?" he asks. I look at the ceiling, trying to think back and recall any moment he might have used it, or any time I may have last noticed it in his wallet. But it was a busy time, and how often does a person take out his license? He wasn't buying booze or getting pulled over recently, so I have no idea if he had it that night or that week even.

"I don't know. He's not the type to go around without it. He must have."

"I just wanted you to know that we are looking at her closely, and it's a good idea if you avoid making contact with her. Just my personal recommendation," he says calmly.

"You think she could be dangerous…is what you're saying? She's too high to think straight ninety percent of the time."

"And she'd do pretty much anything for money to stay that way," he adds. "All I'm saying is, his wallet and phone were not found with him, and his license showed up at her place. Maybe she knows more than she's saying," but I know better. She's a junky, a petty criminal, and an all-round despicable person, but she's not capable of murder. She's not involved with whatever happened to Liam.

"So, the motive would be money?" I ask.

"Partly. She went on and on about finding your father because he was upset with the things you said in your book about your childhood—how it made him look like a monster.

I think she may be projecting a bit," he says, and it's not that I hadn't thought about her being angry about the things I revealed, but she's so checked out of life. She didn't even read the book. Someone gave her the highlights; she's too far gone to care. She'd probably forget the next day.

"I have trouble believing that she'd be capable of doing anything like that," I say, confused about the driver's license, but not really concerned about her. I'm sure she found a way to order a renewal copy through some scumbag she knows. I don't know, but she's been creative with her fraud in the past. I don't want them wasting time going down this track with her. There's no way.

"Well, from what I remember of her and your father, the things you wrote were kind considering the things they've done. I don't think you should put anything past her."

"It's a waste of time. But I guess they're gonna do what they're gonna do." I put my phone in my purse, an indication I'm ready to go. Will puts his hand up to Carl to bring the check.

"The offer is standing if you need somewhere to go. Sylvia designed the guest room with a remote control fireplace and minibar." He smiles.

"You're too bourgeois for me these days," I joke, and stand to put my coat on. "Well, I guess I'll be in touch," I say, starting to go.

"I'll walk you to your car."

"It's okay. I'm close, and I'm gonna use the restroom first," I say.

"I'll wait." He buttons his wool overcoat and makes an "after you" gesture. In the dark, narrow hall there is a single, unisex bathroom. I go inside and look at myself in the mirror in the dark light. I'm too thin, and my eyes are puffy from crying yesterday. I pat on some lip gloss to brighten up my face. My neck is knotted with stress, and I feel like I want to scream. I can't calm my mind. I can't trust anyone. I can't live like this. I dab some cool water on my cheeks to calm myself down and open the door. Will is standing there.

I meet his gaze. We look at each other, our eyes lingering too long. He walks over to me slowly and kisses me, catching me by surprise. When I grip his collar to pull him in harder, he pushes me, lightly, seductively, into the side of the bathroom stall and I lock the door behind us. We pull at each other's clothes. I unzip his pants as he kisses me hard, running his hands down the sides of my body. He lifts my skirt and we bang into the walls, navigating the narrow space.

He lifts me up, wraps my legs around his waist, and pushes into me. I feel all the anxiety and pressure release as we knock against the bathroom stall, rhythmically, pawing insatiably at each other's bodies. When it's done, he keeps me close against him until our breathing slows. Then we straighten our clothes, as I wipe the lipstick marks from his skin and he walks me to my car.

On my drive home, I try not to think of Liam. It feels as though he's watching me, looking down from some high place in the afterlife, and disapproving of the mess I'm making of everything.

TWENTY-SEVEN

I THINK ABOUT BRINGING THE GUN WHEN I GO TO confront my mother the next day, but it seems so wrong. Instead, I decide that even though I might need it, I can't have it in the house because it's too creepy, too unnerving—so I hide it on my fire escape. I pick up the plastic that once housed a plant inside a large terra-cotta pot; it's now light with dead roots and dry dirt from the cold, so I lay the gun in the base of the pot, and place the dead plant back on top. It's better than having it in the house, and it's close enough if I need it.

Sterling has asked me to come down and answer a few questions about my mother to help out the investigation. I plan to find out all the information I can, despite Will's advice.

I draw a scorching hot bath and slip into the water. It's early in the day, and I don't want to take a Klonopin to get through these obligations with Sterling or my mother, so I have a double vodka perched at the edge of the tub, and the lights low so it feels like night, because I don't much care for the long, arduous days anymore. I mostly just wait for them to be over so I can sleep.

I try to relax for a few minutes, but what Will said about my mother loops in my mind, and I try to find ways to explain it to myself.

I like to think of her in those days after my father left when she had moments of kindness, and was almost like a mother. It was the space between staggering grief and the drugs taking hold—that small window when she loved us—that I cling onto, wondering if that was the real her.

But the shift in her was never predictable. Her eyes could go dark without notice. A long-coveted night of girl talk and hair-braiding on the balcony could be halted as soon as she got that look in her eye—as if the vodka, or whatever high she was on, hit her all at once and she needed someone to punish for a whole lifetime of unrequited love. This is when the threats would start. She'd smack my hands away from her hair and loosen her braid—she'd tell me I belong in a psych ward because I'm my father's daughter, and to get my ass to bed before she makes the call and has me taken away. The real her will always be unknowable now.

I hear my phone ringing out in the living room. I know I won't get to it in time, but I still rush out of the bath. I pull a robe around me and am making my way to the living room when I hear something. A rustling noise, like crinkling paper. I stand very still and strain to listen to where it's coming from, and then I see a sheet of paper being pushed under my front door.

I lunge toward the door and whip it open to find out who's put it there, and I see Hilly standing in the hall, wearing a sweatshirt full of cat hair and a startled look.

"What the hell are you doing?" I demand, picking up the note quickly before she can take it back, denying she put something there.

"I tried knocking," she says. I examine the paper she's left with a scowl on my face, and she looks like she's going to cry or run away. After a moment I realize that it's a handwritten invitation to dinner at her place, scrolled on stationery watermarked with a dancing snowman.

"I'm sorry," I say. "I'm so sorry. I'm a little on edge. You just startled me is all."

"I did knock first," she says defensively.

"I was in the…" I don't explain. "This is really nice of you. I didn't mean to snap."

"It's okay," she says, lightening up. "I know you're under a lot of stress. That's why I didn't put a date on there. Open invitation!" she blurts, and gives an insecure gesture with her hands as if she's describing a flower blooming.

"Thank you. Yes, I'd be happy to accept your invitation. Let me look at my schedule and we'll nail it down," I say, and she looks overjoyed.

"I'll let you get dressed then," she says, eyeing my robe and dripping hair. "Can't wait." Then she's off down the hall. My pulse is still darting after she leaves. I rush to pull on some jeans and a sweater so I can get out of the house. I pull up my hair and don't bother to dry it, even though it will freeze into a knot on the top of my head. I don't fuss with makeup, I just pull on a woolen hat and drive back to my childhood apartment, urgently, longing for answers.

When I approach her door, I don't knock. I just wiggle the handle first, and not surprisingly, it's open. I walk right in, but I can't see anything because she has dirty sheets and cardboard from cases of beer masking her windows, and it's black inside.

"Mom!" I call, but no response. I knock over an ashtray overflowing with cigarette butts when I reach for the nearest lamp, which is sitting on a side table. I cover my nose as the sooty ash rises up off the floor where it crashed. I see her, limp, facedown on the couch. I cover my mouth and take a step back. Panic is tapping along my arms and down my spine. I inhale a deep sip of air and then take a few steps forward and shake her. She doesn't feel cold. Then I leap back, hand to heart, as she hacks, sits up, and looks at me.

"Oh. It's you. Did you bring my money?" She reaches for her cigarettes.

"Jesus Christ!" I yell, for lack of anything better to say.

"What?" She furrows her brow and lights a cigarette.

"Do you have anything to say to me?" I ask childishly.

"Yeah. Where's my money you promised?"

"First of all, you told the cops a bunch of bullshit, so you don't get your money. I was gonna pay you to tell the truth, which is that you don't fucking know anything. I shouldn't have to pay you to not make my life worse than it is, but you've already done that. Dad lives in Naperville now. Really?" I say, pushing an empty Big Gulp cup off a chair to sit across from her.

"Want a drink?" she asks.

"Does he live in Naperville? After asking you for twenty-five years where he is, does he live right there?" I demand.

"I don't know. Keep your goddamn voice down." She holds her head, to nurse a hangover I suspect, and picks up last night's beer off the coffee table and downs it.

"You don't know, but you told them this anyway?"

"I gave 'em somewhere to start. They wanted me to say something so I did. It's a good a place as any for them to look. That's where he kept his whore back when he was cheating on me, so maybe he's still there." She wheezes and goes to the kitchen to heat up some coffee.

"What about Florida?" I ask.

"Could be in Florida. Who knows?" I realize quickly that this is the same loop that we'll never be free of, and there is no point continuing the conversation, so I switch gears.

"Where did you get Liam's license?" I stare at her, but she won't look back.

"Oh, come on, Faith. I was trying to make a few bucks. It wasn't gonna harm him any." She sits back down with her coffee and taps the end of her cigarette where the ashtray used to be, but the tiny white pile of dust lands on top of a decade-old *People* magazine instead.

"Do you think I'm fucking around?" I say, standing up.

"What the fuck does that mean?" She coughs. I grab her cigarette from her hand and put it out in her coffee.

"That means look at me and tell me the truth. I'm not gonna do this with you. Where did you get the license? And before you answer that, I want you to know that your careless, idiotic lies have them looking at you for more than credit card fraud or whatever your charges are."

"I didn't do nothin'," she says, looking genuinely scared for the first time.

"His wallet was never found, and now it shows up in your hands. Do you really not get that?" I ask, seething now.

"Well, shit. I didn't know that." She puts down the coffee, the extinguished cigarette floating on top, and picks up her pack to light another, but I grab it from her hands and put in down on the couch.

"That's because you're too self-absorbed to know anything that's going on that doesn't affect you, but now it does, so you might want to start paying attention. Where did you get it?" I yell, and I don't quite recognize the voice that I hear from my own mouth.

"Someone sent it," she says, shrinking into the couch, away from me. I hand her her cigarettes and sit back down. We've made a little progress, so I give a little.

"What does that mean, sent it? Who sent it?" I ask.

"I don't know," she whines.

"Mom. Where did you get it?"

"It came in the mail," she says finally.

"The mail. That's bullshit. All I have to do is call Detective Sterling right now and tell him to raid the place and take you to detox. Done. So maybe elaborate on that."

She points to an envelope lumped in with a dusty heap of junk mail under a half-full Diet Pepsi on the floor next to the couch. I pick it up. There is no address or return address, only her name, *Lisa Bennett*.

"I don't get it. What's this?" I ask. But then I do get it.

"It came in that. Someone sent it. I didn't steal it." She doesn't need to explain anymore. When I look inside the envelope, a tiny slip of paper falls out. It's a clipping from my book: *Have A Bag Packed*.

Whoever is sending these knows where my family lives.

"Did you see this?" I ask, doing everything I can to stave off an anxiety attack in front of this woman. I have to stay focused.

"I didn't know what it meant!" She forces a crying voice that makes me want to punch her.

"You're saying this was sent to you with his license?"

"Yeah."

"You know if there's no address or stamp, it wasn't mailed to you, right? Someone put this in your mailbox. That didn't seem odd to you?" I ask, furious.

"I don't know." She puffs her smoke and tries to look away, but I sit next to her on the couch.

"Instead of contacting someone, you, what? You try to steal his identity to get a credit card. Do they accept credit for dope?" I ask, but she's pouting now. She would have fully shut down at this point if she didn't know she could be in much bigger trouble.

"It wasn't gonna hurt anyone." She sniffles. "I don't know

why someone sent it. Seemed like they wanted me to have it, so I did." Her sniveling is insufferable.

"A dead man's ID and a cryptic note and you don't even know you're being threatened. Your life is in danger and you're too fucked up to know it." I take the envelope and head for the door. I have much more than I expected to leave with, and so much less all at the same time. I open the door, and the daylight cuts through the apartment like a flashlight in the night. I turn to look at her before I go, hoping for some sign of humanity within her.

"Where's my money, though? You promised!" is all I get, and I slam the door, leaving her in the inky darkness of the stale apartment I plan never to return to.

Down at the precinct, Annalise, the front desk woman, gestures toward Sterling's office, and I follow the pretty-named woman with a pin in her sweater. Perfume dotted behind her ears trails her in jasmine-scented wake.

She tells me he'll be right in and so I wait in his office. I notice a small Virgin Mary statue on a bookshelf, so I guess he's Catholic. Never noticed that before. There's one in my mother's curio cabinet. As a kid, I studied her with hunger— her red tunic and blue hooded robe, her somber eyes looking up to God. I thought the tiny Jesus in Mary's arms looked like a small old man, and wondered if Mary resented him for getting in the way of who she thought she'd be. It's funny the things you think about when your life is in crisis, fleeting thoughts that have no business showing up in the situation.

When Sterling walks in, he shakes my hand. Something is different in the way he looks at me. Like an equal more than a suspect. There is almost a trace of respect in his voice when he greets me. Am I no longer a suspect?

"It's not my mother," I say, before he can brief me on what Will has already told me. "This was left for her." I push the envelope, with the ripped-out excerpt from my book inside, across his desk. He opens it, then looks at me.

"Any particular reason she kept this from us?" he asks. I let out an involuntary laugh and shake my head.

"Your guess is as good as mine. She has a compulsion to lie, I guess, trying to somehow cover her ass in some convoluted way. It's the same threats I've been getting, these pages from my book, but I have no idea why they'd send his license," I say. Sterling slips the paper back in the envelope and looks at me gravely.

"This is someone who's closing in," he says. "On you, and now your family. And now they're letting us know that they have something belonging to the victim. This person is getting more aggressive, probably impatient, waiting for an opportunity to strike."

"So you don't think it's me anymore?" I ask rhetorically. I don't expect an answer, but he knows I'm fed up, and that all the time spent on looking at me or my mother is wasted time.

"I'm going to have an officer assigned to keep an eye on your building if you insist on staying there."

"What if this person just enjoys stalking me? What if what happened to Liam…" I stop a minute, swallowing tears before they surface at the thought that someone had hurt him to get to me. "What if it's part of terrorizing me? They could have spent years watching me, threatening me, without ever trying to hurt me, for all I know. What would moving accomplish? They obviously know how to find me," I say.

"I understand, Faith. And you're right. I know you don't want to put someone else in danger by staying with friends or family, I get that. We're gonna do our best to keep you safe." He smiles at me warmly. "That's a promise."

"Is there anything else?" I ask, eager to go home, wrap myself in a comforter and pour a drink.

"Yes. The reason I wanted to talk to you is so I could let you know in person that we located your father."

"Not in Naperville?" I ask, because that's where she told them to look, and I didn't expect him to be found at all.

"No. It took some digging because he lived off the grid for the most part, but I'm so sorry to have to tell you, he passed away." John Sterling pats my hand, which is resting on his desk. He's never touched me before. The gesture is awkward, but kind. I look at it and then to him.

"Oh. When?" I ask.

"Almost twelve years ago. It was an overdose. He was found by a friend in Tallahassee."

"Does my mother know?" I ask. I'm not shocked that he's dead. But if she's been lying to me all these years, making Ellie and me wonder, robbing us from closure, that's what I'm not going to handle well.

"Yes," Sterling says sympathetically. "She was informed at the time he was found. They never divorced, so there was some life insurance that went to her. Sorry, Faith." And just like that, it all makes sense. The reason she shut us out completely wasn't just because she was consumed with her junky life, but because she didn't want us to get any of the insurance money. I always wondered how she still kept that apartment after all these years with no job and only measly welfare payouts. Now I know.

"She's not smart enough," I say. Sterling gives me a puzzled look. "It's possible she thinks she could get some money from my estate if she offed me, and she has friends crazy enough to help with that, but this—" I point to the envelope "—she's not that sophisticated. There are too many details in this whole thing that I am positive she's not capable of managing."

Sterling just listens. Ramirez, his partner, comes in and hands him a stack of files. She smiles and nods at me.

"Dr. Finley," she says before leaving. I greet her back with a nod. It's the moment I finally feel absolved. Not officially, but her face is completely different when she looks at me now. I've received the empathetic expression reserved for victims, not perpetrators. There has been a shift, and for that, I'm grateful. At least it's something. Sterling stands, and so do I, pulling my purse up over my shoulder and heading into the hall.

"I'll send the reports on your father to your lawyer if it's something you want to have a look at," he says, shaking my hand.

My lawyer. I drive home thinking of Will. He knew my father way back when. He'll read about it in the report—another loss. I won't get pity from him, though, which is comforting. I'll just have a soft place to land with him. Then I think about my mother. Is Lisa Bennett more sophisticated than I think?

TWENTY-EIGHT

I GET A TEXT FROM MARTY SAYING THAT HE'S GATH-ered all the info he could find on my father and he's sorry it took so long, but he can swing by if I want to go over it. Of course, I already know what he's going to say, but it would be nice to have a drink with someone, and who knows? Maybe he has more information than Sterling got.

When Marty arrives, I have a fire going and I've changed into leggings and a sweatshirt because I can't get warm. I greet him with a couple hot toddies, and Figgy springs into the room when I open the door.

"Sorry. I hope it's okay that I brought him. He's all worked up right now, and I didn't want to leave him by himself."

"Of course." I pat Figgy's head and he goes to lie by the fire. "What's wrong with him?"

"Oh, he's fine. There was some guy standing outside, and Figgy went bananas barking and tried to attack the guy. I've never seen him act like that before," he says, and I instantly think that maybe he sensed danger.

"What did the guy look like?" I ask.

"Hard to tell. He had a big parka on with a hood. Average height. I don't know. Could be chubby or just the big coat. He's okay though, right, bud?" Marty sits next to Figgy on the brick hearth. I think about Len Turlson. Average height, a little chubby. No one is looking into him. Could there be more behind this than just taking Liam's job? I hand Marty his drink and sit on the edge of the recliner across from him.

"So, finding people isn't so much my specialty as accessing their computer after I find them, so it took a while, but…"

"He died. I know. The cops just told me," I say. "I'll still pay you for your time, of course."

"Oh. Well, I'm really sorry. I wasn't expecting to come back with such bad news."

"It's okay. Was there anything else you found out at all?" I ask.

"Again, it's not really my skill set. All I know is that he didn't use credit cards or a bank. He didn't have a passport, or any of the easy ways to track someone. There wasn't even an obituary. Now if he had a laptop I could get my hands on, I could tell you a lot more," he says apologetically.

"I totally get it." I think of Len again and wonder if there is any way to get Marty's help looking into him. "Do you need someone's physical computer to hack into it? Like if I have the person's place of employment, name, birth date, address, all that… I know it sounds shady, but can you get access and just poke around?" I ask. I have little to lose at this point, but I still hope he doesn't think I'm a total creep.

"To some extent. It's always easiest with physical access, of course, but there is some information I can get that way, especially if I know where he works," he says tentatively.

"You probably think I'm a total creeper." I laugh, but at the same time sincerely try to gauge his reaction.

"Listen," he says, patting Figgy's head. "I don't judge. And considering what you're dealing with right now, I'm sure it's all for the higher good." He blows on his drink to cool it.

"It is," I say. "I don't want a paper trail, so can I just write it down on paper instead of sending it via email?"

"Yeah, I have a couple computer setups in the morning for clients who literally don't know how to plug it into the wall and turn on the power button, but after that, I can work on it."

"Thank you so much. You have been extremely helpful in all this," I say, and he blows it off.

"I was a little late to the party bringing you the info today, but I'll do my best," he says.

I'm startled by my phone buzzing in my pocket. I see it's Ellie. I decide to send it to voice mail and call her back when Marty leaves, but she calls back again right away so I excuse myself. When I pick up, she's so hysterical that I can't even understand what she's saying. I give Marty a look saying "excuse me" and walk across to the kitchen.

"Ell. Ell, I can't—I can't understand you. What's wrong?" I ask, but she's sobbing. I hear the ding of a text coming through, so I hold the phone away to look at it. It's the same Polaroid photo of a woman bound and gagged. Underneath it is a clipping from my book: "Change your locks."

And then, written in pen next to the taped-on clipping, it says, "But you didn't change your locks, Faith, and now I'm in."

"Someone left this on our porch!" she sobs. I see Marty get up. He motions politely that he'll leave to give me my privacy.

"Ell. Okay, calm down. When did you get this?" I ask. Before Marty shuts the door, he mouths *Are you okay?* and I nod, mouthing back *Thank you*, and he slips out.

"I don't know! I just got home from bringing the kids shopping, and I saw it sitting there. Who would do that? Oh my God."

"Does it say anything on the back?" I ask. I hear rustling like she's taking it back out of the envelope to look.

"It says 'Someone's Listening.'" She starts crying and mumbling "oh my God's" again. "Has this happened to you? Is there someone after you or something? You don't even sound upset!" she wails.

"Ell, I'm just trying to keep my wits about me here and figure this out. I did get one too," I say, knowing there is no reason to keep that from her now.

"Oh my Gahhhd!" She's not handling this well. Another text dings. I think she has sent a photo of the back of the Polaroid, but it's not from her. It says I need to talk to you.

I don't recognize the number, but I need to find out who this is.

"Listen, I'm gonna come over in the morning. We'll call Detective Sterling and he'll take a look at it. I can have them send a patrol to have extra eyes on your house tonight, but listen, you're safe okay, you're not the target."

"Target?" she practically screams. "Faith, what the hell is going on?"

"Is Joe home?" I ask urgently.

"No!" she sobs.

"Let me call Sterling, and I'll come over as soon as I can and explain more. I gotta go." I do quickly call Sterling and I have to leave a message, but I explain the note Ellie got and ask him to go over there or send some extra patrol. I think of her fat lip and seeing Joe at Bowen's that night. Is there something right under my nose I'm not seeing about him? I hate that everyone in my life is a potential villain. I'm angry at the invasive thought. It makes my stomach lurch and it's impossible, so I refocus, and I text back the number on my screen.

Who is this? The answer comes back quickly.

It's Carter. I changed my number. Can you meet me at the diner? I don't believe what I'm seeing. What could Carter possibly have to say right now? How could he be involved? I feel my knees weakening. I sit down and text back: I'm on my way.

It's all I can do not to run red lights on my way over to the diner. I can feel the blood in my face and up my legs, hot and percolating, a flash as warm as summer or a swallow of scotch, circulating through my body in one instant. I run a stop sign as I turn the corner to the diner, and I see Carter's silhouette shadowed against a streetlamp in the back alley, waiting for me, exhaling swirls of smoke into the brisk air.

I park, and I'm about to jump out and run over to him, but to my surprise, he approaches the driver's window. I roll it down.

"I'm on break. Can we drive? I shouldn't be seen talking to you," he says. I click the passenger door unlocked, and he climbs in. I drive aimlessly.

"I lied," he says. I don't respond. I wait through his pause for him to say more. "I know you already know that."

"When I came to see you at work, you told me your allegations were true. You said you couldn't believe I didn't remember that night."

"I didn't know what else to say. It was the first thing I could think of," he says defensively, and I remember the uncertainty in his eyes that night, but how his words still made me question everything.

"Okay, well, I'm glad you're telling the truth, but why now?"

"'Cause things are getting out of control now, and I—I don't know. I'm getting sort of scared." I resist the urge to tell him things have been out of control for a long time.

"Scared? What do you mean?" I ask.

"There's this guy. He's starting to send me stuff—like,

threats—because I said I wanted to tell the truth," he says shakily. I pull over next to an empty, frozen strip mall, and put the car in Park.

"What guy?"

"I know how bad it is, what I did. But this guy, I don't know how he found me. He knew I was your patient. He must have been watching your office because he stopped one day when I was leaving. Offered me a smoke, he seemed, I don't know, normal. Said he could get good weed, so I gave him my number...and he called me one day. He offered me money, like, a lot of money, if I'd say what I said. I'm sorry." He hangs his head and fidgets with his cigarette pack.

"You can smoke," I say, cracking a window. "What's his name, Carter? I need to know who he is."

He flicks the bottom of the pack, popping a few cigarettes up higher than the rest, pulling on the protruding brown filter and sliding the white paper tube from the pack.

"He never told me his name. He sent half of the money in cash in the mail and the other half after. I don't know who he is or what he looks like."

"How much did he pay you?" I ask.

"Ten thousand," he says, and I try to think of who would have that kind of money, but all I can think is that I would have paid him three times that much to take it all back months ago. "I told my parents the truth last night. They hate me."

"They don't hate you," I say, although I sort of hate him right now. "They told me I have to tell the truth to the press and stuff." He's trembling; he tries to hold the cigarette steady between his fingers. "If I do, he'll kill me."

"Why do you think that?" I wonder if he's sent Carter those same photos.

"I just know," he says childishly.

"But you can't name him. You don't even know who he is," I argue.

"He wants to ruin you. He said that to me. So, even if he doesn't get caught, it's gonna mess up his plan, and it will be my fault." I think about someone wanting to hurt me so much that they'd put this in motion months ago, before the book signing, before the accident—it had all been according to someone's master plan. Who have I angered that much? These are the answers I've been begging for, but they just bring more questions and worse repercussions.

"I tried to change my mind right after I did it. I felt so bad," he says, and I'm sure he did. He's always been a sensitive kid. "He told me just to get the media all worked up, but not to press charges. He knew there was no evidence, but that this would still do a lot of damage. Then my parents got involved. I told him I'd give the money back and I didn't want to be involved anymore, but he just sent me a list with my parents' names, their daily schedules, some photos of them, just, like, crossing the street or pulling into the garage, like private investigator photos, but on Polaroid."

"So they can't be traced back to a source," I say.

"Yeah. I guess. He didn't have to say they were from him or that they were threats. I mean, obviously. So, I just didn't do anything. I stopped making statements and hoped it would blow over." He flicks his cigarette butt out the window and rolls it up, blowing hot air into his hands to warm up.

"So why now?" I ask.

"Because my parents still believe in the legal system, I guess," he says, flustered. He lights another cigarette, and the smell is making me sick and the cold air is making me uncomfortable, but I don't say anything.

"What does that mean?" I ask.

"I was getting scared, so I told them. My new therapist was urging me to tell the truth, so I contacted the guy again."

"How?"

"I don't know, online, the way he said to, and I said I might want to tell the truth because I was feeling bad and my therapist wants me to do the right thing, and all that."

"And?" I ask impatiently.

"He sent me a photo of a bound and gagged lady with a book clipping. It said I could be next. He sent other stuff too, but that was the worst."

"Jesus Christ," I whisper under my breath.

"I thought it was you in the photo—that you were dead. When I found out you weren't, I told my parents what happened. I was really freaked out, you know. They said the legal system is set up to handle it, and I need to tell the truth and let the guy be found or whatever, so now I have. They're probably making calls and informing police and shit right now."

"He won't go after you," I say. "I'm the one he's after. This isn't your fault, okay?" I say, about to place my hand on his leg to comfort him, and then remember that I can't. Even though he sits here admitting it was all a lie, I have been changed, and I am now afraid to touch people in case it's taken the wrong way. Carter has been taken advantage of and manipulated exactly like I thought he must have been. He doesn't need to take on any more.

"Truly," I say again, "I'm glad you're going to tell the truth. You'll be protected." I cannot believe that my name might be cleared. The truth has seemed so out of reach, but to think that he'll publicly say he lied, and that the same person who made him lie hurt Liam, and I'm not a predator or some crazed, jealous wife. I can't even imagine how it will feel to have the weight lifted—the freedom.

"I'm really sorry," he says again as I drive him back to the diner.

"He got you in a weak moment, and then you were scared. I understand," I say.

"That makes it worse. You should hate me." He looks out the window and leans his head just so, the way Liam did that last night, and I want to cry. I couldn't protect either of them from whatever monster is after me.

"I don't," I say as I park behind the diner.

"He wants to make you suffer," Carter says before he gets out of the car.

"What?" I say, shocked.

"That's what he said. He doesn't want to kill you like he used to want to, because it's more fun to watch you suffer. So I guess maybe he would be after me or the other people in your life because he'd rather watch your life fall apart than kill you."

"Jesus fuck, Carter, he said that to you?"

"Yeah." He looks ashamed.

"Well, what does his voice sound like?" I ask.

"He uses one of those things that changes your voice, you know, to sound like Darth Vader or something so it's not recognizable. Might not even be a guy, actually. That's all I know. Sorry." He opens the door. "Take care of yourself, Dr. Finley," he says, and shuts the car door. I watch his hunched figure as he walks through the alley and slips inside the back door of the diner.

I call Ellie immediately to check on her. She's still bawling, but there is an officer with her taking a report, and I tell her I'll be by later. I call Will. He picks up after two rings.

"I need to talk to you. And I can't stay at my place right now," I say frantically.

"Is it about Carter?" he asks.

"How do you know that?" I ask, confused.

"Because I need to talk to you too. Can you come over?" He sounds a bit frazzled. I'm already in my car, so I race over to Will's.

TWENTY-NINE

WILL ABANDONS A PILE OF SCATTERED BOOKS AND
paperwork on his swanky kitchen table and hands me a glass
of red wine when I arrive. He can see I'm cold, and he pulls a
throw blanket around my shoulders, tenderly. I feel his crisp
shirt and smell the familiar cologne on his sleeve.

I'm instantly brought back to the night when we were six-
teen. My mother never left the apartment for anything, but
on this night she'd finally be gone. Will had driven his truck
as fast as he could, even though the rain fell in torrents outside, because he couldn't wait another day to get me alone. So
he waited in the dark of his truck with the rain thundering
on the metal flatbed, waiting to see a sign of me in the window before I gave him a signal for him to sneak in, and we'd
made love for the first time. He looked exactly the same in
the firelight right now.

"So you know that Carter is going to admit he lied about
me—that the allegations are all false?" I ask as we sit at the
kitchen island on stools.

"His parents called the cops. Sterling called me. Carter's been getting threats in the mail similar to yours."

"Yeah, that's what he said," I say, gulping at my wine like I'll never see alcohol again. Will's phone rings, and he makes a gesture like he has to get it, and steps away. I can tell it's about Carter and that it's someone else at the firm, or maybe even Sterling.

I stand and look at a photo on a shelf next to me. It's of him and his mother. She was always so lovely to me, and I wished she were my mom. She tried out every tip she read in fashion magazines. She dotted toothpaste on blemishes to dry them out, stored little soaps in her underwear drawer so her things would smell better, bathed in raw avocado, pressed wet tea bags on red skin blotches, powdered the roots of her hair so it didn't look greasy. She passed each tip down to me, and I loved her. I'd forgotten how close we all were before life shifted and lurched forward the way it does. Will comes back and picks up his glass.

"The media is having a field day with this already. I mean in a good way, for you, but I worry about your safety."

"Yeah, me too," I finally admit.

"But you're not going back to the condo, right? Please." He says this with a look that doesn't need explanation. He knows I'm stubborn and wants to hear me agree.

"Right. I'm—I don't even know. I mean, nothing has exactly changed. I always knew that someone was after me, but now that Ellie and Carter have gotten threats, I'm more worried for them."

"Ellie got a threat?" he asks.

"We called the police. I'm sure Sterling knows. It just happened tonight. They sent someone over."

"God, Faith, I just—I don't even know what to say anymore—everything you're going through. Jesus. You're a hell of a lot stronger than most people, that's for sure."

"I don't know what I did," I say, almost in tears. "I mean, what could I have done to make someone do this to me?"

"There are crazy, off-balance fucking people out there. I know you know that it's nothing you did. But I'm sure it's hard to keep positive when all this is happening," he says, looking me in the eye. I feel a longing for his touch, just to have him hold me, even though it's not the time.

"I know," I say quietly, pulling the throw tighter around myself. It feels safe to be here, to have the media talking about it, to have Sterling seemingly on my side now. Somehow in the middle of the chaos, I'm not alone now, and I want to stay right here. But then, something occurs to me.

"What if they don't believe him?"

"Carter?" he asks.

"He's lost all his credibility and so have I. I don't know. All of a sudden I can see people thinking I'm the one threatening him and forcing him to change his story. Whoever is doing this has set it up really well. I feel like I lose at every turn, and he's now using my family as bait." I'm starting to stitch together how well planned this was, so I look bad no matter what. And if all else fails, the media can blame everything on my pill habit. There is so much negative stuff out there about me that's been crafted that way. Will this really change it?

"This is a huge step in the right direction, at least. Let's take it as it comes," he says. He pushes a strand of hair behind my ear and I close my eyes and look at the floor, drinking in his touch.

"I have a good red blend a client gave me if you'd like to try it," he says, standing, but then his phone rings again. He picks it up and then excuses himself one more time. "It's in the rack over there if you wanna open it. I'll be back." He covers the mouthpiece on his phone and then disappears into the bedroom. I look to the giant cherrywood wine cabinet he'd pointed to.

On my way to the cabinet, I see his open office door. I hadn't seen his office the last time I was here. It's modern, with just enough character and warmth. I notice a wall of framed photos, so I step in and take a look at them. Mostly it's photos of his family at holiday gatherings and vacations. But there is one of us. His mom took it; I remember that day. We were lying on his front lawn, dissolving Pop Rocks like champagne waves on our tongues and spraying each other with the garden hose. The photo shows us on the deck, his arm around my shoulders. There are slices of strawberry shortcake on the table. I think it was his birthday. We're not looking at the camera. We're laughing. I wish I remembered why.

I run my fingers along his bookshelf and read some of the titles. Mostly law books, but a few classics. Then I see my book, *Someone's Listening*, sitting on his desk. I can't believe he actually read it—I mean, if he did. Maybe he just paged through it out of curiosity. I can still hear him on the phone in the back room, so I sit in his leather desk chair a moment and page through my book. Something falls out.

I look on the floor, and it's a Polaroid of the woman, bound and gagged, with my name on the top. I lose my breath. When I look at the book in my hands, I see scissor marks. There are pages and pages that have sentences cut out. I flip through; they are the very same cutouts that have been sent to me. I can't breathe. I can't move. The book slips from my hands onto the floor. I have to get out of here.

How can this be happening? Why would he do this? As impossible as it is that it could be him, I start to think of all the reasons he would have that no one else would. Love. What could be more of a motive than love that's not returned? I start to piece together facts. When he referred to my condo building after telling me to get a security system, he'd said "my grandma could get over that gate." I didn't think twice about that comment, but now that I'm thinking about it, he'd never been to my and Liam's condo before. How would he know what the gate looked like, how secure it was?

Jesus. He'd shown back up in town the night of the accident; he admits that he's never gotten over how things ended; he has the money to do these payoffs and go to extremes to cover it up. How could I have not seen it?

I need my purse. My keys are in it. I need to get it and get out before he comes out of the back room. My heart pounds in my ears and my limbs feel unsteady as I rise from the desk chair and tiptoe to the door to listen for him. I still hear him talking. I walk into the main room, shuddering. I spot my bag hanging off the back of the kitchen stool. I grab it and I feel like he might grab me from behind at any moment, but I'm able to run down the hall and out the front door.

When I get to my car, I rifle through my bag for my phone to call Sterling, but it's not there. Tears stream down my face, but I'm too frightened to go into full-blown panic, so I drive like hell. He told me that my place isn't safe just to lure me to his, but it's the only safe place to go right now. I do have my backup phone. I can go home and get it and call Ellie and Sterling.

Was that the first step tonight, taking my phone so I couldn't call for help? How did he think he'd ever get away with this right now? Whatever plan was in place, it did not include him getting caught. Every detail has been worked out. That's clear now. I can barely drive through the blur of tears. I loved him for so many years, from childhood, chasing green twinkles of light around the milkweed, collecting fireflies in mason jars, to grad school and grown-up breakups. And he's been my enemy all along.

THIRTY

WHEN I GET TO MY BUILDING, I PARK ILLEGALLY AND run in. The elevator is taking too long, so I run up the four floors and storm into my condo. I run for my burner phone, which I'd stuck in the kitchen drawer, and when I turn around, I see a slip of paper that someone has slipped under the door. My front door is still open, and it's sitting there on the floor. I can't. I can't be here. I run the flight of stairs down to Marty's place. Will would never know to look for me there, and I can make the calls I need to.

As soon as I reach the fourth floor, I look for his unit, 429. I haven't been there before, so it takes me a minute to find it. As soon as I do, I see him, with Figgy on a leash, rounding the turn to go down the stairs, probably to take the dog out. I call out, but he doesn't hear. I assume he just took Figgy out for a quick bathroom break, because he's left his door open a crack. I know I shouldn't, but I push it open to wait inside. I feel vulnerable and completely freaked out, and I know he won't mind.

I wonder if Will could have seen me leave in time to follow me. I click Marty's door shut and stare at the back of it a moment, hoping he returns soon. I wonder how I let my guard down like this. Almost a year without touch, without dry eyes or a clear mind, and he so quickly made me remember what companionship felt like—true, easy love, or something resembling it, I was starting to think—something that would always be there, like the boxes of childhood keepsakes stacked in the garage, not acknowledged every day, but beloved and essential. I'm a fool, I think.

After a few moments, I turn around and look at Marty's incredibly neat and tidy apartment. Very empty and bachelor-looking, nothing like Will's. There is computer and video equipment everywhere, but neatly shelved. The only unkempt part of his place is the kitchen table. I step in and take a closer look, and I don't believe what I see.

A silent scream rises in my throat. I don't understand what I'm looking at, but I can't turn away. It doesn't make sense what I'm seeing.

There are dozens of photos of me. For a split second, I think maybe it's from his research, looking up people for me, something related, but no.

There are shots of me, not from my website or social media, but from inside my condo, or at a café. Just like Carter described. I see pages of my daily schedule in a stack with dates. His kitchen table is covered with me. Images of my face are pinned up on the wall next to the table. I walk up to it, horrified, and I see something that makes my knees buckle. It's Liam's daily schedule and details about the book signing. And a Polaroid photo of a woman gagged and bound. Who is she?

I just saw my book with the cutout pages and a photo at Will's. What's happening? I don't know what's happening! I'm dizzy. I look around the room, trying to steady myself. I know that I felt like the photo seemed real and not a website porn thing, but somehow my gut told me it was staged like a photo shoot, made carefully to scare someone, but now I know that's not what it is. This woman is probably dead. I'm going to be next.

I'm playing each possible scenario over and over. He didn't know who I was until I moved in. It makes no sense. He's not a disgruntled restaurant owner who got a bad review like Hilly. He's not a jealous lover like Cal. He definitely isn't an angry parent who wants revenge. Then what? What did he want with me?

And in the midst of my reeling and dizzying thoughts, I see photos of a woman I recognize. That's it. That's the missing piece. I study her face, and I remember my conversations with her. Marty is in the photo. Suddenly all of this makes sense; it all becomes crystal clear. I was so wrong, and I now I need to run before it's too late.

I turn to run back out the door, but it clicks and locks, and Marty Nash stands in front of it with a terrifying smile on his face.

"You look surprised," he says.

THIRTY-ONE

MARTY CALMLY PICKS UP A CHEF'S KNIFE FROM THE
cutlery block on the counter. He points at a dog crate and
Figgy runs inside. He closes the door.

"This is unexpected," he says, noticing the photo I'm looking at and gestures to it. "You remember my wife, I take it."

"Lettie." I choke and it comes out in a haggard whisper.

"Oh, you do. I wasn't sure if you would." His movements
are so careful and slow. It's as if he's been ready for this his
whole life. His wife was Violet Marie Nash. I'd looked it up. I
look at the woman in the photo on the wall, the woman with
Marty. I remember that I'd met her in the lobby and she'd told
me her story. She was trying to leave him. I'd helped her leave
him—I'd invited her to call into the show. She'd told me her
name was Lettie. Oh my God. A nickname for Violet. The
radio doesn't allow last names, so how could I have made the
connection? I'd walked her through every step of leaving him.

"Have a seat," he says, pointing the knife toward the kitchen
chair. I slink down into it, keeping my eyes on him.

"This is gonna be fun," he says.

"What happened to her?" I ask, trying to keep my breathing steady so I can stay in control. I know now that she definitely didn't commit suicide the way the paper said. I pray to God that she wasn't the woman in the Polaroid.

"Lettie? You should know, shouldn't you? You're the one who made her leave." I remember the things she'd described when she'd called in and when talking to the producers after the call, who were trained to help her with a safe plan and with getting to a shelter. She told us such horrific things—how he'd held her hands to the gas burner, how he made her strip naked and stand there just so he could humiliate her and shame her body. This man in front of me. How is he capable?

"I thought she committed suicide," I say, trying to give him an out of some sort. Anything.

"It looked that way. Your death will too." He is still smiling. Figgy cries and makes circles in his crate. "You think you're so clever," he says. I know that the more I keep him talking, the more time I buy myself, and I need to get as much information from him as I can if there is any hope of talking my way out of this. He'll talk because he assumes I won't leave this apartment alive. He *wants* to talk. He wants to show off his genius after all these months. That much I know for sure. Until now, he was anonymous.

"I mean, how do you take yourself seriously? 'The list of advice to flee from your abuser, by Faith Finley,'" he quotes sarcastically, getting worked up. "What a joke. You know what you did do with your shit advice? You led me right to her. You literally wrote the book on how to find your wife when she tries to run away from you. You could have just drawn a fucking map in the back of the book." I swallow hard. I've put everyone I love in danger, and I'm not in control of this conversation. What if what he's saying is true?

"Marty," I try, "what happened to Lettie?"

But he doesn't answer. Instead, he picks up my book, one of many copies on his table, and flips to the resource list in the back. "Number one, 'Keep loved ones informed of your whereabouts.' Good one!" he shouts. "She told her idiot sister where she was going…who felt sorry for me when I cried and begged for her to tell me, and couldn't keep her mouth shut. Easy. Two, 'Document everything: Keep records of all texts, emails, stalking and harassment. Keep video or written journal, and hide it'!" he continues. "Thanks, Doc! She kept a video journal for proof just like you said. She recorded where she was going to be in case anyone couldn't find her. It wasn't hard to hack into her laptop and find it. That's what I do!" I feel sick.

"'Have a bag packed. Include an extra set of keys, identification, car title, birth certificate,' blah, blah, blah. You think her bag was hard to find in a tiny condo? You led me right to it so I could make sure she didn't get far without ID and money. She followed every word you ever uttered, Doc."

"I don't know your relationship with her, but I…" He doesn't even pretend to listen. He keeps reading, and every word is a punishment.

"'Obtain an order for protection.' Has that ever stopped anyone from anything? 'Secure your PINs and passwords.' Despite the fact that all her goddamn passwords were the dog's name, which she thought was secure, I could hack anything she changed. I mean, come on. Even you have to admit this is shit advice given to sell a bunch of crappy books. But hey, it got me Lettie back, so I can't fault you too much, right?"

"Marty, please. You have to understand that I was doing my job. If she was in danger, I was just trying to help. I didn't know you. It wasn't personal," I say, knowing that someone with this much invested in destroying me would never hear reason.

"She thought you hung the moon. Dr. Finley this. Dr. Finley that. She was pretty fucking surprised when I found her in that motel she overdosed in. Just hours away from moving into a shelter that would never let me near her, but you helped. I think most people will believe that you overdosed too. I mean, you have been under such strain and what with your pill problem already," he says. He moves toward me with the knife.

"Please, Marty. I'll have people looking for me," I beg.

"Not here. Nobody connects me to you." He touches the knife to my neck until the tip makes a tiny cut and he has control over my movements.

"Stand up," he says, and I do, and then he pushes just enough to back me up against a wall, next to a closet. He makes a gesture with his head, indicating that I should get in. I whimper, but he just pushes harder, so I am forced into the hall closet. He slams the door and locks it.

"I wasn't ready for you yet. I need a few minutes to get ready," he laughs.

If full-circle failure looks like something, it's this. A lifetime commitment to helping people led to a psychopath killing someone I advised, and I am sitting on the floor of a closet, weeping, just like I did as a child. *One, two, three, four.* I have to keep control. I can't give way to a panic attack even though there has been no other time to have one as well-earned as this. Mind over matter. I have to stay in control.

I see my father dragging me in by my wrists as I scream and try to wriggle away from his grip. I sat for two days in my own urine, starving and thirsty in the darkness, until my mother remembered I was there and drove my nearly lifeless body to the hospital. I'm back in that closet. It's as if he knows my darkest fear. I cry hard but quietly and mask the hiccups at the end, covering my hand with my mouth. I hyperventilate but force myself to try to control my breath.

Then I remember the burner phone in my pocket. I don't know what Marty is doing or how long I have, but I need to call someone. I can call 911, but I can't talk out loud. My only hope is that I stay on the line long enough for the call to be traced. Maybe someone will know it's me if I can even say a word or two.

Who? Whose number does anyone even actually know these days? When I think of Will, I don't know how he's connected or what I saw in his office and I'm so confused, but his is the only number I remember right now, and the only reason I do is because in some flirty discussion at the bar the other night he said his number was easy to remember because it ended in 1517, and that was the same year the Reformation started in Europe. I called him a huge nerd, and he argued about the significance of the historical event. I remember our first three numbers were the same, and of course the area code is the same, so yes. Yes, I can call him. But I hesitate. What did I see on his desk? Is he involved? I have to try.

I dial and he picks up.

"Will," I whimper into the phone as quietly as I can.

"Faith?" he asks. "What the hell happened to you?" But I can't talk. I hear Marty's footsteps close, pacing. Whatever the hell he's doing, he's close.

"Faith, you left your phone on my counter. Where are you calling from? Hello?" But I hear Marty's footsteps stop, so I cover the phone so he doesn't hear Will's voice come through. I can't answer him.

"Listen. I really hope you didn't get the wrong idea here. I went into the office and saw the book on the desk. If you freaked out because of it, I can explain. I'm sure you're mad I didn't tell you, but I just got it today. Someone left it in my mailbox anonymously. That's the main reason I told you to come over. I was literally about to show you, but I wanted you to calm down a little first. You can't be mad about that, come on." He stops talking for a second. "Faith, come on. I told you I wouldn't keep any evidence secret, but seriously I didn't. It's why I asked you to—are you there?" he says, and it hits me. The reason he knew where the condo was is because we met at Grady's once and I pointed it out. Not because he was stalking me. Carter even said there were other things, threats sent to him, but the photo was the worst. I was fixated on that. I didn't even ask what else. Carter probably didn't know the significance of the cutouts to think it was as important. I can't believe I doubted Will so much.

"There was a fucked-up Polaroid picture inside, and I'm worried for you, so can you please talk to me?"

"Help," I say in a loud whisper. He doesn't hear.

"Okay, I'm not sure where you're calling from, but I'm coming over to your place to check on you, even if you're mad at me," he says and hangs up. I push the burner phone down inside my boot so Marty doesn't know I have it. Hopefully he'll think it's in my purse on the table.

I want to be relieved he knows I'm in danger, but he'll never find me here.

THIRTY-TWO

MARTY WHIPS THE CLOSET DOOR OPEN AND STANDS over me, and all I can see is my father's face. I scramble up from the floor and he takes pleasure in my fear. I've been in here less than an hour, but it still takes me a minute to adjust to the light from the pitch-black.

He still has a chef's knife. It makes me wonder if he also has a gun in the house. He must, but he didn't expect me. He wasn't ready for this to unfold now. Then I remember the gun I have stashed on the fire escape. It's more possible for me to find a way out to his fire escape and up to mine to get it than it would be to get out the front door. But then I think, this guy seems to know my every move; he may have already found it there.

It doesn't matter if all he has is a knife and not a gun right now because he's twice my size. I'm completely at his mercy. He holds it straight out and gives me instructions.

"Can I get you a drink?" he asks, smiling. A drink? What is he trying to do? But I don't answer. I just try to mask the terror on my face. "Let me explain how this is gonna work."

He backs me up with the blade, then takes it away a moment and pulls out a kitchen chair. "Sit down," he demands, but I am frozen, so I just stand there a minute. My mind can't process how I got here, how I could have not seen. He touches the tip of the blade under my chin.

"I said. Sit. Down." And I obey. "I don't want to have to use a weapon and make a mess like last time, but you sort of messed up my plans by coming in like this. If you make me use a weapon, know that I have everything at my disposal to make sure you're never found. I'm prepared for whichever scenario you decide on. But nobody has any idea that your nice, widowed neighbor even knows you, let alone has a reason to hurt you."

"The support group knows," I say.

"Yes, but that was by design. I invited my depressed acquaintance to the meeting to try to be helpful." He takes out a bottle of wine and pours two glasses. "There are witnesses now of your distraught and standoffish demeanor. All that will show is that I tried to help." He smiles a rare, creepy smile. "Plus all those diary entries you kept on your home computer saying how unhappy you are. Those will come in handy." He takes out a bottle of Klonopin and empties it onto the table.

"I didn't make any diary entries," I say naively.

"Oh, but you did. Dating from when you first moved back into the condo. What day was it you gave me full access to your computer? It was about then that you wrote in great detail about how it would probably just be better if you ended it. You discuss your struggle with pills and alcohol. I think you even say once that it would be easy and peaceful just to take the whole bottle," he says, and drops the pills, one by one, into the wineglass nearest me.

He's accessed all of my private documents. I would never know where to look for this journal he's created and hidden somewhere on my hard drive. He's gone to such extremes, and I know that I'm right: he's planned this down to every last detail, and there is no way out. No one knows I'm here. Fuck.

I see the duct tape sitting on the counter, and I'm afraid that he'll tie me up the way he did to the woman in the photo. Lettie.

He sees me looking at it and he smiles.

"Don't worry. I'll get to that. Take a sip," he says, stirring the pills into the glass of wine and pushing it toward me. "I know how much you like your booze."

"Are you crazy?" I whip back. "I'm not going to drink that." He puts the knife to my chin again, and presses just enough for it to cut through slightly. I see a drip of blood land on my white coat.

"Take a sip," he says again calmly. I have no choice. I take the smallest sip I can manage.

"Good girl. See, now, you can make it peaceful the way you talk about in your journal, or you can make it really painful and have your family wondering what happened to you for the rest of their lives. Just like they do Liam." When he says that, I know that he's right. Whatever he did to Liam, no one has been able to find out, and even the best detectives don't suspect him at all. I can't panic, I can't panic. I need to stay strong and think.

He takes the duct tape and moves to bind my ankles with it. I'm trying not to hyperventilate. What if he finds the phone in my boot? Why didn't I put it down my shirt instead? He's pushing and pulling on my legs so tight as he tapes them, I can't tell if he found the phone until he tosses it onto the table.

"Anything else?" he asks, pulling my coat off and checking the pockets, then patting me down. There's nothing else. "Good, 'cause you'll need your hands free for now." He pushes the wine closer to me.

"What happened to Liam?" I ask, hoping that Sterling is right and he's dying to brag about his accomplishments. Maybe I can buy some time. If he's going to kill me anyway, he shouldn't care about telling me everything. He's sick. He'll want to.

"You're so smart and still somehow so clueless. It seems obvious to me. I followed you home from the book party. You drove slow on the icy roads. Do you remember a huge four-wheel-drive truck come up behind you and pass you? You must." I do. I didn't think anything of it. A bigger truck *had* passed maybe twenty minutes before the accident. There was no reason to connect that to what happened.

"I got over the bad roads easily, and when I got about a mile down the road ahead of you, I turned around to come the other way, so I could cross the yellow line into your lane. The nice and unexpected part was that you swerved so fast, I didn't have to. Yours were the only swerved tire marks. The tree you hit was the only collision. They didn't look for another car because there was no evidence of one."

"What if I'd seen you too late and didn't swerve?" I ask, hungry for answers. Maybe they don't matter now, but I still need them.

"Well, if you'd hit me, you'd be dead, which was what I was counting on. A five thousand pound Dodge Ram colliding with your tiny Fiat. Splat. And with all the Klonopin in your system and me sober, they'd be sure to chalk it up to driving under the influence."

"You bought me that drink at the signing," I say in disbelief.

"You shouldn't take drinks from strangers. You never know what's in them." Just then, I smack the drink in front of me onto the floor, and watch the glass shatter as it hits the polished concrete. The wine splashes up and covers him in red, bloody-looking streaks. He grabs the back of my head and smashes it onto the table, hard. I see flashes and bursts of light behind my eyes, and I can feel hot blood trickle down onto my shoulder. I try to catch my breath and not wail in pain. I need to stay in control.

"Okay, you want to make this ugly, we can do that," he growls.

"All this because of radio advice I gave to your wife? She's her own person, she did what she needed to do to—" I scream, and he cuts me off.

"She's a fucking sheep. She did what you said. It wasn't just the radio spot where she told the whole world what a monster I am. It was your books, every show. She was obsessed, and would have done anything you said. She was the love of my life, and it's your fault that she's dead." He spits as he hisses his words at me. I don't ask about why you'd beat the love of your life. I don't say that I was only doing my job. None of that matters now. I need to buy time. Maybe just a little more time, and just maybe, Will might find me.

"But I didn't die, so your plan was ruined," I say.

"I thought you were dead. Your husband woke up, stood up even, so you understand now that since he'd seen me, I had to take care of him. Made a mess of my goddamn truck." He's so proud of this. He drinks his wine and leans back in his chair. Liam was shot in the head, so now I know he has a gun, somewhere. Maybe still in his apartment. I can't hold back the tears, thinking about my sweet Liam, scared, helpless.

"Fuck. You."

"Not very professional of you to speak like that, but I mean, hey, we can do that too, if you want." He comes right up to me, his foul breath inches from my face. He grips my cheeks, and I scramble to back away from him, but he sits me down, his grip so strong, I can't squeeze out of it. He starts to laugh.

"It turned out to be the best possible outcome, really. I mean that you didn't die. Isn't this fun? Your husband wasn't fun. I had to figure out a way to clean up my truck, dump him in a lake. It sucked, frankly, but you. I was pissed at first when you were in the news and alive and well. But I was able to have so much more fun with you, so it really turned out for the best. I can't remember the last time I had so much fun, and how easy will it be to tuck you back in your bed upstairs after it's done? Delicious." He is taking pleasure in every moment of this. Carter, the notes on my door, Ellie, the history he's created on my computer—it's all been his greatest wet dream come true.

"Your stick-it note wall—pathetic. You didn't even have me up there as any sort of suspect, even though I searched 'how many Klonopin does it takes to die,' right on your computer, just feet away from you." He laughs, and I realize that the trail he's left on my computer is probably more complex than I could possibly imagine, and no one will question my death as anything but a suicide—even if he has to kill me with a gun or a knife, and make it seem like I've disappeared.

"You took his phone and you withdrew cash to make it look like he left. Was that letter saying he wanted out—the one on his work computer that Len brought to me—yours too?" I ask.

"Having them think he took off was good, right?" He grins widely and drinks.

"But then they found him. You didn't expect that," I say, thinking maybe he hadn't thought of everything. Maybe there are holes in the plan that I can still find.

"Eh, enough time had passed. Didn't really matter at that point." He kicks some of the broken glass out of the way, and retrieves another glass from the counter, a drinking glass that he fills with more wine. "It doesn't have to be the exact drug you were searching on your computer, if you want to make this hard. Any overdose will do." He takes out an orange prescription bottle with a white lid, pours the contents into the wine, and shoves it across the table again. I couldn't see what it was. Whatever it is, it will kill me.

He's almost done with his glass, and he looks down at mine. If my advice was what led him to Lettie, I need to use it to save myself. Lettie wasn't a fighter; she'd told me that on the radio show. She'd been so beaten down for so long, I'm sure it was easy for him because she didn't fight back, and that breaks my heart. But he doesn't know me as well as he thinks he does.

"Drink up," he says.

"No," I say, but I still don't have a plan.

"Do you know how easy it was with someone her size to force her hand on the trigger and make sure there was close-range gun residue?" He gets close to my face as he says this. "We could do that too, if you want, but this way seems more… you. Don't you think?" I have to believe that he went to great lengths to set up my suicide by Klonopin for good reason, and the last thing he wants to do is steer away from that well-laid plan. He doesn't want to shoot me or stab me. Seeing me suffer would elate him, but the cover-up after doesn't fit as neatly with the master plan. I have to keep refusing for as long as I can. I look to the window leading out to the fire escape. It's only six or seven feet away from me. "I'm done with the Q and A now," he says as he comes closer to me, but I will fight back. I grab the wine bottle off the table and break it. He shouldn't have left my hands free.

"Oh, how fun. Slit wrists is a good ole classic. We can do it that way." As he lunges for me, I try to stand, to run, but I fall hard onto the floor because my feet are bound. I push myself backward until I feel a wall behind me. He laughs and watches, but he doesn't expect me to use the wall to push myself to my feet so quickly, and when he saunters over, arrogantly, thinking he has me where he wants me, I stab the jagged bottle into the side of his neck. He wails and stumbles back, holding the place where the shards are. I use the seconds I have to sit, trying to free my ankles with the small piece of glass I'm still holding. I try to cut the tape free before he recovers. I'm cutting my hands to shreds as I saw away at the tape. It comes free as he lurches toward me. I stand and run.

There's nowhere to go in the small apartment where I won't corner myself. I feel like a caged animal, moving in circles, trying to keep backing away from him. I see the knife he put down on the table. My hands are slippery with my own blood, but I need to try to lunge for it. His face is red with rage as he stands there, watching me feel my way around the room, my hands feeling for what's behind me, so I don't take my eyes off of him. I find myself backed up against the kitchen island. I eye the window to the fire escape, but his body blocks my aim for it.

Once I'm helplessly stuck in the small kitchen, against the counter, he goes immediately for the knife on the table. His neck is bleeding badly. I'm cornered in the kitchen area, so all I can do is grab another knife out of the knife block. My hands are already shredded, and the only knife I can get is a much smaller one than his. There's no way out. He's bigger and he's closing me into the corner of the kitchen. He gets so close I have no escape, so I brandish the knife at him, but I'm trembling violently, and I can tell that he doesn't think I can manage using it, but I thrust it at him, and it slices just below his ribs. He looks shocked as it sinks into his side, and he doubles over in pain.

I make a run for it, but he grabs me as I pass him, and I fall hard, hitting my head on the counter as I go down. Blood runs down the side of my face and he has hold of my leg, but I push myself and wriggle from his grip exactly the way I tried to do with my father years ago. This time, though, I get free. I hear the magnificent howling of sirens coming down

the street, but they'll go to the fifth floor. There is no reason
for them to look down here. I have to get outside. We stand,
facing one another, bleeding, catching our breath on either
side of the kitchen table.

"You don't know when to stop, do you?" he says. "You
made it so easy. All I had to do was put up flyers for services
I knew you needed, and you ate out of my hand, kept coming back to me. I had a dozen plans I didn't even have to use
'cause you just can't help yourself. The harder a guy is to get
to know, the more desperate the bitches get. Now you're
making it so hard, but I kinda like it." He licks the blood that
drips over his mouth. I need to get him to lunge at me first,
so I can bolt to the right and get to the fire escape window.

"She left you 'cause you're a coward and she knew it—she
knew only small-dicked, weak men hit their wives. That's
why she left," I say, looking him in the eye.

"You killed her. I didn't want to. You made me. It wouldn't
have happened if it weren't for you. She'd still be here." His
look has changed, and there is a tone of insecurity or defensiveness in his voice.

"She hated you," I say, and he doesn't lunge; he doesn't need
to, because he's the only one with a weapon now. He walks
to me slowly. He stabs his knife into the top of the table and
picks up the wine with the pills in it. With his free hand, he
clenches my neck and pushes me up against the wall, pinning
me there. He doesn't squeeze yet. He doesn't want to leave
marks if we can do this the easy way.

He puts the glass up to my mouth and tells me to drink, so
I do. I no longer have a choice. I'm caught. I think of Will a
floor up, knocking on my door, and I think of Ellie and how
I didn't go to her right away, and I wonder if she'll be safe.
Will he leave her alone if he gets me? I can't be sure. I do the
one thing I have left to try. I take a huge gulp of the drugged

wine and spit it back in his face with all the force I can muster. It's in his eyes. He lets go, instinctively, and wipes his face. In a split second I charge for the fire escape window and open it.

I'm outside. The air bites at me and numbs my bloody hands. He's right behind me, but I climb up the ladder, the same one I climbed down that first night with a bottle of whisky where I thought I was talking to a new friend—a grief-stricken widower.

I climb, but he has a grip on my leg and he's pulling me hard. I can't keep hold of the icy rail. One wrong move, and we could both fall to our deaths right now. I kick at him and slip away, and I pull my leg up over the last rung of the ladder and I'm on my fire escape. Is the gun there? Has he already gotten to it?

Just as he reaches me, I pull the gun out of the planter and shakily aim it at him. He looks alarmed for just a second, and then, to my surprise, he laughs. He thinks I don't know how to use it. Or maybe, like Lettie, he thinks I just won't, that I'm too scared. He can see that I can barely hold it because I'm shaking violently from cold and from fear. My back is pushed up against my own glass door, so close to the safety of my home, but I can't get inside. He takes one more step toward me, and I shoot.

I can't tell where it hits him, but the impact pushes him with such force that he topples over the side of the fire escape stairs, and almost gracefully, he floats down the six stories until I hear the crack of his landing.

I can hear the knocking on my door inside the condo, and after the gunshot is heard, they break the door to enter. I drop to my knees on the fire escape and let the gun fall out of my hands. I lie on the floor of the fire escape and weep as the police open the window of my condo to find me.

Will is the first to reach me. He picks me up and carries

me inside, and all I can do is apologize to him over and over. He tells me I'm in shock, and when Sterling arrives, he's still holding me and doesn't let me go. I beg him not to leave me alone and he doesn't—through all the medics, and the police station, the statements and tears, he never does.

THIRTY-THREE

HILLY LANCASTER IS THE ONE WHO CALLED THE PO-
lice that day. She heard the struggle inside Marty's apartment,
and by the time they arrived, Will was still outside, trying to
call back the burner phone number and figure out where I
was, and together, without knowing the other was looking,
they found me. I tell Hilly she's my hero, and she just giggles
and tells me to say it again.

When I got home from the hospital a few days after it all happened, there were countless voice mails, and more emails than
I could possibly count. Most were reporters wanting firsthand
accounts, but many were stations offering radio or TV spots.
They promised flashy salaries and my own show, but things
are different now. Maybe the hands-off therapy approach was
something that felt safe because I'd never dealt with the past
the way I told myself and everyone else I had. I'd told myself
I wasn't neglecting my private practice clients and that I could
balance the spotlight, but it wasn't true.

Marty may have claimed that my advice led him straight to
Lettie. But, with my burner phone and the gun I'd stashed,

I'd still managed to save myself through my own advice. And I have to believe that I'm capable, and I don't need to hide behind thirty-second radio therapy and fame to feel like I'm worthy. I don't have anything to prove. After a lifetime of trying to do just that with my mother, I have finally realized that I don't need to, and maybe I can finally get past it for the first time. I turn the offers down.

I bring Figgy over to Hilly's place when I go there for dinner. I know she could use a friend. Her eyes light up when she sees him. She's worried about the cat, but quickly realizes that Mr. Pickle owns Figgy, and they'll get along just fine with that hierarchy established.

"I'm having Christmas dinner over at my sister's," I tell her. I know she'll be alone, but she smiles anyway.

"How nice. She has little ones, right? It's not the same without little ones ripping presents open," she says.

"Neither of us can make cookies very well," I tell her. I bet the kids would like that. "You want to maybe join us? Bring some cookies?" I ask, and I think she's about to cry. She hugs me, and although it makes me incredibly uncomfortable, I let her.

I'm not ready for Will. I know he wants me to be, but I haven't properly mourned the loss of Liam. I only now know the truth, and I need to say goodbye.

I'm on my way to meet a Realtor to arrange putting the condo on the market before I head to the airport when I see Will's name appear on my phone. I pick up.

"Hey," he greets me, with a smile in his voice. "You heading to the Realtor?"

"Yeah," I say. "Just to drop off some paperwork."

"Let me take you to the airport. No reason to take the train. It takes forever," he says.

"Um, okay. If it's not putting you out too much," I say.

He meets me at the Realtor's office, and we make our way to O'Hare. I have my ticket to Santiago. It was Liam's dream trip, so I have to go and bring him there.

"Got your passport?" he asks as we get close to the drop-off.

"Check," I say.

"I'll pick you up when you get back." He smiles as he pulls up to the departure area.

"I really appreciate it." I look at him, smiling shyly.

"I totally know where you stand," he says, before I get out of the car. "But maybe I could make you dinner when you get back…just as friends, for now," he adds.

"You cook?" I ask, surprised.

"No, but I have a YouTube video I have faith in." He smiles, and I can't help but smile back.

"I'd be honored. It's a date," I say, before getting out of the car. I'll let him interpret that how he wants. I need time, it's true, but we can take it slow. He takes my bag out and kisses my cheek before I go. I made a promise to Ellie I'd be there for Christmas dinner, so I only have a few days, but I have to honor Liam's request.

He wanted his ashes spread by the sea, and there's no better place than Santiago, Chile. He'll get to go on the trip he was never able to take.

He stood in the kitchen with open brochures one day and told me that we have to visit Barrio Lastarria first, and so that's what I was going to do. *We'll have coffee and breakfast at Colmado, order a cappuccino and a* pincho de tortilla *and eat in the courtyard*. He was so excited.

Now, I sit in the courtyard with a cappuccino. I order a second for him. I'm laying off the drinks for a while. I've cried all the tears and wept countless apologies to him, and now, it's time to let him go. I hire a car to take me over to Las Salinas. I don't want anyone with me, so I don't hire a boat or anything like that.

I wait until dusk, when the beaches are mostly abandoned, and I wade out to the rocky embankment and sit, looking out over the water.

I open my bag and take out the ornate brass urn. I tell myself I will not cry; this is a celebration of his life. The love of my life. I whisper our inside jokes and our love story to the wind, and then, in one sweep of my hand, his ashes fall and I give him back to the sea.

★ ★ ★ ★ ★

ACKNOWLEDGMENTS

I want to thank the following people, from the bottom of my heart, for making this book possible:

My patient and ever-supportive husband, Mark Glass. My parents, Dianna Nova and Julie Loehrer; my sister (who helped with psychology research) Tamarind Knutson, and her husband, Mark Knutson. My longtime mentor, Kim LaFontaine, and my dear friends Shelly Domke and Justin Kirkeberg for always believing in me. My tenacious and discerning literary agent, Sharon Bowers, and my talented editor, Brittany Lavery, in addition to the whole team at Graydon House Books. And all my hometown, Minneapolis friends and family whom I miss terribly but still feel supported by even though distance keeps us apart.

If you loved *Someone's Listening*,
you won't want to miss the next gripping
thriller from Seraphina Nova Glass,
THE SEDUCTION.

Keep reading for a special preview!

PROLOGUE

The door was open when I arrived. I didn't think it was strange. I thought maybe he left it that way to let in the breezy night air. Perhaps he was enjoying a glass of wine on the porch and ran in for a refill. I didn't know what it would mean that the door was ajar, and I shouldn't have shut it. I shouldn't have touched anything.

I called his name, laying my purse on the counter and cocking my head to listen for maybe a shower running or footsteps upstairs. No answer. No sounds. That's when I noticed his phone on the floor of the kitchen. The glass screen was smashed, but it worked. That gave me pause. Why would he leave it there like that if he'd dropped it? When I looked through into the living room, I saw the couch cushions tossed on the ground. It was so quiet. What the hell was going on?

I called his name again; my heart started to speed up as I began yelling for him and throwing open doors to find him. Was there a robbery? I charted the stairs and started to panic a bit. He should be home. The television in the upstairs family room was on; no one was watching it. When I turned it off, the silence rang in my ears. I saw the French doors to the balcony off of the bedroom were open. It overlooks the back-yard and pool. When I walked out onto the balcony, I felt a tremor of unease even before I saw it.

The backyard was canopied with dripping Spanish moss trees and it hummed with the sound of cicadas, invisible in the branches. The humidity was palpable in the thick night air. I thought to try calling him, but remembered I just saw his phone downstairs. All of a sudden, I wished, desperately, that I could take back every decision I had made over the last couple months that landed me here, witnessing what I could never unsee.

He was there. I saw him in the shadowy blue light the swimming pool cast across the patio. He was lying on the concrete slab next to the pool with ribbons of blood mak-ing a river from the back of his head down to the pool-deck drain. I could tell from the eerie, lifeless stare and gloss over his eyes that he was dead.

ONE

six weeks earlier

The August heat hangs heavy in the wet air. I try to keep Bennett occupied because I feel a meltdown coming, so we sit barefoot on the back steps behind the deck and peel muddy red potatoes and snip green bean ends, discarding them into the rusty buckets we hold between our knees. He loves this. The ritual of plucking off each knotted end soothes him. Inside, I see Rachel and her friend from school eating strawberries over the sink, throwing the green tops into a soggy pile in the drain; she rolls her eyes when I call in to tell her to run the disposal and pull the chicken out to defrost. It's only a few weeks until school starts back up, and I'm using the advent calendar left over from Christmas to count down the days. Bennett helped me tape cut-out images of book bags and rulers over the old Santa and stuffed stocking on the cardboard calendar.

He starts a new school, one he's been on a waiting list to attend because his doctor says it's the best for Aspergers kids.

He should have started in Kindergarten, and now, as he goes into the second grade, I try to curb my resentment at the bougie place for keeping us waiting that long, even after a hefty donation we made two years ago. But, I'm hopeful that they might make some progress with him, at least get some of his outbursts under control. I've read every book, I've gone to every specialist, and still I can't even take him to the grocery store for fear he'll curl up on the floor screaming if a loud announcement comes over the store speakers.

Ben gets the little chocolate Santa out of the pocket taped over with cutouts of colored pencils, and we cheer in anticipation of the exciting first big day (only eighteen days left), and I get a secret reward of my own. I'm a day closer to a few minutes of peace and quiet. I swell with love for him as he opens the foil around the chocolate with the care and precision of a surgeon. He is my joy, but I'm so very tired these last weeks.

The heat is getting to him—making him irritable. I can tell because he loses interest in counting each green bean end, and stares off, rocking ever so slightly—staring at something far away that I'll never see.

"Mom!" Rachel yells from inside the sliding glass door she's cracked open, "I don't see any chicken!" All I have to do is give her a warning look and she shuts the door and goes back inside, muttering "whatever" under her breath. She knows yelling will almost always set Ben into a panic. As recently as last year, she'd be immediately remorseful if she did anything to upset him, but now that she's headed into junior high, the arm crossing and annoyed sighing is constant. The unkindness of puberty has changed her. Now, when we drive past the Davises' house down the street, and their boys are out front playing in the drive (actually "hanging" in the drive because, as she points out, kids don't "play" anymore), one of them will shoot a basket or tackle another boy at that very moment—

like birds of paradise, putting on a show—a primitive mating ritual. Rachel always giggles and avoids eye contact with me. It's maddening. She's just thirteen.

"Bennett," I smile, "I think there's some mint chip I hid in the back of the freezer." I pat his back gently, and even though the signs are there that he may lose control, he just pulls away from my touch and goes inside. Crisis averted. Now he's eating ice cream before dinner, but it could be much worse.

I pile the buckets of beans and potatoes on the patio table and step into the pool. I sit on the edge and close my eyes, letting the cool water caress my feet and whisper around my ankles. It's momentarily quiet, so I allow myself to think of him for just a few minutes before bringing Claire her medication and starting dinner.

He's practically a stranger. It's so shameful. I think about the way we tumbled in his door and didn't even make it to the couch. He pushed me, gently, against the entryway wall and pulled my shirt over my head. The flutter in my stomach is quickly extinguished by the crushing guilt I feel, and I try to push away the thoughts.

"Mom!" Rachel calls from the kitchen.

"Dad's on the phone!" She walks out holding her phone, and hands it to me with an annoyed sigh. My hands tremble a little. It feels as if he overheard my thoughts and interrupted them on purpose. Rachel notices my hands.

"What's up with you?" she asks, standing with a hand on a hip, waiting for her phone back.

"You just startled me. I'm fine. And stop yelling."

"He's in the living room," she defends, glancing in the screen door to make sure Ben is truly out of earshot. She sits in the patio chair and twirls while I talk to Collin.

"Hi, honey. Honey? Hello? Collin?" There is no response. My eyes prick with tears. It's totally irrational, but suddenly, I imagine he knows what I've done and he's too angry to speak. Someone's seen us and told him. I sit, weak-kneed, and strain to hear. "Collin?"

"Sorry, hon. I was in an elevator for a sec," he says, upbeat. The ding of an elevator and muffled voices can be heard in the background.

"Oh. Why are you calling Rachel's phone?" I ask.

"I tried you a few times. I wanted to see if you needed me to pick up dinner. I'm on my way home."

"Oh, I must have left mine inside. I was in the yard with Ben. Um…no that's okay, I've already got things prepped, but thanks." I wonder if my voice sounds guilty or different somehow. I never leave my phone, not with Bennett's condition and Collin's ill mother living with us. So, that seems out of character. He's too kind to say anything, but I'm sure it struck him as odd. It's a pact between us as we juggle all the health issues and crisis calls from school. Both of us will stay available. As a high profile real estate agent, it doesn't look good for Collin to have his phone ping during a showing or big meeting, but he won't let me carry all the weight of this myself. It's his gesture of solidarity, I suppose. The same way he stopped drinking beer when I was pregnant both times. If I couldn't have my wine, he would suffer with me. That's just the way he is.

My face is flush with shame. I can feel it. I turn away from Rachel slightly.

"Pot roast and potatoes. Ben helped," I say with a forced smile in my voice.

"Sounds great. See you in a bit then." When we hang up, Rachel snatches her phone back. She crosses her long legs and hooks a foot inside the opposite ankle, it looks like they could wrap around endlessly. She's always been thin. Her kneecaps practically bulge compared to the rest of her thread-like legs that seem to loosely dangle inside her shorts that are far too short. I don't say anything about them, choosing my battles today.

On my way inside, I stop to smooth her hair and kiss the top of her head. As if each good, motherly thing I do is a tiny bit of atonement for my sins. She smells like sickly sweet Taylor Swift body spray, and doesn't look up at me, just scrolls on her phone.

Dinner is quiet. Collin tells Rachel "no phones at the table" and she fires back.

"You haven't looked up from yours since we sat down."

"That's different. It's work and it's urgent." He gives her a twirly gesture with his hand to put her phone away, and it's true, Collin almost never uses his phone during dinner, but I know he's working on a huge commercial sale and something about a train track being too close to a hospital they invested in and vibrating the building is all he can talk about lately. I pour a little more wine into my glass than I usually would, but take advantage of his distraction. He wouldn't say anything if I drank the whole bottle, but sometimes that's worse— wondering if someone harbors quiet disappointment in you, but are too kind to ever point it out.

"How's Mom?" he asks. Jesus Christ. I can't believe I forgot Claire. "I poked my head in before dinner, but she was asleep. Should I bring her a plate?" he asks. I never brought her her 4:00 p.m. medicine. Shit. I'm so distracted. I leave my phone, I forget important medication. I try to cover quickly.

"I told her I'd bring her something later. She wanted to sleep awhile," I lie.

"You're a saint," he smiles, kissing me.

"Barf. Can we go now?" Rachel doesn't wait for an answer; she gets up, scrapes her plate in the sink, and leaves, too much homework being her staple excuse for getting out of dish duty, which is fine. I usually revel in the quiet kitchen after Collin is parked in front of the TV, and the kids are in homework mode.

"Why don't you let me get this?" Collin playfully hip checks me and takes the plates from my hands.

Recently, he feels like he's burdened me beyond reason by asking to have his ailing mother come to live in the back guest room last month. Of course I said yes to her staying. Not just because of how much I love and would do anything for Collin, but because I cannot imagine myself in her position. She's suffered years with atrial fibrillation, and now lung cancer and dementia. Isn't that what we should do, take her in? Isn't that what makes us shudder? The thought of an old woman sitting alone at a care facility that smells of stale urine and casserole. A woman who spends her days staring out at an Arby's parking lot outside the small window of her institutional-looking room, or sitting in a floral housecoat in the common area, watching reruns of *The Price Is Right* while putting together a jigsaw puzzle of the Eiffel Tower.

Maybe it's human nature to care because it's a reflection of ourselves—what we can't let happen in fear of becoming it someday—maybe it's just compassion, but I could never let Claire be cast off and feel alone in a place like that. Even though having her dying in the back bedroom is breath-stealing and unsettling, and very hard to explain to your children.

I let Collin take the dishes so I can bring Claire a plate and her pills. I pad down the long hall to her room, and tap lightly on her door even though she won't answer, I know. When I enter, I resist the urge to cover my nose so I don't hurt her feelings, but the air is stagnant and the odor is hard to describe. It's vinegary and acrid like soured milk and decay.

"Evening, darlin,' I have some dinner for you." The light

is dim, but I don't switch on the overhead because she complains of the headaches it gives her. I don't see her shape under the blankets. "Claire?" The room is hot and a box fan hums at the end of her bed, propped on a chair. The smell and humidity make me lose my breath a moment, and I notice she's opened a window. No wonder it's so unbearably hot. August in Louisiana and she opens a window. Shit. I should have checked on her at four. I close the window and cover my nose with my arm. When I turn from the window, I can see Rachel down the hall, and her expression is enough to betray Claire's whereabouts. Rachel stares, frozen with tears in her eyes, looking at Grandma Claire standing in an unbuttoned robe without her wig. She's been sick on the bathroom floor, and stands breasts bared and hairless in the hall, disoriented, looking for her room.

"Honey," I try to say to Rachel before I help Claire back to her bed, but she's run off, crying, traumatized no doubt, by what she saw. I should have fucking checked on her at four. What I've done—my distraction—now it's hurting my kids and poor Claire. I need to pull it together.

I help Claire to bed and switch on a rerun of *Frasier*, her favorite. I leave her a tray and give her her pills, then I clean up the vomit on the bathroom floor without telling Collin about what's happened. He'd worry, he'd want to help, but this is my negligence, so I'm glad he has a work disaster of some sort and is drinking a beer out on the patio, making calls.

Rachel has her door closed when I finish, and I hear an angsty, acoustic, festival-sounding song turned up loudly in her room, so decide to leave it until tomorrow.

In the living room, Bennett is sitting at the coffee table, coloring. My sweet baby. I wish so desperately that I could wrap him up in my arms and kiss and hug him, tickle him, and joke with him, but he's the most sensitive soul I've ever known, so I pour myself a little more wine and sit by his side, hoping he lets me have a moment with him. He doesn't say anything for a minute and then...

"You wanna color the Big Bird? You can't have the Transformer page 'cause it's mine, but you can have this one." He pushes a ripped-out page across the table. It's Big Bird with one yellow leg colored in. "It's for babies, so you might not want to," he continues.

"I still like Big Bird. I guess that makes me kinda babyish, huh?"

"Adults can still like that stuff. Mr. Mancini at school calls it nostalgia," he says. I stifle a laugh.

"That's very true."

"Is Mr. Mancini in the mafia?" he asks, without taking focus off his transformer.

"Pretty sure he's not. Why?"

"'Cause his name is Mancini, like Vincent Mancini."

"Vincent Mancini?"

"You know. *The Godfather.*"

"You watched *The Godfather*?" I ask, wondering when he would have seen this.

"It's only the best movie ever written."

"Says who?" I laugh.

"Uh. The internet." He looks at me, hoping that I agree.

"Oh, well that's a good point. But I don't think he's any relation."

"That's good," he says, the topic apparently resolved.

"Yeah." I agree, coloring the rest of Big Bird and I'm so incredibly in love with my son in this moment. The times I see the true Ben come out, and he's totally himself are breathtaking. I don't ask to hug him because if he changes his mood and says no, it will ruin this.

When the kids are asleep, I take my time before getting

into bed. I gaze past myself in the mirror, removing eyeliner with a makeup wipe and closing my eyes against the intrusive heat I feel between my legs at the thought of him. I push the thought away and undress, pulling on a T-shirt and clean underwear. In bed, Collin is on his laptop, but he closes it when I sit down.

"Hey, beautiful."

"Hey, hon. Everything okay with work?" I ask, knowing the answer.

"Eh. It will be. Sorry I got busy there." He puts his readers away and shakes his head. "We sold a hospital building and the goddamn train is too close, so the surgeons' hands vibrate when it barrels by. Can you imagine having a spinal fusion and a goddamn train full of Amazon Prime packages paralyzes you? It's unfathomable." He says this like I'm hearing this for the first time. I smile at him.

"Sorry," he says, holding his hands up in surrender. "No work talk in the bedroom. I promised."

"It's okay," I pull the down comforter over my legs and rub lotion into my hands and up my arms.

"No. It's a sanctuary. Who said that? Someone wise, I think," he pokes fun at me and my insistence that no TV, work, or arguing belong in the bedroom. He pulls me over to him and kisses me. So comfortable, so innocent. I breathe into that familiar, faded scent of Dolce & Gabbana left on his neck, the feel of his sharp whiskers, grown out from this morning's shave, sandy against my skin, and I want to cry.

All I see are threads of memory strung together from the other night. The ride home I should have refused, a benign acquaintance turned more, his mouth on mine, the keys unlocking his door, every time I said yes, never trying to stop it. I can't bear it. As tears run down the sides of my face, I push them away quickly before they fall on Collin's bare skin.

Sweet Collin, kissing down my neck, his discarded readers about to tip off the side of the nightstand in front of a photo of Ben and Rachel. What have I done to us?

TWO

seven weeks earlier

Gillian Baker, one block over, holds a book club at her house once a month. Reluctantly, and at her insistence, I have finally decided to join. I squeeze a cylinder of cookie dough out of its plastic tube, cut it into disks, and put a tray of artificial-tasting cookies in the oven, so I have something to bring and pass off as my own. Collin thinks the book club idea is great, and might inspire me. I tell him it's just a kid-free night for the neighborhood wives so they can drink wine and make vapid, uninformed comments on great literature, but he still thinks I will be in my element and should give it a try.

I was going to be a scholar once upon a time, but I dropped out of my master's program when we learned about Bennett's condition. I wasn't forced to stay home, but we decided it made sense. It was for the best, and even better than a degree, because I could write books from home and still pursue that dream. What a gift! All the time in the world to write the great American novel. Except, I haven't written any books, have I? What the hell do I really have to say anyway? Life has gone out of its way to ignore me in many regards. Shelby Fitch two doors down was in the Peace Corps in freaking Guatemala for two years before she married into this neighborhood. She should write the book.

What will my topics be? "Mom cleans up kid's barf during carpool."

"Mom waits half a day for dishwasher repair guy, and guess what? He never shows."

"Mom tries a Peppa Pig cake recipe from Pinterest, but it looks like deranged farm swine with a phallic nose and makes son cry." I have nothing to say. The other day I thought I'd get serious again and try to really sit and brainstorm some ideas. I ended up watching videos of people getting hurt on backyard trampolines and a solid hour of baby goats jumping around in onesies. So, I guess maybe at least getting my mind back into the literary world can't hurt.

At my dressing table, I pull my hair back and slip on some dangly earrings. It's my first time out of yoga pants this week, and it's nice. I apply lip gloss and press my lips together; I can hear the chaos begin in the background. The oven is beeping nonstop, beckoning Collin to take out the premade dinner he's heating up for the kids, but he's arguing with Ben about a video game he's refusing to turn off. He still has to make a plate for Claire and survive the inevitable meltdown Ben will have before homework. That is if he can even get him from the TV to the dinner table. I feel guilty leaving, but when I appear in the front hall in a sundress, he lights up and gives me a kiss, telling me he has it under control. I know he ultimately does. It's not rocket science, it's just exhausting and emotionally blood-sucking, and he's already had a twelve-hour day of anxiety at work.

I carry the plate of cookies and a copy of *Catcher in the Rye* as I walk across the street. They're already trying too hard. Why not start with *Fifty Shades* or a cozy mystery? When Rachel had to read this book for English, she called it a turd with covers. I, on the other hand, spent hours making meticulous notes, so I could be sure to make comments that were sharp and poignant. I rehearse them in my head as I walk.

I'm the last to arrive. There are about four other moms from the block. We all do the obligatory cheek kisses. Gillian's living room looks like she's hosting a dinner party rather than a book club. Chardonnay is chilling in ice on the kitchen island next to a spread of food that could have come from a Vegas buffet. I wish I could hide these pathetic tube cookies.

"Wow, Gill. Did you do all this?" I ask, impressed.

"Oh, hell no. Are you kidding? It's catered, silly." I can't believe she's had her book club catered. Everyone has wine and something fancy on a toothpick in their hands. She puts my sad cookies next to the beautiful chiffon cake on the island, and I'm mortified. There's cling wrap over them for God's sake—on a Spiderman paper plate left over from Ben's last birthday! Kill me.

She pours me a glass, pretending not to think anything of my trashy offering, and I walk carefully over her white rugs as we make our way into the sitting room. Of course she has a "sitting room." It's a bright space in the front of the house with vaulted ceilings and a blingy chandelier. We all perch on the edges of pale furniture. I never quite know how to feel about these women. They've welcomed me so warmly, but they sometimes seem like a foreign species to me. Yes, I live in this neighborhood too, but it's because of Collin's success, not anything I've done. I guess they can probably say the same. I still feel sort of like an imposter. I don't lean into it the way they seem to.

I didn't intend to stay home, of course. Ben's condition forced me to and it was mutually agreed upon, but I still feel like I was destined for a career, never dependent on anyone else. I don't feel dependent on Collin. That's not the right word. What we have is ours. The way I contribute is something he could never handle, but I guess I don't take it for granted the way they seem to. Gillian is constantly remodeling her house and upgrading things that you'd think it impossible to upgrade. She had a stunning outdoor kitchen next to a pool that appears damn near Olympic-sized. It was even highlighted in the local home tour magazine. One day she gutted the whole thing because she wanted the pool to be teardrop shaped instead. Here I am using Groupons for my facials.

Even that sounds indulgent. Facials. I grew up in a double-wide trailer in Lafayette with a mother who worked the night shift at the hospital and an alcoholic father who spent his days quiet and glassy-eyed on the front porch staring at some invisible thing—another time, maybe. It will never feel right to buy five-hundred-dollar shoes or drive a luxury car, although I'd never want to lose the safety of it and I'm grateful my children will never have to struggle the way I did. This comfort is for them. This safety is for them. That's the bottom line, so I brush away the negative thoughts.

Tammy comments on Gillian's bracelet. She holds her wrist, examining it. Everyone guffaws as Gillian explains that it's an early birthday gift from Robert and she got it insured. I have never understood tennis bracelets. An ugly soccer ball hangs off of her silver chain, but I make my face look delighted along with the others. After we settle in, I think the small talk is over and we will dig into a great piece of literature. Kid-free, wine-lubricated, I'm ready.

"Oh my God, you guys, did you see Bethany Burena at Leah's wedding?" Karen asks. There's mocking laughter. I was at that wedding, but I don't know what they're referring to, so I stay quiet. Liz chimes in.

"God, it looked like someone stuffed a couple honey baked hams into the back of her dress."

"And the worst part is she did that on purpose." Tammy says, placing her glass of wine on an end table so she can use her hands to talk. "That ain't too much buttercream, y'all!" Then she holds her hands to her mouth and pretends to whisper sideways. "Although did you see her shoveling it in at the cake table?"

"She had those babies implanted," Karen laughs.

"No!" Gillian gasps.

"Yep. Ass implants. Ass-plants." Everyone roars with laughter. I force a chuckle so I don't stand out. I hate these people, I realize right in this moment. I long to leave. I could fake a headache, or check in at home and say there's a problem with Ben. Why don't I? Why do I need their approval? Karen keeps the gossip going.

"That's not as bad as Lily. She brought the guy who cleans her pool to the wedding!"

"What do you mean?" Liz asks.

"As a date."

"No!"

"Scandal much?" Tammy is delighted she has everyone in hysterics.

"Lily Berg?" I ask, not understanding the social sin she's committed. "Isn't she single—like divorced, I thought."

"Yeah, but she brought The. Pool. Guy. Sad."

"So sad," Karen echoes.

"Desperate," Liz adds. She notices the book in my hands. "What's that?"

"What do you mean? It's *the book*," I say with a lighthearted scoff.

"Oh, Mel. I'm so sorry I didn't mention it, I guess I thought everyone just sort of got it—especially since the book was something so random," Gillian says.

"Got what?"

"We don't, like, read it. We just need an excuse to get rid of the kids and hubbies for one night. I think we deserve at least that?" she says, glancing around for allies.

"Damn right, we do." Liz holds her wine up and gulps it down, a sort of toast to herself. "You didn't read it, did you?" but I don't answer. I feel like an idiot. I was joking when I said it was an excuse to drink and have a night away. I was at least half-joking. I thought that, surprisingly, I may have found a few kindred spirits, perhaps. What a joke.

"I just skimmed it," I say. I'm probably visibly blushing, so I pick a strawberry carved into a rose shape from the table, and pick at it.

"Mel has a master's in literature. Did y'all know that?" Gillian says, maybe in an attempt to redeem herself from indirectly embarrassing me.

"Oh my gosh, smarty-smart pants. Look at you." Karen swats my leg and smiles, supportively. I want the attention off of me as soon as possible, so I don't correct her and say that it was creative writing…and that I never finished the degree.

"You should give me the name of your caterer," I say, picking up a skewer of chicken and taking a bite. "I was gonna do a thing for Collin's birthday. Maybe a trip, but if we stay in town we'll have people to the house." The subject is officially changed. Her eyes light up.

"Oh my gosh, I have their card. I told them they should pay me for how many referrals I'm getting for them. Their almond torte is totally to die for. Seriously. If you don't do a cake, maybe mini tortes."

"Oh, cute!" Liz says.

We talk about mini tortes, whose phone carrier is the worst,

Karen's daughter's modeling career, and Botox for the next two hours until I walk home, unsteadily, with my plate of cookies that Gillian gracefully sent home with me. I toss *Catcher In The Rye* in Brianna Cunningham's garbage can which she failed to pull back into the garage (Tammy actually made mention of that particular oversight earlier in the evening), and I don't know if the crushing disappointment of the evening is worse than going back home to Claire's bedpan and Ben's bedtime screaming. I wish I could just sit in the Millers' yard, drunk for a little while, but someone would see, and it would be discussed at some other neighborhood book club.

The temperate dusk air is dense with mosquitos and the chatter of crickets. I take my time walking back. When I approach my house, I see Collin in an orange rectangle of warm kitchen light. He's washing dishes, helplessly. I concentrate on appearing more sober than I am as I enter the kitchen. I sit at the table, pulling off my shoes and he sits, offering me a glass of wine.

"No, thanks." I fill a plastic Bob The Builder cup under the tap and sit on a counter stool. He pulls one up next to me.

"Was it fun?" he asks, hopefully, wanting me to find an outlet—some joy in my life while things are so tough. I don't know if I should tell him the truth or make him happy, so I go down the middle.

"It was okay."

"Just okay?"

"Eh. Not exactly the literary minds I was hoping to connect with."

"I'm sorry," he says, squeezing my hand. "I took Ben to pick out a new chapter book at Bookland tonight."

"Oh, fun. What did he pick out?" I say, thinking he's changing the subject, but he's not. He hands me a little postcard advert. "There's a writers' group starting next week." I look over the glossy square and it has details welcoming any local writers to join the weekly Thursday group to workshop their writing. Before I can dismiss the assertion that I'm a "writer," he points to the bullet point that says "all levels welcome." It's so incredibly sweet that he wants to not only encourage me in pursuing something I care about, but is also willing to hold down the fort every Thursday. I kiss him.

"That's very thoughtful of you."

"But?" he asks, anticipating a "no" brewing, but I don't have a reason to say no. I mean, except that I have no writing to present to the group. I could write a critical essay on *Catcher in the Rye*. That's about it. It sounds thrilling though. Maybe some accountability and pressure will be just what I need. I glance past Collin into the living room and see Bennett asleep in front of a WWE smackdown on the TV. I give Collin a look.

"Well, he's asleep, isn't he?" he defends. I smile and shake my head, pressing my thumb into the crumbs on his plate, and tasting the remnants of the cookies I left behind for them.

"I guess I can try it." I say, standing and rinsing the plate. Words I'd give anything to take back.

THREE

six weeks earlier

I feel like they're looking at me, like they know something. I find a place away from where most of the moms sit and I spread a blanket out on the matted grass behind right field, and lay out snacks. Ben forgot his cleats. He gives me a wave from the dugout to tell me he's borrowing a pair. He points to his feet, smiling. He loves baseball practice. Maybe only because he gets to use allowance money to stop at Dairy Queen on the way home for a frosted fudge Blizzard. Whatever the reason, I'm grateful he's found an activity I don't have to drag him to, howling. All the other kids are special needs too, so there are a lot of social rules in place by the coaches that he handles better than the free-for-all that basketball was.

I see Marcy Tritto and Carrie Rivard sitting in camping chairs on the other side of the dugout. Marcy waves. Her son, Trevor, has Downs and always tries to hug Ben, which doesn't go over well. Carrie fans herself with a coloring book and tries to look interested in the kids as they find their spots on the field. She gives a little clap and thumbs-up to her kid. I can never remember his name, but he bites.

I feel a prickle of heat climb my spine. Of course they don't know anything. It's strange how intensely it feels as though they are looking at me differently. I'm the one who set my chair away from them, but they didn't wave me over either. I'm being ridiculous. Everything is okay.

I wait a little while until everyone seems to settle in and no one is going to sit near me. Then I pull out his book and hold it in my hands. *His book. He wrote it.* It's a romance, and on the cover there is an image of two lovers entwined in a crimson bed sheet. His name appears in bold letters beneath the scantily clad couple, and the title *Summer Heat* has an artistic drop of sweat dripping off the S. I'd usually scoff at this sort of trashy, drug-store novel, but it's different when you know the person who wrote it. It's so…impressive. I have the cover masked with a different book jacket—a respectable Jonathan Franzen cover. He's too smart for most people to get, so I feel safe that no one in this crowd will ask about it because they won't know who that is.

I turn each delicious page with shaky fingers, stopping after every paragraph or two, to peer over the book and make sure no one hanging out behind me. Linda Singer likes to creep over with her purse-wine and try to hand it out to all the moms. She could be lurking along the fence trying to be sub-tle. I feel totally paranoid. It's hard to look away from these filthy pages. Each one lustier than the last—inner thigh ca-resses and nipple sucking.

I hear Ben in the distance, so I hold my hand over my eyes and squint against the sun to see him. Oh no. A kid pushed him and now he's crying. Shit. Practice is from five to seven and it's barely 5:20 p.m. I have been looking forward to these two hours of reading time all day. Sometime, if Coach Joe can get everyone to quiet down, the meltdown will pass. Nope. Ben's lying next to third base, kicking his heels into the orange clay; he's got Gavin Waters and the biter kid crying now too,

all feeding off of one another's howls. That's it. Joe looks my
way, and I nod, stuffing my portable chair into its vinyl carrying case and crossing to third base.

I kneel and go through my steps to calm him. A calm voice,
and praise.

"You're doing a great job, bud," I say, lightly touching his
shoulder. I hand him his Dumbledore action figure. He takes
it and twists its head, but it's not going to be enough today. I
tell him that we can go if he wants and he charges across the
field, a small, marching silhouette, headed toward the car. I
see him sit on the curb and make Dumbledore walk across
the bumper while Joe talks to me.

"Maybe he'll want to come back after a little time," Joe says,
but I know my son, and I can tell when there will be a quick
recovery, and when he's done. His eyes change when he's about
to vehemently refuse to do something. Forcing him is not how
to handle it. Joe blows his whistle abruptly, causing me to yelp.

"No spitting, Jason!" His attention is across the field, pointing at, presumably, Jason, who shrugs and looks around to pass
the blame. "Sorry." He realizes he's blown my eardrums out
with his aggressive whistling.

"It's fine." I dismiss it and dig for my keys.

"New haircut?" he asks. Even Collin didn't notice the layers I added. I think I blush a little.

"Oh, sort of."

"Looks nice," he says, smiling. Joe Brooks has one of those
personalities. He always asks people about themselves. Maybe
a police tactic, because who doesn't love to talk about themselves? It makes people feel good, open up. I thought he was
an asshole in high school. He was popular, always had something to prove, and girls threw themselves his way. He asked
me out a couple times junior and senior year, but I rejected
any interest he showed…out of principle. I was not going to be

SERAPHINA NOVA GLASS

another girlfriend of Homecoming King, Joe Brooks. I guess that was just a part of being young, his obnoxious arrogance, because here he is now: local cop, volunteer coach for special needs kids, of all things. One of the moms, Julie Fenton, says he does it because it attracts women more than if he'd gotten a puppy. He does play a large part in the moms' fantasy lives, but he smashed all of these rumors by actually just being a stand-up guy over the years.

"Thanks, Joe," I say, involuntarily smoothing my hair with my fingers.

"I can try getting him back in the game if you want me to take five and go and talk with him." Not many people would go out of their way to deal with him. It was so kind. I feel bad about all the bias I held about Joe over the years without any real justification.

I might have said yes, but I already know it's not happening, and maybe if I get him to the promised DQ and then home early, I can sneak in a chapter or two before Collin and Rachel get home.

"Thanks, but I think we'll just try again next week," I say and he puts his hand up for a high five like I'm part of the team. I reluctantly slap his hand, feeling a bit condescended to, but it's just his way, I suppose. His hand lingers on a mine a moment longer than it should.

"All right," he says and hollers over to Ben. "Good job, champ!" Ben doesn't look up from his fantasy world. I get him in the car with the promise of ice cream and leave, wondering if I've just been flirted with or if the guilt I'm wrestling with is causing delusions.

Collin calls after picking Rachel up from cross-country practice and they decide to meet us for a burger and ice cream. It's a rare occasion that we veer from our local, organic dietary guidelines. Collin and I both cook and share a love of the farmer's market. We bonded over the belief that a child's palate is largely developed depending on what they're exposed to early in life, so we have been strict about leans and greens at every meal, but lately, I've been a little lax. The news of now burgers and ice cream has Ben in the back seat whooping and singing a song about waffle fries that he's composed, impromptu. He sees a woman hollering at her kid, blocking the only parking spot as we pull in.

"Fat ass, fat ass, fat ass," Ben starts to repeat. "Waffle fries. Fat ass thighs!"

"Ben! That's not very nice to say, is it?" and he is quiet, afraid burgers may be taken from him if he continues.

"Ricky!" the woman called. She was carrying a full tray of large Cokes in one hand and three greasy DQ bags in the other.

"Ricky Junior, you get your skinny little butt right out of the way, right now." The child pays no attention. He just continues mimicking Karate Kid moves, kicking high and creating his own sound effects. "Whaaa. Kwaaah." The woman is stuffed into blue sweat pants and a long stretched-out, stained, tee-shirt with "Got Milk?" scrolled across the front. She's helpless to catch him. She waddles off the curb and moves closer to him, giving us an anxious wave of apology.

"Now Ricky Junior, I mean right this very second, or you will not have this Blizzard. I'll give it right to your sister, and don't you think I won't!" Ricky still didn't seem convinced. "And no fries. You'll eat a salad!" Ricky scurries to his mother's side and quickly shifts his attention from karate moves to jumping up on her, trying to snatch a Coke from her tray.

After negotiating a spot in the packed parking lot for some time, I stand in line at the walk-up window. There are four red, plastic tables with attached benches where Ben sits, on his best behavior, watching the busy patio with delight. There are families—moms and dads bent over dripping cones, children running around them in circles or calling emphatically for them to "Watch me, watch me" while they performed some unimpressive activity like jumping off the six-inch curb or dabbing a dot of ice cream on their nose and laughing as if it were a great accomplishment.

A Celine Dion song pipes through the speakers and I feel inexplicably depressed. I treasure family nights like this, unexpected and serendipitous, but I want to be anywhere else right now. I want to be by myself. Just for a little while. I shouldn't have suggested this. Another out-of-character moment for me, eating junk food. I don't want Collin to think anything is off.

When we are all finally finishing up and Ben is delighting in crumpling up the oily burger wrappers and making multiple trips to the trash with each plastic tray, Rachel is weighing the pros and cons of trying out for cheerleading when school starts. The paper tray liner has two columns she's written in crayons pilfered from the Kid's Corner. She's treating it like the most important decision she'll make in her life. Collin is ever attentive and indulges her.

"I'll look like the biggest loser though. I can't even do the splits. I'd be like the only one on the team who can't do the splits." She looks at me sideways for a moment as she goes off on her diatribe, harboring anger that I didn't put her in dance when she was young. All the other girls started at five years old and she didn't show interest until twelve, so it's my fault she "totally sucks."

"You're tall," Collin tells her. "It's much harder to do the splits when you're tall. Girls would kill for your height." He always says the right thing. She softens.

"Really?" she asks, self-consciously.

"You'll get the splits down. It just takes longer for tall people," I add. Her dance teacher, Linda Waters, I happen to know, is looking for extra cash, offering private lessons; it came up at a brunch with Gillian and the girls recently. Linda happens to have the misfortune of being young and very pretty, so naturally, all the ladies hate her. "Why doesn't she just work the pole at Bottoms Up Gentlemen's Club across town," Liz had once joked.

"Why don't you take some private lessons to get you ready for try-outs," I say. I wish I could take it back. Now I am unabashedly buying my child's adoration because I feel guilty about something she knows nothing about. Three out-of-character moves in a few days. Shit. But it's already out there.

"Really? Are you serious?" She looks to Collin who shrugs in agreement! "Oh my God!" She flings her arms around me. "I'm gonna go and call Katie and tell her, can I?" She's almost across the parking lot before I nod. She leans against the car, gesturing wildly as she talks to her friend.

"You're feeling pretty generous today, huh?" Collin asks lightheartedly. I redden.

"I guess. I'm not sure why I said that. I just hate seeing her down on herself... I don't know."

"I think I know why," he says. The blood in my face drains. My hands shake, involuntarily, and I hide them under the table.

"Sorry?" I ask.

"I think this writing group stuff has really boosted your confidence—made you—I don't know…happier. You need the time away, you know, just to have something that's just yours. I think it's great. You seem different."

"I do?"

"In like a really good way."

"Oh." I smile at him, and then look down, picking at the paper corners of Rachel's list on the table. Ben saves me from having to respond. The tower of wadded up wrappers he's constructed on top of the trash can was knocked down my some asshole kid, and Collin leaps into dad mode, distracting him, showing him the elaborate ice cream cakes in the display case. I gather up our things quickly and meet them near the front door so there is no danger in resuming our conversation.

Yes, I do have something that's "just mine," and I need to get rid of it.

When we get home, I tiptoe into Claire's room. The canned laughter from her sitcom underscores her snoring. She's fallen asleep in her wheelchair with her head back, mouth agape. I remember a Mother's Day, years ago, when Collin took the two mothers in his life to Woodhaven country club. Claire and I sat sipping brandy alexanders in sundresses while Collin swam in the pool with the kids.

She held a long white Marlboro in her thin fingers, and through threads of exhaled smoke, she spoke about her work at the university. She taught anthropology, and was explaining all of her exciting research and her upcoming trip to Uganda. She was lovely. I aspired to be like her. Whenever she visited us from Santa Fe, I doted on her. I was captivated by her stories, her worldliness. She was charming, sophisticated. Not the big house, ugly charm bracelet, married into fortune, fake sophisticated. She'd earned it.

Now, when I take off her soiled diaper, I try not to think about that woman who jet-setted around the world and told dirty stories we laughed and shrieked over on the deck at night, pinot grigios in hand. I clean the mess and shift her into her bed. I slip a surgical mask over my mouth, for the smell. No matter how much disinfectant one can use, dying is a smell that just refuses to be cleaned. I hate to offend her, so I only cover my nose when she is fast asleep.

When I place a clean sheet over her and turn off the television, I notice it's faintly dark now. The kids must be in their rooms because the only sound is ESPN on in the living room and Collin on another call about the hospital that's too close to the goddamn train track.

I slip out onto the deck for the fresh air. The light over the door attracts masses of insects. Thick beetles drop onto the thin concrete stoop and collect themselves. The temperate dusk air is dense with mosquitos and the chatter of crickets sound from the tall prairie grass and the jungle of weeds in the wooded area just beyond my view. It's peaceful.

I sit at the edge of the pool, looking ahead, past the rusted-through jungle gym set, resting my focus on a dilapidated pool table in one of the storage sheds along the long, fenced yard. Boxes of Christmas ornaments, a calcified fish aquarium, and last autumn's garbage bags of leaves with pumpkin faces are all piled up on a work table, brittle with neglect.

I try to understand the reason for this finger of pain pressing against my throat. This is not out of control. It was a minor lapse in judgment. I'm not the only one to have felt this. I'm sure this sort of thing happens all the time. It was stupid, yes. So stupid, but, it's done. "Get it together," I say softly, to myself, and then go inside to start Ben's bedtime routine.

Need to read the rest? *The Seduction* will be available Summer 2021 wherever you buy your books—pre-order your copy now!